ELEVEN HOUSES

ELEVEN HOUSES

COLLEEN OAKES

SIMON & SCHUSTER BFYR

NEW YORK   LONDON   TORONTO   SYDNEY   NEW DELHI

An imprint of Simon & Schuster Children's Publishing Division
1230 Avenue of the Americas, New York, New York 10020
Text © 2024 by Colleen Oakes
Jacket, interior, and map illustration © 2024 by Jingkun Qiao
Jacket design by Chloë Foglia
SIMON & SCHUSTER BOOKS FOR YOUNG READERS
and related marks are trademarks of Simon & Schuster, LLC.
Simon & Schuster: Celebrating 100 Years of Publishing in 2024
For information about special discounts for bulk purchases, please contact
Simon & Schuster Special Sales at 1-866-506-1949 or business@simonandschuster.com.
The Simon & Schuster Speakers Bureau can bring authors to your live event. For more information or to book an event, contact the Simon & Schuster Speakers Bureau at 1-866-248-3049 or visit our website at www.simonspeakers.com.
Interior design by Hilary Zarycky
The text for this book was set in Jenson.
Manufactured in the United States of America
First Edition
2 4 6 8 10 9 7 5 3 1
CIP data for this book is available from the Library of Congress.
ISBN 9781665952583
ISBN 9781665952606 (ebook)

For my dad, my lighthouse.
I wish we could have kept you forever.

**STORM YEARS ON WEYMOUTH ISLAND
ARE RECORDED AS FOLLOWS:**

1790, 1800, 1809, 1817, 1827, 1836, 1846, 1856, 1864,
1876, 1882, 1890, 1899, 1908, 1916, 1926, 1935,
1945, 1953, 1963, 1971, 1980, 1990, 1998, 2000, 2012 . . .

THE ELEVEN HOUSES OF WEYMOUTH

 Cabot: First House to the Sea. Control and Power. Descendants of the People of Iron.

 Pope: Second House to the Sea. Art and Defense. Descendants of the People of Paper.

 McLeod: Third House to the Sea. History and Language. Descendants of the People of Iron.

 Pelletier: Fourth House to the Sea. Faith and Eccentricity. Descendants of the People of Salt.

 Nickerson: Fifth House to the Sea. Modern and Proud. Descendants of the People of Salt.

 Mintus: Sixth House to the Sea. Medical and Macabre. Descendants of the People of Paper.

Bodhmall: Seventh House to the Sea. Piousness and Duty. Descendants of the People of Iron.

 Gillis: Eighth House to the Sea. Brightness and Fertility. Descendants of the People of Salt.

 Des Roches: Ninth House to the Sea. Elitist and Literary. Descendants of the People of Paper.

 Grimes: Tenth House to the Sea. Militant and Clever. Descendants of the People of Iron.

 Beuvry: Last House to the Sea. Secretive and Winsome. Descendants of the People of Salt.

Our people shall not linger here, for this is a place of death.
—Unknown Mi'kmaq Grand Chief, circa
1710–1720

Historical note by Reade McLeod: As the Mi'kmaq were primarily oral storytellers, this quote is according to local legend and cannot be verified.

Weymouth Island
30 Miles East of Glace Bay, Nova Scotia
May 20, 2018

CHAPTER ONE

The dead that wait underneath the sea are unusually loud today—or perhaps it just seems that way since I'm always walking alone these days. Either way, their howl roars like an airplane engine in the background: the ambient noise of my life.

The morning air is crisp as I hike toward the end of the island, wishing for the hundredth time that I could be homeschooled like my sister. I've tried begging, but Jeff says no, that I have to be here, walking to school with elbows tucked tight. He probably just doesn't want me hanging around the house all the time asking for biscuits. My hair blows over my swollen eyes in a wild tangle of wind and curls. I didn't get much sleep; one never does when one has a manic sister who wants to talk all night. I'm a mess this morning. The noise from the sea grows louder.

"Bloody hell, shut up!" I shriek at the dead, but they don't listen. They never do.

At the top of the slope, I check my watch; I have three minutes before class starts, which means I'll have enough time to chat with Norah but not too much time that I'll have to deal with strange looks. I hear chattering voices down the hill, my peers excited to be talking, always talking. I love them—I do—but the kids I've grown up with on this island have never understood that "alone" doesn't always mean "lonely."

Once I cross a field choked with Queen Anne's lace, the one-room Weymouth schoolhouse comes into view over the ridge. I exhale the breath I'm always holding—the one that feels like I'm waiting for something—when I see something bolt away from the schoolhouse like a bird released from its cage. It's Norah, and she's moving fast.

I'm almost halfway down the hill when Norah rushes up to me, long honey braids flapping behind her. At first, her intensity makes my heart clip. *Why is she running like that? Has something bad happened?* Norah never runs—it's something we have in common. But the closer I get to the schoolhouse, the more I can see the thrilled smile spreading across her face, the one that makes her look like she's twelve years old. I watch with folded arms as she scrambles over the low wooden fence that runs past the school, her sweaterdress getting caught on a nail.

"Dammit!" she shrieks, loud enough for me to hear, followed by a ripping sound, and I grin; it's so like Norah to not be able to wait for something as simple as untangling a dress. Her poor, sweet mother cannot mend her clothes fast enough.

My best friend moves like a hurricane of sunshine headed right at me as I brace for impact. Norah surges forward, a line of gray yarn trailing out behind her like a ribbon, still attached to the fence nail.

"Oh my God, Mabel—where the hell have you been? You will not believe what happened this morning! Literally, you're not going to believe it. No one can," she sputters, her voice so loud. I gently reach around her to fix her snag.

"You know it's *really* early for all this excitement, right? Is someone dying? Is Mr. McLeod out sick today?" I try to watch my tone with her, to not sound bored or judgmental. It's not her fault; I've never been as excited about anything in my entire life as Norah has been every second of hers. It's a wonder we're friends, but I'm always grateful—true friends can be hard to come by on Weymouth. Especially when you remind them of things they would rather forget, like a dead moth lingering on a windowsill.

We're nice on Weymouth Island, but wary. Grief is catching here.

"No, no one's dying—it's even better! And yes, we still have school, unfortunately." Her cheeks flush underneath a smattering of freckles as she takes a minute to compose herself. My friend loves a big reveal, but I am running out of patience.

"Norah . . . out with it! Tell me."

"You aren't even ready, Mabel Beuvry, because there is a *new boy sitting in our classroom*." That was definitely not what I was expecting, and so I pause, taking in what surely should be a lie.

"*What?* No. Norah, that can't be right. . . ." I let the sentence trail off as she frowns at me. "But *how?*" I finally blurt out, and she shrieks with joy at my obvious bewilderment.

"I know, completely against the rules, right? But it's true!"

I shake my head. No. A *new boy* can't be real, because a *new anything* isn't allowed on Weymouth Island, ever. Sure, we get the occasional conspiracy-obsessed American tourist who ignores their better instincts and makes it past the Lethe Bridge, but that's different. Besides, the second that tourist crosses the bridge, an unexplainable dread settles into their heart and they find themselves hightailing it back to Glace Bay. Their mind won't let them stay. In all our years here on Weymouth, there has never been a new young person in town, and certainly not a new boy our age. Thoughts tumble incoherently through my brain as it struggles to connect to this new information. But there is something stranger about this news—an alarm sounding off in my heart. It feels like there is an unraveling in my disbelief.

"But—who is he? Does the Triumvirate know?"

"Who CARES?" Norah fires back, one eyebrow raised. "I'm sure the Triumvirate does know, but the real news is that he's here, and he's kind of cute, actually. Not my type, but yours maybe?" Norah is always desperate for romance—any kind of romance. It makes sense—our island is very boring until it's not.

I frown. "And what is that, Norah? My type?"

She ticks them off on her fingers. "For one, he looks kind of grumpy. Two, he seems sarcastic and edgy, and three—and most importantly—he's not from here." What she really means is *He doesn't know about your weird family.* Shame floods up my cheeks, but Norah doesn't notice.

"His name is Miles. That's all I know. Eryk is already in a snit about it, of course."

I roll my eyes. "Of course he is. God forbid anyone draw attention away from His Majesty Eryk Pope. He's been pissed all year." I'm desperate to change the subject, trying hard to ignore the fact that Norah nailed my type on the first try. I try to keep a placid face to throw her off.

Norah grabs my wrist. "I see you pretending to be chill about this, but sod off, Mabel Beuvry. This could stir things up here. Just what you need, perhaps?"

"Norah, calm down. I'm fine." She gives me a look, disappointed as always with lackluster Mabel, who gives her much less drama than she wants. I'm constantly struggling to maintain strict control of my mind and heart, whereas Norah whirls through life, not unlike the winds that batter our island. I envy her, but I do not want to be her.

I figure vulnerability is pain—let her have all of it.

I *do* have questions, though. "Why did they let him stay? Where is he living? How did he even get onto the island?" I blurt them out rapid fire, my fingers rubbing nervously at the small scar that traces up past my ear, a gift of the last Storm. Norah pulls my hand away.

"You only touch it when you're nervous, love." She brushes my brown curls away from my face as I slap at her hand, and she slaps back, and for a moment we playfully flap at each other, echoes of the children we once were.

"Come on, yeah? The bell's going to ring, and Mr. McLeod will have a fit if you're late." Norah doesn't look back as we make our way down. "You should see the new boy's hair *and* his backpack."

"What could possibly be interesting about his backpack?" I sigh, pulling my own like a suit of armor across my back.

"Oh, you'll see." She grins.

"Fine, but I'm not running down there like some deranged fan. You embarrassed yourself galloping over here. Boys—even when they're new—aren't all that grand. They break your heart *and* make you watch them play video games." She shoots me a dirty look that means *Don't talk about Edmund*, but I pretend not to see it.

The first seeds of heather crunch underneath our boots as

we go. It's late May on Weymouth Island, and only a month ago this grass was laced with morning frost. But as May winds down, summer is almost here; I can taste it on my tongue. Weymouth summers taste like campfire smoke, salty lobster tails, and stolen blackberries from the Des Roches garden. Summer on Weymouth must feel like how the outside world must feel all the time, like there is a sense of possibility lurking everywhere.

The bell tower on the schoolhouse looms bright against the mottled sky. The symbol for Weymouth Island sits proudly right above the heavy brass bell: a sigil crest in the shape of a tall gate, with eleven different spears making up the bars, one for each family.

The bell tower is supposed to be this iconic thing, a relic from the Storm of 1846, "a pillar of our community," but truthfully, I've always found it gloomy and more than a little bit phallic, but that's not really what the Triumvirate wants to hear.

I duck in behind Norah as she explodes through the double doors of our school. Mr. McLeod, our sole educator and historian since I was in primary, stands near the front, his head buried in a book like Ichabod Crane. He doesn't look up when we enter—he never does.

Twenty wooden desks line up in front of him like weary soldiers. I see our school as if I'm looking through the new kid's fresh eyes, and I think about how strange this must all look: the old Colonial school house, the bell tower, Mr. McLeod's expensive computer humming at the front. He won't know that the warped wood under our feet was laid by the hands of my ancestors or that the quilted banners hung around the room show the pride of our eleven houses. I squint at them. Edmund and Sloane Nickerson's banner is by far the most lavish: a quilted gray river winds up the middle, with gold on one side and ash on the other. I'm pretty sure their mother ordered real gold leaf to get the effect just right.

Also, I'm pretty sure Anjee Nickerson straight-up made it.

Cordelia Pope, my least favorite classmate and Eryk Pope's sister, is a pretty good artist herself, something I begrudgingly admit. Her banner is made up of crudely cut strips of black shale, pasted in geometric shadows that form a deadly wave. Abra Des Roches's shows a clock made from body parts; Van Grimes's banner shows a moat made of curled paper and salt, probably because the Grimeses actually *have* a moat.

At the end of the row, tucked near the back door, is mine: a badly sketched-out version of my house on a black background, and around it, two swirling ghosts drawn with smeared chalk. It really says, "minimal effort." Mr. McLeod was not impressed when I turned it in; I got a C–, which bought me an entire weekend of shoring up at home with Jeff. Personally, I felt like a C– wasn't terrible, considering I'd made it that morning from old art supplies I'd found floating around Hali's room.

Norah brushes past me as I set my backpack down and unconsciously run my hands over the carved graffiti on the bottom of the desk. It says *Isla was here.* It reminds me that once upon a time my mother sat here in this very classroom. I run my fingers over the words when I'm bored in class—which is often. I like thinking of my mom with her brown high ponytail pulled taut, eagerness shining out of every pore.

That was before the Storm.

Beyond my desk, I hear whispers echoing at the front of the schoolhouse. The girls—and a few of the boys, I suspect—can't contain their excitement about the new kid. Norah bolts up to them and begins chatting; she will not be denied being a part of the group's excitement, not even for a moment.

That's when I notice his silhouette. The new kid is hunched over the farthest desk in the corner, the one that no one has sat at since Charlie Mintus died in the Storm of 2012—the same Storm that took my dad. The new kid with terrible posture is staring at the banners with confusion, definitely wondering where the hell he is. His head tilts, and a lock of black hair falls into his face, and my heart skips a beat. *He really isn't bad-looking,* I think, but then I notice that he's looking at my banner with a look of disgust. *Oh God. It really is so bad.*

After pausing a second, I decide to go over and sit at the vacant desk next to him. It's bold and not my normal vibe, but I know what it's like to be stared at in this schoolhouse. I try not to look directly at him as I sit down casually, like I belong back here instead of at my usual desk. Norah shrieks at the front, and I think, *I'm going to kill her,* but before I can open my mouth to say hello, the new guy beats me to it.

"Hey," he says, and everything slows.

Thomas Cabot, May 1790

I suspect that we Acadians were mistaken of our purpose here on Weymouth. The mutual expressions of animosity between families that were here when we arrived have vanished in an otherworldly storm, but I am loath to tell you that most families are gone—only eleven remain of the hundreds that came. We have all been drawn under its dreadful veil.

May the good and noble God of our former land watch over us, for we fear we have arrived on the devil's shore, and there is no mediator to save us.

Historical note by Reade McLeod: This is the first recorded instance of a Storm after the arrival of the Acadians in 1790. The document was found tucked inside a wine bottle, unearthed in the Cabots' root cellar in 1862.

CHAPTER TWO

"Hello," he says, his voice deeper than I thought it would be. I turn to give him a mildly interested smile, but in a second every intention dissipates, because . . . *Jesus.* He's just so new and shiny. I can't tell if he's actually good-looking or if it's because all my life I've seen the same boring faces, but I can't stop staring at him. He's of Asian heritage, with olive skin and thick jet-black hair that is slicked straight back over his head like a wave on either side. It has height. He has a handsome and sad face, a jutting nose paired with sharp cheekbones. He radiates intelligence and cool; he's the clever kid in movies who winks across a table, who persuades you to pull a heist or join a cult. His eyes are a deep, secret brown, and wrapped around his wrist is a clumsy tattoo of a black ribbon. I find myself wanting to run my fingers along it. No one on this island has a tattoo. He drapes himself over the desk like a blanket, and he's staring right at me.

As his lips form a half smirk, I'm suddenly aware of my own lack of edge: my crazy pile of brown hair, the black turtleneck tucked tight against my throat, jeans tucked into green Hunter boots. Someone should have told me that today was the one day *of my entire life* that I might want to think about what I'm wearing. Instead I'm rocking my standard "outdoorsy kid on an island" look. I could have at least tried to have edge and not be the person Edmund Nickerson once described as "the girl you see reading at a bus stop."

The new guy leans forward, one hand curling around the edge of the desk. There's an intensity in the way he's looking at me that makes me want to either lean into it or run for the door. I'm not sure which. After a second, he seems to realize that he should chill and leans back.

"Interesting . . . uhhh, school building you guys have here. I particularly enjoy these haunting parchments; they really add something to the atmosphere." When he speaks, I glimpse perfectly straight teeth inside his crooked mouth. When I don't say anything, he forces an awkward smile, probably one of dozens that he's given today.

Say something back, you idiot!

"I'm Miles," he says finally, moving through my awkward silence and reaching out to shake my hand. After a long pause, I take his hand in mine. It's a strange, businesslike gesture, but I like the way his warm fingers slide over my cool ones. An unfamiliar electricity spreads through me, and I quickly jerk my hand away.

"I'm Mabel of House Beuvry. And that . . . uh, human tornado over there is my friend Norah Gillis." When I point, Norah waves before burying herself in a cluster of three other girls. "I promise she's normal *most* of the time."

"What does that mean? House Beuvry?" he asks, and I pause, thinking, *Oh God, why did I say that? It sounds so weird to a normal person!*

"Oh, umm, sorry—that's where I live. You know, the last

house to the sea." He nods, and I think he's not following, but then:

"Well, I guess that makes me Miles of House Cabot. I moved here three days ago, and yeah . . ." He lets his voice trail off, implying the weirdness of it all, his name left swirling in the air particles around me. He's a Cabot. *Jesus, the way he said it*—plain as day, like any other name. He has no idea what it means to be a Cabot on our island, no idea that the name Cabot means that you're held in the highest regard, that your house is the first house to the sea, the most important defense on the island. The Cabots have their finger on every small axis of power that exists on Wey-mouth. No wonder the entire schoolhouse has a buzzing, frantic energy about it; they must already know.

"So, are you a cousin or . . . ?" I struggle to keep my voice light even though I'm practically twitching with fascination. I see a flash of watery eyes as he looks away from me sharply.

"Nephew. My mom, Grace, grew up here. She . . . um, died of breast cancer about a month ago, and now I'm here, which is . . . frakking awesome, I guess?" His voice is sarcastic but undercut with sadness. *Grace Cabot, holy shit!* My mother was friends with her once upon a time, but Grace is never spoken of here. No one who leaves Weymouth ever is. I had forgotten she existed until this very moment.

Miles tries to find his next words, struggling to push through some very fresh grief. I want to say "It's okay" or some other junk like that, but I don't. I know from experience that you don't push it or try to fill the silence. I can wait.

He finds his voice again after a few seconds, tears disappearing from his eyes. "We lived in Seattle, my mom and me, but I didn't even know about Weymouth until about two weeks ago. My uncle—her brother—who I've seen exactly one time in my entire life, lives here."

"So, Alistair Cabot is your uncle?"

"Yeah. Do you know him?"

I laugh. "Trust me; everyone knows everyone on this island." There's also the fact that Alistair Cabot is perhaps indirectly responsible for my father's death, but I'll keep that bitterness to myself for today, a thistle perpetually growing in my heart.

Miles Cabot (!) doesn't seem to sense my mood shift. "Apparently, I have no other relatives in a good position to take me. That's what the social worker said—and believe me, I looked. But it was just my mom and me, always. So now I've been sent up here for two years before I can leave for college." He gives a meaningless laugh, the side cut of him nothing but hard angles. The undercurrent is clear: he hates it here. "Two years. I should be able to make it two years, right? Hey, can I ask you a question—Mabel, right? Does your cell phone work here? I haven't been able to get any service or any internet."

I shake my head. "There's no service on this island at all. Cell phones don't work until you're over the bridge. It's why we use walkie-talkies and landlines."

He groans, slamming his head back. "This island is so fuck—"

He's cut off midsentence by a frowning Mr. McLeod, who definitely overheard Miles's choice words. Mr. McLeod clears his throat. "Ahem. Sit down, everyone, please. Girls, take your seats. Sloane, put your comics away." I can tell by Mr. McLeod's strained voice that he's annoyed at the distracting energy Miles is bringing to class. "Now, I realize that it's not every day we have a new face joining us, and so I would like to take a moment to officially welcome Miles Cabot to our classroom."

At his last name, there is a sharp intake of breath, and every eye in the room turns to him. Miles smiles nervously, but it fades as he takes in the piercing stares around him.

Mr. McLeod, a man oblivious to the emotions of others, barely seems to notice.

"Welcome to Weymouth, Miles! It's been a few years since I've had a Cabot in this school, and it's nice to say your family name once more." He smiles proudly as Miles looks like he wants to slide out of his seat and die.

I force myself to quit staring at him.

"Now I need everyone to grab their copy of *The Castle of Otranto* and pick up where we left off. Can someone remind me of what page that was?"

Cordelia Pope's hand shoots up; she's always the first to answer. "We left off on page thirty-two, where Michael shows up to help Miss Isabella."

"Yes, that's right. Let's move along. Cordelia, you start." Mr. McLeod leans against the dusty old organ at the front of the schoolroom, the position he always assumes before falling headfirst into the classics. I imagine Cordelia's voice drifting out through the classroom windows, past the stony shore, and down toward the horror quietly waiting under the waves. Maybe they hear her. *Maybe they listen to all our stories.*

Next to me, Miles stares down at his book, no doubt thinking that *something is not normal about these people.* He's not wrong; our island, this schoolhouse, these people, we are definitely not normal. But then I glimpse Brooke Pelletier staring hungrily at

Miles from across the room, her wispy blond hair curling around her fingertips. As her eyes drink up the delicious mystery of him, I think, *Well, in some ways I guess we are completely normal.*

It's really not my problem, this new boy and his grief, his obvious confusion, and those lost eyes. *God, those eyes.* Yes, definitely not my problem, especially when other girls in this class really want it to be their problem. The last thing I need to do is draw more attention to myself, 'cause when they come for me, they'll come for Hali—and that can't happen. Cordelia keeps reading.

"He was persuaded he could know no happiness but in the society of one with whom he could forever indulge the melancholy that had taken possession of his soul."

"Incredible." Mr. McLeod rocks back on his heels, his eyes half-closed. "*Wow.* Really take that in." Behind him, the massive wooden clock ticks back and forth above his head. On the top of the clock, two carved foxes sway in time with the pendulum swinging below. When the pendulum hits the twelfth cycle, a cloaked figure of death rises slowly out of a bed of wildflowers. Real subtle-like. This morbid clock—carved by the Grimes family, of course—exists to remind us that the Storm is always coming. Practically everything on this island exists for the same reason.

Apparently, I'm not the only one watching the clock: After hooded death sinks back down, Miles sighs and buries his hands in his hair. I ache for this lonely boy with a dead mum, sitting in a weird school on the edge of the world.

The morning ticks by in a haze of literature and math. Lunch is spent outside on the craggy hillside above the Soft Shore (Jeff packed me tuna and biscuits—hooray—with a bag of large carrots for a snack—boo) before we begrudgingly go back inside for Weymouth history. When we get back inside, each student grabs a journal, cataloged chronologically by Storm year. I can see that Miles is confused, so I snap one up (Storm of 1916) and lay it gently on his desk, tapping it with one finger. *Just read,* I mouth, with a shrug.

Thanks, he mouths back. I quickly finish reading the Storm of 1846—an account I've read a dozen times, written in a shaky hand—when our morbid clock finally hits three thirty. At the solemn chime, Mr. McLeod dismisses us with a wave of his arms.

"I'll see you all in two weeks, yes? Don't forget to take your historical readings with you." A gleeful energy shoots through the class at his words—in all the Miles excitement, I had forgotten that today is the beginning of our spring solstice. A smile stretches across my face: More than anything else, Hali will be thrilled by this. Two weeks with no school for me *and* someone new to gossip about. I couldn't give her a better gift.

Miles angrily bolts up from his chair and grabs his backpack—a leather messenger bag with band patches on the straps (dammit, Norah was right, *a very cool backpack*)—and bolts out the door before anyone can talk to him. I watch the door slam behind him.

Norah strolls over a minute later and rests her head on my shoulder. "Cheeky bastard, he hopped right out of here! I was hoping to talk to him after class, get the scoop."

"I have the scoop," I say, pulling on my windbreaker. "He lived in Seattle. His mum is Grace Cabot, who just died of breast cancer."

"That's so sad!" Norah's face falls. "My dad and her were pals back in the day, I think. Maybe he fancied her. Don't tell my mum."

I shrug. "It sounds like he has no other relatives, so he came here. Alistair is his uncle." I think about the way Miles stared at the clock, shoulders squared against his own existence. I would recognize this needless defiance anywhere, the act of trying to will your grief into ambivalence. It never works; we all find better ways of coping.

"Poor kid." Norah shakes her head as she stands back. "Can you imagine? First you're just living your life in Seattle, and then suddenly you're on Weymouth Island? Living in that haunted Cabot mansion? God, does he know what we do here, you think? Christ on a cracker. His entire worldview is about to be shaken. Can you even imagine?"

"I can," I whisper softly. "Yeah, I can."

CHAPTER THREE

Even though it's perpetually gloomy on our little island—all of Nova Scotia can at best be described as "uncomfortably wet" and "perpetually gray"—Fridays in Weymouth still seem like a regular Friday—especially when it's break. The rest of my small class scampers out ahead of me in a wave, each making their way up the main road that cuts Weymouth in half like a knife, heading back to their respective homes and enormous families. From where we are standing, I can see a number of their gates from the road. Gates are a big part of Weymouth; the town is chock-full of barriers to represent what it is we do here—as if anyone could ever forget.

A few years ago, my curiosity—and boredom, too, if I'm honest—got the better of me, and I found myself climbing the tallest trees of the Blackseed Forest, surprising even myself when I reached the top. I had lived here my entire life, but the bird's-eye view of Weymouth took my breath away.

From above, our oblong island juts proudly out into the sea, a defiant piece of land standing where only water should be. I could see the Lethe Bridge at the west end, the only thing connecting us to the rest of the world. The Beuvry house—my house—sits a mile up from the bridge. The Cabot mansion is the first house to the sea, and the Beuvry house is the last one. Our houses are the bookends of the island. From the bridge, if you follow the narrow two-lane road snaking east, you'll drive past the nine other houses on the island, even though some are well tucked back from the road. Beyond the houses, the Dehset Sea looms angrily in the distance, the never-ending mist lying over the deep.

Eleven houses. Eleven families. Eleven traps. From above, I could see how each house flows into the next and into the next—a pattern.

More than a dozen generations have been housed in these buildings of stone. I once asked my father why there were eleven houses and not thirty, not two hundred. A smile formed underneath his mustache as he pulled me against his side.

"What good questions you ask, Mabel-leaf. Eleven is the stroke before midnight, the last chance before night comes. It's the hour when all the world holds its breath, waiting for the dark." This wordy, metaphorical answer was not what I was looking for at seven years old, and so I leapt off his lap and scampered away, looking for Hali.

Just over the Lethe Bridge is the rest of the known world— the mainland—though there isn't much. The town of Glace Bay (an hour's drive away and *barely* a town) is our only mainland link. There are a few businesses, a handful of restaurants, a gas station, and a couple hundred houses scattered around the bay. With cigarette stains on their fingers and empty cans of copper lager at their side, the weathered old men of Glace Bay whisper about us late into the night. Some say we're a cult. Some say we're descendants of the old Guardians of Nova Scotia. Some say we're rich isolationists. They're all a breath away from the truth.

"Mabel?" Norah jogs up beside me as the memories of my dad and the treetops drift away. Up past the lighthouse, I see Miles Cabot speed walking toward the arched Cabot gate, his shoulders hunched protectively. The Cabot house hides its enormous Gothic beauty behind a thick line of trees around the property. I'm surprised at how disappointed I am when he disappears from my sight, a blur in the pine needles. Why am I so drawn to this stranger?

"I wonder what he's thinking." Norah's voice interrupts my thoughts. "It must be lonely in that big house with just Alistair, Liam, and Lucas; a veritable pool of testosterone. I'll bet he needs a distraction." Norah kicks a rock as she walks, rolling the sole of her worn boots over the pebble. She's always moving, never still. "Maybe that distraction could be *you*."

"Actually, he's probably thinking that he wants to go back to Seattle and get off Weirdo Island."

"Hey!" Norah loves it here and never wants to leave.

"Sorry," I say. She hates when I talk about leaving—but it's not like I could anyway. That would mean leaving Hali. We make our way up the hill from the sea.

"So, I have a question, and I want you to *actually* consider it before you give it your typical no-way-in-hell answer." Her face brightens when she looks at me, hoping for a mimic. Girls like Norah are always working overtime to pull sunshine out of rain, and it can be exhausting. However, I'm sure it's *also* exhausting to be friends with the rain.

"I'm sure Jeff told you that the Nickersons are having a party tonight to celebrate our little spring break." I nod. I've heard about nothing else lately. There are no secrets on Weymouth. "Did you know it's Gothic Victorian themed?" She claps her hands. "A theme party! That's so very American of them!"

Theo Nickerson came over from America almost forty years ago, and Norah is obsessed with everything the family does that relates to that. Sparklers on the Fourth of July? So American. Sneakers instead of hiking boots? So American. Edmund Nickerson not calling her back when he says he will? "You know how they are. Americans."

"Mabel. Can you please go? Please?" She points at my face. "And don't say I can go without you. That's not the point. I'm going no matter what, but I *want* to go *with* you. I'm tired of not having my best friend there." She takes my hands with a pout. "At some point, you have to join us. It's been six years. People miss you."

Sure, so they can talk about me, I think.

"A theme party, though?" I sigh. "It's probably so Noah and Anjee can relive the 1980 Storm with the rest of the Triumvirate." We both moan. Parents and grandparents constantly reliving their Storms is one of the worst things about living on Weymouth Island. The stories never stop, and most of the time you aren't in the mood to listen to so-and-so's parents talk about the time they used an iron spear from the porch as a lance.

"Sure, but . . ." She pauses for effect. "My mum found a pattern online for this gorgeous white lace dress, and I'm going to wear her pearl earrings. She's probably sewing it right now." Norah, it should be noted, lives in a different world from the rest of us when it comes to fashion. While the rest of us mostly wear the standard Weymouth uniform of jeans and North Face jackets, Norah wears floral dresses with big gardening boots or green train overalls with a sports bra, or a sweater covered with tiny

yellow pom-poms. Somehow things that look ridiculous on anyone else work on her. In another life, Norah would be walking the
streets of New York and sipping chai while she sketches runway
designs. Now she cinches her arms around her waist and shiv-
ers; it's almost summer, but that doesn't matter. A wind from the
Dehset always brings chills. I offer up another idea.

"You know, we could stay in and watch a movie with Hali. I
bet Mum will let us use the movie room." My friend turns her face
up to get the first splatter of rain on her freckles. I am grateful for
her pause; Norah is the only friend who doesn't act weird when I
talk about Hali. Everyone else doesn't know how to talk about my
sister's "delicate situation."

"No offense, Mabel, but as much as I love Hali time, I would
rather go to a Gothic-themed party in the Nickersons' *sweet*
house than watch a movie. Also, you know those couches are
deeply uncomfortable, right? I literally hate sitting on them." She
levels me with a pleading look. "Mabeellll . . . please. You owe me."
And just like that, I know I won't be winning this one. I can tell
already. And she's right. I owe her a thousand times over.

Finally I surrender. "Fine, we'll go to the Nickersons', but I
really don't have any Gothic attire, since I live in thoroughly modern times and always have."

"Might your mum?"

I rub a finger across my forehead. "Honestly, she'll probably
be three drinks in by the time I get home, so I doubt she'll be
much help, but maybe Jeff would like a project." Jeff always likes
a project.

Norah frowns. "I'm sorry, Mabel. I shouldn't have asked. I—"

She's interrupted by the crashing of branches to our right,

just inside the wood. I put my hand up for her to stop talking, and we pause on the road. Occasionally we do have bears on Weymouth Island that make the swim across the river.

"Is that—" We both jump as a tall man trips out of the woods barely fifty feet in front of us. He stumbles forward, dragging an enormous bag behind him that sounds like it's full of metal. I breathe a sigh of relief. It's Will Lynwood, the Guardian for House Pope.

Norah waves cheerfully. "Hi, Mr. Lynwood!"

He glances at us, and I see that time has not been kind to him lately. His face is hollowed and worn and hanging open at the mouth. He has dark bags under both his eyes, and he's much too thin. His white hair sticks out in all directions as he looks up at us as if he can see through our bodies.

A minute later, he blinks, coming back down to earth. "Oh, hi, girls. How are you?" he asks, as if he has not just burst through the trees looking like a wild man.

"Er, good," Norah replies.

"We're fine," I reply. "Are . . . are you okay?" He does not look okay.

He snorts. "Yeah, I'm fine. Don't tell Cordelia and Eryk, though. They're always worried about me, going on and on about what I should be doing, cleaning up the house, preparing for the Storm, like there's anything you could do to stop a Great Storm, silly children!"

Lynwood's voice rises, and then he's ranting, not looking at us anymore as we stand frozen, unsure what to do. He points at the Dehset Sea. "Sadly, all of you gullible lambs—all of you— so blind! The deception is in the Triumvirate, the Guardians, everyone. If they would just read the journals, they would see the truth. It's clear! You can't silence the voices of our ancestors! The first and the last, they'll bring it around, you understand?"

Then he points to me. "You'll need it to work before the *boom*. Needs to be high."

"I don't understand," I say softly, but he doesn't respond. It's like he doesn't quite see us. A second later, he gives a groan and then begins speaking random numbers, shifting from foot to foot. This man is not okay.

"Eight, one, sixty-seven. No, six then seven. One, eight first. It's there." Norah and I have never seen anything like this on our island. He turns around, and then it's like a switch is flicked, and his ranting stops. His face softens to the familiar, kind one I've known all my life. His madness passes as quickly as it came.

"Whelp, good to see you girls. I'm heading into Wasp Wood. Hope I don't get stung! Have a nice afternoon, Mabel, and say hello to Hali for me." Apparently, now he's back to the man who brings my family a homemade Christmas ornament every year. Lynwood shuffles his way across the road and disappears into the trees, dragging his enormous mystery bag of metal behind him. Norah and I look at each other with wide eyes.

"Well, that was normal," she deadpans.

"What should we do?" I whisper. "He doesn't seem okay!" His words make me uncomfortable. Something about what he said makes me feel vulnerable, exposed, like the words to a fairy tale I once knew. I want to ask him more, and I turn to follow him, but Norah stops me.

"Let him go. He knows his way around. I'll talk to my dad about it as soon as I get home—he'll call the Popes, and they'll come get him." This sounds like a good solution, because what was my plan? Drag him home?

It's such a sad, strange encounter that we walk home in silence for a few minutes before the most unexpected thing pops out of my mouth.

"Maybe I should invite the new boy to the party." I shrug as I say it, my hazel eyes on the road in front of us. In the distance, I hear the quiet lull of the Soft Sea. Norah whips her head around.

"Did you just say what I thought you said? MABEL! Oh my gosh, YES, absolutely we should invite him. I *knew* you liked him!"

"I don't even *know* him. He could be a total psychopath. You saw his backpack. Seems like a lot going on there."

She twists her fingers in her hair. "Maybe, but at least he's new. He'll mix up the group dynamic here."

"Not if Brooke Pelletier devours him first."

She snorts. "As if Brooke could ever top you. Not with those freckles and those curves."

"Or this jacket." I do a little spin, and she wrinkles her nose.

"I hate that jacket."

"Well, Brooke does have a distinct advantage in that no one thinks her family is unhinged."

Norah's voice remains steady. "What do you mean, Mabel?"

"Nothing, just that I'm sure he's hearing all kinds of things about the Beuvry family."

Norah rolls her eyes. "He's probably hearing about every family on the island, gobs of gossip straight from Alistair's mouth. He's like an old woman." She pauses. "Do you think Edmund will mind if he comes?"

"Do we care if he does?" I ask, knowing full well her answer is yes. "And if I recall, everyone on the island was invited. That means Miles, too." Also, I don't give a single care what Edmund Nickerson thinks.

Her eyebrows rise. "Even if he's annoyed, I bet Edmund will get over it. I doubt the Nickersons have ever had a *Cabot* at their party before."

"There's a reason for that," I remind her. Not everyone on this island is an Alistair Cabot fan; you're either in his group of yes-men or you're not. Basically the entire Triumvirate are his yes-men. My family—the Beuvrys—are not, and the Nickersons aren't really either; it's one of the things we have in common. The Guardians of Weymouth tolerate him.

We reach the edge of the Gillis property, and with a few clever clicks of her fingers, Norah opens the lock. On its surface, their gate is lovely: bluebirds circling a wooden cutout of Weymouth Island, blowing green ferns painted underneath it. The cheery paint job hides protection, however: The bluebirds are etched with iron, and folded papers are tucked and hidden underneath the island cutout. Iron is laced through the paint. The house it protects is much too small, however. Norah is the second youngest of eight children. *Eight!* Most families on Weymouth Island are very large. There are two very notable exceptions: my family and the Cabots.

"I'll call you later, yeah?" Norah calls, latching the gate behind her. "And, Mabel—whether or not you invite Miles, just breathe tonight. You're seventeen—it's okay to make mistakes once in a while." Her voice drops as she leans forward. "Don't let Hali give you too much grief, yeah?"

I smile, thinking, *You don't understand,* as she sprints up to her house, no doubt on her way to work on her outfit for this evening's revelries.

I head back out to the main gravel road that runs down the center of the Weymouth. My boots scuff the mud as I loudly exhale the breath I've been holding since I met Miles this morning. Now that everyone is gone, I'm finally able to take in the sodden air, the softly whispering woods. My pulse slows as I make my way home, but the panic on Will Lynwood's face stays with me.

CHAPTER FOUR

B eing the last house to the sea gives me exactly twelve minutes of quiet between Norah's house and mine. I hum lightly as I walk, an old Weymouth lullaby about the sea—because they're all about the sea. I see Hali as I come up the road, waiting for me on the porch like an eager golden retriever.

The peaks of House Beuvry loom against the gray sky. I walk off the road and put my hand on our gate. When I was little, one of the first rhymes I remember learning was:

Mist, sea, white rocks. Close your gate; check the locks.

It's deceptively simple, an easy refrain for a three-year-old to remember. I recall a young Mr. McLeod watching over us as we chanted the words, our little legs kicking at each other. Nothing has changed since then; we will always be those children, learning rhymes and lore, circling each other forever. Until today there have never been new faces inside the circle.

Miles's face flashes in my mind. Maybe he'll see me differently than the rest of this island does. Maybe he won't see sad, strange little Mabel Beuvry. I think of what Alistair, his uncle, probably says about me. *She watched someone in her family die, you know.* But . . . haven't we all at this point?

I make a right onto our little driveway. Our house gate, rather than being symbolic or beautiful, is really morbid. Pieces of iron soar nine feet above my head, and the bars themselves are carved to look like thin bones. Cloaked figures of death swirl around the town's crest in the center, and iron-sculpted ivy drips down to the ground. My great-grandfather ordered this gate from an ironworker in Louisiana in the States, and it always feels that way to me: a little piece of voodoo here in our chilly part of the world.

I press my finger against death's skeletal foot, and the small lever inside clicks to the right. The gate groans as it opens, and I slide through the narrow opening. *Welcome home.*

My fifteen-year-old sister waits for me with an embroidery hoop clutched in her hand like it's 1912. When I come up onto the porch, I can't help but laugh. She's embroidering a comically bad portrait of Ryan Gosling inside her small hoop. She holds up two spools of thread when I come close.

"I can't get his hair right. Do you think this calls for golden thread or classic umber?" I look down into the deeply unsettling face that she has made in her hoop. He looks like a deformed horse.

"Umm . . . classic umber?" I suggest, raising my eyebrows. "You know, for that swoony vibe."

Hali is undeterred by my amusement. "Yes, that's what I thought too. The golden thread is too dark." I drop my backpack onto the porch and sink gratefully onto one of the Adirondack rockers that line our porch.

"How was today, *mon ange?*" I ask, touching her shoulder

COLLEEN OAKES

lightly. I miss Hali when I'm at school. She shrugs and focuses back on her needlework, her short ginger hair practically glowing in the afternoon light. Hali is all gossamer and mood, a phantom that tip-toes through our house. Like my dad, she's very attractive; people are naturally taken by her. I, on the other hand, take after my mum: I'm long and a bit swarthy, with heavy eyebrows and strong, long legs. I carry an intensity in my steps and in my hips. Good eyes, long lashes (wild hair), but no one would ever call me delicate.

"Don't act like you care about my day, Mabel—it's the same as every other day." Hali's voice is sharp; she's in a bad mood. It hangs around her like a thundercloud. "In order: books, clean-ing, crafts, TV. Mum lay down at two, and Jeff has been putzing around. . . ." Her voice trails off.

We both know what Mum lying down means: she's at least a bottle in and down for the count.

"How was school for you?" She brightens at the question, anticipating all the details of my day, and because of that, I spare her none. Hali's life is lonely, and so my mundane details—and gossip—are treasures. But unlike every other day, today I actually have something *special* for her.

"You're not going to believe this, but there was a new boy in class today." Her face doesn't register, and she laughs with a scoff.

"What do you mean, a new boy?" The concept is as foreign to her as it was to me several hours ago.

"There is a *new* boy in our class. His name is Miles . . ." I pause for full dramatic effect. "Cabot. He's Alistair's nephew." Her mouth falls open, and I can't help but relish her absolute shock.

"NO! A new Cabot? For real?" Questions fall out of her mouth rapid-fire. "But . . . how? God, does he know what it means to be a Cabot? Wait—his mother was Alistair's sister, right? The one that ran away a while ago, the one Mum talks about sometimes. What was her name? Grace?" She takes a deep breath. "I am freaking out. The main question is—does he know what we do?" We are silent for a minute, thinking about *what we do*. I reach out and link my hand with hers. It's small, light as air. She yanks it back. "Ugh, Mabel, stop being all sentimental and *just tell me*." I lean back against the porch chair.

"Well, I don't think he knows yet, because he seemed pretty bewildered by our school banners and the death clock." I pause, remembering the sad look on his face.

His very handsome face.

"I hated that clock," hisses Hali. "The foxes always look evil."

"I felt sorry for him." I don't mention the fact that when our hands touched, it felt like the world was opening up, just a little.

"I was thinking of inviting him to the Nickersons' party tonight. Do you think you would have enough time to whip me up a quick Gothic dress?" I laugh lightly, trying to delay her anger. Hali's left eye twitches suspiciously. She ignores my lighthearted request and aims her needle right at my heart.

"You're leaving? Again?" She stabs her needle through the hoop. "First of all, *no*, I cannot sew you a Gothic dress in the next two hours. I'm not magical. And second of all, you hate parties, so the only reason you want to go is because *you like him*. Tell me I'm wrong."

There is desperation in her last word. It cuts sharp as I look out over our gardens, the ones that hide a gauntlet. The lupines are cutting up, royal purple peeking up through the green. I clear my throat.

"I don't even *know him*, Hali. I spoke to him in class for about three seconds while the rest of the girls stared, and the boys circled him like lions. That poor kid has no idea what he has stumbled into. But if anybody needs a friend, it's him. You know what it's like to be the odd one out."

She sighs, propping her feet up on the deck. "I suppose. So, what does he look like? Come now, tell me. Spare no detail." She flutters to my feet, her intense green eyes peering up at me.

An uninvited smile creeps across my face. "Well, he's Asian. I think. Loads of black hair. He has a nice smile and narrow shoulders." I pause and shrug as if it's nothing. "A good face, overall, I guess." *Incredible cheekbones, long hands that could make a girl move. A calm, sad energy. A hint of mischief; a body he doesn't quite know how to control yet.* Hali is not fooled by my show of disinterest. She's smelled blood in the water.

"A nice smile? Nice how?"

I think back to how his lips rose on the right side first, sliding open like a secret. "Hardly any decaying teeth at all."

"So he didn't climb up out of the Dehset? Interesting." Hali climbs up and leans her head on my shoulder, and I inhale the slightly pungent hint that implies she didn't shower today. "I wish you didn't have to go to a party tonight. I thought maybe we could stay home and watch *Dolores Claiborne*. I'll ask Jeff to make popcorn!"

I reach up and pat her cheek, her skin as soft as it was when she was a girl. Sometimes it seems like Hali's illness has suspended her somewhere between a child and a teenager, stuck there forever. "Maybe later this weekend? Norah's dead set on me going."

Hali sighs. "Of course she is. What would she do with her life if she weren't chasing after Edmund Nickerson?"

"I have a crazy idea," I mutter, watching the sun begin to lower itself in the sky. "Why don't you come with me?" As I say it, I know what her answer will be, but I always ask anyway. Hali needs to know that I *want* her there. It's not about her physical presence. It's about me noting her absence. It's a complicated dance that never ends.

The wind hurtles up from the lower gardens, and the tiny silver acorns of our wind chime titter in the wind, the soft sound of home. I've heard them go silent only once, and that was the night our father died.

I gently shrug Hali off my shoulder and climb to my feet. "I'm going to say hi to Mum. See if she can rally off her effing pillow."

"Be nice, Mabel. She's trying. You're too hard on her."

I stretch my arms over my head. "She needs to try harder." As I head inside the house, Hali speaks to me in a low voice that no one else can hear.

"A boy in the mix. Just what we need. You're selfish, Mabel."

I let the door slam hard behind me.

Eustace Mintus, October 13, 1817

I write in this journal from amongst the debris of the most unthinkable night of terrors. Around me sit the white-shrouded bodies of men, women, and children wrapped in damp, dirty linen; my own Daniel is among them; my mother also.

His small body is curled beside her in the mud, my heart alongside them. It won't belong to me ever again.

Charity's and my pain is unimaginable. Pieces of houses have been swept out into the Dehset, leaving behind only the marked stones underneath. It was as if the heavens crashed down on us; only instead of angels, they contained all the demons of hell. Everything is gone; everyone is dead. Why have we been called to this godforsaken place?

Historical note by Reade McLeod: The Mintus family suffered great losses in the Storm of 1817. Eustace Mintus himself would pass away in a fortnight from an infected cut he received during the Storm.

CHAPTER FIVE

E
ntering the Beuvry Estate is a dramatic affair. When I walk through our carved double doors, I sometimes imagine that we live in a charming place like Carmel-by-the-Sea, a town I read about once. When I walk into my imaginary bungalow, Mum is waiting for me with a plate of cut fruit. She's sober, no wineglass clutched in her trembling hand. Hali is hanging out with her friends, something unimaginable at this point. I hear my dad's boisterous laugh echo through the little house. There is no legacy binding us, no Storm, no ancestors to honor. This dream gets left behind as I climb the steep staircase to reach the first wing of the house.

I knock softly on her door.

"Come in, Mabel." She isn't abnormally cheery yet, which means she isn't too far in today. *Good.* I push open the door.

"Hi, Mum." She's in here, buried somewhere. Her room is like the backstage of a midcentury play. Thin pieces of fabric are draped everywhere: on the walls, over mirrors, on the backs of couches.

"How was school, lovie?" My mum is seated at her vanity, turned halfway around.

I stand awkwardly in the middle of the room, not wanting to give the impression that this interaction will last longer than it has to. "It was fine, a normal Friday. We read some of the journals today."

My mother brushes back her pale toffee curls, streaks of gray at both of her temples. "I always loved reading the journals. The account of the 1876 Storm is *dynamic*. There was something about that Storm, bigger than the rest."

I think of Will Lynwood, mumbling about a Great Storm. I hope Norah's dad called the Popes. Mum looks up at me from the mirror.

My mother is still lovely, but drinking has aged her prematurely. Her skin is stretched thin, lines at her mouth pronounced. She lowers her voice to a conspiratorial whisper as she takes a drink. "Funny you didn't mention there is a new Cabot in town! I thought that would be the first thing out of your mouth. I've been dying to hear about it! Was he at school?"

I roll my eyes. "Of course you know already. Did Anjee tell you that?"

She shrugs. "We may have had a brief phone chat." Anjee Nickerson and my mother are very close; they chat on the phone every day, which is why I generally avoid Anjee Nickerson.

Her eyes grow curious. "Well, was he there today?"

I rub my fingers across my forehead where a headache is forming. "Yes, the new Cabot boy was at school today. He seemed overwhelmed . . . and sad." My mother taps her cigarette on the edge of the chair, like a silent film star. It's not lit—she hasn't actually smoked since my father died—but she loves the feeling of a cigarette in her hands, and as she says, *It keeps the demons at bay*. I don't blame her—we all have our vices.

Tap, tap, tap. She leans back and sighs.

"Unless his mother told him about the island—which she couldn't if she left—I doubt he knows anything." That's something fun about Weymouth. If you leave for a long time, you forget about what we do here. "Still, even if she forgot about Weymouth, it was always calling her back." *Tap, tap, tap.* "Mabel, you should tell him before he finds out about us in some other, dreadful way—like if he's hazed for his iron whip." I hadn't thought of that, but she's absolutely right. What a nightmare that would be. The boys on this island wouldn't. Would they? I think of Eryk Pope's smug face.

As I turn to go, Mum pulls me close in the same way she did when I was a girl, and against my better judgment, I lean into her touch. Her wine breath washes over me with its sharp taint.

"Are you going to the Nickersons' party tonight?" she asks, and I shrug. When she points my chin up, I see the remnants of crusted golden eye shadow at the corners of her eyes, which makes me so sad inside, I can hardly bear it. My mother always wakes with such hope; she showers and puts on makeup, but then it's noon and one glass becomes three, and by the time I get home from school, all her good intentions have sunk to the bottom of a bottle.

"Please go, Mabel. At least one person in this house should get out and have a nice time. Be a kid, make some mistakes. Get kissed behind a tree."

"MUM!"

She tucks a strand of hair behind my ear. "Sorry. When you get there, make sure to tell Noah and Anjee thank you for the invite. I'm not up to it today."

And you have a long night of drinking ahead of you.

"I'll tell Jeff to make something to send with you. Or perhaps he's going?"

"It's just families. Not Guardians," I mutter. "Besides, if he goes, who will stay with Hali?"

Her eyes darken. "I'm here," she snaps. "That's all you need to worry about. I'll wait up for you."

"Sure thing," I mumble, the pesky ache in my heart wishing that she *would w*ait up but knowing that she won't.

After I leave my mother to continue her self-destruction, I climb to the uppermost level of the house, what some would call a widow's walk but we call Cloudbreak. We have to check Cloudbreak every day, and by "we," I mean Jeff and me. I let myself out the narrow door that leads to the walk high above our house.

It's pretty up here. To the east, a sharp wind moves tips of blue pines, fine as needles. On my left, the Soft Sea waves lap gently against the rocks. I watch silently as the sky dyes itself a pomegranate pink, reminding me of harvests and hearths, things of old. Just like this house. Just like this island.

There is nothing on the horizon to note, so I go to the small steel box on the ledge and pull out a walkie-talkie, turn it on, and switch it to channel 11. "This is Mabel Beuvry from Cloudbreak, over."

"Mabel, this is Alistair from the Cabot house, over."

Ugh, of course *he's* on tonight.

"There's nothing to report from here. Again. Over."

"Thanks, Mabel, I've noted it in the journal. Would you mind measuring the air density for me? Over."

I roll my eyes but do it anyway. The small red Kestrel environmental meter tacked to the wall measures air velocity, density, and evaporation rate. I dully read Alistair the numbers. We measure these in hopes that they will help us predict the next Storm, but so far they haven't.

Alistair's voice crackles over the radio. "Thank you, Miss Beuvry. It seems like nothing is amiss tonight. Over."

I go to turn off the walkie, but I hesitate for a second, and against my better judgment ask, "Mr. Cabot?"

There is an awkward pause. "Errrr . . . yes?"

"Would it be okay to invite Miles to the party at the Nickersons' tonight?" I cringe at my nervous, too-high voice and smack the walkie-talkie against my forehead: so stupid, so stupid. In the long pause that follows, I pray for the earth to open and swallow me whole. Finally the walkie crackles once more.

"Uh, sure, Mabel, I'll pass that along. Have a good night. Over." I barely have a second to soak in my shame before the radio beeps again.

"Yes?" I say too quickly. I hear static, followed by the voice of James Gillis—Norah's pesky little brother—over the waves. He's always creeping on the channel.

"Miles and Mabel, sitting in a tree, *K-I-S-S-I-N-G*."

"Eat shit, James! I'm calling your mum," I hiss. God, this is a *public* channel. "JAMES! Hang up!" He makes a fart sound and clicks off the radio, laughing as he goes. I sink back against the decrepit stone chimney that forms the spine of Cloudbreak and let out a groan. If James knows, everyone will know soon enough.

What did Alistair say? *I'll pass that along.* God, I hate that guy.

I take a last look at the blotchy sky and head back into the house, latching the door behind me.

39

"Fancy trying that again?" I leap out of my skin when I hear a male voice just behind me. I jerk backward, hitting my elbow hard against an iron railing.

"Oww! Jeff! Subtly announce your presence before you speak in a dark hallway. Geesh." Our House Guardian, Ser Jeffrey—*Jeff*—stands below me, blending in with the shadows on the staircase. His features are rounded, his chin growing a little heavier with each passing year. His brown goatee is dusted with gray. The light from the window reflects off his large tortoiseshell glasses. He's built like a stack of bricks: strong, unshakable. I trust him with my life.

He reaches behind me to wiggle the lock. "Check locks once; check them twice; less than four will not suffice." He smiles.

"I know, I know." I sigh as I flip the lock four times and add my and Hali's personal rhyme: "Check the locks with a sigh; check the locks until you die."

"Mabel." He frowns at the refrain. Man, I love annoying him. House Guardians—in my opinion—are one of the best perks about living on Weymouth Island. Jeff's family has served House Beuvry for generations. His grandfather served my grandparents. His father served my father, and for a while, he did too. Jeff was getting his PhD when the Storm took my father, but he returned so his father could retire after his stroke. His father lives off-island now, in Vancouver, and now Jeff serves Mum, Hali, and me. His father was a kind man, but Jeff is, how do you say . . . ? *The bomb.*

Being a House Guardian is a choice, of course—we're not monsters—and Jeff is paid through a living trust. Literally the last thing I remember from *that night*—inhuman wails tearing from my chest—is Jeff's father's arms carrying me away from the body in the hallway, my mother slumped over it. I remember the feel of the thick wool against my cheek, the smell of his sweater covering up the metallic tang of blood and salt.

That man's son now hands me a small cheese wheel with a happy face drawn on it. Jeff's not our father, but he's not far from it either. He's always reminded me of a stocky owl, fluttering around our house, checking in on things. But he's also a bird of prey who has sharp talons for anyone or any*thing* that would threaten us. Without him, this old mansion would fall apart, quite literally. With all the constant structural changes we make, it has a lot of weird quirks that only he knows. It's kind of like our family.

Old House Beuvry creaks when I plop down onto a small ottoman, shoveling tangy cheddar into my mouth as Jeff looks down at me with amusement. He's handsome for his age (which could be anywhere between forty and fifty, though Hali believes he's ageless). He sighs as he watches me inhale the snack. "Reade McLeod doesn't feed you any snacks at school, does he?"

"Never," I mutter.

"You would think he would have heard of biscuits by now. I mean, what else is he doing?"

Teaching us everything, I think, but I stay silent. Jeff always has a lot of thoughts about Mr. McLeod given that they were once *romantically inclined.*

He dramatically leans over the banister. "I heard there's a new Cabot in town."

I close my eyes. *Why is everyone talking to me about this?* Of course Jeff knows; House Guardians chat with one another all day. Their topic this and every week is probably Shoring Up and Freaking Out.

"I really don't want to talk about it. I've already heard from Mum and Hali."

"Fine. I won't mention it." Jeff drums on the railing, and I change the subject.

"Norah's begged me to go to that Gothic gathering tonight at the Nickersons'."

He rolls his eyes. "Oh yes, the party, so garish. If it was All Hallows' Eve, it would be one thing, but in the middle of May? Please."

"I thought all gay men loved theme parties."

"Well, I haven't checked with our official handbook, but sometimes we do, when they are tastefully done. The only thing good about the Victorian age was the clothing. The rest was just Eurocentric racism and dangerous medicine." He rubs his temples as if the very idea gives him a headache. "In my opinion, the Nickersons are always looking for new ways to entertain us because they're bored on Weymouth."

"Nothing wrong with that. Weymouth is incredibly dull."

He raises an eyebrow.

"Until it isn't," I stammer, realizing the error of my words. Thankfully, he lets it pass.

"Right, then. SO, what are you going to wear to this theme party?"

"This, I guess?" I gesture to my jeans and nondescript top, and he looks devastated. "Or not! I asked Hali if she would put something together for me, but she refused. Too busy with needlework and being mad that I'm leaving." I let out a strangled sigh. "Every time I walk out the door, it's a betrayal."

"You know what I think about that? You cannot live your life for Hali's sake! She'll be all right here with us, I promise. Worrying about her won't do you any good. Go out. Spend time with Norah and Sloane. Maybe talk with the new boy?"

Guilt over Hali worms its way into my chest.

"And, Mabel, you know you can call me at any time if you decide to have a drink. Notice I said have 'a drink.' Not six. I'll come get you with the car, no judgment included." Of course. It's not like I could call my mum. You don't call a drunk driver to save you from a drunk driver.

I wave him away. "You're assuming I'm much more popular than I actually am. I'll leave after a half hour, like normal. Then I can come home and spend time with Hali." I would rather shove a needle under my fingernails than deal with the sister guilt coming my way.

Jeff pauses. "Of course. But first, I think I can help you with a Gothic outfit. Your grandmother has some vintage dresses in a trunk in the attic. She loved to dress up in the evenings and pace Cloudbreak—very *Flowers in the Attic* of her. Let's go see what we can find; I've needed to shore up that area for weeks anyway."

I grin. Now, this *actually* sounds kind of fun.

Two hours and much arguing later, I'm standing in front of the mirror in my bedroom as Jeff proudly looks at his handiwork. "I'm not one to pat myself on the back, but you look wonderful, Mabel. Absolutely marvelous."

I stare at myself, unsure what to say without hurting his feelings. I do look great. *I just don't look like myself,* and honestly, that's why I look great.

My normally unhinged brown mess of hair has been swept back into a high, curly bun with loose tendrils falling all around my face. I am wearing an old black lace dress of my grandmother's.

She was much more petite than I am—most of my family is—and so the dress is unzipped in the back but hidden by a tasseled black shawl. Around my neck is a thick gray ribbon with a small porcelain bird in the center. Pearl earrings dot my ears; black-and-white Converse sneakers sit on my feet. I look like someone who would live in an old mansion bursting with secrets. Oh, wait, that *is* my life.

I touch the brooch cautiously as I turn in the mirror. This is not the Mabel who fades into the background. She's who I wish I could be.

Jeff smiles. "You should probably head out. The Nickersons are weird about lateness." As he leaves the room, Hali comes in, ducking underneath his arm and giving him a nasty look.

"Wow, you look different." Hali's voice trails off when she sees the dress, but it's me who spins around in shock. Hali is *dressed*—dressed like she's going to leave the house. She's wearing a pale pink dress of Mum's with ballet slippers on her feet. Her short ginger hair is brushed to the side and pinned with a pearl clip. The freckles spattered across her face are no longer childish; they've become beautiful.

"Hali . . . ," I say softly.

"I'm going to try." Her voice wavers on the last note. "It's time, right? I can't stay in this house forever."

I say nothing, but I give her a big smile. If I react with too much excitement, it will tip her scales into anxiety. If I act like it's no big deal, Hali will deflate like a popped balloon. We have done this dance many times.

"You look gorgeous," I say. "Pale pink is your color."

"And you look like a high school production of *The Woman in Black*." She smirks.

"My God." Jeff stands in the doorway, his eyes on the mirror. "You look just like your mother." Hali gives him a proud little spin in her dress. His eyes meet mine.

"Handsome, too, like your father. You have his strong chin."

Oh good, just what a girl wants to hear. "Hali's going to be coming tonight," I tell him.

"Two Beuvry girls at the party would be just the thing, wouldn't it?" Hali smiles at him, but I can see her breaths becoming quicker as reality begins to sink in.

The people. The noise. The questions. I watch as a flush runs up her tiny neck.

Holding up our dresses, we make our way down the hallway and past my mother's room. I rap my knuckles against the door as we go, where I can hear her frantically humming inside.

"Mum, we're leaving for the party!"

"Have fun!" her strangled voice rings out; I can tell she's been crying.

"I love you, Mum," I whisper softly through the door. We're so close to and yet so far from each other: ships on different sides of the same ocean. I have no idea what I'll do if the Storm comes when she's like this.

I hear Hali's breathing pick up as we make our way toward the front door. I take her hand as we walk out onto the porch, still well within her safe space. She begins muttering a stream of quiet monologue, a skill that she has picked up from a self-help book she found online.

"I can control my fear. I am not alone." She repeats this over and over again. "I can control my fear. I am not alone." She looks over at me, every step slower than the last as her eyes grow wide and a cold sweat breaks out on her forehead. Jeff stands calmly on the porch, watching us go.

Across the wildflower fields in front of our house, the sun pulls itself down into the sea. We make it halfway across the yard before Hali loses it completely. She begins clutching at her chest with fingernails painted a pale pink to match her dress. Her breathing becomes shallow as she tries to find her center, and her eyes fill with desperate tears. There's nothing I can do, no way to stop it. She has to stay, or everything comes apart. I hold her arm as she falls to her knees; it's all too much: the sweat, the nausea, the anxiety. *She cannot leave.*

"I'm sorry, Mabel," she rasps, turning back to the house, where Jeff waits patiently for her. "I'm sorry. I wanted to come. I really did."

I wrap her in my arms, heart aching for my sister, the one who is the bones of my bones. I wish I could fix her, could give her back to the world. "I know. I know. You tried so hard. But look how far you got; this is the farthest out from the yard you've been in a year! That's not nothing, Hali; *that's everything.*" She leans against my chest, her head covered with shiny sweat.

"Let me go," she whimpers finally, and I release her arm. She rushes toward the porch.

"I should stay," I say, turning back to the house.

"No. Go on ahead, Mabel. You're going to be late," Jeff says carefully, his eyes steely. "Just go. I've got it. Say hello to Norah for me." I stand frozen for a minute, trying to balance the emotional weight of what happened with the knowledge that this is a normal day.

When I turn to go, the porch light winks off, leaving me trapped between two worlds.

CHAPTER SIX

E dmund and Sloane Nickerson live only a few houses down from ours, which is nice because I'm wearing a dress, the wind is strong, and I'm basically naked underneath. *This is why people don't wear dresses.* Halfway there, I almost turn around because of how awkward I feel, shuffling down a gravel road wearing my late grandmother's dress. It's ridiculous. I am ridiculous. But I make myself keep walking toward the Nickerson Estate.

Their enormous, modern house appears through the trees, sitting cozily atop an ivy-covered stone embankment. The Nickersons have the newest house on the island because their ancestors tore everything down to their sacred foundation stones and rebuilt it after the Storm of 1980. I often find myself staring when I'm inside it, wondering what it's like to not live in a house so old that you once found an actual sword buried in the garden, a house where nothing works the way it should. Up close the Nickerson house is an enormous white Craftsman with gray stones and mixed shingles. It's classic and bright, just like their family.

Their house is a very pretty trap.

Glowing luminaries lead the way toward the house, marking a clear path. When you're visiting any house but your own on Weymouth, you stay on the marked path. I'm seized with a sudden fear: What if no one else dresses up? I'll be stuck here looking like Morticia Addams while everyone else is wearing normal clothing. *God, I should go.* I turn back, hoping to sneak away, when Norah appears around the side yard.

"Mabel, you came!" She's wearing a white gown with a turquoise butterfly pinned in her hair. She's a Gothic romance come to life, only a breath away from being a dead bride. Immediately she assaults me with questions, dragging me toward the house.

"Was Hali pissed? Is that your mum's dress? Do you think that my dress is Gothic? What do you think Edmund will think of it? I heard you invited Miles. Do you think he will come?" I don't even have time to respond before she waltzes me through the front door. *Clever girl.*

Inside the house, I hear the tinkling of piano keys and I can't help but smile; John Nickerson is an excellent piano player, the best musician on the island. The closer I get, the easier it is to recognize the song: "Dance Macabre" by Camille Saint-Saëns, one of my favorites.

I turn to Norah, feeling actually excited for the first time in a while. "Ever think how weird it is that we know these songs deep in our soul, even though they aren't part of *our* history or *our* culture? Almost as if we know them through our biology. Do you ever think about that?"

She looks over at me with a combination of love and utter disappointment. "Mabel, I love you, but we are at a party, an *actual* party. Maybe it's not the time to discuss music passing through our biology."

"Sorry." I bite my lip and remind myself *not to be weird.* It's been a while since I've hung around lots of people outside of school.

"No worries." Norah remains undeterred as we pass through the foyer. "You should see Edmund tonight; my heart almost stopped when I saw him with his suit and pocket watch." She sighs lustfully but lowers her voice as we pass by several Weymouth families. The eccentric Pelletiers are here. So are the awkward but loveable Grimeses and the snooty, artistic Popes.

"Hey, did your dad ever call the Popes about Lynwood?" I whisper.

Norah nods. "Yeah, he told them, but Eryk's dad said that his blood sugar was high and not to worry about it, that they would check on him."

I frown, thinking of how Lynwood was raving about the Great Storm. *That didn't seem like high blood sugar.* The trio of families glances over at me as we pass, probably whispering about Hali. In the corner, Liam and Lucas Cabot—Miles's cousins— are getting sloshed on Moscow mules. I don't see Miles anywhere, and I let my heart feel a twinge of disappointment.

The main room of the house looks incredible, filled with vases of wildflowers and low, rich plates of food: cheese and fruit, huge dark grapes glistening seductively on the silver platters. Mirrors have been draped with translucent black fabric, and candlelight flickers in from every surface. Several adults sway together to the low, mournful piano music, drinks in hand. People from all eleven houses—now that I'm here, anyway—congregate around the kitchen, laughing a bit too loudly as they raise their wine goblets.

It makes me want to die inside.

"Norah! Come dance with your father!" Oliver Gillis, Norah's boisterous father, calls over to us. He's chatting with Laurel Des Roches, who is dressed in an old green smock with a black net over her face. Norah jumps in with her dad, and they sway awkwardly together. At first it's cute, but then Mr. Gillis accidentally steps on her foot, and as they laugh, an ache for my own dad passes through my heart. "Mabel, you want to join us?" he asks, and I'm so choked up that I can't even answer, so I wave them away and head to the kitchen to hide.

Except there is no hiding here. Anjee Nickerson, the matriarch of their family and my mom's best friend, is lording over the kitchen.

"Hey, Mabel! I didn't expect to see you tonight." She looks stunning in a navy Victorian dress, which brings out the gorgeous shades of her dark brown skin. Edmund's mother, without a doubt, is the most beautiful woman on our island. I'm sure it didn't take much for her to find a person off-island (John, currently playing the piano) to give up everything, move to Weymouth, marry her, and stay forever.

It doesn't hurt that Anjee is also incredibly nice. "Hey, how's your mum doing? I so wish she would have come. This is the kind of party she used to love!"

The sympathy in her voice fills me with a small fury. *You know she's drunk,* I think, but instead of saying this, I smile and reach for some Brie. "She's fine. She, Hali, and Jeff are watching a movie."

Mrs. Nickerson shakes her head as she refills a silver water pitcher. "Well, that sounds nice too. Nothing wrong with a night in. The rest of your classmates are downstairs, but they'll be coming up for food pretty soon here. Can't keep them away—you know them."

Of course I do; they are the only kids I've known since I was born. Anjee walks over to the staircase and yells, "BOYS! FOOD!" which is amusing, seeing how she is dressed like a proper duchess.

The Nickersons are the only Black family on Weymouth Island, and from what I know from Edmund, it hasn't always been easy. Decades of old, ugly racism run through Nova Scotia and pockets of our island as well—as brittle as the bones of our ancestors. We live in one of the whitest areas in the world. When Adelaide Nickerson married a Black man from America—Theo— it was a huge scandal. Their family grew, but not without harassment. They didn't flinch. It was a dark time in our island's history, a shameful note in our canon books.

As if we didn't need every house, every family.

As if anything else mattered other than the Storm.

At the time, Weymouth didn't know how lucky we all were to have the Nickersons. Their house—more than any other— brings fresh life and innovation to the island. We are an old, honor-bound people and as a result can be as cold and unfeeling as the seas that crash against our shores. The Nickersons are friendly—all *twelve* of them—and Anjee Nickerson is an engineer the likes of which this town has never seen. We are safer because of her, and the Cabots' power-wielding techniques aside, I would say that the Nickersons are the most popular family in town. Two of those reasons—Sloane and Edmund, their youngest boys—come thundering up the stairs a second later, looking for food. They are *always* looking for food.

"Mabel, you came!" Edmund doesn't try to hide the shock in his voice. "I bet Norah's over the moon. You going to stay for a while, unlike last time?" I blush, trying not to think about the dozens of social gatherings that I've left early, only because some-one asked too pointed a question about Hali. Honestly, I'm never sure where I fit, and yet I remember the moment earlier today, shaking Miles's hand. The way warmth spread through me; I felt like I fit there—with him. I shake the ridiculous thought away. What am I, a character in one of Mom's romance novels? Jesus, I'm sure dressed like one.

"Sure." I laugh lightly. "Though, hopefully I don't go home in a body bag."

Edmund's face is puzzled as I try to explain myself.

"You know . . . Gothic party. Murder. A big house. Never mind." As he stares at me, his other hand sneakily slides a wine bottle into his jacket. He winks at me, and my heart gives a tiny, meaningless shudder. Edmund and Sloane Nickerson are what many would call "golden boys." They are tall and hearty, with their mother's glowing brown skin, deep amber eyes, and clever white smiles, just on the other side of pretty. Edmund, one year older and the whole purpose of Norah's entire existence, is athletic—a runner and a baseball player. (We have no official teams here on Weymouth—obviously—but there is a small group that plays in the summer.) Edmund has an intensity that's hard to stomach, but he can be kind in quiet conversation.

Sloane, the youngest, has an aloofness that draws you near. He's my other *actual* friend on the island, though we don't hang out as much as we used to. Sloane is more intellectual, more styl-ish than his older brother. If he didn't have to stay here in Wey-mouth, I could see him feeling at home in NYC or Vancouver. Every sentence ends with a clever quip.

Norah has been enamored with Edmund since she turned

twelve, and when I look at Edmund tonight, I at least understand her obsession. He's dressed in tight tweed pants, a white button-down shirt with a black suit vest over the top. The boy cleans up well.

Mrs. Nickerson doesn't even look up as Edmund attempts to slink back down the stairs. "Boy, put that bottle of wine back in the fridge."

He flashes his million-dollar grin at his mum and shrugs. "Did you know that back in the early 1900s, kids started drinking as early as eight years old?"

She tilts her head. "Edmund, just because you know how to Google something doesn't mean it changes the existing rules in our home." She shakes her head at me. "I tell you, Mabel. These boys . . ."

Edmund puts the bottle back. "Fine, I'm going."

Anjee waves a kitchen knife at him. "Have some water, and make sure those kids out by the fire are drinking water too. I don't need anyone ending up face down in the Soft Sea. I'm not cleaning up that mess." Edmund leans over and gives his mum a quick kiss on the cheek, and I wonder what it's like to be a part of a family that's so lighthearted.

Is it nice? Annoying? A little bit of both?

Edmund sees me staring at them out of the corner of his eye. *Don't. Be. Weird.* "Hey, Mabel, grab that cheese plate, will you?"

I follow him to the stairs.

"Sorry, my mum is too much sometimes."

"It's fine—she's so nice."

"Yeah, she's all right, I guess. I know she worries about you and your mum."

I don't know what to say to that, so I silently follow him down the staircase. It's lined with iron rails that disappear into the ceiling. The doors on either end can be shut, effectively making this a cage. It's a clever trap, barely noticeable to the naked eye.

We round the corner into the basement, which is unlike any other basement on Weymouth. There is a big-screen TV, a pool table, and a granite bar filled with soda pop. Double doors lead out to a walk-out patio with a stone hot tub, tables, and a cobblestone firepit that overlooks the Soft Sea. It's the perfect spot to hang out with friends or find a quiet corner to make out with someone. I know because I kissed Sloane there once. We were thirteen and curious. It was warm and nice, and we've never been interested in doing it again.

Sloane is standing behind the bar, throwing cans of soda around like he's a mixologist. He gives me a wave and goes back to chatting with Cordelia Pope and her minions, all eyes turning to me. Their gazes burn as they size up my dress and hair, whispering among themselves. *Weird Mabel, always alone. Did you hear about the messed-up sister in the house?*

I ignore the sinking in my stomach, trying not to think about what they are saying. *It doesn't matter. They don't matter. Screw them.* All the faces in here are dully familiar: Hudson Pelletier is lying on the couch with Abra Des Roches perched on his lap. Eryk Pope, the island's resident d-bag, is playing pool with Van Grimes and Brooke Pelletier. Fallon Bodhmall bounces in from outside and shouts at Sloane in French.

"*Vite, barman, servez-moi un verre!*" Quick, bartender, pour me a glass. We all speak a little bit of French here. Sloane flips him off. Norah explodes down the stairs, her loud giggle turning everyone's attention to her. She makes eye contact with Edmund for a second and then turns away with a smile. I watch it all play out, somehow removed from it all. I have known the people in this room since birth, and that's the problem.

Sloane frantically waves me over. "Hey, BEUVRY! That dress looks great—looking like Mrs. de Winter over there. I'm so glad you came."

I give him an awkward hug and lean against the bar, feeling very grown-up. Sloane shares my embarrassing love of books. As we talk, I feel myself unwind around him; his humor puts me at ease, and it makes me remember who I used to be—before Hali's agoraphobia and my mother's drinking.

"Well, that's what I was going for, you know: a mysterious woman, living in a creepy house on a windy moor, communing with the dead on a normal basis and having a lot of tea."

"Yeah, you've definitely got that sexually frustrated widow vibe going on."

I make a face. "Errr, thanks, Sloane."

"What do you want to drink? We got soda, ginger ale, water . . . soda with a dash of rum?" He winks just like his brother.

I look at him exasperatedly, daring him to remember that my mum is an alcoholic. "Yeah, alcohol's not really my thing." I know he knows. Everyone in this town knows.

After a second, it dawns on him. "Oh right, sorry, Mabel. I was feeling the bartender thing. I've been thinking about it as a part-time gig in college. I'm getting pretty good at it—watch this." My eyes glaze over as he attempts to spin a glass over the back of his hand; it falls to the ground and explodes. Sloane doesn't even look down. He just shrugs lightheartedly and grabs another. *A part-time gig in college.* What dreams.

College is the far-flung dream of every single kid in this room, the dream of every kid that has ever lived on Weymouth Island. It comes up in the schoolyard, whispered in bedrooms after the lights go out. *What if we could go to college?* they whisper. *What would you major in? Where would you go if you could leave?*

Biology, they say. *Creative writing*, they muse. Cambridge. MIT. Stanford. Queen's University.

"Apparently, none of us are going to a local Halifax community college?" I once joked to Norah, before she leveled me with a stare.

"Why would you dream of a local school when you know it's just a dream?"

She's right. None of us can leave, because what if we're not here when the Storm comes? Because when you leave, you leave forever. I used to be one of those people who had dreams of college, of leaving this island for four years, seeing new places, experiencing new things. When I think about the person I was before the Storm that took my dad and broke Hali, I feel a hint of envious rage. That Mabel was so free. Her heart wasn't heavy every day. It was able to dream.

I take my fancy vintage Coke from Sloane and turn to look for Norah, but she's escaped outside with Edmund. I don't know what to do next, so I stand awkwardly in the corner, watching everyone have fun as I try to blend in with the wallpaper, wondering what Hali's doing and how soon I can sneak out the back door.

CHAPTER SEVEN

I pass the next painful hour making small talk with Abra and Fallon. They're both nice people, but we have nothing to talk about. After listening to Eryk Pope brag about the new, radical defenses that Lynwood is creating around their house, the crackling firepit outside begins to look particularly tempting.

"I'm heading outside," I say to no one in particular as I slip through the open patio doors and head toward the chairs around the firepit. My plan is to hang here for a few minutes and then silently head home. *I came. I tried. And Miles never showed.* My disappointment at this surprises me. I barely know this kid—hell, have barely even talked to him—so why does it feel like I'm waiting for him? He has a gravity that pulls me down. I shake my head. I don't have room for this in my life or in my heart, which carries so much already. A crush is messy. Hali's waiting for me at home with Jeff's homemade carrot cake, and Norah is sucking face with Edmund somewhere, so yeah . . . it's time to go.

I'm going to ghost this party like it's no one's business.

Weymouth at night is always a harsh pleasure. There's a keen bite in the air. I'm thankful that my dress has long sleeves as I sink down into one of the Adirondack chairs. The sound of a haunting piano score floats out the window, but underneath, I can hear the crash of water against the Dehset Shore, always the wicked undercurrent to our joy. I close my eyes and lean my head back, trying not to think about Hali, about the memories that have trapped her in place. I'm sinking into some deep places when a familiar male voice interrupts my thoughts.

"If I sit here, will every single person on this island know by tomorrow?" I open one eye and see Miles looking down at me with a grin.

My heart speeds up, and an uninvited heat rises through me. He came. I'm secretly thrilled but then mad at myself for being thrilled. I am a strong island girl who doesn't need this in my life, so why is my heart racing and why are my hands clammy? The flicker of the fire catches his crooked smile. I try to keep my voice level.

"Of course they'll know. We'll be the main topic of the Guardians' lunch tomorrow," I say.

Miles shrugs. "I don't know what that means exactly, but I'll take your word for it. You just looked so cool sitting out here alone, I couldn't resist joining you. And thanks for the invite— you're the only one who asked me, out of all these kids. My uncle told me about it in the most awkward way possible."

"Oh God. I'm sure he did. In my defense, there's not a way to not be awkward on a walkie-talkie." My face flushes as I glance down at my black Converse perched up on the firepit and let out a quiet laugh.

Without invitation, Miles Cabot slides into the chair next to me. He occupies his space with ease, radiating confidence. Hell, he didn't attempt to even dress to the party theme. Instead he's wearing tight jeans, maroon sneakers, and a dark green sweatshirt with a bear on it. He scoots his chair up next to mine, and I freeze. Up close he's taller than I thought, and thicker, too, with arms that could really wrap around a person. A muffled laugh breaks through my lips at the thought. *Jesus, Mabel, get ahold of yourself.* But at the same time I think, *He called me cool.*

"Should I be flattered, to be called cool by a city kid?" I ask.

"Well, for starters, don't say 'city kid' if you're trying to be cool. It sort of defeats the purpose."

I raise my Coke bottle to him. "Said like the cool city kid."

His eyes glitter in the dark. "My real question is, who exactly are you avoiding out here by not being in there?" He tilts his head with curiosity and takes a sip of his drink in a way that lets me know that he's had a beer before.

I absentmindedly touch the brooch at my neck. "No one, really. They're all nice people. . . . Well, except for Eryk Pope. Might want to steer clear of him. I'm fine out here, though. I like my own company. Not everyone does."

Miles leans back. "I like my own company too, though I've had a bit more silence than I would like lately. The Cabot house is quiet, and I fear deeply haunted."

I have just taken a sip of my Coke when he says it, and the laugh comes out of nowhere. It forces the soda up my nose. I cough loudly, simultaneously snorting and dying of embarrassment. A real smile breaks open on his face, gloriously transforming it from jadedness to playfulness. I see a youthful energy, a quick laugh. I like it. But then he disappears again as he thumps my back. I could not feel more mortified if I tried.

Finally I gasp out the words blocked by soda fizz. "Trust me.

Ghosts that would haunt a house are not the kind of dead you have to worry about."

He stares at me in confusion, and I wonder why the hell I brought up something so complicated. He's just trying to make small talk, and I'm dropping conversation bombs. I'm so bad at this. I've never flirted in my life. Around the time everyone else on the island was having crushes, I was dealing with Hali's spiral into anxiety. When my classmates were playing spin the bottle, I was making sure she was okay.

"What does that mean?" Miles asks. His tone is light, but I can hear the concern underneath the words.

"Don't worry about it."

He shakes his head with an angry sigh. "That's what I keep hearing."

I don't know what to say next, so I blurt out the first thing that comes to mind. "Sorry your mom died."

He looks at me in shock, and then it's quickly replaced with a shake of his head. "That's one way to open a conversation."

"I'm not very good at this."

He doesn't say anything in response, and I nervously roll the Coke bottle between my fingers. There's a tension thrumming between us, like we're mad at each other for no reason whatsoever. Eventually someone in the basement breaks something, and a chorus of "oh shit" echoes out through the night. We both chuckle quietly before looking back at each other. My eyes trace down his jaw, down his cheeks flushed with cold. He leans back in the chair, letting his body drape, and looks over at me with an intensity I've never experienced. I feel my breath catch.

"So what ghosts *do* you have, Mabel Beuvry? You're the last house to the sea, and I'm the first, so does that mean we get married and have island babies?" My mouth falls open at his presumption, but he keeps going, like he's dead set on barreling through the awkwardness like a wrecking ball. "Sorry, isn't that what you all say when you introduce yourselves? First house and all that? And yours is the big gray mansion before the bridge, right? I asked Alistair about you, but he didn't have much to say."

My stomach drops. *He asked about me.* He knows where I live. Of course he does. There are only eleven houses on this entire island. I swallow, trying to ignore the way his hand is resting on the edge of *my* chair, and so I hit him with the least sexy thing I can think of: facts. "The Beuvry Estate, yes. Built in 1834 by my great-great-great-grandfather, updated in 1974 by my actual grandfather, who died not long after that. It still has our original foundation stones and original stonework in the cellars. It's the second-biggest house on the island . . . after yours." I sound like a history tour guide but can't stop myself. At least it makes him stop talking about us getting married and having babies.

"But . . . you don't like living there?" Miles asks, his face open and curious.

I pull my feet back from the fire; my soles are burning. Do I like living there? No one has ever asked me that before. I think of the leaves turning red in November, of Hali rocking on the porch swing, of the giant Christmas tree that fits in the foyer. And then I think of my dad's study, of the stain on the floor. I take a breath. "Yes . . . and no. I *do* actually love my house and the people who live there. But sometimes I imagine living in a house that's actually *just* a house; a place where not every inch, stone, and room serves a greater purpose. You know what they say: move a foundation stone, die alone."

"Do they say that? Do they? Anywhere but this weird island?"

Weird island. It is a weird island, but it's also my island, and I'm surprised at the defensiveness that rises inside my attraction to him. Who is he to make me feel this way? My voice has an edge when it reappears. "Weymouth is built on a hundred little rhymes that keep us safe. Trust me, you'll learn them soon enough."

"Poetry is officially my least favorite subject in school. I'm more of a calculus and science guy."

I lean over, and our hands accidentally brush.

"Oops, sorry!" he says, in all honesty, and then he curls his hand around mine with his other cradling underneath it, like he's protecting our hands. "I'll just move that over there." He puts my hand back on my chair and lets go, my hand burning like fire.

I rush to fill the silence, flustered by his touch and nervous that it's only me who felt the heat, the rush of touching him. "Speaking of poetry, did you know that George Barteux, the famous poet, once made it to Weymouth Island? Many of his poems—which are considered the first known poems *of horror*—are not symbolic poetry about the nature of death in late age, as believed, but were rather literal thoughts about his time on this island."

Miles bites his bottom lip. "So, Mabel, I have to ask. Are you always this fun at parties, or do you save the horror poetry conversations for when things really get wild?"

"Imagine if I had had a real drink. I might talk to you about the continuing lack of journalistic curiosity about this town." I grimace, unable to stop myself from being awkward. "Sorry. I've been told I'm too serious sometimes."

Miles presses his shoulders back against the chair. "Don't apologize. I like serious. Serious is what I need right now. Back in Seattle, after my mom passed away, everyone kept trying to cheer me up all the time. Like, I don't need to smile right now, *Brad.*" We both laugh, but it walks the razor edge of gallows humor. His words are playing on a loop in my head. *What I need right now.* Miles is actually the last thing I need right now, so why does it feel like the opposite? Here, in this crackling firelight, he looks like a moody hero stuck in a fantasy world.

I notice he's fiddling with something in his pocket. A second later, he pulls out a small white rock marked with dark, glittering veins. I sit up at the sight of it. *Why does he have that?*

"This is my mom's rock. I carry it with me; is that lame?"

I shake my head. "Not lame at all. Also, I know exactly where that rock came from, if you're interested."

"Really?" His eyes widen, but at the same moment, the sliding-glass doors open, and Sloane slips out, leading Cordelia Pope behind him. I want to strangle them both.

Cordelia Pope looks over at us with surprise. "Her? Really?" she whispers, followed by a naughty giggle. Sloane shushes her, yanking her behind him as they head toward the Hemlock Dock on the Soft Shore—the island's local make-out spot. Shockingly, I've never been there.

I'm mortified. Nothing like the island's resident mean girl to bring me back down to earth. But when I look back at Miles, he doesn't even seem to have noticed them. Instead he's just staring at me in the firelight. My breath catches in my throat as he reaches over and softly curls a tendril of my hair around his finger. *What is happening?* I'm delighted, but also, I sense something wanting in his smile that I automatically don't like.

"So, Mabel, I was hoping that you would level with me. . . . What's the deal with this place?" I turn my head, so close that I can see the chestnut-brown color of his eyes and the slight bags underneath. Up close, Miles looks tired—and disingenuous. "I was hoping maybe . . . we could get away from this place, and you could give me the real scoop." The joy inside me evaporates into thin air, and I push his hand away from my hair.

That's why he's out here flirting with me, complimenting me, making chemistry flow through every inch of my veins. He thinks he can pump the weird girl for information. He's using me; it's so obvious. The party is full of loud, excited girls who would love to talk *at* him about everything in the world, and he's out here with me, alone? I figure it out so quickly. He thinks I'm the weak link—the one with no friends. He must have heard something about me, about my family.

Well, I have news for him. I may be alone out here, but I'm not keen on being manipulated. Miles doesn't notice when my eyes go cold, and why would he? He's not really looking *at* me. A lock of jet-black hair falls onto his forehead as he leans in conspiratorially.

"I'm asking because no one else will tell me. Not my uncle or Liam and Lucas. My two older cousins just keep blowing me off when I ask what the hell is going on here, and Alistair keeps saying he'll tell me 'when the time is right.'" He moves his chair closer to mine in the darkness, which just ignites more anger inside me. Who does this kid think he is?

"I saw you sitting out here alone, and I thought: *She's the one. Mabel.* I mean, you seem about as far away as I am from these people." He laughs as he gestures to the house, the party, everything, as if we are united against them. His hand creeps up the arm of my chair near the crook of my elbow. He's so close, I can see a sprinkling of freckles across his nose like tiny stars. I freeze at his proximity, at the way my skin seems to rise to meet his. The air around us smells like burning wood, and in his pupils, I see the reflection of the embers in the firepit.

This guy, this kid who knows absolutely nothing about me, is trying to seduce me for answers. *Are you kidding?* I take an angry breath in.

"All right, here's what I know so far: This island is full of the weirdest *crap* I've ever seen. You have a one-room schoolhouse like it's 1912, but it only has about fourteen students. The people on Weymouth talk about themselves like they're the only people who exist in the universe, like there's not a world beyond the bridge. You all live in these enormous mansions with these gates in front of them." The closer he gets, the more I resist my attraction to him, my blood pressure rising with each word.

"Everything on the island feels like a Gothic painting—the spires on the houses, the ocean, the trees. . . . It's too fucking beautiful, all of it! It's not natural! And when I woke up this morning, my uncle was shoving folded pieces of paper under my floorboards. In my house, there's an elaborate lock on the fireplace—the fireplace! I've found a dozen strange doors that are *always locked, never opened.*"

He's growing louder and more intense, attracting stares from my classmates and a few adults on the balcony. An embarrassed flush rises up my cheeks. Miles is drawing attention to me, and that's something I cannot afford.

"Can we talk about the fact that I can't find this island on any maps? Or on the internet? I mean, come on, the internet has *everything*. . . ." He trails off for a second. "There's one exception. A small conspiracy site that I found on a random back-end server. The owner seems to think you guys commune with the dead."

I know exactly who he's talking about: David Schmidt, a local looney who lives down in a trailer on the shore in Glace Bay. A few times a year he tries to land his boat on Weymouth Island, and he's always quickly—and gently—escorted home by the Guardians.

"And lastly, what's up with the ocean here? It's so loud that I can hear it everywhere. When I sleep, I hear it in my dreams. Am I the only one who hears it, that roar that never goes away? I've never heard an ocean that is so . . ."

"Angry?"

"Yeah. Like it's trying to spit up the devil."

I can see that he's confused, but that does nothing to quell the anger I feel inside that he's trying to use me and use my attraction to him to do it. *This is why I stay home*, I think, which is where I want to bolt at this exact moment.

He runs his hand down his face in exasperation. "I don't know what the hell is going on here. I mean, I don't even know why *I'm here*." He pauses, and for a moment I see grief slide across his face. "I don't know anything about my mother's family. She was secretive about where she grew up, and now that I'm here, I think I understand why. And, Mabel—"

He says my name like he knows me, and for some reason this makes me incredibly uneasy, because he doesn't. I'm not sure why it feels to me like we are connected, but he is not allowed to use that. I feel the need to be away from him, to clear my head, anger and pity mixing together into something I can't sort out in front of him. I need to end this conversation.

He leans in, not reading my signals. "I know we just met earlier today in class, but I felt like you and me . . . that we . . ." He shakes his head. "I don't know, but if you could tell me anything about this island, it would really help me. Please." Miles reaches for my hand, and the movement ignites a reaction inside me.

"Stop trying to touch me!" I snap. "What makes you think I'm the weak link?"

"What?"

"There are a ton of people in that house that you could ask. Instead you targeted *me*. Why? Because you heard something about me, about my family?"

"*What? No.*"

I shake my head. "You think that just because I'm out here alone, you can come out here looking like that, touch my hand, and that I'll just fall at your feet and tell you all our secrets?"

"You think I look good?" he asks with a flash of delight, but I'm off and running.

"No one is telling you anything because you haven't proved yourself yet. But if you don't want to be here, on this so-called weird island, you should *go*. And trust me, you probably should. We can't leave, so you can take your . . . flowing hair and hands and go. I can barely leave my own goddamn house, let alone fix yours." Did I just tell him to take his hands and go? *God, what is this kid doing to me?* Miles flinches at my curse. What was a lovely moment ten minutes ago is now burning.

When I turn to face him, he's already leapt up from his chair. His posture is defensive as I am curling into myself. *Why am I arguing with this stranger?*

When he speaks, his voice is balanced on a knife's edge. "You know, you could have just been nice to me. I heard you were strange, but I didn't hear that you were mean."

"I'm not the one trying to use someone," I say softly.

"Fine! Sorry!" With that, Miles Cabot dramatically takes off in the direction of the woods behind the house. I watch him go, stomping like an angry scarecrow ambling toward the trees.

I can feel Norah walk toward me, feel her lean over my shoulder, a cascade of loose blond hair tumbling down around me. Her lips are swollen and her face flushed. "Where the hell is he going?" She looks down at me. "What did you do, Mabel?"

"I'm not sure." It's an honest answer. I see Miles's eyes in the firelight again, pleading with me for answers. Have I called this wrong? "He tried to, I don't know, *seduce me* in order to get me to tell him about the island, and I called his bluff."

Norah curls over the side of my chair, thumping down onto my lap with a little whoosh. "Well, just before he came out here, Edmund caught Miles trying to creep around their library, so they had a little bit of a dustup, if that helps."

"A dustup?"

"Yeah, basically Edmund told him to get the hell out. I mean, God knows how many traps are in there. It's really not safe. And then Miles said he was looking for information and bumped Edmund's shoulder on his way out! Can you imagine?"

"Yeah . . . I can. He seems to go through life like a wrecking ball."

"After he shoved past Edmund, Eryk Pope yelled, 'Weymouth doesn't need new blood!' and Miles stormed down the stairs, grabbed a beer, and came out here. *He was pissed.*"

Oh no. I lean my head back against the chair and bang it twice. Suddenly it all makes sense: the heat I felt coming off him when he sat down, the desperation in his voice, the need to use his considerable charm when anger hadn't worked. *I'm such an idiot.* I finally get out of the house, and the first thing I do is be unkind to the first boy to interest me in a very long time. I flash to Hali, staring up at me from the porch with jealous emerald eyes. *You're selfish, Mabel.* Maybe I can prove her wrong. I move Norah aside and painfully climb out of the Adirondack chair.

"I have to go after him." I'm uneasy about my pushing him away; the feelings he awoke in me were just too much. But he's as lost as I am.

"What? I just got out here." She pouts. "I have so much to tell you! Mabel, come on. You're here, at this party, and that makes me so deeply happy." She shines all her drunken radiance on me.

"I wasn't very kind to him, and it sounds like I wasn't alone in that. I can do better."

She tilts her head toward the woods where Miles disappeared. "Fine, go, but only if I get *all* the details later."

I lean my forehead against hers as the wind rushes past us, whipping our hair together into a tangle of blond and brown. "Promise. Want to come shore up with Hali and me tomorrow?"

She settles back into the chair, her eyes on the flames. "Hellllllll no. Call me later, though, yeah?"

I can barely hear her as I take off after Miles, jogging awkwardly toward the tree line at the rear of the Nickersons' property.

Thank God I wore sneakers, I think as they pound over the forest floor. I don't want to seem desperate, but at the same time, I don't want to lose him in the woods.

No one wants to be alone in the Weymouth woods at night.

"Miles?" I hiss under my breath as I duck into the forest. "Hey, wait up!" The moon pokes through the clouds, giving off a little light.

As I run, I think how this night got so stupid so fast. Here's what I was supposed to do: go to a party, have a good time, and flirt with a cute boy. Here's what I'm doing: chasing that cute boy through the middle of the woods in the dead of night, the bottom of my dress tangled with leaves. *Par for the course, Beuvry. This is why people stay home with their sisters and do puzzles.*

I hear some bracken crunching behind me, and I spin around.

"Miles?" I say, a little louder, hoping to God it's him.

An annoyed voice emerges through the trees. "First you tell me to piss off, and now you're following me? You've got some nerve, Beuvry."

Miles emerges from the trees looking a bit nervous. It's hard to take him seriously, though, because he has a gigantic leaf stuck in his hair. Something shifts in me at the sight of it.

He frowns. "Oh, you're here to laugh at me, are you? I see. Well, you can piss off too, Mabel Beuvry. I might be hopelessly lost out here, but I still have a shred of pride left."

I shake my head. "I'm sorry, Miles. It's just . . ." I walk over to him, surprised at my own boldness. "Hold still." I gently reach for him. Our eyes stay fixed on each other as my fingers fumble for the brittle stem of the leaf. I feel the soft texture of his black hair brush my fingertips.

His breath washes across my cheeks, and I'm drawn toward him, excited to be this close to him. His hand comes up and wraps gently around my wrist. His fingers are light and soft, and I can feel so much with just this simple embrace.

Does he feel it too?

"What are you doing?" He chuckles, ducking to avoid my touch.

"Stop moving! You have a leaf in your hair, and I can't take you seriously until it's gone."

"Oh. Well, proceed, I guess." A second later, I get it untangled from his black waves and step back, twirling it in my fingers.

"See?" He blushes, and I take a breath. "Look, I'm sorry about before. I don't like being manipulated. I already felt like going to the party was a step outside my comfort zone, and then you were saying all sorts of things and . . ."

He nods softly. "Yeah, I'm sorry too. I guess I got a bit upset as well. I had already asked a few people at that point, and it didn't go over well, so I figured I would ask *nicely*. Heavy on the charm." He sighs. "I should have just come right out and asked you genuinely. Can we start again? Hi, I'm Miles. I'm normal, promise." He sticks out his hand in apology, and I take it and give it a firm shake.

"Mabel. And I know what it's like when people whisper around you—it's what they do around me." I bite my cheek. *Screw those people and their whispers.* "So . . . you want answers, Seattle?"

"God, yes." He's pleading now, all pride vanished.

"Okay. I'll tell you, but you have to let me show you something first. I'm not hanging out in the Nickersons' woods all night—God knows what traps they have out here. Lesson one about Weymouth: It's never safe to be around or in another house unless a member of that family is with you. Trails between the houses are neutral ground. No traps."

"Do you mean like . . . wildlife traps? Bear traps?"

"No, Miles, not like bear traps."

I nervously gesture for him to follow me as I begin making my way away from the Nickersons' house, aware that every step he takes is one of the last steps he'll take in his "normal" world. "It'll make more sense when I explain things if I can *show* you, though you're not going to believe me anyway."

"Where are we going?" he asks, stepping gingerly over a root to avoid marking up his fancy shoes.

I laugh. "You're such a city kid."

"I told you that wasn't a cool thing to say."

"Listen, I have no intention of ever being cool. Haven't you heard? I'm the weird Beuvry girl. It's who I'll probably always be." I glance back, and he's closer than I thought. His hand accidentally brushes mine, and both of us let them linger there for a few seconds.

"And where is this weird Beuvry girl leading me?" he asks, breaking the moment.

"To a graveyard." And to my utter surprise, Miles doesn't even flinch—he just sighs.

"Figures."

CHAPTER EIGHT

We follow the trail for ten minutes, tracing our way through the dark. In the moonlight we can see the shadows of tree branches stretching above our heads. It's like walking under a cracked lake. It feels like that, taking Miles here—like I'm about to pull him under.

A few minutes later we pass under an archway made of iron laurel wreaths and enter Weymouth's graveyard, affectionately known as Sentry's Sleep. Blindfolded Guardians carved from imported Cork marble stand on either side of the arch. A hundred small paper notes tied underneath the archway flicker back and forth in the breeze. White shrikes—Weymouth's most common bird—like to make their nests among paper we've tied there, entwining our words with sticks and leaves. During the day, the graveyard is lovely; tonight it seems eerily still.

Miles gently touches one of the notes with his hand as we pass underneath the arch. "Sure," he mumbles. A funnel of wind blows up from the Soft Sea as we enter one of the oldest landmarks on the island.

"So . . . this is Sentry's Sleep. The graveyard began in 1792 with simple stones marking the resting places of the dead. Now it holds the sacred remains of the eleven families on Weymouth Island, each one in their section. The Cabots—your family—are buried in those dramatic mausoleums." I point to a few marble squares rising up out of the ground.

"Seems about right," Miles deadpans.

"The Des Roches prefer monoliths, whereas the Popes like angels."

"What about your family?" Miles asks, and I look away from our sector of the graveyard.

"The Beuvrys prefer gently sloped tombstones adorned with marble thistles."

"I mean, it's all kind of creepy, isn't it?" Miles mutters.

He's not wrong. Sentry's Sleep is lit only by two single lampposts, the light stretching out over the graves like in a nightmarish Narnia.

When I look over, Miles's shoulders are pulled tight, his breath coming out in nervous puffs. I understand where he's coming from, but I don't feel the same. To me, Sentry's Sleep has always been a comfort. When we were kids, it was our favorite place to hang out, a place away from our parents where Norah, Hali, and I could play Trap and Hide, our favorite childhood game. I step farther into the cemetery, ignoring the twist in my chest, and beckon for him to follow. I raise my arms, my black lace dress catching the wind. "It has a certain loveliness, no?"

Miles shakes his head. "'Lovely' is not exactly what I would call the place where you sacrifice me before being named queen of the island."

That gets a deep laugh out of me, and for a minute he looks delighted.

"Blood sacrifices are only on Mondays. On Fridays, it's just a regular graveyard. But let me say, if I *were* queen of Weymouth, I would definitely make some changes around here, or at the very least get out of shoring up."

"I've heard people mention that—shoring up—but don't know what it is." He follows me behind the array of mausoleums to find a simple white marble bench, adorned by foxes on either side. This is it, a good place to start. I brush the dust off the bench before gesturing for him to sit. Miles leans back on the bench and rests his hand on the fox's head like he's some dark lord of the manor. I watch him carefully, wondering why it seems like I've known him my entire life.

Below us, the Soft Sea laps gently against the rocks, while on the other side of the island, the Dehset Shore screams. I take a deep breath, knowing that I am about to break a bunch of Weymouth rules. But if Miles is staying here, he has a right to know. My loyalty is to my family and to the island—but I have too many hidden places in my heart already. Maybe I don't need to hide from him. Besides, I'm not sure I have the strength to resist those sad eyes for much longer.

I look over at him. "You have to promise to listen *to the whole thing first*. After that, you can ask me any questions you want, and I'll answer the best I can. But once I tell you, you are bound by the island to keep it a secret."

"I'm sorry, what?" He looks terrified.

I ignore him. "For instance, you won't be able to talk to anyone outside the island about what I'm about to say. You can't post about it on a chat room or drive to the diner in Glace Bay and start blabbing about it to the waitress."

"Can't or shouldn't?"

I pause, weighing his question. "*Both.* From what I've heard, if you leave the island for good and try to talk about it, you'll find yourself forgetting most of what you know. But we're getting off track." I run my hand nervously across the scar by my ear. "Look, what I'm saying is, don't tell anyone I told you, okay? Your uncle should be the one to tell you, not me. I'm overriding him."

"Why are you?"

"Because your uncle isn't my favorite person," I reply honestly. "And I know what it's like to try to hold it together when everything falls apart." Saying this feels vulnerable, so I immediately divert.

"Miles, how much do you know about Nova Scotian history?"

He gives a small laugh. "Literally nothing, like everyone else in the world."

I smile. *Fair enough.*

"Well, for starters, Nova Scotia is very old, much older than the Americas. Nova Scotia itself is a place of old magic and spiritual dogma." I gesture out over the sea. "Our island is a place at the end of the world. They say the gods of Nova Scotia, after they created this continent, used their remaining strength to form a gate between our world and the next, and that gate is Weymouth Island."

"A gate, you say. Sure. This is all completely logical." Miles's face is skeptical. "Though, could we maybe skip forward from the actual beginning of time itself?"

"No. It's important to understand where you are before we jump into why you are here." Though, I can't shake the strange feeling that he's here *for me.* "For a long time, this island was empty.

The Indigenous people—the Mi'kmaq—knew that the gate was here, but they wisely did not live on the island. For a period, there was only wildlife occupying it. But when people finally did settle on the island in 1790, they came from three separate groups of very different people, all *called* here from distant shores. Those three original groups are called the Triumvirate."

Miles makes a face. "I've overheard my uncle talk about them."

"Uh, yeah, your uncle is the head of the Triumvirate—it's a fancy word that means 'three.' Anyway, the first group of people to land on our island was the Novantae. They came from the southern shores of Scotland, a mystical, sensitive people who were drawn to the shores of Weymouth. They were desperate men and women, sailing across a violent ocean to find their purpose. The Novantae wrote in their records that they heard 'the call to Weymouth come up from the salt of the sea.' Those men and women knew their destiny was here, but they didn't understand why." I smile proudly. "Those were my ancestors, the 'people of salt.' We're descended from the Novantae, not that it matters very much. Since then, all the bloodlines of the original Triumvirate are mixed. It's the best way, eliminates any tribalism."

Miles makes a face. "Are you all . . . intermixed? Like . . . in a diminishing returns type of way?"

I laugh. "No. At least one child of every family generation *usually* marries someone from outside Weymouth. That way we aren't . . . yeah, marrying our cousins. We're not the royals. But back to the history lesson. During that same exact time period, a group of monks and nuns was also journeying here. They were called from Our Lady Monastery in Canada. These humble men and women were at the fringes of their religion. They said they were called here by the scrolls they wrote the scriptures upon, the 'people of paper.' After a long journey that took many lives, these holy people stumbled right into the middle of the Expulsion of the Acadians."

"I think I learned about that in history class back in Seattle; it sounds familiar, but I probably wasn't really paying attention." Miles strikes me as one of those infuriating kids who doesn't pay attention in class and still gets As.

I continue. "The British during that time—you know, always the heroes of history—were forcing the removal of native Acadian people from what is now present-day Canada. Some of the Acadians escaped their imprisonment, and among those was a small group that found themselves called here, called to this place, by—"

Miles interrupts me. "By the iron of their chains! There's a plaque over our front door that says, 'By the chains they came; by duty they remained.'"

I grin. Maybe this won't be so hard. "That's exactly right. The Cabots are descendants of the people of iron. So anyway, in the middle of this Great Upheaval, in 1790, these three groups all mysteriously descended onto Weymouth within the course of a month." I tick them off on my hands. "The Novantae from Europe, the Acadians from Nova Scotia, and a bunch of monks and nuns from Our Lady Monastery. Salt, paper, iron." From far below us, strange, loud bellows come up from underneath the sea. Miles jumps up with alarm.

"What the hell was that?"

With a smile, I pull him back down onto the bench. "It's just blue whales. They sing sometimes," I whisper. "Take a breath.

These three groups, *the Triumvirate*, had nothing in common except that they had been called to this strange place for reasons they didn't understand, refugees essentially. Eventually, though language was a barrier, they did find that they had something in common: they were all people who had unique—and what some religions would call heretical—ideas about the spaces between the living and the dead." I pause to take in his face. He's listening, but I can see the disbelief growing in his eyes. "Remember, this is the Friday-night version of our history. It would be better told to you by Mr. McLeod."

"I only want to hear it from you. Continue. Please," he insists, and I see him watching my lips very closely. The thought makes me want to drink all the water in the world.

"What these groups didn't realize was that they had been relocated to the island for one purpose only." I exhale, my breath puffing out in a small cloud. "Miles, have you heard anyone mention *the Storm?*" My whole body tightens at the words.

"Yeah, like, I've heard people talking about the weather."

I groan; I had hoped for that, at least. *Hell, this is going to be more difficult than I thought. How can I explain something impossible to imagine, devastating and exhilarating, and the very thing this life is based around?*

I close my eyes and prepare to shatter his world, one that has already been broken.

"In the spring of 1790, a few weeks after the groups had arrived on the island, an unexpected Storm rose up off the Dehset Shore. It was like a hurricane, more violent and devastating than anything they had ever seen in their lives—and they weren't prepared. Hundreds of these people had traveled across oceans and continents to live here, and after that first Storm, only eleven families remained."

"Eleven. That's why there are eleven houses on Weymouth Island. Oh!" He brightens at his own connection. He thinks he understands. He's adorable.

"Every person on this island—aside from Guardians—is descended from those families in some way. The eleven families of Weymouth Island are Cabot, Beuvry, McLeod, Gillis, Nickerson, Pope, Pelletier, Des Roches, Bodhmall, Grimes, and Mintus. Eleven."

Miles looks at me with wide eyes. "So, you guys are like . . . a Weymouth ancestry club? New people aren't allowed on the island—"

"Unless they are brought in through marriage from the outside world."

"Fine, so if they aren't brought in that way, everyone treats them like a pariah?" He's obviously speaking from experience. "My cousins treat me like I'm some fungus they deign to live with."

I twist my hands together. "It's not that we *hate* new people. It's that we don't get new people here. *Ever*. But that's for a good reason."

"Is it rich privilege?" He snorts.

I ignore him as a slight panic rises in my chest. I've never had to tell anyone about the Storm before. "See, when that first Storm came, something else came up from the depths of the Dehset Sea. Something terrible." I meet his eyes, so he can see that I am serious, that there is no hint of a smile on my face. "The Storm brings up *the dead*."

Miles blinks twice and stares at me, waiting for a smile to crack across my face. When it doesn't, he erupts with a harsh laugh, sharp as broken glass. "I'm sorry, what did you say?" He looks incredulous.

I'm out of my depth—the Storm has always been a fact of my life. I lace my fingers nervously together.

"The Storm *usually* comes every eight to twelve years, but it never comes on the same date, and it's never the same Storm. It's tricky that way, always shifting. We never really know *when* it's going to be or what it's going to look like."

Miles pushes up from the bench and begins pacing back and forth, growing more agitated with every step. He thinks I'm playing some game with him. "Sorry, but I don't really care about the average time between years—"

"Between Storms," I gently correct him, and when he looks back at me, his eyes are wide with shock.

"Yeah, obviously, I'm sorry. I'm really not trying to be a jerk, Mabel, but CAN YOU PLEASE CIRCLE BACK TO THE PART WHERE YOU TALK ABOUT THE DEAD?" He's getting louder, so I drop my own voice to a whisper.

"Shhh, sorry, no one can know we're out here. Look, I know it's a lot to take in, but try to relax. *Try to listen.*" He turns quickly, and before I know it, he's kneeling before me, his hands on either side of my thighs on the bench. My entire body goes hot as I'm aware of every inch of space between us.

"I'll try to keep my voice down, but, Mabel, I need you to explain right now. . . . What do you mean by 'the dead'?"

"When the Storm comes, the dead that live underneath the Dehset Sea move across our island, from the sea to the bridge. They are attracted to and guided by the foundation stones inside our eleven homes. Our job is to trap them and diminish their strength and numbers as they move across the island. Moving them through our eleven houses buys us time as we wait out the dawn." I pause. "One night. One purpose."

Miles has not moved. "Explain what you mean by *the dead that live underneath the Dehset Sea*. Is that a metaphor for, like, technology or something?"

I wish. Instead it's the uncomfortable, tragic, and beautiful truth of our lives on Weymouth. It's a terrifying story and a fact of life, all at once. It's the reason we have this gorgeous island, hidden away from the world. And it's the reason I don't have a dad anymore. I want to laugh and cry for Miles. Nothing could have prepared me for how out of my depth I feel at this moment, and my feelings for him are making it even harder. "Um, nope, not a metaphor for technology. The dead come up out of the water, where they bide their time between Storms. They don't really walk per se—it's more like a float. . . ."

He points toward where he thinks the Cabot house is. "Do you mean THAT Dehset Shore, like the ocean right outside my bedroom window?" Oh boy, this kid has no idea where he is. I gently take his arm and redirect him.

"It's this direction. And yes, the Cabot house is the first to the sea, so yes, *that* Dehset Shore, the one outside your window."

He chuckles nervously. "Mabel, stop messing with me. None of this is real. I mean, ghosts aren't real."

"Maybe in your world, but you're not in that world anymore, not once you crossed the bridge. Miles, I'm not messing with you, I promise. I know this sounds insane, but this is what—who—we are. Weymouth Island is the gate between the living and the dead. When the Storm comes, these eleven houses are the only things that stand between the rest of the world and a *flood* of the dead. We have to survive the night. We have to keep them here until morning, moving through our houses—" I think I'm doing well, that I'm being clear, when Miles interrupts me.

"When you say 'the dead,' do you mean zombies?"

I try to find the words when all I can think is, *You'll know them when you see them.*

"No—and yes. They don't look like zombies from the movies. They're more similar to ghosts, only they are much more solid and gruesome than you would think." I close my eyes as fear shoots up my spine, as sharp as a needle. "They are mist and bone, shadow and water and rotting flesh—all of it."

He snorts. "You say that like you've seen them."

His careless words send me spiraling through my own memory as a black vortex swirls in my vision.

My sister's sweaty hand in mine. My mother pleading with the old gods to save us as she clutches both her children to her chest. Sweat and blood dripping off my father's forehead. An iron whip, sinking below foaming waves. Glowing orbs shrouded in mist. A scream. I'm circling in a depth of darkness; I see marble flowers on a grave, a ribbon floating on the water, and long hands reaching for me as fireworks explode overhead.

"Mabel! Hey!"

I make a gurgling sound in my throat, trying to call back to the voice, when I realize that Miles is leaning over me, cradling my cheek, calling my name. I see spindly branches overhead, the cold moon beyond them. *Shit.* I'm in the graveyard.

"Hey, hey! Oh my God, are you okay? You fainted!"

I'm mortified as I sit up, working to quell the nausea rising inside me. I gasp for air, my heart pounding against my chest, the fear lingering like a scent. Miles kneels beside me.

I try to calm down, remind myself that I'm not there anymore, a child, knee-deep in water, screaming.

I take a deep breath. "Sorry. I . . . er . . . Give me a minute," I whisper. I curl my hands around my knees, not meeting his eyes. I feel his hands on my shins.

"What happened?" he asks, so gently.

I shake my head. "It's been a while since I've talked about it." I feel myself return to my body, feel my blood pumping through my veins. "To answer your question, yes, I've seen them. They killed my father. And . . ."

Miles leans back, realizing that he's drawn up a very real trauma in me. His anger vanishes, and pity takes its place. I look up at his face, one that I've grown so fond of so fast, and I know I have to tell him the truth. The fact that I feel drawn to him like a magnet doesn't matter, not in the big scheme of things.

"They'll kill you, too, if you stay here."

"What do you mean? Mabel, look at me. What happened? Talk to me." His finger brushes my cheek. He's trying to reach where I'm at, but I'm suddenly aware of how useless I am tonight. *I can't be the person to tell him this, this innocent kid who doesn't even know what lies beneath the water.*

God, I want Miles to stay here so badly, to breathe new life into Weymouth—and into me—but the sharp lash of memory reminds me what the Storm really is: a night of death and terror. It's nothing an outsider should have to experience. *Ever.*

"Miles, you should go." It's humiliating that I can't seem to power through my emotions right now. I feel dizzy, undone, and like I'm all out of words. This memory has wrecked me in the same way it always does when it comes out of nowhere, a wave of grief and trauma.

I tell myself that at least Miles knows why they all say *Mabel Beuvry is a little out of her mind*. It doesn't matter that it was so many years ago—the brutality of it leaves me twisting in its wake. I can't rapidly adapt to social nuances. I don't want to cry in front of Miles, this new face that has awakened a complicated hope within me, like opening a door into the light. I'm humiliated.

"You should leave," I whisper.

He turns to me, desperate. "But where am I supposed to go?" His voice breaks my heart as we stare at each other. "Where?" He has just stepped closer to me when I hear a high, clear voice calling through the trees. Relief washes through me. Hali is my exit.

"MABEL?" Her voice grows louder as she yells from our front porch. Norah must have called the house and told her I was out here. "Heeellooooo? You out there?"

"I have to go. My sister is worried," I say, the mud leaving its mark on my palm as I push myself up.

"Wait, *what*? Please, don't go. You just started telling me about the island!" Miles is pleading with me, but I'm moving on automatic, pushing my way through a blur of fear. I don't meet his eyes.

"Do you know how to get home from here? Walk down the path we came from, the one with the lanterns, and you'll hit the main road. Just follow that down to your house. Watch your steps; the roots out here can grow pretty high." I pause. "Miles, I'm sorry. I shouldn't have tried to tell you. It's too much."

"I don't believe you," Miles says quietly as I turn to go, each word a dagger. "People would know. *The world* would know. I can't tell if you are playing a cruel joke on me or if you actually believe this, but I can't decide which is worse. Did the other kids put you up to this? I heard that the boys on this island have some initiation. Is that what this is?"

I jerk back. "God, no! I would never do that."

His face darkens as he steps toward me. "You know, three months ago—*three fucking months ago*—I was playing video games in my apartment with my friends, and my mum was putting out veggie quesadillas for us. I liked my life. And now you're telling me I'm stuck on an island full of ghost hunters?"

I keep my eyes on the soil in front of me. "On the night of the Storm, we aren't the ones doing the hunting."

"I don't believe you, Mabel," he snaps. "*I don't believe you.*"

I feel the failure of this moment swell around me. "You asked me earlier why the sea sounds so angry here, why it roars. It's because the Dehset keeps the dead at bay until it's our turn. You can hear it because you're a Cabot. It's in your blood. Which, by the way—do not go into the Dehset Sea. If you hear me say anything tonight, let it be that."

Tears blur my vision as I turn to go, with one foot in my most painful memory and the other in a hopeful dream of being a normal teenage girl with a normal little crush.

This was never going to work. I begin making my way down the trail.

"Does it go silent then?" he calls after me sarcastically. "The Dehset? Does it stop roaring after the dead leave?"

"No," I reply. His heavy gaze of disbelief sears into my back. "It screams for us."

CHAPTER NINE

In my dreams I'm chasing Miles as he runs through the houses of Weymouth, dashing through the Pelletiers' looming Colonial and the cement tunnels of the Grimeses' contemporary monstrosity, until finally we end up in my own garden. Wherever Miles steps turns first to flames and then to ash. Flames lick up through our tulip beds and freshly planted walls of ivy. Peach roses wither to black, and thistles burn like meteors against the night sky. I chase him relentlessly, screaming his name into the wind, but he never looks back. The most horrifying part: as I'm chasing him, something has started chasing me, and as the gardens around us burn, I see the wave of a tsunami on the horizon. When Miles takes my hand, I open my mouth to warn him, and black mist streams out in a plume. *It's here. It's in me.*

I wake up with a terrified cry and fling the quilt off the bed. My sheets are tangled around me, soaked through with sweat. I roll over onto my side, trying to slow down my heart, which pounds relentlessly against my chest.

"Just a bloody dream," I mutter to the dark room, hand on my chest. Of the entire thing, the part I remember most clearly is not the predictable horror of the Storm but the feeling of Miles's hand in mine. I flip my pillow over to the cool side and close my eyes again, but I can't shake the feeling that Miles is next to me, even now. Why can't I escape him? It's not just that he's new and shiny, though at first I may have thought that. It's as if there's a deeper, ancient thread running between us that only we can feel—a thread that I can't let pull me any closer. It's that I can't look away from him. It's that he makes the hairs on my arms stand up when he's close, that he could derail every careful thing I've built here. I'm not Norah—I can't afford to be interested in him, even if it feels like the island is pushing us together.

As I'm lying there, the enticing smell of something baking hits my nose. Beside me, I hear a small snort, and I push my curls back from my sweaty face. I need a shower—and so does she, probably.

Hali is lying on the couch in my room under her own antique quilt, curled on her side and snoring loudly. She always ends up here at around four in the morning—just around the same time our dad died. It can't be a coincidence. Four nights a week or so, Hali shuffles in, lies down on the couch, and falls immediately back to sleep. There are some mornings I wake up and stare at my sister, taking in her perfect face and her little tulip mouth. On other days, my first instinct is to shove her violently out the door and take back my space. I've done both things, but today I decide to let her sleep. She tried hard yesterday. I'll let her rest.

I pull on the fancy gray robe Jeff gifted me for my birthday last year and wrap it over my tank top and pajama bottoms. I grimace as I pass the mirror; it's better not to linger on how wrecked I look. My hair stands up from itself in a massive tangle—I must have been thrashing around in my sleep.

Downstairs I'm greeted by the most comforting of scenes: our House Guardian, wearing his apron, whistling happily while he cooks. I slump down onto the kitchen stool, and before I can say anything, he places a steaming mug of coffee in front of me.

"Extra creamer." Jeff points.

"Thanks. I didn't sleep well," I mumble, leaning my head on the table and wrapping my hands around the warm mug. I have a hangover. A Miles hangover, caused by a rare combination of emotional turmoil and failure to act normal.

"Oh, I know. You got in pretty late if I remember correctly." He grins as I take a small sip. *God, it's good;* Jeff makes his coffee in a ceramic pour-over from France because Jeff is extra and can't do things like normal people. "So, how was the Nickersons' party?" he asks, raising thick eyebrows as he ladles waffle batter onto spitting iron squares.

"It was fine." I blink, trying to recall it all. The party. Miles. Sentry's Sleep. His hands on the sides of my legs. Fainting. *Oh God, that's right.* I flinch as I remember the utter care and worry drawn upon his face as he looked down at me. I cringe even more when I remember the way I left him standing in the middle of the woods.

I'm pretty sure the only time I'll be seeing Miles again will be in class. If that. He's probably on his way back to Seattle as we speak.

I shudder, and Jeff glances over at me. "What is it?"

I know it's better to tell him the truth before he ferrets it out on his own. "I maybe . . . uh, told Miles about the island."

Jeff pauses for a moment, ladle hovering in his hand, and continues. "That's interesting. Shouldn't telling Miles about the island be Alistair's job? The last thing you want to do is upset a Cabot."

I snicker. "It is, but he hasn't told Miles *anything*, and he's been here, what—about a week? Can you imagine moving here to Weymouth and THEN you learn *what we do?*" I sit back, wrapping the robe around me. "Trust me, I tried to make the explanation as basic as I could, but . . . he still freaked out—of course—and he absolutely did not believe me." I leave out the part where I couldn't handle my own memories of the Storm and passed out like some delicate handmaiden.

Jeff shakes his head. "Of course Miles didn't. It's outside the realm of possible for regular folk. None of us believe it when we're first told, not unless you grow up here, inside this culture." He smiles crookedly. "You're lucky. There was never a time you didn't know about the Storm. I remember when my father first explained what the Guardians were and what we were protecting the world from. It sounded like something from an old fisherman's tale. The dead coming out of the sea. It was ludicrous." Of course; the Guardians are the only ones on this island, besides the eleven families, who have access to our entire history, who know what we do. Our protectors.

"How old were you when your dad told you?" Jeff's father was a kind man with crinkly skin and a full white beard, a high-pitched laugh, and hands always ready with grapes. Rain patters softly outside the window. This quiet time with Jeff is precious. Hali will be up any moment now, and she's very loud. My mother, however, won't be up until around noon, what with her "allergy" headache, aka, her own proper hangover.

Jeff's round chin catches the shadow of raindrops against the window. "I was about nine when my father pulled me aside and explained what the Guardians did. Up until that moment, I thought he was a glorified butler. I thought he brought your parents tea and trimmed the bushes every now and then." He chuckles. "I should have known, though; he also had an elaborate weapons room that I dusted regularly. I thought all butlers had one."

We both laugh. The line between Guardian and servant here on Weymouth is a fine one and can be exploited if the families aren't careful. In most houses—like ours—it is the Guardian who dictates what he does and does not do. Jeff feeds and cares for Hali and me, but he does not clean our bathrooms. And that's why they are disgusting.

I run my fingers lightly around the edge of the mug. "Last night I told Miles to go back to Seattle—because why wouldn't he?" I pause, not wanting to voice the possibility that he may be gone already. "Do you ever dream of leaving? Of finding a handsome husband, moving to a modern city, and raising heirloom tomatoes? Of living in a place with a single lock on the door?" *Please don't ever leave us.* He's the glue that holds this family together.

Jeff shakes his head while sliding a golden waffle onto a blue-and-white chintz plate.

"Mabel." His voice plucks at my heart like it has strings. "You know that the Beuvry Estate is my home, right? I grew up here. This house is a part of my family legacy too. And I hope you know me well enough to know that I don't do anything I don't want to. My life is dedicated to my Guardianship. That's a choice I made when I took my oath to protect House Beuvry. I'm not going to give up saving the world so I can go to an organic grocer in Vancouver."

I blush, hiding my relief as I proceed to cover my waffle with maple syrup straight from Norah's farm. *Our island may be strange*, I think, *but there is also a wild magic to it.*

Perhaps I can make Miles see that. Maybe that's part of the problem. Miles is trying to understand the island, while it's something that has to be felt. I also am unsure what I want. I have a burning desire for him to stay, but also there is a fierce need in me to keep him safe—and that means his leaving. Ugh, I have had more conflicting feelings in the last day than I have had in the entire year.

"What made you believe in Weymouth then? In the Guardians? What was the selling point?" I ask, hoping for tips.

Jeff shoves half a waffle into his mouth. For being such a proper Canadian gentleman, he has the appetite of an ox. "At first I did it to please my father. But after I saw the Sacred Line, I knew that there was no greater purpose in the world than this one. I decided right then that I would serve the Beuvry house until I died."

My mouth drops open. "Oh God, Of COURSE. Why didn't I take Miles to the Sacred Line? Instead I took him to Sentry's Sleep."

Jeff looks aghast. "You took him to Sentry's Sleep?" He shudders. "Ugh, God, I always hated that you and Hali played there as children. There's something terrible about that place. So many dead islanders. So many snakes."

"Maybe it felt that way earlier, but now Dad's there. For me, it's always felt like home—and now even more so. My family is there."

His face falls as he stirs a spoonful of sugar into his own coffee. "Oh, Mabel, I didn't think about that. I'm sorry."

"No, it's fine. I'm pretty sure Hali and I are the only ones on the island that still enjoy a seaside picnic at Sentry's Sleep." I take a drink of milk to wash down the saccharine sweetness of the syrup. "But you're right, the Sacred Line *is* impressive. I wonder if I could get Miles out there. Maybe then he would listen . . . and maybe I could be better at explaining."

"There is something staggering about it," Jeff says. "Also, it has an incredible view."

"Maybe I should head over to the Cabots and see if I can try to talk to him today. But that would be silly . . . right?" The suggestion hangs in the air awkwardly. No Beuvry has set foot in the Cabots' house in a very long time.

Jeff takes a drink of coffee, his face furrowed. "You know, bad blood can only exist so long before it turns to actual blood. Maybe it's time to open ourselves to the Cabots once again. Unfortunately, Mabel, you're not going anywhere today." He points to his meticulous calendar that hangs next to our fridge, and I see the giant red *X* on today.

"NOOOOOO." That's right. It's shoring-up day. *Bloody hell.*

Jeff lets out an evil cackle. "Incredible how it catches you off guard every month, even though it happens every month. So unless you want to go after you're done, perhaps tomorrow would be a better day to visit the Cabots. And save me the whining. None of us enjoys shoring up, but it is a necessity." That's a lie. Jeff totally enjoys it. In fact, I'm pretty sure it's his favorite day of the month. Suddenly it all makes sense: the unnecessary pep in his step this morning, the waffles, the humming, all of it. I know what he's going to say next, long before he says it out loud, and it begins with "Fares well. . . ."

"You know what they say, Mabel: fares well the house that's ready! Let me know if you want another cup of coffee to boost up that serious lack of energy."

As I scowl at him, he shrugs, and I sense the satisfaction wafting off him at the laborious day ahead of us. He grabs a long list off the fridge, tucking a Sharpie behind his ear.

"All right, let's trap some dead!" he shouts in a booming voice.

It's too early for this.

Holland Des Roches, February 16, 1846

My heart mourns this Storm, for Weymouth
itself is a most beautiful place, a paradise of land
and sea. The Storm, while thankfully taking only
six lives this year—not a Des Roches among
them—did take the land with it. I am full of woe
at the state of the island, one week ago a host to
mild horrors; now the only remainder is what
the land tells us. There are rock-strewn clefts
where lush land once sat, and the shore is dotted
with the corpses of birds displaced by the great
wind, the valley, full of overturned pine trees and
torn-up brambles of primrose. The shore holds
the lingering scent of the dead. Our two seas seem
to have been spread to the very edge of the earth.
The main road we have been carving along the
island has been washed away, taking with it all
pine and hedge, rock and wildlife. Everything has
been pulled back toward the Dehset. I suppose one
should be thankful that our Sacred Line of stones
has remained and that the wails of the dead would
not shake them. The island, though, is deeply

wounded. I feel her cry in the depths of my chest. From want of regular rest since the Storm, I have been repeating the passage in Lear—"Do you not hear the sea?"

To which I say, this sea haunts me. Intensely.

Historical note by Reade McLeod: While Holland Des Roches is surely not the first woman to record her thoughts on Weymouth, she is the first female author to appear in our historical records. Holland Des Roches lived a long life on the island and is responsible for many of our gardens and trails that stand today.

CHAPTER TEN

H ali and I start shoring up an hour later, at exactly eleven a.m., when the sky looks like a layer of cement. Wind swirls underneath the cloud cover, battering against the house. Once my mum stumbles out of her room wearing green overalls and hastily applied concealer, we begin the process by breaking into two teams. Jeff and my mother take the outside of the house—as always—and Hali and I take the interiors. Securing the exterior of the house is more difficult, but the interior is much more intricate. I'm always thankful for the latter assignment. Subconsciously I know Jeff will go over everything we do with a fine-tooth comb later, but we still have to try. Well, I do, anyway. Hali is lazy as shit.

As Jeff and Mum head outside, the woman who bore me gives me a sympathetic look, trying to unite against a common enemy, but I choose not to meet her eyes. If I see her pupils, I may be tempted to ask: *Why are you always drinking? Why have you left me alone in our grief?* Instead I look away.

Hali and I start in the basement and work our way up. My backpack holds a collection of new and old power tools, electrical wiring kits, and old masonry hand tools. My hands grip a tote stocked with thick paper, scissors, ribbon, and twine. Underneath all of that is a basket full of shaved iron pieces, fine as sand and jagged as razors, complete with the thick gloves we use to handle them.

"Got the bag?" Hali asks, totally uninterested. As much as I hate shoring up, she hates it more.

"Check," I reply. Things are still a bit awkward because of last night: I refused to talk to her when I got home, didn't tell her what happened with Miles. I know she's dying to know, but I can't bring myself to talk about it again. I choked. I flailed. We both lost. Why does it feel like the stakes are so high with him?

We use our ancient passageway to get downstairs, checking the pulleys and the iron gates that shut it off from the rest of the house. Then the real work begins.

There is always something sacred about the moment we start shoring up. Light pours through small crescent windows as our feet press into ancient foundation stones. We take each other's hands, Hali's soft palms pressing into mine.

"If we don't start soon, this will take forever," I finally say, giving her hand a squeeze, and Hali squeezes back, pushing out her silliness.

"Okay fine," she moans.

According to Weymouth lore, the words we speak call out to the Beuvry ancestors who came before us. When we speak these words, our bloodline whispers back, and in the refrain, the protections of our home are reinforced.

We have no idea if it actually works, but Jeff is probably listening to us from the top of the basement stairs, so there's no getting around it. Besides, it's been six years since the last Storm, which means we need all the help we can get.

Hali and I stand face-to-face, becoming a mirror of each other as we begin the ritual: Our fingers cross over our chests four times, making an x symbol—similar to a Catholic genuflection. After that, we grab each other's opposite wrist, binding ourselves to each other. We make a gate as we lean our foreheads together. Hali's lip curls, and a laugh rises through her. She's about to lose it, and I shush her with a whisper.

"Hali, shut up! We have to take this seriously."

"I know, I know. It just . . . I feel silly every time."

I calm myself by thinking about how every house and every family on Weymouth is doing the exact same thing. Our words together should have power.

"Let's take this seriously, yeah? Otherwise . . ."

"Otherwise what?" Hali's voice drops for a moment, and she leans forward, whispering into my ear. "What if we can't stop them again? What if they take more of us?" In the basement, I feel a sudden drop in the air pressure, and the hanging bulb overhead gives a flicker. The island does not like us to speak this way: full of doubt and fear. *Doubt opens doors.*

I squeeze her hands. "Remember what Dad said? Fear cannot take away the time we've put in. Our house will keep us safe." I push the memory of dead bodies in the hallway out of my mind. "C'mon, let's begin." We close our eyes and begin chanting in hushed voices.

"When the sea begins to scream, close the shutters.
When the wind starts to rush, lock thy doors.
Reckon your gaze on the Dehset Shore.
Fares well the house that's ready.

Watch the water; watch the trees.
Check rations; bend your knee.
When mist is on the rise, say a prayer.
Fares well the house that's ready."

The soft cadence of our words seeps into every empty crack and rotting stone, fortifying, solidifying. I hope it calls to the strength of our Beuvry ancestors, or at the very least, makes up for Hali's and my somewhat indifferent will.

After our rhyme is done, we pull on white gloves and face the enormous task in front of us. I pull a dusty boom box out of the corner; we aren't supposed to listen to music while shoring up, but the task is unbearable without it. I fiddle with the dial and find an alternative station out of Halifax. A minute later, Alanis Morissette's deep voice fills the basement. When I turn around, Hali hands me a hammer with a sigh.

Our basement cellar is a cavern; sound bounces off the chalky foundation stones, the very thing that attracts the dead to our houses. If I look closely, I can see the words carved into them. Hali and I tap each stone three times with the silver hammer, making sure they don't crumble or have any weak spots. If we find one, a good chunk of our day will be spent filling it with iron dust and cement, a backbreaking chore. Luckily, all the stones look the same as they did last month, so we're in the clear for today. We tap all three hundred and twelve stones that make up the foundation, and by the end my back aches.

Next we check the entry points: trapdoors that can be pushed open from the inside and sealed on the outside. The door that leads down to our canning cellar (barely used and not a safe place to find yourself in the Storm). Doors on Weymouth aren't built like regular doors. They are built to withstand the worst environments possible. Most everything in our house has various layers of material: wood, plastic (for waterproofing), and inside that, poles of iron that run from top to bottom. Clever traps hidden inside antiques.

Singing loudly, Hali and I inspect every door with a flashlight, looking for any cracks and running our hands over each inch. Jeff ordered this particular door from the Mintus family, who specialize in creating protective measures like this. They are not generous with their knowledge, but they will part with certain items for a high price.

On the door is a latch shaped like a small egg. I glance at Hali, who gives me a tired thumbs-up, and turn the latch clockwise one time. The iron spikes hidden inside the door shoot up out of the top and bury themselves in eight open slots in the ceiling. What looks like a normal door is now a fortified barricade; a car couldn't get through this. Also, there is the small fact that *the dead hate iron*.

"Next?" Hali says lazily, biting her fingernail. Shoring up, when you've done it your whole life, is terribly boring. Furry black spiders scurry back into their corners as we sweep through the basement, checking everything: folded paper hidden in chests, iron axes buried under drop cloths, fire extinguishers and water bottles tucked up on the shelves.

After the basement is done, we head up the stairs and face the rest of the house, taking the boom box with us.

On the main level there are four points of entry to check, along with every window. Hali and I run our hands over the front

COLLEEN OAKES

door, checking for flaws; inside its normal facade are two sheets of iron, and inside those is an ancient papyrus from Israel, some of the finest paper in the world. It's not a normal front door; it's basically a safe, and it locks like one.

Hali wipes her sweaty forehead with the back of her palm. "Are we done yet?"

"Your whining definitely makes it go faster," I snap. "God, Hali, go get a lemonade or something." She does, and while she's gone, I quickly check the windows. They are all reinforced with a glass-plastic combination and iron top rails, all locked firm.

The only exception is the stained-glass window that sits at the very top of the stairs. That, however, has a different protection. Inside the stained glass, tiny threads of iron have been melted into the wave-shaped glass. When I was little, I thought it looked like a blue flower, but now I see water, flowing out in a thousand directions. The heart of the Beuvry house is the same thing that brings the dead.

"Here." Hali hands me a lemonade, and we both stare at the window.

"I wish it were a rose or a sun or a saint even," she says quickly. "Literally any other thing." With a grimace, we pass underneath the wave, taking our sweating lemonade with us.

The hours pass slowly. Finally the end of shoring up nears as we head out onto our old-fashioned porch, which wraps around the entire east side of the house. This is our place—mine and Hali's. It's where we lie around all summer, sitting in rocking chairs, eating puffs until our fingers are stained with cheese as we thumb through our single worn copy of *The Witch of Blackbird Pond*. The sun streams through the windows like pale honey, and

102

beyond us, the Soft Sea whispers against the rocks. And while the sun porch carries magic for Hali and me, it is also the most vulnerable place in the entire house during the Storm. If the dead reach us on the porch—which doesn't always happen but can—it's basically their easiest entry point.

On the left interior wall, next to a terrible painting of my grandfather, a set of headphones perches on a small hook. Once I put them on, Hali gives me the thumbs-up, and I kneel on the porch floor and slip a wooden panel sideways. Inside is a vintage silver button, the kind our grandmothers would sew onto our coats. My finger lingers above the button as I whisper the words I once sang as a child, circling around a white elm tree with the rest of my classmates:

> Iron, paper, and salt;
> all fill thy breath with dread.
> Mind your house to keep the dead.

I pause. *No wonder Miles thinks we're crazy*, I think. *Listen to yourself.* I push the button down into the floor, where it spins once before sinking down into a keyhole. A loud screeching sound fills the porch; the sound is horrible (hence the headphones), and my teeth grind in its wake. As my sister and I watch, huge metal shutters swing down from above, sealing the porch windows tight. Metal doors drop down in front of the entrance to the porch, and everything clicks shut. The light is swallowed, and once the doors latch, small lightbulbs overhead buzz to life.

Below each metal shutter is an open latch. One by one, Hali and I latch each window shut, effectively putting a layer of metal between the window and us. Metal is good against wind and water but not so good against the dead, so on the inside of each door are a dozen pieces of paper clipped with magnets in neat rows. They are covered with poems and lines of literature, thoughts, curses, dreams, even recipes. The dead hate paper.

I push the button once more. The metal sheeting rises back into the ceiling, and light floods in through the windows, turning my sister's hair to shining red-gold. For a second I wish the world could see Hali as I do. I wish they could see how fearless she is, even though she is a person defined by her fear. I wish they could embrace her in the same way the light does.

She cocks her head. "Why are you staring like that? You're such a weirdo. No wonder Miles ran for the hills." I almost laugh. Whenever I lavish love on Hali, she usually makes me regret it.

We head back inside, where the shoring up continues. We check the kitchen: iron rods in the curtains above the windows that double as lances, the plastic in place of glass, weapons in half the drawers and candles in the others, the oven we can hide inside.

Next to the kitchen sits our salt pantry. I quickly duck inside, half-assedly checking the barrels, filled to the rim with fine salt, shipped straight from one Dead Sea to another. *If it's good enough for Jesus, it's good enough for us*, Jeff once told me, pushing a barrel over the lip of the pantry.

Above the salt barrels, tucked back on a shelf, sit long silver pipes with trigger hinges at the bottoms. These are our salt guns. Hali and I do iron, paper, salt (Weymouth's version of rock, paper, scissors) to see who gets to clean them out. I lose on iron. She watches smugly as I refill them with fresh salt, all while carefully facing away from her. Edmund Nickerson once shot Sloane in the elbow with his salt gun while they were playing, and Sloane has the scars to this day. Our defenses are good, but they aren't safe. *The dead hate salt.*

After we check the salt guns, Hali and I sift through each barrel with our hands to make sure there is no salt rot; I relish the feeling of salt siphoning between my fingers. After that, we count to ten and race through the rooms of the house, checking the canister of salt in each one, seeing who can finish first.

The bathrooms are quickly checked; each one has several iron locks and clever cabinets that can be used in an emergency. Trapdoors are open and shut, and secret passageways are checked for decay. The formal sitting room (a long room full of creepy paintings and uncomfortable furniture that we never use) is checked by Hali, while I check the removable iron bars that make up our twisting stair rail. I cast a wary eye at the ballroom, the one interior room that my mother checks. It's enormous, and I've seen both bats and mice inside. *No, thank you.*

We do our bedrooms. I check the iron bars that cover our windows. There are protections under our beds, and beneath our vanities, a secret door leads between my and Hali's rooms. In the bathrooms, I fling open the medicine cabinets not to find tampons or pill bottles, but two paper chains, an iron dagger, and a few small bags of salt, tied neatly with a lavender ribbon.

"Well, at least if those bastards get us on the toilet, we'll be ready," Hali deadpans.

When I get to my mum's room, I hesitate at the door, dreading what I will find in there: empty wineglasses, the smell of rotting flowers, clothes strewn about like in a brothel. I always end up feeling sad when I shore up in there, and so after checking over my shoulder for Jeff and getting approval from Hali, I wiggle the door lock and move on.

Hali nods as she passes. "He'll never know," she whispers.

The last room to shore up is my father's study, a room that no one goes into ever. I hear voices from outside as I pass by a window. I look down and see Jeff laughing with my mother. He's the only one who can still make her laugh. I watch as Hali approaches them, perhaps hoping to steal some of Mother's sunshine before it disappears into a mixed red with an oaky aftertaste. I watch as they congregate together, Hali making excuses as to why she's not helping me finish.

I'm alone up here. I exhale, tell myself that there are no such things as ghosts—even though I know that personally to be a lie—and push open the door of my father's study.

CHAPTER ELEVEN

J ack Beuvry, my dad, was a big man, with thick forearms covered with dark hair, a barrel chest that filled up with deep
laughter, and a sly wink. He swept through the world like a
warm, confident wind. He was also obsessed with the dead.

When I move through the study door, I sense a change in
depth, and there is a hollow ringing sound in my ears. My heart
quickens when I remember what happened here. Through his
double-paned glass, I can see a hint of the Dehset Shore, the
murky blue contrasted against a gray sky. This end of the house
is sour; I glance into the corner of the room, where a new rug
hides the bloodstain beneath it. Behind the stain sits a closet,
permanently sealed shut by wood planks—the place we hid as
my father died.

My eyes flood with hot tears, and I force myself to look away.
But it's a mistake, because I focus on something even more dis-
turbing: my father's charcoal sketches of the dead. My eyes trace
the skeletal hands, hollowed-out eyes, the bones that clatter on
the breeze. His art hangs on the wall, a nightmarish gallery, yellowing with age and flapping in the wind.

Flapping in the wind? I jerk around, my heart clenching

nervously. The windows in front of me are shut tight, but some-how a slight breeze flutters through the room. The pelican skele-ton that hangs from the ceiling turns slightly.

"What the hell?" I mutter, making my way behind my father's desk, a behemoth thing, carved like a ship's prow. Three deep scratches mar the surface—grooves made by his axe as he fought desperately for his life and ours. A drift of cold air kisses my ankles, and I crouch down, pushing aside my father's bench.

"Well, hello there," I whisper. Near the floor, a fist-size hole has been blown out of the farthest window. I spot the culprit a second later: a large white stone, jaggedly cut and laced through with black veins, lying on the carpet, surrounded by a few pieces of broken glass. I glance out the window. From up here, it's a long way down to the ground. A broken window is a minor inconve-nience everywhere else, but on our island, breaking the protection of our house is another thing entirely. I curl my fingers around the unnaturally cool rock and realize where I've seen it before—in Miles's hand. This is his mother's rock. So why is it in my father's study? My breath catches in my throat when I hear quick foot-steps in the hallway, and for reasons I can't fully explain, I tuck the rock into my pocket.

Jeff appears in the doorway looking frazzled. "Mabel, your mother and I are making biscuits for lunch! What's taking so long up here?" He freezes. "And why do I detect a breeze?" The man misses nothing.

I try to sound casual. "Something broke the window . . . maybe a bird?"

Jeff cocks his head. "Well, that will be a dead bird for sure. I'll check the garden for it later, right after I order a new pane of glass.

It's always something with this house. Will you grab me a broom and a dustpan?"

"Sure thing." I nod, happy to be away from his prying eyes, and scamper out the door. I pass Hali on my way downstairs. She stops humming when I grab her arm with a pleading smile.

"Hali, will you do me a favor and grab Ser Jeff a broom and a dustpan? I need to go see Norah about something really quick. He's in Dad's office. There's a hole in the window."

Her face crumples. "You're leaving *again*? I thought we were going to hang out! Mum said we could each pick out fifty dollars' worth of clothing from the catalogs. Fifty dollars!"

I smile, the rock heavy in my pocket.

"That sounds really fun. I promise I'll only be gone for a few hours, and we can pick out some clothes and watch a movie together." I can see the hurt in her eyes when she turns away, utter abandonment in the curve of her mouth.

She starts to say something cruel but then thinks better of it. "If you're not careful . . . You know what, never mind. Do whatever you think is *most important*."

"Halifax Amelia Beuvry!" I use her whole name to reach her, but she's already stalking away from me, headed toward the kitchen in search of a broom. "Stop being a brat. You could come with me, you know."

"That's not fair to ask me, *you know*," she snaps in reply.

Guilt bubbles up inside me. She's right—I shouldn't have said it—but by the time I open my mouth to apologize, she's gone.

After a quick shower, I pull on soft jeans, Keds, and a long-sleeved gray shirt before making my way downstairs. No one is around—

thank goodness. I dart outside and head around the side of the house, to where my bike leans lazily against the garage. This new mystery has me motivated—and I need to understand. Why was Miles's rock in my father's study? I need answers, or maybe I'm just making up excuses to see him. But either way, I'm going.

I wheel my bike away from the house, the bright yellow paint and brown leather seat gleaming in the sun. I love this bike with a passion, especially since Jeff brought it home for me a few months ago when I outgrew my old one, the one my dad taught me to ride on. It's a fact: kids with dead parents always get lots of presents.

I snap up the kickstand and fly away. The gloom of the morning is clearing up, and it might actually be a nice afternoon on Weymouth—a good day for a ride. As I escape, I glance back at the house to see Jeff watching me suspiciously from my father's window. *He misses nothing.* I wave and pedal as fast as I can away from the Beuvry house, the wind pushing my bangs out of my face, the rock hanging in my front pocket. I need answers, but more than that . . . I need a buffer. I need Norah. Five minutes later, my tires come to a screech in front of her house.

Each time I visit, I'm struck by how different the Gillis house is from the rest of the estates on Weymouth. The rest of the houses are built to be fortresses of safety and power. They say, *We stand against the dead.* The Gillis house says, *Oh my gosh, come on in; shoes are optional here!* It's probably the reason I wanted to be here so much as a child; instead of the cold grief that consumed our household after the Storm, I craved the chaotic warmth of their home. Norah's mother is the cheeriest person I know, displaying the typical Nova Scotian kindness that can sometimes be lacking in Weymouth. I don't even knock at their house anymore.

"Hello? Norah?" I call out, and Lorraine Gillis is on me in a second.

"Mabel, come in!" she shrieks, bustling out of the kitchen as she wipes her hands on her jeans. Lorraine is curvy with wide hips, and she takes up all the space in the best way possible. Her curly hair is pinned up on the sides, and she's wearing a bright teal sweatshirt. Her jewelry jangles loudly, announcing her presence before she even reaches you. She sweeps me into a strong hug, and I'm embarrassed at how much I want it. Instead I pretend to be shy and step backward.

James, Norah's twelve-year-old brother, saunters out of the kitchen in an oversize T-shirt and baggy shorts, the ravages of adolescence dotting his face. He rolls his eyes when he sees me.

"Thought I heard a moooo-vry."

"Hi, James." I raise an eyebrow in his direction. The last time we talked, he was harassing me on the walkie-talkie about Miles.

"'Sup, buttface." I watch as he shoves a whole piece of bacon into his mouth. "What are you and Norah doing today? Talking about Edmund Nickerson and your periods?" He snickers.

"JAMES GILLIS!" his mother screeches.

"What? I thought we were supposed to be open about them. That's what you said last week!"

I narrow my eyes as I look down at him. "That's exactly it, James. Edmund and periods. I mean, what else could women possibly have to talk about?"

Crumbs hurtle out of his mouth as he protests. "That's what I'm saying!"

When Mrs. Gillis turns away, I punch James hard in the shoulder. He's the little brother I never wanted.

"OW! That hurt! What the hell?"

I lower my face to his. "That's for being such a *little shit* the other night. Also, you can't be creeping on the nightly shore report. Alistair's going to make you pay for that."

James sighs, eternally put out. "He already called my dad. I'm grounded from the walkie for a month . . . which means I can't do the nightly shore report, which is kind of great and was maybe my intention in the first place!" He wiggles his shoulders back and forth. A little god of mischief unleashed.

Mrs. Gillis bustles back out of the kitchen. "James, go finish your homework and stop bothering Mabel! That boy, I swear. If he had been my first child, he would have been my last child."

"Bye, Mabel! Tell Miles hi for me!" He makes smoochy kissing sounds as he goes.

Mrs. Gillis sighs and hands me a muffin I did not ask for. "Sorry about him. He needs a friend besides Hunter—they're equally terrible. Also, don't tell him I said so, but I think he may have a wee bit of a crush on you, Mabel."

I smile tightly, knowing that's not actually the case. James hasn't told his parents yet, but he's told Norah: James prefers boys. There's no crush at play here. He talks to me like a douchey twelve-year-old talks to his sister's best friend. I know that when he does decide to tell his parents, Mr. and Mrs. Gillis will shower him with public declarations of support, which is exactly what he doesn't want right now. Norah says that he'll do it when he's ready, but James seems in no hurry. Instead he's too busy pissing off the head of the Triumvirate.

I hold the muffin awkwardly in my hand. "Hey, I was wondering if I could steal Norah for a bike ride today?"

Mrs. Gillis claps her hands. "A bike ride, oh, that sounds wonderful. It's been so long since Norah's taken her bike out; she's so preoccupied with those Nickerson boys these days."

"Uh-huh." I'm already halfway up the stairs at that point; the last person I want to talk about Norah's love life with is her mum. I rap on the bedroom door as two of her older siblings thunder past me on their way downstairs.

"Come in." The low tone of her voice lets me know exactly which Norah I'm getting today. *Great.* I push open the door and walk inside. Norah's room looks like a kaleidoscope exploded. The walls are a deep coral, speckled with bits of color in the corners. Colorful yarn garlands stretch out from side to side. Her enormous bed takes up the center of the room, strung with little fairy lights and pieces of tissue paper. She's standing in front of the mirror wearing her mom's high-waisted green pants and a cheery mint T-shirt with a rainbow on it.

"Hey!" She looks back at me from the mirror. "You never came back last night to the party. I waited for you!" *Ah, that's why she didn't call me this morning.*

"Sorry. I took a walk with Miles, and when I got home, I went right to bed. And then surprise, when I woke up this morning, it was shoring-up day!"

"We finished this morning. Done by ten, not too bad."

I don't say anything, because I can tell she's already on edge by the way she is tightening her ponytail over and over again, but everyone knows the Gillis family is terrible at shoring up. When the Triumvirate does its annual audit, the Gillis home always fails the first round. Their Guardian, Ser Martha—a sweet woman who has cared for their family for thirty years—is now in her sixties. She's basically their grandmother and lives to dote on all the kids. She is, however, terrible at keeping the house ready, which is why Jeff pops over here every few months to help them. Sure, they may be carefree and terrible at checking locks, but families like the Gillises keep us from throwing ourselves into the Soft Sea because we're all so damn melancholy.

"Here." I set my muffin down on her dresser and walk over to the mirror. "Want me to braid it for you?" She nods. I take her thick, golden hair into my hands and begin. It's a routine we've done since we were four years old. "Tell me what happened with Edmund at the party." I prepare for the story I've heard a hundred times before.

"After you left, I went back inside to see where Edmund was, but he wasn't there. I looked all over the house, but upstairs was just parents, and they were all arguing about the next Storm and someone was yelling about the Pelletiers' gate. . . ."

I groan.

"Sloane said I should go look outside on the deck, and so I did . . . and I saw Edmund walk out of a bedroom, and guess who walks out two seconds later?"

I don't have to. "Brooke Pelletier?"

Norah looks down, and I see tears gathering in her eyes. "I mean, maybe they were just talking?"

"More like kissing." It comes out blunter than it should.

"Oi, Mabel, I know, but you don't have to say it."

"Sorry." I finish her braid and tuck it over her shoulder.

"It's like, I can't breathe without thinking of him and he barely thinks of me at all. He's, he's"—a sob wrenches up her throat—"indifferent to me! I wait by the phone all day, and when he calls, I'm there. The worst thing is that somehow he's the only one who gets to decide that."

I give her a half hug. "It's hard when the intensity of your feelings is not equal." I say it gently. "Maybe it's time to ask yourself if you can live with the difference, or if he just hurts you." They are harsh words, but I hate seeing her broken like this all the time; I feel defensive for my friend, who deserves only good things. Watching her heart break again and again is so hard and so unfair.

Norah drops her head sadly. "He pulls me in like gravity. I have no control."

"But you do," I sputter.

She spins around, focusing all her intensity on me, and in her placid blue eyes I see sparks of anger. "I know you're trying to help, Mabel, but you don't know what it's like because you've never been in love."

I flinch.

She's right. I don't know about this, and that embarrasses me. I've always felt like a little girl when Norah has relationship problems, because I don't know. But it doesn't mean I wouldn't like to. Besides, I understand that pull now that Miles is here.

"Sorry." Her voice lowers back to its normal, kinder register. "But someday you will, when you're ready to move forward."

"I just don't think he deserves you," I say softly.

"He doesn't. But that doesn't make me want him any less. Anyway, I'm glad you're here, but . . . why are you here?"

I put my hands together and make a pleading face. "I don't suppose you'll come to the Cabot house with me? And maybe up to the Sacred Line? I'll explain on the way."

"The Cabot house? Why on earth would we want to go to that old haunt?" A second later she grins naughtily. "Wait, Mabel, are we going to see *Miles*? You have to tell me everything! EEEEE! And yes, let's go have a fun day at the Cabot house, see how many gargoyles we can count." She does a little shimmy as she backs up from me. "I knew you liked him. I knew it! Admit it! Do it!" She sits on me, and I push her off, laughing.

"Fine. I like him. A bit. Now let me tell you how I ruined everything last night." I reach down, pull the white rock out of my pocket, and hold it out to her. "Also, I'm pretty sure Miles hurtled this through my dad's study window. So let's just say I have some *questions* for him." I raise an eyebrow. "Want to take our bikes?"

Norah's face lights up. I know we're getting older and leaning more into the grown-up responsibilities of our island, but honestly, nothing beats a bike ride with my best friend.

"Hell yeah." She reaches for her windbreaker.

CHAPTER TWELVE

From our end of the island to the Cabots' house, it's a plea-
surable ten-minute bike ride. We fly past the lines of trees
on either side of us; beyond them, wild water swells around
our island. The sea is everywhere here: in shells found in the
middle of the forest, in the salty smell that lingers in your hair.

Up ahead in the distance, I can make out the gray-and-white-
striped Weymouth lighthouse, just on the edge of the Dehset
Sea. Our gilded cage sure is pretty.

Cool wind snaps against my cheeks as we go faster, and I
howl, letting the exhilaration of flying down a hill on a bike fill
me right up. Norah answers back with a joyful shriek, and suddenly we are seven years old again, holding our hands up from
our handlebars as we careen down the hill. Back then, the Storm
seemed like a faraway dream, something our parents talked about.
We were free and we didn't even know it, just regular children at
that point. I raise my hands above my head and close my eyes for
a second, relishing the sun on my skin and the gravel grinding
beneath my tires.

"Look, no hands!" I yell. We are whooping as we round the
bottom of the hill, to where the road curves slightly north before

turning onto the Cabot property. The sun on my skin disappears as I'm swallowed up within the giant shadow of the Cabot house. I put my hands back on the handlebars and look up just in time to see Miles sitting on the front step as if he's waiting for us. The sight of him throws me off. *Shit. Shit.*

I remember the awkwardness of last night, when my memories flooded my brain, and the look of disbelief on his face. From somewhere in front of me comes a shout. Norah's slowing down to avoid the sharp turn, but I'm going too fast, and I realize too late that I'm going to hit her back wheel. I wrench my handlebars sideways and narrowly miss her, but the movement opens up chaos. My bike tips forward, and the stone wall that divides the Cabots' property rises up before me. The back wheel of my bike goes careening sideways as I squeeze my brakes hard. The tires skid, and I feel them leave the ground as the bike is pushed out sideways from underneath me. All I can think is, *Too fast, too fast.* I hear Miles shout my name.

The next second, I'm flying through the air, watching my handlebars move away from me and the expensive river rock of the Cabot driveway rush up to meet my face. I twist around before meeting the ground with the force of a meteor. There is a second of blackness as my body rolls once, twice, and then skids to a stop. A painful ache explodes up my wrist. My head scrapes on the ground, which sends spikes of pain shooting up through my teeth. Gravel carves itself into my arms and cheeks. I don't move, letting the pain radiate through my body. Every inch of me is shocked. Ow.

Norah is on me in a second. "Oh my God, are you okay? Mabel!" She is checking my face, touching my cheeks as she lifts my head up.

I blink twice, the bright sky blinding me. *Am I okay?* I let out a loud groan as I fully understand what happened: I just went ass over teakettle in front of Miles Cabot.

"*Uhhh*, I think so." I push my legs out from underneath me and bend my knees up to my chest; they seem fine. I roll my neck around. It's fine—stiff, but fine. But when I lift my head up, I see Miles sprinting toward me from the porch. "Oh God," I mutter when he reaches me, shame firing on all cylinders. "Please have somewhere else to be right now."

"Not a chance, Beuvry." He kneels down in front of me, his face so close to mine that my breath catches. I watch the way the wind catches the edge of his black hair, his peach lips parting ever so slightly. His hand curls around my chin as if we've done this many times, a familiarity with my body that feels right.

"Can you hear me okay, Mabel?"

"Miles, I didn't lose my hearing—I fell off a bike."

Miles rolls his eyes. "Right. That was stupid to ask. Maybe not as stupid as forgetting to brake, but . . ."

When he looks down at me with a pitiful smile, I feel a warm reassurance that everything is going to be okay between us. Even if I am totally mortified right now, praying for the earth to swallow me. He reaches out his hand, and I immaturely push it away.

"I guess you'll get up yourself, then."

Miles might take this motion as disgust, but really, it's the opposite; as long as he's touching me, I can't process what just happened. Bike, rock, blush, it's all too much. Norah gingerly reaches to help me up. I take her hand because that is safe, but when she pulls on my hand, a shot of pure pain jolts through my wrist.

"Ow. Oh yeah, that's tender." I bark out an awkward laugh,

and Miles looks even more concerned. "I'm fine. I'm rolling it out." I grit my teeth, trying to rein in the tears that have sprung to my eyes without permission. "Okay, yeah, it hurts, and honestly, I'm a bit dizzy," I finally admit, throwing my pride down beside my spinning bike wheel. I lean forward, putting my head between my knees, willing the nausea away.

"Bring her up here." The new voice that speaks from the porch is authoritative and deep, fueled by decades of power. Alistair Cabot looks down at me in immaculately cut clothing, the lines in his face as sharp as the eaves on his house.

With a grimace, I wipe at the wet spot underneath my chin and come away with blood on my fingertips. "Shit," I whisper.

That's when Miles sneakily makes his move; he sweeps me against his chest and heaves me up into his arms. The pain in my wrist when it knocks against him distracts me momentarily, but that feeling is followed by the deep, utter shame of this moment. The new kid is carrying me, and he's looking down at me like I'm the only person in the world who matters. My blood rushes to my cheeks as immense pleasure fills up my entire body at being scooped into his arms. But my temporary insanity is short-lived when I realize what is actually happening—and then I'm mortified.

"Oh, for bloody sake, put me down!" I snap. "I'm not some damsel who needs a man to carry her up the porch stairs." I hope my words drown out the quick thrill of it: his lean muscles against my head, the fact that he is cradling me. It feels like my hormones are betraying me because it feels so good.

As he mounts the steps, I catch the slightest hint of his smell: strong and clean, like the pressurized air after a storm. I shake my head. *Yeah, that's enough of that.*

When he gets to the top of the stairs, I look up at him with gritted teeth.

"Down now, Miles Cabot, please and thank you."

"My lady." *My. Mine.* His words cluster around my heart.

He gently sets me down on an enormous black wicker seat on the porch. I sink gratefully into it, settling into a place that I haven't been since my father died: the Cabot mansion. It's a house that has clawed its way out of a dark fairy tale—and was once one of the favorite places of my childhood. It's hard to imagine now, but my dad and Alistair would hang out almost every weekend. As a child, I spent many hours on this porch, gazing with wide eyes at the snarling gargoyles while Hali pretended to feed them wild blueberries. Everywhere I look awakens a memory: of salmon cookouts overlooking the Dehset, of Hali doing cartwheels in the driveway. Our fathers constantly talked of how our families were meant to be friends, how our destinies were intertwined because of their friendship . . . and then the Cabots didn't come when we needed them. *And now my father is gone.*

Tears blur my vision as I try to distract myself, staring up at the iron rods shaped like cobwebs that secure the vast corners of the porch. When I look past the porch, I can see the entire perimeter of their property. The high stone fence surrounds the grounds, and past that, the Dehset. Like in a Gothic fever dream, the house sits at the edge of the sea like a foreboding monolith, all black with gray shutters, a tall tower at its peak. The man who helped build it is now staring down at me with something that isn't quite caring, isn't quite hatred. It's disappointment almost, paired with confusion as to why his nephew seems intently interested in the state of my ankles. His voice is steady when he speaks, but it is not kind.

"Mabel Beuvry, I have to say, the last thing I expected this morning was to look out the window and see you flying through the air over my driveway." He takes a sip of his coffee. "Did your blood get on my paving stones?"

"Alistair! Jesus." Miles looks over at him in disbelief, but honestly, I was expecting this ambivalence. Anger curdles inside me. I want to remind him that he left my family to die. I want to remind him that not only did he leave us once but that he never came back around afterward; instead he just started sending a check to our house every month to assuage his guilt. But money does not a father return.

But I don't remind him of this. Instead I stare at my bloodied knees.

"May I take a look?" Alistair asks, and I nod reluctantly. He gently takes my wrist between two fingers, and I hold back a whimper as he turns it in a gentle circle. He looks like a professor, a careful man with a kept beard and cool undertones. A thick scar loops across his right cheek, but that's normal on Weymouth. We all have scars—some are more visible than others.

"Does this hurt?" Alistair asks, and I shake my head. "Can you move your fingers?" They curl easily. He bends my palm backward, and I wince. "Yeah, that's the spot." He carefully places my wrist back on my leg before stepping away. *Is it hard to look at me? The daughter of your best friend? Does it bring you pain?*

"I don't think it's broken, rather just a wrist sprain. Still, you might want to have Dr. Mintus check it out." Dr. Mintus is our island's doctor. He is about a thousand years old, is uncomfortable talking about periods, and *I will not be seeing him, thank you very much.*

Miles pokes his face into my frame of vision, and for a second

I'm absolutely shocked by the resemblance. *My God.* The elder and younger Cabot share the same nose and the same prominent cheekbones. The features of a man I hate have been resurrected in a face that has upset the delicate balance of my life.

Great.

Miles looks down at my swelling wrist, a look of concern on his face, before snapping his fingers. "Wait! I think I have an old wrist brace from my skateboarding days upstairs in my suitcase."

"Did he just say his 'skateboarding days'?" asks Norah, laughing. "Who is this kid?"

He thunders into the house, taking all the ease with him as he goes, leaving the three of us—Norah, myself, and Alistair—in a cesspool of awkwardness.

The head of the Triumvirate rocks back in his black boots. "So . . . Norah, how are your parents faring these days? Is your mother still painting?"

I want to roll my eyes. Of course Alistair acts like we're at a dinner party or something.

"Aye." Norah comically crosses her arms in front of her. She's trying to be short to him on my behalf but is struggling against her positive nature. Her arms quickly unfold. "Well, if you must know, my mum started a series on the wildflowers that grow underneath the bridge! It's turning out quite beautiful."

Alistair perks up a little. "Ah, yes, that is a lovely little piece of land. The bluet and the rhodora are particularly stunning this time of year, the ones that grow up right near the pylons." He eyes me cautiously before delivering the passive-aggressive statement of the year. "I hope that bridge is being checked regularly; you never know when we may need it."

I steel myself against him. "You could check it yourself, you know. Stroll on over."

He frowns. "The bridge falls under the Beuvry Estate, as you well know. Every house must stand for itself during a Storm." I see a flash of panic in his eyes after he finishes his sentence; he's realized too late the ugly door he's just opened.

"Don't worry. The Beuvrys know that very well," I snap. "My father especially."

He stirs angrily, hoping to change the subject. "Speaking of houses, have both of you finished your shoring up today? Truthfully, I have to say it's fairly early to be done, but then again, the Cabot house starts shoring up at five a.m. to make sure everything is done correctly. Liam and Lucas ran the shore at three thirty just to prep for the day. Miles . . . had a harder time getting up for it. He obviously has a lot to learn, but we don't want to overwhelm him."

"Miles can handle it," I whisper, watching a blossom of red slowly leak through the knee of my badly ripped jeans. Alistair's face remains hard, but his retort is cut short by the sound of Miles coming back down the stairs.

"Did you finish the list I gave you this morning?" Alistair asks him, one hand on his shoulder.

"Yeah, dude, chill. I finished that insanity an hour ago."

Alistair gives us a withering look. "Then I would advise you to take your *friends* and leave. Liam, Lucas, and their mother have much more work to do here today." His face looks up to the sky. "Fares well the house that's ready." I roll my eyes.

The iron door slams shut behind him, sealing Alistair inside his own defensive mausoleum. Miles turns back to us and gives a dramatic bow. "My uncle, ladies and gentlemen." He reaches out to check on my wrist.

I jerk back like some sort of feral cat. Amusement washes over his face.

"I'm just putting on the wrist guard, Mabel." As he pulls open the guard, Norah inhales sharply behind me, like she's watching some Victorian-level drama unfold.

"I know. Sorry. I was just surprised," I stammer quickly, loving the intensity of his gaze on my face.

He gingerly slides my hand into the wrist guard, his palm tracing warmth over the places that hurt. Then the boy from Seattle kneels in front of me, takes a wet washcloth out of his back pocket, and begins tracing it over the bloody scrapes across my knees. His hands gently move behind the spot where my knees bend, and I feel, ever so slightly, the tiniest stroke of his fingertip in the soft crease there. It's the most erotic thing that has ever happened to me, and he doesn't even notice, as evidenced by his doctor-like focus on my cut. His being this close to me has opened some sort of need within me that I didn't know existed until this moment. I lean my head back, trying to hide the blush spreading over my cheeks. Norah's face has faded into pure, unadulterated voyeurism as she watches over his shoulder.

"There, that's better!" Miles remarks, and for a second I swear he's going to press his lips against my wounds. But instead he somberly produces a Band-Aid. I'm mildly disappointed as he sits back on his heels and sighs. "Now that you aren't bleeding profusely, can I ask why you were flying alone onto my driveway, screeching like some sort of banshee?"

Norah coughs. "Uh . . . I am also here, Miles." He looks up

with a start, and I realize that he actually forgot she was here.

I pause, weighing my words. "Well, um, we were wondering if anyone has taken you out to the Sacred Line yet?"

"No. What's that? Is that the line of boats on the north end of the island?"

"Oh my God, Miles, the Sacred Line is not *the harbor*." Norah laughs.

I press my fingers across my forehead, fielding an oncoming headache before it feels like my head is smashing against the ground. I feel the weight of the white rock in my pocket and remember the anger in his eyes at Sentry's Sleep. I don't want to spook him.

"Norah and I were headed there this morning and wondered if you wanted to come with us. Your house is on the way, so we figured we would invite you." *And I haven't stopped thinking about you since the other night.* "The Sacred Line is one of the most incredible places on the island, and essential to understanding our history."

Norah brightly pops into the conversation. "Well, that *was* the plan, and then Mabel decided to re-create the Tour de France and ended up face down in your driveway."

"That was a truly unexpected start to the afternoon," Miles says with delight. "And one that probably saved me from more— what do you call it? Shoring up? I have to say, Mabel, you're always surprising me, whether it's flying down my driveway or fainting on me in the woods."

"I'm sorry, what?" asks Norah.

"Look, do you want to come or not?" I snap, hiding my nervousness under a layer of unpleasantness, rule one of Mabel's failed seduction book. I'm alarmed at how much I want him to touch me again, so instead I push backward. Makes sense.

Miles smiles. "Yeah, that sounds interesting. But riding a bike might not be the best idea for a certain someone. Can we walk?" I close my eyes to block out his intense stare.

"Only if we can walk slowly." I sigh.

"Deal." This time I surrender and let Miles help me up, but I find myself steadier on my feet than I expected.

William Gillis, November 28, 1882

This morning I carried the bodies of friends to the shore and piled them into a large bonfire for the dead. The sea has finally receded, leaving with it an endless graveyard. At last we are rid of this nightmare, a respite of peace to follow a never-ending night. It will come again; we all know it. As the sun rose, the Acadians, the Novantae, and the monks met together; we can no longer weather this darkness, this epoch of evil apart. We do not understand our foe, but the truth is that we must band together, in whatever distorted form that may be. The Cabots have a theory of why we are here: we are to bring our separate principles of religion and ancestry under one peace to align the three—a triumvirate.

It is true, what they say: without one another, the island will swallow us whole; without one another, this inevitable evil will march forward. We must learn from the mistakes of other families and share wisdom with one another as we fortify our families and our houses.

This Storm was not like others. I wonder if they are growing worse. So few of our people have survived more than one. The thought chills my bones. I am stating here that I will go to this meeting with my family's best interest at heart, as will each soul on this island. Because of this conflict, I will put forth a motion that each house has a guiding force to both steer its course and consult with other houses, without putting the families at odds. Guardians, if you will.

According to Cabot, each family has its part to play, but we will not be told ours. Our legacy is our family, and we need a guardian to protect us.

Historical note by Reade McLeod: This account by William Gillis, kept safe in the Gillis household for over a hundred years, is one of the most important historical documents in our collection; it is a comment on the Storm of that year, but more crucially it is the forming of the Triumvirate and the creation of the Guardians.

CHAPTER THIRTEEN

From the Cabot property it's a ten-minute walk to the Sacred Line, an essential barrier nestled between the houses and the shore. Above our heads the day grows gloomy, thick clouds tempted with rain. We head northeast from the Cabot mansion, climbing down a gradually sloping trail as the ocean horizon grows closer. As we walk, Miles quietly peppers Norah with questions about the island, acting like he's not dying for answers as I limp behind them, trying not to notice the way Miles walks, the way he moves. He takes the jagged stone steps overlooking the shore two at a time, and I marvel at the ease with which his body occupies this island. His physicality matches the landscape: moody, strong, determined. I have the strange thought that he belongs here, that he's been brought here at this time for a reason. It's a wild thought, but our island moves in mysterious ways. Maybe it needs him. Maybe I need him.

I shake the thought out of my head and will my knees to take another step.

After a few minutes, Miles sees me lagging behind and waits for me to catch up as Norah plows determinedly ahead.

"Hey, daredevil queen, is your wrist feeling better? I've seen some falls in my life, but that one took the cake." He pushes a lock of black hair out of his eyes, and behind his humor I sense real concern, and my embarrassment disappears into his contagious smile. It turns out that the tough guy beneath that hair and that tattooed wrist is *generous*.

"I did lose touch with gravity for a few seconds. It was liberating before it was terrifying."

"I'm glad you're okay," he says with sincerity. "I was worried about you after you left me in the graveyard." Oh, that little thing. "I shouldn't have pushed you to keep going, especially after you fainted. I'm sorry. I just needed answers."

"And you deserve them." I mean it. None of us should be gatekeeping the truth.

"This morning was—well, different," he says. "My first shoring up."

A crisp wind blows up from the Dehset, almost as if it's trying to shush him.

"And how was that?" I ask cautiously.

Miles grits his teeth, pushing a stray white-flowered branch out of my way. "You would not believe the strange shit I did today. Like, totally bananas. Alistair really believes in that stuff."

"Oh yeah? What a bloody nutter. Can't imagine why anyone would believe this stuff." He starts to apologize, and I hold up my hand. "Miles, everyone on the island did that strange stuff today. *That stuff* is your legacy." We continue toward the Sacred Line.

"Oh right. My momentous Weymouth legacy. Lucky me."

I want to tell him we don't have to talk about this. We can talk about a thousand other things. I want to talk about what kind of books he reads, what is his most embarrassing moment, what kind of movies hurt his heart. I want to know about his first and last kiss and what his childhood was like. I wish we could start slowly, making small talk as we wait in the popcorn line at a movie theater.

But those conversations are for girls who don't live at the edge of the world. And so instead I walk down the hill in silence, the chill wind whipping at my cheeks. Norah waits at the bottom for us and lovingly loops her arm through mine.

"Are you sure you don't want to go home and lie down?" she whispers to me, and God, *yes, yes, I do*. I want to let my sore body sink into my oversize bed and let Hali—*who's going to be so bloody pissed when I get back*—and Jeff fret over me with biscuits. I do want that . . . but I also want to be here. I want . . . I glance over at Miles.

To be here.

He's looking at the lighthouse rising up in front of him, the rest of the forest at our back. This tall, wild kid looks like he belongs here. His hair is the color of the black rocks on the shore, his skin the very shade of the sand of the Soft Shore. It's as if the island created him. For me. For itself.

"How come no one comes here?" he asks quietly. "I was thinking about it all night. If they can't come over the bridge, couldn't outside people come from the sea? Could you *leave* by boat?"

When I step up beside him, my hair tangles in the wind. "They don't come here from the sea because, on navigational charts, Weymouth is a sailor's worst nightmare: a shoal of jagged rocks and strong currents. Literally they would be risking death to come to an island with no trade and no outside purpose. We're already off the beaten path. Few have reason to be up this far north anyway."

Norah chimes in. "Also, the island itself keeps them away:

sextants, compasses, and chronometers all go bloody mad when they approach us."

Miles takes it all in with a dose of patient skepticism before pointing up at the lighthouse. "But that's fricking huge! How can people miss that?"

I run my tongue over my cracked lip, tasting blood. "Weymouth Island protects its own, but the lighthouse is not without use. It occasionally helps fishing vessels blown off course from Glace Bay, but that's not its main purpose. Our lighthouse is one of many warning systems on the island. She's our stronghold; when everything else falls, she gives us light. When the Storm comes, it may be the only light you have."

"It's a she?" Miles laughs.

"All lighthouses are shes," I say helpfully.

"Duh," Norah adds unhelpfully.

"One more thing I guess I should have known." Miles's eyes are indiscernible as he takes in the shoreline stretching out below us. His body goes rigid. "Whoa." *He sees it.*

"Behold the Sacred Line," Norah says in a dramatic voice. Our own Great Wall of China appears down the steep hill.

Miles takes it in for a second and then turns back to me. "That's really steep. Here." He uncurls his long fingers toward me. I stare at his hand like an alien, while behind him Norah makes frantic movements indicating I should take it. I've never held a boy's hand before—especially not one I'm interested in. The thought is thrilling—and seems a bit dangerous.

I pause a second too long, and Miles sighs.

"Look, you literally already beefed it once today. I'm not going to let it happen again."

I smile. "Okay, but if you trip, I'm not going to be much help."

He laughs as he delicately encircles my wrist with his fingers. His skin is warm, even though it's cold outside, and our hands slide together like puzzle pieces, his fingers latching through my own. "I figured as much."

With small, careful steps, he helps me down the hill, ending up in front of the towering wall of marbled stone.

The Sacred Line stretches from one side of the Weymouth horizon to the other, like a snake crossing the island, a line between us and the Dehset Shore. In the low afternoon light, the stones have a subtle sparkle as the sun reflects off white quartz marked with gray veins. Miles seems dumbstruck.

"*Jesus*, this is huge. I mean—I've seen this from our widow's walk, but it looked so much smaller from there. I literally thought it was just a big fence." He reaches out slowly and rests his hand flat against the stones, a compulsion with hundreds of years of history behind it. He breathes in, and I know he must sense the subtle magic pulsing out from it. Does he feel that he belongs here? Or does the strangeness of it scare him? Does he feel that way about me?

"What does it do?" asks Miles, a hint of strain in his voice.

Norah pushes herself between us. "Glad you asked, Miles!" I know Norah has been waiting her entire life to be a Weymouth tour guide. She takes a deep breath, summoning all her knowledge, like an old dragon of lore. Then she unleashes.

"The Sacred Line was our ancestors' official first defense against the dead. It stretches the entire length of the Dehset Shore, a grand total of three point seven miles, end to end. The stones are called *cloche geala*."

"They're beautiful," Miles says softly.

"Almost every morning for twenty years, these giant stones washed up on the shore of the Soft Sea; sometimes there was just one, but sometimes it was ten or more. It took our people five years to figure out what they were for and then ten more years to build this wall, stone by stone. These stones aren't found anywhere else on earth. They are delivered to us by our gentle sea—one of the island's many gifts to us."

"You're really laying into this," jokes Miles, but Norah ignores him, swept away by the dramatics of her story.

"The early families of Weymouth Island formed the stones into the barrier you see now. This line has stopped many dead over the years."

"Or they're *just stones*, shaped into squares and stacked. Like Legos."

"Not . . . like . . . Legos," I say through gritted teeth. He does not get it.

Norah's voice is full of awe as she looks at the line. "When the dead come ashore during the Storm, these stones break the first wave, and some years it has been enough to stop the whole wave. And we, like, have tea and crumpets. Every Storm is different, but the Sacred Line *always* buys us time. Sometimes the dead break their way through, but not always. Some stones are weaker than others, and the dead always seem to figure it out."

"And then . . ." Miles trails off, his face pale.

"And you find your iron whip. And pray," I deadpan.

"Helpful, Mabel," Miles teases me, but his smile is not unkind. He stares at the wall, and then, moving so quickly that neither of us has time to protest, he lodges his fingers into a deep crack and scales the wall like some sort of freakish rock climber.

"What the?" Norah sputters.

And then He. Sits. His Lazy. Ass. On. The. Sacred. Line.

My mouth drops open. "What are you doing?" I demand. "Miles, get off!"

"Why? Are some ghosts gonna get me?" The playful look on his face disappears as I stalk up below him, all pissed off.

"Miles, get down!"

"The view from here, though." He whistles through his teeth.

"Dude." A word I've never said before and meant tumbles out of my mouth as my jaw clenches. "Get down." Norah looks like she's about to have a panic attack, glancing around to make sure no one sees us. We could get in so much trouble for this with the Triumvirate.

Miles laughs. "Come on. Either you're all playing a joke on me or your parents are lying to you. This has *got* to be some ludicrous fantasy of deeply secluded families. They want to keep you here. Haven't you ever thought of that? This isn't real."

I feel my anger quietly rising to the surface, one of the many feelings he seems to awaken in me. The Storm has cost me everything. How dare he mock it? His long hoodie is hanging over the edge of the Sacred Line. I walk over and grab the back of it.

"Does this feel real?" I growl, yanking downward. Miles has time to let out a surprised "Hey!" and then he's tumbling off the wall. Luckily, he pushes himself nimbly off the stones and lands hard on his feet.

"What the hell, Beuvry?" he sputters. But he freezes when he senses the storm brewing in my eyes.

I'm so furious with him that I don't mind the space between

us. From here, I can see the light hazel flecks in his brown eyes. I can't figure out whether I want to punch him or kiss him. I'm hoping for both, maybe. But for now, rage wins. Norah watches us with wide eyes.

"My father died in the Storm. He died protecting us, so don't sit on our sacred relic, claiming that it's not real." My voice gets choked up. "This whole island—this lore—is older than everything you've ever known. Weymouth Island was here before you, and it will be here after you. Our *job* is to protect the entire world. We've all sacrificed a lot for it. It's all grand and it's all terrible, so if you're going to come out here and mock us . . . then . . ."

"I can piss off?" I can see something like an apology forming in his eyes.

"Exactly. You can piss right off. This island doesn't have to prove anything to you."

"She's right, you know," says Norah quietly, stepping between us, her presence a cooling balm. "Miles, it's true. During the 1998 Storm, my grandfather drowned steps away from our front door. When we finally found him, he was missing both his arms. Before he died, he managed to trap hundreds of dead. He was a hero. This wall is a part of him."

Miles looks back at us, caught up in the moment. I understand him. He needs to make light of the intensity, because if he believes it, what then? His heart and his mind are battling inside. His body knows it's true; I can tell by the way it leans into the wind, the way it feels at home here. *How can I make it easier for him?*

I soften my voice. I don't want to push him away like I did at the firepit. "Whether or not you believe it, it's still real. We don't

COLLEEN OAKES

need *you* to make it real." I gently reach out and rest my palm on his shoulder, feeling the sinewy muscles there.

"Mabel." The way he says my name puts me in my grave. "I don't know what to believe. Are you lying to me? Is everyone?"

I look him straight in his stupid, beautiful face. "No one is lying to you, Miles. I promise."

"Fine, I won't sit on your holy wall, but I mean, come on? The dead?"

"The dead *must* be trapped," adds Norah. "The foundation stones that lie in the bottom of each house attract them. That's how we keep them from getting to the bridge, to the mainland. We can't have a flood, so instead we create a river of the dead. Our houses act as well-placed dams." Beyond the wall of white rocks, the Dehset Shore hurls itself against the rocks. It doesn't like what Norah is saying.

"Why doesn't the military take this over?" Miles asks, and in his question, I see the beginning of acceptance.

Norah snorts. "Like we would trust any nation to do this. Weymouth Island is technically a part of Nova Scotia, but it's not under the jurisdiction of any nation. We need to stay completely independent of any country's politics, anywhere wars would be waged over control of this. No one would agree; the island would be torn apart. My mom says that we have to trust the island. It chose us; the fate of the world can't be manipulated by the hands of anyone else. The world taking over would mean our doom."

Miles shakes his head. "But how does the internet not explode about this?"

I hold up my finger. "One, it sounds so unbelievable that it's always completely dismissed as a conspiracy theory. That works in our favor. Two, the island has a way of keeping things away from it, whether it's attention or people. If a visitor tries to come here, they'll feel the overwhelming creep of uncomfortableness. It's the same with people searching the internet; they will inevitably find somewhere else to be."

"I felt that when I crossed the bridge with Alistair. It felt like wanting to vomit," Miles says sadly. "At the time, I thought it was because my mom died."

Norah's face grows empathetic. "Oh, Miles, I'm *sure* it is grief as well. Everyone on this island has lost someone they love. You're in good company." I take her words into my heart and lock them in my own secret places.

"There's also a different alarm on this island—it's called the dread," I say quietly.

"Do I even want to know what that is?" Miles asks nervously, and I sense the tide shifting from disbelief toward fear. As it should.

I hate giving him this, but he needs to understand all of it. "The dread is our internal warning system. Each of us has it inside us, honed from generations on this island. When the Storm approaches, it will warn you first; you'll feel it in your bones, in your chest."

"I remember it from the last Storm," Norah said. "It felt like being sucked into a black hole." I look over at Miles teetering on the edge of belief and calling us charlatans. It's probably the right time to bust out the rock.

I meet Norah's eyes. "Do you think we should put *it* back here?"

She grins, the wind circling her blond hair around her. "Ooooh yes! It's always so fun to watch!"

Miles's eyes narrow. "What are you two talking about?"

"Oh, I think you know." I pull the rock I found in Father's study out of my pocket; it's blindingly white and sharply cut, as if someone took a pickaxe to it. His mother's rock, the one he showed me yesterday. Miles pales. "Got anything to add, Cabot?" I ask.

He looks down guiltily at his feet. "Shit."

I sigh. "The line can get a bit crumbly in places, but the thing is, a senior member of the Triumvirate walks this line *every single day to make sure it's solid.* This big a piece did not simply fall out of the wall—it has to be yours. And *you threw it through my window.*" My voice is compassionate, all anger left behind. I know he's hurting, he's confused, and he is trying to make sense of all of it. I have been in that place, when you desperately need to create sense out of tragedy.

"We're not here to rake you over the coals," Norah says nicely. "We're here to understand why you would throw a rock at the Beuvry house."

Miles looks at my eyes, pleading silently. "Maybe whoever did that was really angry. Angry that his mom died and left behind only a stupid rock to understand his history. Angry that he has to live with an uncle he barely knows and two asshole cousins. Angry that no one wants to tell him the truth about this place. Angry that the only girl who seems like she could understand him left him standing alone in a graveyard."

I hold the rock up, my voice kind. "It's completely understandable. But maybe whoever did this doesn't need to be so angry. Maybe they need to replace their anger with curiosity."

"And perhaps some new friends?" Norah chimes in. "Like us."

Miles circles his foot on the grass. "Perhaps the person who threw that rock had better aim and a stronger arm than they thought and ran home in the dark, wondering how the girl in the house would think about him now."

Our eyes meet, and it's as if the entire island holds its breath.

Norah lets out a groan. "Okay, you two, this is getting weird. I'm going to give you a minute while you 'someones' sort it all out." She slips away from us, mumbling something about "just kiss already." *I'm going to kill her later.*

Miles's hair blows in soft curls around his head, his brown eyes squinting in the sun. "I'm really sorry. I didn't know about all this. I realize now that breaking a window here is a big deal. I wasn't trying to hurt anyone, but I wasn't thinking. I've had a month, let's say."

"You're not going to do it again, right?"

"Never."

I smile at him, a big, wide, truly Mabel smile. "Then you're forgiven."

His whole body deflates with relief, and he yanks me into a hug. I still, shocked at this sudden embrace. My face is pressed up against his shoulder, fitting perfectly into the small of his collarbone. As he exhales, I feel a barrier lower between us. He's no longer the cool new boy; I'm no longer the girl holding back all the answers. We are Miles and Mabel, real human people, and it seems like we are meeting properly this time. *This is where we begin,* I think. I reluctantly pull back, my heart pounding.

"Do you want to see something amazing?" I ask, and he doesn't miss a beat as he stares into my eyes, lighting up everything inside me.

"I am," he replies with an intensity that scares me.

I laugh awkwardly. "What I meant was, do you want your mom's rock back, or is it okay to return it to the line?"

Miles carefully considers. "I think my mom would love to know that it is back where she came from. Her home." This is what I was hoping he would say, because I'm about to show him something that will change everything.

Norah and I walk down the line until we find a small divot in the wall—the perfect place to return Grace Cabot's stone. As I lean over it, the cloudy light hits the cleave in the rock just right. As we step closer to the wall, Dehset screams as wind wraps around our bodies and pushes us away from the wall.

"They don't like that we're fixing it," I say quietly, before kneeling down. *Ow. God, my body hurts.*

"They?" asks Miles, looking nervously toward the sea. "THEY?"

I nod.

Norah and Miles kneel beside me as I lean toward the wall and bring the rock up to my lips, speaking quietly to it.

"I call upon the island who brought these rocks from your sacred altar under the sea to save us. I ask our ancestors to look down on this new protector." I look at Miles. "Help his wounds heal and please accept this offering from . . . Seattle." I laugh. "Let his gift help protect us from the dead and welcome Grace Cabot's son home." I press my bloody lip to the rock. I see Miles wipe a tear away as I dust my hands off.

"Now watch closely—and don't forget to breathe."

CHAPTER FOURTEEN

A soft grinding sound fills the air; like teeth cracking over a piece of ice. We don't see it happen—Weymouth's magic is shy—but when we blink again, his veined rock has been absorbed into the wall.

Miles stumbles backward, his hands over his mouth. "Holy shit! Holy shit!" Every ounce of cool swagger has been sucked out of his body. Instead he acts like a raving lunatic for the next few minutes, asking rapid-fire questions and answering them himself.

"How did you guys do that? No, you couldn't have done that—*you couldn't have done that*—I was watching you! What was that sound? Did you hear it? Like a . . . grinding? Is it some sort of special magnetic rock that clicks into place? No, that's ridiculous. This whole line can't be magnetic rocks. But that idea is no more ridiculous than . . ."

He crouches down to get a closer look at the rock, and I see his body go still as he runs his fingers over the spot where his mother's rock has been absorbed, as if it were never separated from the whole.

"How is this possible?" he whispers to himself, and I see it on his face. He finally believes.

"You act like you've never seen a little bit of magic before," I say, my voice gentle beside him. Miles's face goes bloodless as he sinks down onto the cool grass, head hung between his knees.

"Oh my God. It's all true." He looks like he's about to vomit. I understand the feeling.

Norah gives him a sympathetic smile. "This isn't all some elaborate plot to deceive you, and suggesting that we all exist to fuel your confusion is, like, really condescending."

"I didn't . . . I mean . . ." He closes his eyes. "I have this memory, one I never thought about before coming here. I was eleven. That year, my mother had appendicitis. When she was coming out of the anesthesia, she was saying the craziest things. She was ranting about *the island* and how it was calling her home. She kept saying 'No house alone.'"

I clear my throat. "'No house alone, every house alone' is a saying here. It means 'we need all the houses on Weymouth to stand united through the Storm. No one house can do it alone, but each house stands alone when the Storm comes.'"

"This is all true." He keeps muttering to himself. "Which means if this is true, then that"—he points to the Dehset—"is true too. Aghh!" He circles his arms around himself and leaps up to his feet to pace in front of the wall. "God! Everything in my life makes sense now—why my mother never talked about her childhood, why we had no family to speak of. And if the Storm happens every ten years or so, then . . ."

"Your mom was here for a few Storms," Norah says quietly.

Miles looks up at the sky. "And if it's all real, that's why you came down here today, all hot and bothered and flying through the air. You wanted—needed—to show me."

"Yeah. You deserve the truth. We all do." *Also, I wanted to see your face.* "It's spooky and weird and unnerving, but it's our life here, and I think it could be yours, too. I won't walk away from you again, I promise. I'm here for you as you process all of this. I may not be the best person on the island to explain this to you, but—"

Miles doesn't move. "No. You're the only one I want to learn it from. And honestly, I don't like to see you leave." Our eyes meet, and I feel everything around us blur: the trees, the shore, the line. There's just his face and mine and something flowing between us. I think, *We are the first and the last.*

The moment is lost when I hear a soft crackle, followed by a male voice. "Oi, Norah, you out there?" Norah pulls the walkie out of her pants. We both blink, but Miles doesn't lean away from me. Ugh, leave it to Edmund Nickerson to ruin this moment.

"Edmund?" Whenever she talks to him, her register goes through the roof.

"Norah? Hey! What are you doing right now? You want to come over? Later tonight me and the boys are planning something, but I could hang during the day."

Crumbs. He gives her crumbs.

"Is that Edmund Nickerson?" Miles asks quietly. Norah's face goes from normal to swoony. "Does she like him? That guy's a real—"

I cut off whatever he's about to say with my hand. "Literally, she'll kill you."

"I'll be there in a second. I'll cut through the woods—it's faster." Norah looks up from the walkie, her face flushed. "Yeah. Soon." She clicks it off before turning to me. "Edmund wants me to come over! Is it fine if I head back? I have to go home and change. I'm all sweaty, and I think I still have some Mabel blood on me."

I grimace. "Eww, sorry about that."

"It's fine! Miles and Mabel, you guys stay here, yeah?" She says it in a singsong voice. "Hey, 'Mabel and Miles' has a nice ring to it. There's something to that."

"Norah! *Stop.*"

Miles smiles. "We can stay awhile. I have a couple hundred more questions."

"Of course you do." I say it nicely, thrilled and equally nervous at the idea of spending an afternoon alone together. "Take the trail through Wasp Wood," I tell Norah. "You'll shave about five minutes if you take a right past the hollow."

Norah flutters. "Oh, right, I forget about that trail sometimes." Everyone does. Wasp Wood is the creepiest place on the island.

I give her a quick hug; there's really nothing I can do to keep her feet on the ground, and no one likes an anchor.

"I'll call you later, all right?" she says, chin digging into my shoulder. "See you around, Miles! Thanks for the rock!" She darts toward the trees. That's what Edmund does to her; he makes her run for his affection. I will never be like that. Opening your heart is like opening a door in a hurricane; it invites chaos in, so it's best to keep it sealed, keep it safe. Like our houses, hearts should have exits and traps that only you know. And yet here I am, bruised and bloody from chasing a boy across the island to give him back his rock.

What is happening to my life? I feel like I'm perched on the edge of a chasm.

Miles stretches his legs. "So, resuming interrogation. If my mother left the island but I've returned, does that mean the island called me back? Does that mean the island killed my mother?"

I shake my head vehemently. "No, it's not like that. Cancer killed your mother. But if you're asking if the island is glad you're back, then I would say probably yes. We're her children, in a way, so it's like you're returning home. She's glad to see you."

"Do I have to give anything to her? Like a sacrifice?"

I grin naughtily. "Yes. A blood atonement. Why do you think I brought my knife?"

His smile disappears, and I laugh.

"You really are the most gullible thing. It's so refreshing." *And I'm not sure I can resist it.* "Some people like to put their first blood during a Storm into the soil, but there's no sacrifice needed. Some may say surviving the Storm is the sacrifice we all give, though, every ten years or so."

"How do you get supplies here if no one can come on the island?"

"The Triumvirate goes into town and shops for everyone once a month, or maybe your Guardian does. It depends on the house. We catch most of our fish from the sea and grow a lot of our food in our gardens. But you know, we have crisps and stuff. We're not bloody Amish."

Miles starts to ask another question before he suddenly turns his head, his back straight as an arrow. "What was that?" he asks. "Did you hear it?" I tilt my head and hear a faint wailing cresting off the waves.

"It's the Dehset," I say. "Remember?"

"Oh yeah," he says softly. And now he is looking at me.

Staring. Without warning, he reaches out and tucks a lock of hair back behind my ear. "Have I ever told you that you have the wildest, most fantastic hair I have ever seen?" I hear the water below us, frothing with want. Or maybe it's me. For so long I've denied myself friends and fun; I've denied myself life. But he's here now, and it feels like holding back my feelings for him is like trying to stop a tsunami. My tongue is heavy as I lean closer to him, aware of every inch between us, a distance to be closed. Two weeks ago I didn't know he existed, and now he's consuming everything.

Maybe I understand Norah better than I think.

"Mabel." He says it under his breath, in a very American dreamboat way, *and Jesus, this kid*. Suddenly the Dehset screams so loud that we both jolt away from each other. The hairs on my arms stand up when I realize that the high-pitched wailing isn't coming from the Dehset.

It's Norah.

CHAPTER FIFTEEN

Without a word, Miles and I both sprint toward the woods, my body screaming with each step. Pain grinds up through my knees and throbs through my wrist. Miles is practically a bullet, and he's at the edge of the woods in less than a minute. I run awkwardly behind him, my pain-filled breaths loud as I pass into the shadows of the trees.

Wasp Wood—aptly named for the angry wasps that fill it each summer—is darker than the rest of the woods on the island due to its heavy canopy. Moss grows heavily on the trees here, and the soil is moist and dark. The number of branches stretching out overhead makes it easy to lose track of where we are. *Although, Norah should have been on the trail. . . .*

"The trail is over here!" I shout to Miles, and he follows me along a path overrun with ferns. Through the trees, I see where gray sky meets green forest, and to my left I can see where forest meets a steep cliff drop. *God, did she fall?*

"Norah!" I scream hysterically from the top of my lungs, my heart pounding furiously. *Where is she, where is she, where is she?* The woods spin around me; I cannot lose another person. I cannot lose her.

"Mabel?" I hear Norah's quiet voice peep through the trees, and my heart rises in relief. Finally we come upon her, standing perfectly still just off the trail; to her left is a small wooded glen, a place where families picnicked a hundred years ago, before the Triumvirate wisely left it to the wasps.

"Hey!" Miles runs toward her, but she stands still, unmoving.

"Norah!" I wrap my arms around her and pull her face toward me. "Hey, hey. Look at me. What's wrong? What happened?" She blinks twice, her eyes pointed at the ground.

"He . . ." She whimpers, her voice trailing off. *Something is very wrong.* I check her body. Physically she seems unharmed, aside from her face, which is drawn and pale. Her dark lips tremble as she struggles to get words out.

I give her a gentle shake. "Norah! Look at me! What's wrong? What's—"

"Mabel . . . there." She chokes on her tears as her finger points at something deep in the trees.

I follow her finger with my eyes, up past the trail, up past the gnarled branches to where I see something—a body?—slumped over some gray boulders. Above us I hear a metallic sound clanking among the branches. I choke down a wave of nausea as my brain struggles to connect what I'm seeing. Miles's arms are suddenly circling around us both, pulling us against him. A cold sweat appears out of nowhere, drenching my forehead; and I get the strange sensation that we are being watched. I can't look up, so I focus on the soft earth behind Miles's shoulder, where a small foxglove has popped through some salty hunter sprigs. An emotional numbness shoots through my system, and after a minute I'm able to breathe again, able to *think* again. I pull back from

Miles, leaving Norah to sob against his other shoulder, and look at what I cannot unsee. Dead bodies are like that.

Will Lynwood, the Popes' older beloved Guardian, is lying face up on a pile of boulders at the base of one of Weymouth's tallest trees. His body is crumpled, his neck turned unnaturally. There is a dark stain beneath his head. Rivulets of blood drip onto the dark soil below. His bare feet are coated with mud and bloodied. He's wearing a familiar maroon windbreaker with the Guardian emblem embroidered on the breast—Jeff has the same one. Underneath the crest, the words "Servir Pour Combattre" are visible. *Serve to fight:* the motto of the Guardians. A moan from somewhere deep inside me escapes; this scene is awful.

"He must have fallen," I whisper. I look up, deep into the pine tree, and I see something metal and whirling at the top of it, some scientific instrument that he has attached to the tallest branch. It blows and circles in the wind, causing a clunking sound that fills the forest.

"It's so awful! He made our family a birdhouse last year. We just saw him a few days ago, Mabel! Remember?" Norah whimpers.

I flash back to his vacant eyes, to his sack of metal, his madness. Should we have gone after him? Was this what he had in his bag?

"Who is that?" Miles asked, horrified.

"Will Lynwood. He's the Popes' Guardian," I answer, not able to look away.

"Did you know him well?" Miles asks.

"As well as you can know another house's Guardian." I shake my head. *Poor Jeff.* Will Lynwood was a friend of his, a mentor who shared his love of gardens. My face crumples at the idea of Jeff's pain. Lynwood's pale, sightless eyes stare upward toward the sky. I try to imagine him falling, hitting every branch on the way down. This does not look like a peaceful death. The wind circles around us.

Miles stares stoically ahead as Norah sobs.

"It's okay not to look," I whisper to him. He follows my suggestion, still holding on to Norah as he turns away. Somehow, I'm able to bear it. I slowly walk around the body, and when I get closer, I can see the small trickle of blood that trails down from his ear and pools at the top of his white shirt collar like a small red poppy. Broken branches lie in a pile around him; it looks like it happened fast. There is something carved in the tree trunk, some numbers, spiraling around one another again and again: eights, sixes, ones, and sevens. I trace the numbers with my hand and step back, the fog of shock taking over.

"We have to tell the Popes right away."

Norah is standing beside me, frozen to the earth; her sweet heart is struggling to process this. "Do you think . . . ? Do you think he fell while we were just out there, by the Sacred Line? Could we have saved him?"

I glance at his lips, which are a pale shade of purple. "No. He's been dead for a while, I think. We would have heard him scream." I stare for a minute.

"What are you thinking?" Miles whispers.

"How did he get up there with his contraption?" I whisper. "There's no ladder, no branches low enough that he could have climbed, right? Or I guess he could have freehanded it?" I tilt my head to get a better look.

Miles frowns. "That seems like a lot for that old man, but I don't know, maybe he was fit."

"No. He was a mess." I hug a shaking Norah and pull the walkie out of her pocket.

"Are you calling the police?" Miles asks hopefully.

I shake my head as I switch the channels. "No. We don't call the police on Weymouth." It seems wrong as the words leave my mouth. "We *should* call the police, but as they near the bridge, they'll forget why they're coming. We have to call the Triumvirate." Miles's face tells me everything I need to know—that he thinks we are all misguided. That's fine. I switch to the island's emergency channel. Eleven, one hour before midnight.

"This is Mabel Beuvry, emergency calling for a member of the Triumvirate, come in?"

There is a long second before I hear Alistair's intensity crackle back.

"This is Alistair Cabot. What is your emergency, Mabel?"

I take a breath. "Uh, we . . . um found something—a body— in Wasp Wood. It's Will Lynwood. . . . I think—I think he fell trying to put up an instrument. He's . . . dead." My voice betrays me at the last second, choking up. It's all so horrible; I want to wrap my arms around the person I was five minutes ago, before I saw a body crumpled on the rocks.

There is a long pause. "Will Lynwood of House Pope is dead? Are you sure?"

I pause sadly. "I'm sure."

After my father died in the Storm, Will Lynwood came over to our house and quietly gathered all my father's shirts. My mother had locked herself up in her room with bottles of wine for days, and it was just Hali and me, silently watching him clean out our father's drawers. Two weeks later, I had a beautiful quilt on my bed made from my father's old shirts. It smelled like him. It felt like him. It was one of the greatest comforts I had during that time—and one I still use to this day. That man, that artist, is now lying face up, broken like a rag doll across a pile of boulders.

"What? My God. Is Miles with you?" Alistair's voice is shocked.

"Yes, Miles is with me. We're past the trail near the old fern hollow in Wasp Wood, over."

There is a long pause. "I know it. I'll be there as fast as I can."

My voice trembles, but I have one last request. "Could you, um, bring Jeff with you? Please."

There is a long pause, and then Alistair confirms. "Yes, of course. Over." The walkie clicks off. I sigh, trying not to look at the body. Beside me, Miles takes my hand.

"What was he doing up there?" he asks, and I flash to his interaction with Norah and me from yesterday, the fear and madness in his eyes, his mention of something called the "Great Storm."

"I'm not sure," I say honestly. "But I hope he's at peace, wherever he is." I know exactly how far we'll all go to find our peace.

Thirty minutes later it seems like the entire island descends on us. Alistair and the Triumvirate arrive first, their loud voices signaling their arrival in the woods long before we see them. We are quickly pushed aside, and honestly? I'm grateful. They are followed by the Guardians, all of whom are visibly upset and racked with disbelief.

Everyone is messing everything up with their footprints and their touching; there are too many people, too many things happening all at once. There won't be an investigation. This is Weymouth, and most likely this was an accident. But the question keeps sticking in my brain: *How did he get up there?*

When Jeff sees the body of his old friend, he lets out a cry of utter disbelief that punches a hole in my heart. I watch as my Guardian kneels next to the rocks and rests one trembling hand on Will Lynwood's shoulder. I ache for him, this man who gives us so much love.

I walk up beside him and take his hand. "I'm so sorry," I whisper. He looks over at me, his face grateful.

"Oh, Mabel," he utters. "What a sadness this is." He curls his fingers around mine, pressing our hands against his forehead as he cries. Something about that gesture makes me desperate for something I will never have again: I want my DAD. I want him here with us, a pillar of strength among all these excitable men, who are so desperate to do *something*. I search for my father's face among the Triumvirate for a delusional second before I remember that he's not coming. *He's never coming again.*

Alistair walks up beside Jeff. "I'm sorry for your loss, Jeffrey." *Jeffrey?* I've never heard anyone call Jeff that *in his life*, and the strangeness yanks me out of my grief spiral.

"I need a moment with Mabel, Norah, and Miles." Alistair pulls us aside, sitting us down on a picnic table dotted with moss. Not a second later, Jeff is standing protectively behind us.

"I'll sit in here, Alistair, if you don't mind. They're minors and should have a Guardian present." Alistair gives Jeff a strained smile.

"I can account for where these three were about two hours ago, so there's no need to discuss that." He turns to Jeff. "Mabel took a tumble on her bike in our driveway this morning. It was quite a sight."

Jeff turns to me, his face concerned. "Mabel, were you hurt?"

"No, not really," I say, just as Miles interrupts me.

"Yes. Her wrist and knees were both injured. She should probably ice them for the rest of the day."

Jeff gently tilts my chin up, inspecting my face, taking in my cut lip and bruised cheek. "Hmm. I'll treat these at home, and maybe we'll have Dr. Mintus look at your wrist. You should have called *me*," he says sharply. There is much more he wants to say but doesn't.

Alistair continues. "They left my house around two p.m. I didn't know where they were going or why, though I probably should have asked."

Miles and Norah look over at me, and without speaking, we all agree to a lie. We aren't going to tell them about the rock. It's too much.

"I wanted to show Miles the Sacred Line," I blurt out. "And beyond the Cabot house is the best place to see it. We literally hung out by the wall and talked. Miles had a lot of questions. *Questions that should have been answered already.*" I keep my gaze on Alistair.

"I said you could ask me anything you needed to know about the island!"

Miles shrugs. "I wanted to talk to someone my age about it."

Jeff leans forward. "A perfectly normal thing, Alistair. Sometimes we need to hear hard truths from those most like us."

Alistair's eyes narrow. "So that's all of it, then? You hung out by the Sacred Line for an hour and walked into the woods? Why?"

"Norah's friend called and invited her over. She wanted to

head home right away, so she took the shortcut through Wasp Wood. Miles and I stayed behind."

"What friend?" Alistair asks Norah, and I watch a flush go up her cheeks.

"The call was from Edmund Nickerson. I was going to see him," Norah says softly. I see Alistair soften—Norah can win anyone over with her earnestness.

"Oh, of course. That makes sense. I know you're fond of him," he replies. Norah looks mortified. Of course her lifetime crush hasn't escaped the notice of the adults on this island. "What happened next?"

Norah continues. "I was running through the hollow, and my eye noticed something glinting, over there at the bottom of the trees. Something gold. At first I thought it was maybe a bird with a trinket in its mouth. I left the path to see what it was, and that's when I heard the clanking sound. I couldn't see very far—the mist and the trees were thick, so I didn't see him until I was standing right by him. And I looked over, and . . ." She lets out a strangled sob and buries her face in her hands. "I must have panicked. I think the wind was flapping his clothing, because in my mind I thought he moved. I tried to climb up the rocks, but then I saw that he was dead. I must have screamed at some point because Mabel and Miles came running, but I don't remember actually doing it."

Alistair's shoulders slump. "You poor girl. I'm sorry this happened to you."

Norah can't speak anymore as she begins heaving big, ugly sobs, and while I hold her, a flash of jealousy runs through me. To be able to grieve like this, to let your emotions wreck you in this way, is such a gift. While Norah is able to drown in a flood of her tears, my own grief rages internally, creating things to hold on to.

"Mabel, is that about how it went?" asks Alistair, like I'm going to suddenly sprout a surprise confession about how we murdered a Guardian.

"Of course." Our eyes meet, and where I think I'm going to see righteousness, I see only a deep sadness.

"All right. Why don't you two head on out? Ser Jeff will see you back. Miles, you stay here with me." Miles is pulled away from us as Alistair awkwardly wraps his arm around his nephew's shoulders. The last glimpse I see of him is Alistair leading him past the tree line, where he will no doubt question Miles on his own. Poor Miles, far from home and missing his mother, stuck on an island so different from the rest of the world. And now: a dead body. No wonder he hates it here.

Jeff drives us over to the Cabot house, where we grab our bikes and throw them into his truck, and we all ride up the main road in silence. Norah hops out at her house, and I give her a quick hug from the back seat.

"I'll call you later," I say, and she blinks as if she's seeing me for the first time.

"Oh, yeah, sure." She unlocks her gate. I can see her mum standing in the doorway with a cup of tea waiting for her, the warmth of her silhouette reassuring. I can't shake the feeling that something inside Norah has been broken, maybe forever. I wave goodbye, but she doesn't see me.

There is silence in the car for a second before Jeff takes my hand. "A girl your age should not have to see so many bodies in her short lifetime. It's not fair, and it's not right."

No, I think bitterly, *it's Weymouth*. I'm struggling to keep flashes of Will Lynwood's body out of my mind. *His neck, hanging to the side. The small blossom of blood on his collar.* Details I'll never forget. A wave of nausea passes through me, and I roll down my window, letting in a tunnel of crisp air.

"I can't believe Will's gone," he says softly. "And on such a beautiful day."

He's right; the sky is mostly clear now, with a peppering of fluffy gray-blue clouds hanging over the horizon.

"Was he confused? Did you know? Why would he climb that tree with that huge metal pack? What is that thing?" I ask Jeff.

He shakes his head angrily. "I'm not entirely sure. Mental illness can be a liar, you know. I know Will had some struggles lately. He was getting older, and he was very afraid, I think, of the next Storm."

"I saw him on the road the other day. He was talking about a Great Storm and mumbling. It was like he saw us, but he also didn't." I pause. "Maybe he thought no one would listen to him. The Guardians are never supposed to show weakness." I should have listened better.

"Will knew me better than that. I would have listened." As Jeff stares out the windshield, my mind is a million miles away. *What was Lynwood doing up there? Why was Alistair acting so strange? How did Lynwood get up the tree?* The beginnings of doubt press down on me, one cold thought at a time.

When we get home, it's not my mother who is waiting for me on the porch but Hali. Jeff gives her a sad smile as I sink into her arms with a sob. For the first time since I saw the body, I take a real breath of relief as her neediness pulls me down.

CHAPTER SIXTEEN

The next few days pass quietly; I don't hear from Miles, and we don't hear any new information about Lynwood. Jeff spends a lot of time whispering into the phone as Hali and I become sloths, moving only to get toast, find new books, and rearrange ourselves. I worry that this thing with Lynwood broke whatever new magic Miles and I had together. How do we go back from here? How do we find each other when we found *a body?*

Then somehow it's Thursday already; our break from school is flying by. I'm almost at the end of *The Giver*, listening to the rain patter against the porch shutters, when Hali finally brings up Lynwood. I hear her mutter something under her breath, and I look up from the book.

"What did you say?" We're sitting on the couch together, both wearing our soft green pajama sets dotted with orange flowers and trimmed with lace edging, rubbed thin by years of use. The pajamas were our last Christmas gift from our father. Jeff has let out the waists—twice. Hali and I have never talked about it, but we always choose to wear them on the same day, like there is some unconscious thread running between us. We both miss him at the same time.

"Nothing," she mutters, but I can tell it's not nothing. It never is with her.

Thunder grumbles outside as I bury my feet under her thighs. She shrieks in return.

"Ow, Mabel! You pinched me! Get away." She swats at my foot, and I stick my toe in her face.

"This pinched you? This toe?"

"Oh my God, stop! You're so annoying. Go find some lotion." She bats her book at me, but I can tell she loves the attention. I yank my leg back, hoping to stay in the silly mental place where I don't have to think about bodies at the bottom of tall trees.

Hali begins tapping a single finger on the glass, which is something she does when she gets anxious about the outside. As the weather weeps, her boredom grows, and so does her anxiety about leaving, a vicious cycle, a snake eating its own tail. *Tap. Tap.*

"So what did he look like? Will Lynwood?" she asks curiously.

I grimace. "Do you really want to know? It was hard to see."

She nods slowly. "I think it would help you if you talked to me about it."

I sigh, closing my eyes. "He looked sad. His face looked like he had clay mixed into his skin, like he wasn't quite real, like a movie prop. His lips were plum colored. There was blood coming out of his ear, dripping down to his shirt collar. He hit his head on the rocks; they were soaked with his blood."

"That sounds awful." Hali is trying to look sad, but I can tell she's excited by this.

COLLEEN OAKES

My sister is nothing if not morbid. My mind crawls back through the muddy soil, back out to Wasp Wood, to the body on the rocks. I see the palest blue eyes I've ever seen, staring upward through broken blood vessels.

"I can't stop thinking about the fact that he didn't have a ladder. Also . . . it felt like someone was watching us, but that might have just been how creepy the scene was."

"Do you think it was murder?" She's practically frothing at the mouth.

"No, it didn't feel like that."

Hali sits up, a blanket falling from her shoulder. "But who would be watching you? How would they know you would be out there?"

"I know. It sounds stupid." I focus my eyes on a small raindrop inching its way down the window. "Why would he climb that high, though? He was an old man, for God's sake."

Hali frowns. "Maybe things aren't good at the Pope house. We've always known they're a bunch of high-strung maniacs, even if they are talented." Hali chews on the end of her ragged fingernail as she thinks about it. "Don't forget about Miles either. It can't be a coincidence that this happened when he arrived—I bet the Triumvirate is wondering the same thing. Something's not right with him. I know it. I mean, how did he even get out here to the island?" She tucks one of her tendrils behind her ear, not succeeding at hiding the jealousy in her voice.

Rage rushes through me; no one else can get me angry as fast as my sister can.

"Alistair went and got Miles, remember? Also, he's a Cabot. He belongs here. Why would you *say* that?"

Hali suddenly doesn't look so sweet. "Maybe you should reconsider hanging out with him, Mabel. I'm just saying—maybe the island is trying to tell you something."

"What are you even talking about? The island is trying to tell me something by an old man falling out of a tree? You really think Lynwood's death was just a message? I hope nobody tells Miles that. Those things aren't related, Hali. It's disrespectful to suggest they are!" I slam my book closed with a huff. "Also, you don't even *know* Miles. You haven't even met him. He's definitely a strange kid, but no more than we are. He belongs here." I think about how strange we would look to anyone from outside Weymouth, these two awkward girls living in this enormous, half-used Victorian mansion, waiting for the dead to come, dressed in old pajamas. *God.*

Hali curls her lip. "Is 'he belongs here' French for 'I want to make out with him'?"

"HALI!" My mouth drops open. She never talks to me like this.

"I see the way you light up when you say his name, even though he's *an outsider*. He doesn't belong here, not the way we do. We were born to defend this island. He's a cute interloper. If he leaves, maybe things can return to normal around here."

"What do you mean, back to normal?" I ask, trying very hard not to punch my sister.

She angrily grabs her mug of tea, her long fingers perched lightly on the ceramic like they're longing to scratch something. "Can't you feel it? There's something in the air, like a pressure change. Everything seems a bit off in the house. I haven't heard birds lately. You probably haven't noticed because you've been all moony about him, but I think he's bad for the island. I should have known that the second a new boy shows up around here, you would fawn all over him. Of course you want something new. He's all you've been waiting for."

"Hali. You're talking nonsense." I get it—it's hard to not be on the edge of sanity when your life is a series of fences, but that doesn't mean she gets to be cruel. "You're jealous, but you have no reason to be. *You're my sister.*"

She snorts. "Jealous of Miles? No thanks. He sounds like a scarecrow met a boy band." It's a pretty solid burn. But I can still meet her fire.

"No, Hali. Jealous of *me*, of my time. It's never enough for you. It's always been the two of us, the Beuvry girls, but it can't always stay that way." Hali holds my stare, my fearless sister who is afraid of the whole world.

"You're always gone," she whispers finally, vulnerability seeping out from every pore. "One day you're going to leave Weymouth, and I'll be stuck inside these walls forever. I'll stay here with the memory of Dad and the ghost of Mum, and you'll only come back to visit my grave."

"My God, Hali, that's so dramatic."

"Piss off," she snaps, angrily heaving herself up from the couch, flipping me the bird as she goes. "I wish it was Miles on those rocks."

"Hali, Jesus!" I follow behind her. "Seriously? Why are you getting all worked up about this? Come on, we can hang out!" I follow her up the winding stairs until I come to the outside of her room, but before I can say anything more, she slams the door in my face.

"Fine! Really mature of you!" I yell, slamming my palm

against the door, my face flaming hot. "You don't have a life, so I don't get one either, isn't that right?" It's mean, but it's true. On the other side of the door, Hali has gone silent.

How dare she? What Hali wants is for me to live like her: to never laugh at a party or hang with friends on the beach. I let out a moan. How can I so deeply *love* my sister and *hate* the cage of her own making? I'm so exhausted from carrying it.

I stomp back down the hall, pausing outside Mum's door. I close my eyes for a second, wishing she would yank the door open, head down the hall, and take Hali in her arms. That she would make it all better. This is who I need, the mum I know she can be, the one from our childhood. Instead I walk away from the door, lonely in a house full of people.

I'm about to push open the swinging door of the kitchen when I hear Jeff's hushed voice. It's when I catch the worry in his tone that I pause and crouch down, my ear near the crack at the bottom of the door. I've always been keen on eavesdropping.

"Tobias, *for Pete's sake*, we don't know what he was trying to do. Stop suggesting outlandish theories just because we don't understand this yet."

Tobias is the Guardian for the Mintus family, a sharp-tongued, efficient hunter who provides the island with a lot of its meat.

"Yes, I know that's what Janet implied, but she was wrong. And yes, I've heard about his journals, about what's going on in the house, his Great Storm theory. To be honest, I'm not going to wave it away as superstitious nonsense. Will was in his right mind when he wrote that, and his theories deserve an investigation at the least. Information can't hurt, is what I'm saying, and contrary to what the Triumvirate says, *Alistair Cabot doesn't always know what he's talking about.*" I hear him shift his feet. "It's suspicious that they are trying so hard to lead us away from what he was trying to prove, right? Alistair chooses to believe whatever makes him safe; he has enough to worry about with his nephew's arrival."

Miles? The Great Storm? His journals? Suddenly nothing matters more than hearing the end of this conversation; I feel the undercurrent of his words tugging at something in my brain. I inch closer to the door.

Jeff's voice grows dark. "The Guardians knew Lynwood better than he did—and yes, I know about the ladder. I have those questions too." There is the sound of a glass slamming down on the counter. "*Fares well the house that's ready.* That's our job—to be ready! And that's what Lynwood was trying to do! Now his family is alone."

I shift, and the hardwood floor underneath me creaks softly.

"Hold on, I think I heard something."

I scramble backward, launch up to my feet, and am unsteadily swaying on them as the door pushes open. Jeff stands in front of me, our landline pressed tightly against his chest.

I plaster a hopeful look on my face. "Hey, you still got those muffins from yesterday lying around?"

Jeff sighs, all the weight of the world going out of his shoulders. It's the crabbiest I've ever seen him. "Yes, hold on, Tobias. *Mabel wants a muffin.*" He disappears behind the swinging kitchen door and comes back slinging a carrot muffin with a delicate swirl of cream cheese.

"Mabel, can you eat it on the porch or something? I'm on a private call." I pretend to go, but I creep back and listen until

I hear the details I'm looking for: "Tomorrow we're all meeting at the lighthouse, Guardians and Triumvirate, ten p.m. . . . Yes, Tobias, I know it's late, but have a goddamn coffee or something."

I hear the phone slam down, and suddenly I'm flying out onto the porch, my heart pounding as I shove a huge bite of the muffin into my mouth. Jeff leans out the door, his intense voice replaced by the gentle one I have come to depend on.

"How is it?" he asks.

"Ahhmazing," I mumble, my mouth full. It's not a lie. "Thanks! Oh, hey, Mum's out, I think. You should maybe check on her later?"

He sighs and leaves. With a relieved smile, I kick off to make the porch swing move. Only when I'm rocked into a quiet place do I let myself put words to the feeling in my stomach: *Something is happening on the island.* There's a whisper in the air, a malignant breath that runs up my spine. When we found Lynwood broken on those rocks, some fabric of the island shifted. This isn't the Storm. It's not the dread. That I know. So why can't I shake the uneasy feeling that maybe it does have something to do with Miles? Is it my anxiety driving me into conspiracy theories? Is the first light I've felt in years too good to be true? Hali, even in her jealousy, was she onto something? There is a feeling like being punched in the gut when I wonder if it's not just Miles that's making me think this way, feel this way. This instinct that it has something to do with him and . . . *me?*

Is that why Hali was really being so strange?

I angrily take another bite of my muffin. If Jeff and the rest of the adults on this island are not going to give us answers, I guess we'll have to find them ourselves.

CHAPTER SEVENTEEN

I leave my house at nine the next night, and right up until that moment my entire body is twitchy at the thought of seeing Miles again. The morning at home was slow and lazy, spent playing a card game with Hali (who is still barely speaking to me) and reorganizing my room to the sounds of a Black Prairie CD. Jeff bribed me with a trip into Glace Bay next month in exchange for an extra hour spent shoring up the porch (measure the iron rods that run along each tiny bevel, then shove them into the openings before covering them with a paste made of fine salt and water).

Even though I spent the entire day with her, when I told Hali that I was sneaking out that evening, she had the predictable meltdown. It was too much; I walked away, leaving my sister in her own fiery coil of anger, my threshold for her ridiculousness extra low.

In my bedroom, I yank on rose-colored sneakers, dark ripped jeans, and a gray shirt, and pull my curls up into a ponytail, then top the outfit off with a thin parka. I wish I had something lighter, more girly—but then I think how ridiculous that is. I don't live in a place where we wear ruffles.

I pinch my cheeks to bring out some color underneath my freckles; they dance across my face like a disjointed collection of stars. I lick my finger and try to smooth out my eyebrows, but after a minute, I give up trying to tame them. I'm a northern girl through and through, and no matter how much I wish that I had a bit of Hali's summer shine or Norah's smooth mane, I'm just Mabel—and Mabel is kind of swarthy.

I tiptoe down the stairs, skipping every fourth step (there're traps underneath every fourth stair), hoping to avoid anyone on the way out. Jeff has already left for his top-secret meeting, Mum is watching TV down the hall, and Hali is most likely reading Harry Potter for the ninth time. I'm in the clear. The Beuvry Estate is silent as a tomb as I edge out the front door. When I turn around, it's lovely outside. The night edges on a row of clouds hanging patiently above the Dehset shore. *Almost there.*

My movements are careful as I make my way down the outside stairs. I don't want to have to explain myself, don't want any conversations about where I'm going or why. When I turn toward the garage, I almost leap out of my skin when a human shape bleeds out of a dark corner. My heart knocks against my chest, and I skitter backward with a shriek.

"Argggh! What the hell!" I trip, almost knocking over our two stone gargoyles (Lestat and Louis), which stand guard at our front door, my hand held defensively out in front of me. I almost land on a bed of iron needles that sit low in the ground, hidden among our mums and chrysanthemums.

"Oh shit, Mabel, sorry!" Miles leans forward, wearing all black. His hair is pushed forward into a small tangle at the front of his forehead that definitely took time to achieve. When Miles reaches out to steady me, all I can think is, *It would be grand to not fall down around this boy.* I let him take my arm and then don't pull it back; instead I let the heat race through me.

"Rule number one: don't scare people on Weymouth. There's a good chance you'll end up with an iron spike through your eyeball."

"I wasn't trying to—you're jumpy!" After he steadies me, he keeps his fingers laced around mine for a second longer than he should.

I glance up at him. "What are you doing out here, lurking around in the dark, looking like a vampire?"

"I wanted to sneak into the Triumvirate meeting. I came over to ask if you wanted to come with me, and when I was walking up to your porch, I saw you tiptoe out. Great minds think alike, I guess."

"Or we both desperately need to know what happened to Lynwood."

"Or we were hoping to run into each other on the way."

I smile shyly. "Still, you shouldn't be sneaking around Weymouth. It's not safe."

"Says the girl sneaking around outside her own house."

"Yes, but this is my house, and thus I know where all the deadly things are." I gesture to the deadly flower bed.

"What if you live in a house and you don't know where all the traps are?" he asks.

"Then you're screwed, I guess."

He chuckles. "That's what I figured. *So,* I've been checking out your incredibly weird porch while I was waiting for you." He squints at the rafters, where thousands of paper cranes shift in the wind. "Explain," he says plainly.

"The dead hate paper," I say, pointing to the cranes. "They especially hate paper with penned Brontë quotes."

"Is it because *Wuthering Heights* is insufferable?"

An unexpected laugh escapes from my throat. This boy knows his books, and I can't show how incredibly and deeply sexy that is.

"My dad once told me it's because *art* is the crux of living, the peak of mortality. Most art starts with paper: music, words, paintings. Paper reminds the dead of everything they once had . . . and can never have again. It undoes them."

As a breeze whips past us, the cranes move slightly in the wind. His weary eyes watch them sway, a mix of skepticism and resignation on his face.

"My mom liked origami. She would always be folding little animals out of napkins. If I found pretty paper, I would bring it home for her, and ten minutes later I would have an owl or a little boat on my bed. I never knew what to do with them, and so I put them all on this little shelf above my bed." I watch his face as he processes the memory, passing between a happy nostalgia and pain at speaking of it.

"One day, not long before she got sick, we had a big fight about something stupid: I wanted to go out, and she wanted me to stay in. It made me furious that she was always so suspicious of my friends. She couldn't understand why I wanted *more* people in my life; she was so secretive, so closed off to others outside our circle. Anyway, the day we fought, I took all the origamis and tossed them into a dumpster outside our apartment building. Like a little shit." He curls his body defensively, steeling himself against his past actions.

"Later, when I got back from my friend's house, I sprinted to the dumpster, but someone had grabbed the trash already. My mom never said anything, never made me feel bad about it." His eyes fill with tears. "She was a better person than I am. She should be back here, not me." Then he smiles. "She would have loved this porch. I feel her here, and at so many places. It's like she's the island sometimes."

I know exactly what he means. There's a moment, a pause, and we take each other in, and I wonder: *Does he feel what I do? That something is pulling us together?*

"MAAABEL?" A shrill voice cuts through the night as we stare at each other. When I look up, my mother is drunkenly leaning out her bedroom window, her robe fluttering open in the wind. I can see her bra. *Oh my God.*

"Mabel? Is that you out there?"

I cringe. "Yes, Mum, it's me."

"Is there someone out there with you?" Damn, she must have heard him.

"Yeah. Miles is here. Miles Cabot."

Her face lights up. "Oh, okay. Hi, sweetheart!"

Miles waves sheepishly back at her, and I see that he's a charmer with parents. Of course. "Hello, Mrs. Beuvry. Nice to meet you!"

She gives us an impish smile as I die inside. "Nice to meet you too. Welcome to Weymouth! Sorry to interrupt, Mabel. For a second, I could have sworn I heard your father out there. Silly me. Must have been Miles!"

Yeah, because Dad's dead and you're drunk.

"Yeah, Mum, it was just us," I mutter.

"Come inside and go . . . go back to bed." Her words are slow and heavy, mingled with the wine. "It's late, and I'm tired."

"Then go back to sleep!" I order, bouncing between pity and mortification.

"Okay, okay." She retreats, chastised.

I turn back to Miles, who has smartly kept his face neutral through all this. "Let's get the hell out of here. The meeting is at the lighthouse—they're always there. I figured we can ride our bikes down there?" I gesture to the garage. "You can ride Hali's bike."

Miles shakes his head. "Uh, I'm not gonna fit on that. And the last time I saw you on a bike, you were not *on the bike*. I figured we could take my car, if that's okay. I know it's a short drive, but probably worth it to let that wrist heal. I like my Mabel whole."

I like my Mabel whole. It's kind of romantic, but I can't even linger on it because—"YOU HAVE A CAR?" I burst out, not able to contain my excitement. *A car. A CAR?* Words are exploding out of me as the embarrassment over my drunken mother evaporates. "Are you serious?"

Miles is amused by my excitement. "Uhh, yeah? Alistair had it towed up to Glace Bay and then drove it from there. He brought it back two days ago. Most teens in the States do, in fact, have cars."

A look of unbelief leaps across my face. "Okay, well, *most teens* in Weymouth do not. None do, in fact." Miles does not realize the social clout he has just leveled up. With that face and a car, he's unstoppable.

"Well, it's parked under that creepy light over there."

I laugh. We have an old lantern that sits at the edge of our property, before the hill to the bridge. It does look like something out of Narnia.

"That's not just a light, though. It's an inlet-heated, wind-shielding rain gauge configured with three cell sensors to monitor wetness and will burn blue when it senses a dramatic spike in those elements."

"Nerd alert," he teases good-naturedly.

"Everything on this island serves a purpose."

"Even me?" He raises his eyebrows.

Definitely you, I think.

"We'll see—but the fact that you have a car doesn't hurt."

I approach the beat-up gray Honda like it's a wild animal, falling deeper in love with each step. The car is gorgeous: banged up rightly, covered with bumper stickers. Good Lord. Forget about Miles. Perhaps this is the thing I really wanted.

"Look at it," I whisper, voice heavy with awe. It's not an official rule that teens can't have cars on Weymouth, but a cultural one. It's not without merit—everywhere we go on the island is within biking or walking distance. The adults on the island rarely use cars as well; whenever someone is driving one, everyone wonders where they are going and why.

Miles reaches forward and unlocks the car, banging the door with his hip to get it to pop open. "It's basically a piece of crap, but I love her."

"It's a she?" I ask with delight, running my hand along her dirty flank, where cool metal meets an unknown desire.

"My mom got me the car when we lived on Galer Street in Seattle, so . . . meet Gale. My mom taught me to drive in the bank parking lot."

"Gale," I whisper. "Absolutely brilliant. But listen, if we take a car down to the shore, there has to be a plan. No headlights, no music. We can park beyond the trees at the edge of the lighthouse grounds. Can you cut the engine and . . . um, drift up the hill?"

Miles snorts. "That's not really how cars work."

I give him a dirty look. "Sorry, I don't have much car experience. I walk everywhere."

"Or grab air on your ten-speed."

"It was a twelve-speed, I'll have you know." Our banter is so electric, it lights up the night. "Anyway, an unknown car on Weymouth Island draws plenty of attention is all I'm saying."

Something flies through the air toward me, and I snatch it above the roof of the car; it's the keys. My eyes are wide when I look up at him. *No way.*

"You're kidding," I say softly. It's insane. It's selfish. God, it's a need.

Miles pauses. "Have you ever driven before?"

I shake my head. "Not even once." Jeff has an expensive SUV car for supply runs, but it sits in our garage gathering dust most of the year. It has never occurred to me to even ask to drive it.

Miles considers for a moment. "Look, Gale may not look like much, but she's my soulmate, and if you hurt her, I may have to hide your body in the woods—" He stops short, both of us freezing at his words. *A body in the woods.* Lynwood.

"Shit." He breathes. "I'm sorry. I didn't mean it."

I let out a long breath for both of us. "It's okay. Are you really saying I can drive?"

After a second, Miles nods. "Yup. I mean, it's not like you're going to hit another car."

My heart lifts out of my body. *I'm going to drive.*

"I'm going to regret this, aren't I?" he asks as we switch sides.

"Probably." I yank open the door and fall into the ripped driver's seat. It's even smaller inside than it looks outside and smells like aluminum foil and stale cheese. *It's perfect.*

I note the empty Starbucks cups, discarded homework folders, and mounds of broken CD cases that litter the back. A small Pokémon ball dangles from the rearview mirror, and above his dashboard is a tiny white heart sticker; it looks like a navy tattoo and says MOM. My heart clenches. Seeing this messy, unkempt side of Miles makes me like him so much more. He's a person, not a new character in our Weymouth book. He looks embarrassed as he shoves the pile onto the floor so he can sit.

"Sorry. I didn't have time to clean before I came."

"Have you been living in here? The Cabot mansion too small for you?" I kid as I slide across the worn leather

Miles adjusts his seat to accommodate his long legs as I settle my hands on the wheel.

"Now, what do I do next? I only did this on my dad's lap a long time ago, and we never left the garage." The sentence should gut me, but it doesn't. I'm too excited; something magical travels up through the steering wheel and pours into my palms: the tingle of golden possibility. This beat-up wheel feels like freedom, like I could drive away from my enormous house filled with secrets and my island drenched in death. I could go anywhere. Toronto. California. South America. *Anywhere.*

Miles leans over and moves my hand to the gearshift, wrapping his fingers around mine over the knob. His hands are warm and long, and they swallow mine completely, and I love the way it feels to disappear into him.

"Gearshift," he says softly near my ear. "First we're going to *slowly* back out of the driveway." I glance over at him, incredulous, and he leans back. "I've seen you smile more in the last five minutes than I have the entire time I've been here. I have to say, it's kind of addicting. I like this side of you." There is a feeling here, more laid-back than it's been.

The compliment goes right to my head, but I focus back on the car for a minute. "Did you say 'back out'?"

He gives me a slightly naughty grin, the same one that pierced through me at the firepit. "I think this island may be affecting my sanity, but yes. You're about to surprise yourself."

I take it very slow, which is absolutely maddening, since I can feel that Gale wants me to drive, *really drive*. I fantasize about a long highway under an open sky at ninety miles per hour.

Instead I take slight turns at seven miles per hour, and Miles claps condescendingly. But I don't care. *I'm driving.* It feels exhilarating, like freedom. *Like living.* Like I could leave my past behind me and go anywhere, be anyone. He tells me when to slow down, and once when I hit the gas instead of the brake, he yells "BEUVRY, BRAKE!" and I want to laugh forever. I almost forget why we're out here until I see the lighthouse rise up ahead of us and I think, *Oh that's right. We have a reason for sneaking out at night.* I know we have to go, but I want to keep driving.

I clumsily maneuver the car off the main road onto a small access road. Inching the car forward as slowly as I dare, I pull Gale close to the heavy tree line. When she comes to a final halt, I hit the brakes too hard, and Miles flies forward into the dashboard. I grab his arm with a laugh and don't let go.

"Oh my God, are you okay?"

When he looks over at me in disbelief, I let out a barking laugh, which dissolves into carefree laughter, which then dissolves into hysterical tears. I can't stop laughing, can't stop even to breathe, and so I'm gulping air and he's doing the same until he crumples forward and surrenders with a moan. Ever since I met Miles, we've had one weird thing after another, but now all that awkwardness is released in our laughter. I don't care how I look or what he sees; all I know is that I can't remember the last time I laughed this freely. He unlocks something in me—a joy I didn't know could be there. Miles clutches his arms around his stomach.

"Oh God, I needed that," he gasps. I wish I could take this moment and seal it between thick pages, the tiniest piece of a fairy tale.

"Ow, my ribs hurt," I mumble, still laughing as I unbuckle my seat belt and turn off the engine, the keys swaying in the dash.

Gale jerks awkwardly and dies on the road. Miles gets out of the car as I let adrenaline radiate out of every part of my body. I didn't know that I wanted a car. I didn't know that I wanted this joy, but now that I've had a taste, that's all I want. I glance over at Miles, who is muttering to himself as he makes his way around the car.

Well, that's not the only thing I want.

As he comes around to the driver's door, my body freezes and pushes against the seat. He opens my door and bends over; my pulse escalates as he reaches over and yanks the keys out of the ignition. I blink; embarrassed at how my body reacts so strongly to him. I remind myself that I can't have this, that being with Miles opens all kinds of doors that I don't want it to. Doors that can't open. It's too terrifying and too complicated.

Right?

"I'll be taking these, thanks," he says.

My face flushes as I swallow hard, desire running from my heart to every part of me. I practically vault out of the car. "We can hike down to the lighthouse from here, but we should probably hustle."

Miles runs his hand through his hair and plops on a heathered navy baseball cap, and boy, I am not ready for how sporty and ultra male he looks in it.

"What is that?" I say nervously, running a single finger along the brim of his hat, wondering, *Is this how a human flirts?* "Is that your disguise?"

He shrugs. "You never know when you might need one. This is basic spy stuff, Beuvry."

"I hear that driving a very loud car to the location and wearing a baseball cap that has the words 'Seattle Public 54' on it are a very good disguise."

Miles leans over me, and I forget that he is tall—much taller than me—and grins, the curve of his mouth swallowing the entire night. "You know, Mabel, if you keep giving me shit, I may have to seduce you, spy-style."

God, the idea is so delicious that I can't even think, and so my knee-jerk reaction is to deflect. The fight between my head and my heart is beginning. "I don't kiss Cabots," I say, looking up as everything inside me burns, hoping the indifferent stars above will cool me.

"Who *do* you kiss?" he asks.

I shove one hand into my pocket and zip up my coat, sealing myself off from my own desire. "I don't kiss anyone. Come on."

I head toward the lighthouse. When we top the ridge, we hear the sound of voices pouring out of the lighthouse, faint chants passing through old layers of stone and tradition.

The meeting has begun without us; our island has no patience for fumbling hearts.

CHAPTER EIGHTEEN

We follow the chanting voices. I keep my flashlight pointed at the ground to avoid unwanted attention as gravel slides under our sneakers. The air smells like salt, but there's another scent underneath it, deep rot with a hint of seaweed—the smell of the dead. I hear a scattering of rocks behind me, and when I glance back, Miles is pushing himself off the ground from where he has fallen, his face flushed.

"Nothing to see here. I'm fine. Don't worry about it."

"Take wider steps—you'll fall less on the shale. We're almost there."

The closer we get to the lighthouse, the more apprehensive I get; this is a big deal, spying on a Triumvirate meeting. I'm not sure anyone has done it in the history of Weymouth. But how else can we get a full picture of what's happening? I saw Lynwood's body broken at the bottom of a tree; if I'm old enough to experience that, I'm old enough to understand the gravity of what's happening. The kids on this island fight just like everyone else; it seems like we should have all the information.

Moving slowly and carefully, we make our way down the switchback in silence until we find the footpath near the base of the lighthouse. It's barely wide enough for one of us, and without a guardrail, a slip means falling onto the rocks below.

I switch off the flashlight once we clear it; from here, the spinning lantern of the lighthouse is bright enough to illuminate our path.

"What are they singing?" Miles hisses as the eerie sound of dirges rises up through the night. I can understand why he's uneasy, but to me the haunting sound is oddly comforting.

"It's the Triumvirate; they're chanting some of the old island prayers and songs. They sing them in hopes that the sound reinforces any cracks in the lighthouse. They're calling on our ancestors to fill in the gaps. It's tradition."

"Well, that's totally normal and not creepy at all." Miles crouches behind me, and I feel the soft wash of his breath on my neck. My hairs stand on edge.

You can just be friends, I tell myself. *Breathe.* "We're going through the maintenance room." I can see the small window emitting a faint light at the base of the lighthouse, the cozy glow standing in stark contrast to the monolith looming above it.

When we get to the door, I try the brass handle. It's locked. *Of course.* "Thought I would give it a try." I shrug before pointing overhead to the small window. "But I'm pretty sure I can squeeze through that if you lift me up."

"How do you even know about this place?" Miles asks.

"The Guardians take turns maintaining the lighthouse. Jeff would take Hali and me along with him sometimes."

"Could we get arrested for this?"

I laugh. "By who? No police in Weymouth, remember? The

most that will happen is that we'll get yelled at by your uncle."

"Uh, I think I would prefer the police," Miles replies as I motion for him to boost me up, trying not to think about the fact that he is about to hold my entire body in his hands. With a sly grin, he hooks his knuckles together, and I put my foot into his hands and rest both hands on his shoulders. Our eyes lock.

"To the moon," he whispers, and I hold back a snicker; it's so stupid, but it makes me laugh.

My face is so close to his that if I leaned forward, our lips would touch; I can see the drop of sweat at the tip of his crown.

"Up you go," he exhales, and he shoves me upward, too fast, much too fast.

After a brief moment of terror when I'm flying through the air, I'm able to get my hands up onto the dusty windowsill. I grip it and lodge my foot up onto the wall. Rock particles shower his upturned face, but Miles holds me steady as he coughs.

"This seems like a lot of work"—he grunts, my knees smooshing into his face—"to listen to a meeting."

I finally get my fingers under the gap and yank upward. The window gives a second of resistance before sliding open. I step off Miles's shoulders and awkwardly slide my legs through the opening. Below me is a dusty room filled with tools for the upkeep of the lighthouse: bulbs and glass, stone and caulk. I gingerly test my weight on the table below me before gently dropping down. A few seconds later, I swing the door open for Miles, flashing him a smug, self-accomplished grin.

"Look at you, so proud of yourself!"

"I really am," I whisper, before yanking him into the room

with me. The walls are covered with yellowing blueprints and outdated safety instructions. A lonely desk sits in the corner with a black coat on the chair.

At the back of the room sits a large red door, the entrance to the lighthouse. It's a good thing the Triumvirate are still singing, because we aren't the quietest as we trip our way through the cluttered room. As we reach the door, their melancholy song wraps around us.

> 'Tis late in the season, the island in no hurry.
> My love, till I lie awake beside you,
> Remembering your purest heart, thy fullest breath,
> Before the water came, before the waves and bones,
> I'll sleep eternally now that I'm alone.

Miles turns to me, his face ashen. "What the actual fuck?" he whispers.

I shrug. "It's an old hymn."

Miles shakes his head. "Just when I thought this place couldn't get any more strange." I hold my finger to my lips, and with a grimace, I nudge open the door. It creaks loudly, but luckily the last verse of the song covers the noise. We slip through the door and out onto a stone staircase, crouching down as the song ends, hidden by the iron banister that swirls around us.

Voices echo up from the basement as Leona—the Pelletier Guardian—claps the meeting to order. Conversation quiets down when people take their seats; Miles's legs press against my back as I carefully maneuver myself onto the stair below his. As we get situated, Alistair Cabot stands.

"Yes, take a seat, everyone. Please. Tobias, there's an extra one there, by Leona. Thank you." He clears his throat. "Friends and Guardians, I know we're all devastated by the sudden loss of Will Lynwood. He was our friend, our companion, and the truest Guardian in every sense of the word." Several people voice their agreement. "While I know that the Guardians are preparing their own private ceremony for him, I wanted to say that the entire island feels his death acutely and grieves him deeply." There is a moment of silence. Alistair leans forward and speaks the same soft rhyme that he chanted over my father's casket.

> *"May those who fight above*
> *Rest below*
> *Whilst we plead, 'Don't go.'"*

It catches me completely off guard, and I close my eyes, pushing the memory of my dad's funeral as far away from me as I can, because there's something wrong with it. This time, instead of one coffin there are two. Lynwood's body flashes through my brain. I blink the image away, thinking, *Focus. Be here now.*

The elder Cabot continues. "I want to address the various rumors that have been drifting around Weymouth since the discovery of his body. Some people have even suggested bringing in outside police from Glace Bay. I'm here to remind you that we cannot in any way draw attention to ourselves from the outside world. What good is having outsiders meddling in our affairs? What we do here matters above all, even due process. I have spoken at length to the Pope family, and they confirm that Lynwood was struggling with his mental health. It is a tragic accident and nothing more, despairing as it may be. We've never lost a Guardian outside of a Storm, and it's been a jarring experience for all of us."

Below us, Crake Pope, Eryk and Cordelia's father, stands. "It's true. Our Lynwood was not fully himself in his last few months." His hands are paint-stained, his nice shirt smudged with charcoal. The Popes are artists, and talented ones at that; their paintings of the Storm (which the *New York Times* has called "a brutal metaphor for unchecked capitalism") sell for hundreds of thousands of dollars. The Pope house is a midpoint safeguard on the island, made of clever, artistic traps.

"He had spent the last few months working on his barometer contraption, and he believed that it needed to be mounted at a great height. He was confused and nervous about the upcoming Storm and had lost touch with reality a while ago. What matters is not his end but that we loved him dearly."

One of the Guardians stands; it's Katherine, the Guardian for the Des Roches house and a notorious thorn in Alistair's side. I've always liked her spirit and the way she has become a beacon of what a woman can do in a Guardian position.

"I've known Will Lynwood my whole life. I don't believe this was anything other than an accident. But can we not look deeper into the circumstances surrounding his death? Or what he was thinking of when he went into the woods that day?"

Joseph Mintus stands. "Will Lynwood was my friend, but he hadn't returned my calls for weeks. There is nothing to overthink here. Looking into this will take precious time and resources that this island doesn't have. All of us should be keeping our eyes on the sea, including you."

"Hear, hear!" shouts someone else. The crowd gets louder,

and my heart starts to beat faster in my chest, but not because of their words. Miles is slowly, carefully, pushing my ponytail over to one side of my shoulder. I feel the tip of his finger trail softly over the small hairs at the back of my neck and around to the valley where my neck meets my collarbone. The finger pauses there as he slowly secures my ponytail against my shoulder, a whisper rather than a touch, so light that I could be imagining it. He leans forward.

"Your hair was in my face," he whispers.

He dips his head down next to mine so that our cheeks are almost touching, and I lean slightly back so that I am in between his legs, his knees on either side of my shoulders.

"You're warm," he whispers. In the lighthouse, grown-ups speak of serious things, but in our tiny, cobwebbed corner, there is just the two of us, a delicate world of want. Miles leans forward and trails one finger across my upper collarbone. When my cool, exposed skin meets the heat of his touch, everything inside ignites. But then he sits back as if nothing happened, and I burn inside. It's better, though, to not be so close; it confuses me, the way my body reacts to him. It makes me feel like I have no control.

Below us, members of the Triumvirate are sniping at one another.

"*I don't see what the harm is with doing a small investigation into his theories. What if Lynwood knew something we didn't?*"

"*You didn't even like Lynwood, and now you're so concerned about him? That's rich!*"

It's as if a fuse has been lit. The room erupts with voices. There are accusations of a cover-up, of murder, of a conspiracy theory among the Guardians. Michael McLeod leaps to his feet, one polished fingernail pointed at Alistair. McLeods have always longed for the Cabot position.

"What you're pointedly not saying is that Will died right after *your boy* arrived on Weymouth. Since his arrival, things feel like they are falling apart. It can't be a mere coincidence. Perhaps the island is trying to tell us something. I know you can all feel it!"

When Alistair turns toward him, radiating that Cabot power, it seems like the entire room steps back.

"How *dare* you accuse my nephew in all this?" he hisses. "He's a Cabot through and through, even if he didn't grow up here. Miles might be naive and a bit different from what we're used to, but he's just a boy who has suffered the loss of his mother. You all remember Grace, if I recall." He angrily eyes Michael McLeod. "How could you think his *mere presence* has something to do with Lynwood's death?"

Crouched in the darkness, I think of Hali, of her anger radiating at Miles. I turn toward Miles, but he doesn't see me. Instead he looks furious, his jaw clenching angrily as his name rings out below.

"How about you let us—the Guardians—at least question the boy about Lynwood? See if he knows anything else?" Katherine eyes him. "The Guardians will not relinquish their duty because of your personal relationship. It's our job to protect the eleven houses of Weymouth. It's probably nothing, but we must examine every possibility, regardless of your delicate position."

Alistair snarls. "I'll sooner throw you lot into the Dehset than let you question a grieving child. And may I remind you that Mabel Beuvry and Norah Gillis were also with him. Norah found the body first, so perhaps you should question her, too."

Behind me, Miles has gone very still, and I think, *We should leave.* Finally my Guardian stands. At his presence, everyone goes quiet. Jeff has always been a bridge between the Guardians and the Triumvirate and is well respected on both sides; when he speaks, they listen.

He clears his throat. "There is another possibility we must explore as well. We know that as we change, so does the Storm; it adapts to us, to our defenses. When we built the walls, the water surged higher; when we planted pure herbs and wildflowers in their path, the dead began to float just above the earth. We've built gates, and the dead grow stronger. They aren't stagnant in the sea; they're preparing; they're adapting. Perhaps Lynwood knew something we did not, and I believe that is worth exploring. We know he had his theories. . . ."

"It's a myth. The Great Storm is a myth. Lynwood was not in his right mind," snaps Alistair.

"The what?" I hear Miles whisper, fear an undercurrent in his voice.

The Great Storm. Exactly what Lynwood mentioned to Norah and me that day before he disappeared into the woods, muttering to himself. The ravings of a madman? Or something we need to understand and don't?

Jeff continues. "Perhaps. But we need to know why Lynwood was so afraid of it. Knowledge can only help us! That is the reality."

Alistair levels Jeff with a stare. "I'm not sure you're one to lecture on accepting reality." The room goes silent. "As for Miles, he *has nothing* to do with Lynwood; in fact, I don't believe they ever met. That we would question him shows something ugly about our island: that even someone who belongs here will be treated like an outsider. The Triumvirate grants permission for the Guardians to lead a small investigation into Lynwood's theories. We'll start with his journals and proceed from there. And I don't want to hear one more word about Miles. This island has enough to worry about for the next few years without baseless rumors."

My shoulders sink in relief; Miles is in the clear. I turn around halfway to take a good look at him, and sure enough, he looks like he wants to bolt. His jaw is tensed, his hands clenched. What I just heard swirls around in my mind: Lynwood, the Great Storm, the journals.

His body, broken on the rocks. We deserve more answers than these people are giving us, and I know they won't share it with us when they do find something—not even Jeff. I lean back against Miles.

"Are you up for breaking and entering one more time tonight?" I whisper.

"Absolutely," he says thankfully. "Whatever gets me the hell out of here."

CHAPTER NINETEEN

We slip back into the workroom, shutting the door quietly behind us. In the flashes of light that rotate through the window, we trip over tools as we make our way through, shedding the loud adults below us. This time, though, we go out through the door rather than the window, and within a few minutes we are away on foot, leaving Gale hidden next to the lighthouse. Lynwood's phrase keeps repeating in my head: *The Great Storm. The Great Storm.*

Miles blows warm air into his palms and shoves them into his pockets.

"Are you going to tell me where we're headed?" he asks.

"We're going to the schoolhouse. It's only a five-minute walk from here. I need more information."

His breath puffs out, a tiny cloud. "The schoolhouse—*just* where I want to be on a weekend. Will Mr. McLeod be meeting us there for some midnight lessons?"

"We only do midnight lessons on weeknights." Miles doesn't crack a smile, and I can see that he's not sure of anything right now. "I'm kidding. It will be you, me, and a classroom full of ancient journals."

"You're looking for Lynwood's journal. Is this about the"—he puts finger quotes up—"Great Storm?"

A chill passes through me, and I wonder why this phrase affects me so. Could it be because of when Lynwood spoke of it with Norah and me? Or the fact that we found him? Or is it something else? I can't forget the fear on his face.

I nod, trying to act like I'm not affected. "It's probably nothing, but I want to look at his journals before everyone in town descends on them. I don't like secrets." *Even though I have some of my own.*

"Do you think they're hiding something?"

"Yeah. Can you hurry?" I can't explain the strange urgency I feel. "I've only heard whispers of the Great Storm, which is kind of strange if you think about it. Normally we beat our history to death."

"That's true," Miles replies as I push my sweaty curls out of my face. "Also, the Popes are super shady, so there is a good chance they're hiding something." We shuffle over a rocky embankment and weave through a small patch of oak trees and fireweed. When we emerge, we're standing at the east end of the island, right above the valley that lovingly enfolds our schoolhouse.

"My last high school was like half a city block, two thousand kids, two hundred staff and armed police that roamed the halls. One could say it was a uniquely American experience. And now I go to school in a one-room schoolhouse." He reaches for my hand as we make our way down, cradling it beneath his other hand. It feels alarmingly natural. "Do you ever feel like Weymouth exists outside of time? You don't exist in the *now*, but also, you're not living in the past. You have computers but a one-room schoolhouse.

Advanced weaponry in the house, goats for milking out back. The roads are made of dirt and gravel, but the bridge is made of expensive steel." He peers at me with fascination. "What is it like to grow up outside of every cultural trend in the world?"

I think about his question as we move through the high grass. In the distance, I can hear the slamming of the lighthouse door as the Triumvirate and the Guardians head out. We have to hurry; I begin to jog.

"It's lonely . . . but also freeing. Most of that stuff is pretty stupid anyway—and it's not like we don't experience the outside world. We get movies and books. But when I think about how the whole world doesn't know what we do—or that we even exist— that seems really scary. When the Storm comes, we're all alone—a flare of light against a sea of darkness."

Miles groans as he runs beside me. "Well, that's a terrifying thought."

Try living it, I think.

We're at the doors of the schoolhouse. I lean against one of them and turn the iron handles counterclockwise a single time. Inside, a latch unlocks.

"Mr. McLeod takes access to information very literally." We slide through the open wooden doors. I can sense the Triumvirate on my tail—they are most likely headed this way to grab Lynwood's journals, so we have to most fast. On the right side of the school, perched above a row of blackboards, sit enormous bookshelves, built out of pine and worn with years. I rush over to them.

"These are the Weymouth Canon. They contain our history, our legacy. They're the journals of everyone who has ever lived here and contain everything we have learned about the Storm . . .

or so I thought, until today." It has never occurred to me that there might be information that is hidden from us by the Triumvirate. The idea takes my breath away. Our island's history is built on trust—or at least it is now. It wasn't always that way, though, so should I be surprised?

I yank one of the journals down. "Before the 1970s, these were only available to the men of this island. You could read them once you received your iron whip."

Miles glances over his shoulder, checking the door. "Do I want to know what that is?"

I anxiously dust off some titles, looking for what I need. "You will, maybe in a few years. The Storm of 1971 changed everything. It killed many of the men between the ages of fifty and eighty, and only younger men, along with women and children, were left standing. To the whining of the surviving men, the women stormed this schoolhouse in order to read the canon and reformed the Triumvirate to include women. It's not a coincidence that since then we've had a *much* smaller loss of life." I check one spine after another. Nothing, *nothing*!

"Crazy how a variety of voices is best for battling against great evil." He looks back again. "Hey, not that I'm not down with chatting about women's liberation through literature, but should we speed up? I don't want to be caught here, especially when I know those on the island are so fond of me already." He's joking, but there's an undercurrent of hurt in his voice.

I stop joking for a minute and, feeling brave, look him straight in the eyes. "I'm fond of you, Miles. The island is fond of you. Can't you feel it?"

He looks like he wants to say something more, but then I

move past him, focused again on the bookshelves. Leather-bound journals are kept on the top shelf, shoved among history texts of Nova Scotia and a few volumes of dark, terrible poetry from House Mintus. I scamper up the bookcase ladder and am balancing precariously on the top rung when we hear the faint din of voices coming over the hill.

"Hurry! They're almost here!" Miles steadies the ladder below me. When I glance down, his eyes are trained on the enormous embroidered tapestry that runs along the west wall. Stitched on it is the story of the first Storm: waves roaring upon the shore, gray threads of mist swirling on the Dehset Sea, and upon the waves sits the cloaked figure of death, sitting straight astride a pale horse. The years of the Storms are printed at the bottom of the piece, the names of the dead below that. When my eyes flit to 2012, I look back at the ladder, my breath caught in my throat, tears in my eyes. I know well the names on that plaque.

Miles's strained voice comes out of the dark. "When I first saw that *thing*, I thought it was a weird piece of folk art. I didn't know I was looking at a documentary."

I'm rapidly pushing books aside, looking for the right one. "During the Storm, we have to last the night. It's somehow as complicated and as simple as that."

"You make it sound easy."

"It's . . . not." *I'm not sure I can survive it again.*

I slam a book down, frustrated by what I'm not seeing: Lynwood's journals. "They're not here, but they should be. Dammit! I bet they're at his house." I'm about to move on when a row of Storm journals catches my eye. I lean forward, a memory flashing through my mind.

"Do you remember the random numbers carved on the trunk of the tree when we found Lynwood? One, six, seven, eight."

Miles squints. "Yeah, I thought they were measurements for his instruments."

"Me too, but maybe they weren't measurements." Adrenaline filters through me as an idea pops into my head. "Maybe they were *years*." With a smile, I reach for the Storm of 1876 journal. This could be something. It could be nothing, but it's worth a try. As I pull the journal off the shelf, the glare of a flashlight bounces off the stained-glass window.

They're coming.

"Mabel, we have to go!" Miles yells. I tuck the book into my coat and start to climb down the few rungs, but instead of waiting for me, Miles lifts me off the middle of the ladder. My sneakers dangle inches from the ground, and his head sits below my chin as he looks up at me. His eyes ask permission, and mine say, *Yes, yes, please.* His hands slide up my back as he lets me sink lower and lower, until our eyes are level, our noses almost touching. I want to stay this close to him. It feels so right, like we've always been moving toward each other, but we have to go. The world can't stop just because I want it to. My feet aren't touching the ground—metaphorically or literally, since he's holding me in his arms. His eyes are huge brown chestnuts. Our faces move toward each other in the dark schoolroom, but then the loud voices are near the front door. We jerk away from each other, a rush of fear passing through me. They can't find us here. He lets me go, and my feet—and mind—crash back down to earth.

"Where do we go?" he asks, his voice frantic.

"There's a back entrance. Come on," I whisper. The front door to the schoolroom creaks open as we duck behind Mr. McLeod's desk.

"Lynwood's journals should be in here," I hear Alistair say. I begin to crawl quickly toward the back door, Miles behind me.

I pause when we get there; they'll surely hear the door open, so we have to be ready to run.

"One. Two. Three." I kick open the door, and we stream out into the dark night, both sprinting as fast as we can away from the schoolhouse. We move like shadows, high on each other and the adrenaline coursing through our veins like fire.

It's late when Miles pulls up in front of my house. "You'd better head inside. Someone's probably waiting for you."

I see what he means through the dusty windshield: Hali is sitting on the steps, hugging her knees against her chest, her small body silhouetted in the porch light. Hali sarcastically overwaves to Miles, but he ignores her.

"I know. My sister is kind of a lot," I say.

Miles shifts uncomfortably, and the mood in the car changes, the playful warmth I felt radiating from him the last time we were in the car disappearing in a second. He leans over and opens the door for me.

"So, I guess I'll see you around? Maybe in class after break." His voice is cold and distant, and I'm not sure why—just a minute ago we were holding each other close, something sparking between us. Did I do something? Is it Hali, the look she's giving him? I look at him quizzically, confused and hurt, tears blurring my eyes.

"*Are you serious?* I guess I'll see you around? What about the journals? What about . . . ?" I leave the phrase hanging, but it's there.

What about what just happened between us?

Miles forces a smile, and suddenly I see the cool, detached kid I met that day in the schoolhouse. Apparently, he can turn on a dime. I'm panicking. I don't understand.

"Well, we didn't find the journals, so . . ." His eyes stare straight through the windshield; his voice is robotic, though his fingers are twitching. I sense a foreign panic rising through him as well. What is happening?

"Why are you being like this? You wanted to figure out the truth of what the Triumvirate is hiding as much as I do, and now it's *I'll see you around?*" My anxiety and anger swirl inside me, my mind shifting to before driving lessons, before Miles and I were hiking through woods, before wounds being cared for and us laughing until it hurt. I think of Miles's first day at school, of the campfire the night of the party. Of him seeking out the weird, strange girl on the island for answers.

My voice shakes, but I try to hide the hurt. "You don't want to be hanging around a Beuvry, that's all."

Miles's head snaps toward me. "It's not you, Mabel."

"That's bullshit."

"It's just . . . I don't even know if I belong here. Especially after tonight. I'm sorry—it's all hitting me right now. Just as I was trying to process the Storm, we are adding a 'Great Storm' to the mix. And why is my name being thrown into the middle of all this madness? And, and . . ." He looks at me.

I feel his walls shooting up, like physically feel them piercing any hope I had about us. About anything. Suddenly he seems like every other person on this island. Not the special Miles with his bright, crooked smile that makes me think of freedom.

"I have to go," he says, breaking the silence that's like a chasm between us.

I stare at him for a long moment, wondering how this can be the same boy who stared so hungrily into my eyes in the schoolhouse. His hands grip the wheel, and he leans his head against it. "Please, Mabel. You're making it hard for me to leave."

He doesn't look up at me again. I slam the car door so hard, he probably feels it in his teeth. He watches me as I make my way up the stairs and then angrily peels out.

Hali is standing, astonishment on her face. "That's the guy you're over the moon about? Him?"

"Let it go, Hali. I'm not in the mood." I pray she won't notice the hurt and confusion written on my face as I walk past her. She follows me inside, and together we find our way to the kitchen.

"So . . . how was your night?" Hali asks, sharp as a rusty nail.

My stomach hurts when I think about it. *What happened?* How is it possible that today was one of the best days of my life and is now one of the worst? I try to downplay it. "Miles and I snuck into the lighthouse and listened to the Triumvirate meeting about Lynwood. They're looking for his journals." I'm desperate to change the subject, away from Miles. "Hey, do you want tea?"

"Yeah, the honey spice."

Oh good, *a smile.* I step off the eggshells between us, my body sagging forward in relief. I could really use a friend right now.

"Were the Guardians *and* the Triumvirate there?" she asks, green eyes glued to mine.

"Yeah. Long story short, Miles and I dashed over to the

schoolhouse to try to get Lynwood's journals from the canon before the Triumvirate did, but guess what?"

"They aren't there."

I grab a mug off the hanging rack above the sink. "Exactly, and so the conspiracy deepens. There's really only one other place they can be."

"Ugh, but if you go to the Pope house, that means you have to see Cordelia and Eryk." We both groan. I feel like I'm watching myself from the outside, putting on a show, while inside I want to cry at the way Miles reacted to me. What the hell?

"Hanging out with the worst people on the island is not exactly my cup of tea." I put on the kettle, trying not to betray the quiver in my voice. Even from a young age, Cordelia and Eryk both were sharp and cruel, bitter for the love they didn't get from their parents (two beautiful, artistic, and narcissistic people) but had been lavished on their seven older siblings.

I would feel bad for them if they weren't so *damn mean*. Cordelia used to be friends with Hali, but she doesn't come around anymore; she doesn't want the messiness of Hali's reality interfering with her careful world. She left my sister behind, and every time I see her face, I want to punch it.

The steam from my tea curls into the air, and my sister sinks against my side. Outside, crickets murmur as the night grows deeper on the island. For just a minute, we're perfect. Then Hali breaks it.

"Can I ask you something? Why do you care about this so much? I know finding Lynwood in Wasp Wood was upsetting, but you *can* let the adults figure this out."

How do I explain to her that since the moment I saw Lynwood, I felt other elements at play? That Miles brings out something unnatural in me, and I can't help but wonder if it's tied to what's happening on the island. Life feels like a winding labyrinth lately, and I'm without a map. "Well, for one thing, some of the adults at the meeting accused Miles—not of anything to do with his death, per se, but with messing with the order of things on Weymouth. They don't want him here."

"What if they're right?" she asks, and I give her a withering glare.

"Don't. Hali. Just . . . don't." I'm too exhausted for this.

Why did I even mention his name to her?

My posture turns defensive. "Before he got here, I was just numb, going through the motions. I've told myself I can't have this joy in my life because of my family, but I'm tired of trying to deny myself. Why do you have to taint it? This isn't about you."

I think of Miles leaning his head against the steering wheel. *What happened?*

Hali sighs. "Mabel, I worry that your *need* for him is clouding your judgment. Besides, what does he have that I don't? We only have each other! You and me and Jeff, and maybe a little bit of Mum. We're the ones that matter."

I shake my head. "I'm not *replacing* you, Hali. I'm making room for another person. Besides, I don't want to kiss you."

She makes a gagging sound before heading up the stairs. "Now that you're home safe, I'm going to bed. Make sure to lock up. Sorry you didn't find what you were looking for." I watch her climb the stairs and hear her bedroom door shut.

I'm left alone in the dark kitchen, my mug steaming on the island.

"You okay?" I leap up to see Jeff standing at the kitchen door, his round face tinged blue by the pale fridge light. "Sorry. I didn't mean to scare you. I thought I heard a voice down here, so I wanted to come check it out. When did you get home?"

"What do you mean?" I ask with a straight face, and his kind demeanor drops into skeptical annoyance.

"I know you were out with Miles. I saw his car leave our driveway just now—what a heap of junk, by the way. Does it even have working seat belts? Forget it. I don't want to know." He focuses his intense gaze on me as his glasses slip down his nose. "Do not take me for some naive parent, and it would be unwise to assume that Alistair is either. We know what's going on—it's as clear as damned day. And while I am *very* glad that you're getting to know Miles, you two should be careful about making your relationship known, especially so soon."

My face burns. "We're just getting to know each other. I wouldn't call it a relationship, not yet anyway." I remember the way Miles wouldn't meet my eyes when he dropped me at home, his sudden, disengaged coolness in the car. Maybe he saw the truth: I'm just weird Mabel from the big house on the hill. Maybe the truth is that there was nothing at all, and this is all in my head, a fantasy that the new boy has eyes only for me. "What are you saying? Is there some specific reason we shouldn't let people know we're interested in each other?"

Jeff watches me cautiously. "A relationship with Miles might bring *certain things* to the surface. And there are some things the Beuvrys don't want the entire island talking about."

"Like what?" I ask him.

"Well, I think you know we don't want them to talk about

Hali. It would be . . . hurtful," he says carefully. "You know what, never mind. It's late. Why don't you head to bed? I don't like you hanging out down here in the dark." He looks out the window. "Be mindful. Weymouth's unbalanced lately. I sense it in the air." A chill rises up my spine; it's not like Jeff to exaggerate. Before I go, he touches my back. "I want you to be happy, Mabel. I hope you know that. It's my greatest desire. I have loved seeing you light up since Miles arrived." He looks like a proud dad, which twists a thorn in my heart. I don't want to tell him that this might all be for nothing. "Did you find anything in the schoolhouse, by the way?"

My heart stops as I turn on the stair, the journal of 1876 tucked against my chest.

"Like I said"—Jeff switches off the kitchen lights—"don't ever mistake me for some naive parent."

Sister Mary Rose Pelletier, April 1908
A Prayer Against the Damned

Hail Mary, full of grace, our immaculate Mother,
bless our cursed shores; kiss the sand with the
 footprints of the damned.
We give you thanks for iron, salt, and paper.

The material of gates, of bread, of stories
and yet, in your wisdom, powerful gifts.
Holy Mother, please intercede with the metal in
 my hands,
the salt in my bowl,
the paper folded in my book.

In your great wisdom, our eleven houses will stand
 on these tools
born from the earth, trees, and ground:
iron, salt, and paper.

Historical note from Reade McLeod: Sister Mary Rose Pelletier is
a local legend. She was indeed the first to document iron, salt, and
paper as possible defenses against the dead. Some whisper that she
is perhaps even the one to have discovered them.

CHAPTER TWENTY

My hand reaches deep into a bag of salt, the sharp crystals rolling pleasurably between my fingertips. I pull out a handful and blow on them gently, sending them spiraling down onto the plants at my feet. Hemlock, thistle, and wild phlox are beginning to poke up around the house, which means it is time to baptize them with salt. In gardens across our island, salting plants has become an art form; too much can dry out the land and kill the plants; too little does nothing. The right amount hopefully infuses these plants with a touch of protection—not enough to keep the dead at bay but maybe enough to help.

My braid falls over my shoulder as I sprinkle a tiny bit onto the lower petals of a new tulip. I stand up, salt bag hitched around my waist, and raise my face to the morning sun. Being out here is nice; Jeff is quietly reading a historical novel on the porch, my mum is still sleeping—no surprise there—and Hali is upstairs, logging into her agoraphobic chat room.

It's been three days since I talked to Miles. He's called a few times, but I instructed Jeff to tell him that I'm busy, which he has done with a snarky flair that was *not* requested.

The morning after our little adventure, I decided that Miles's coolness was unwarranted and that I needed to take some time to sort things out. It hurts less this way. The worst part is that every time I reject his calls, I see Hali's smugness grow in the curl of her mouth, the lift of her eyebrow. I've purposely turned my attention elsewhere: shoring up the house with Mum, catching up on my schoolwork over the break, and trying my best not to think about Miles Cabot. And then there is the Storm journal. The Storm of 1876 was a living nightmare, the worst Storm account I've read. I had read this journal before, years ago, but it took on a new meaning this time. It wasn't just a Storm; it was THE Storm. The fog came without warning. Six houses washed out to sea, seventeen deaths, mostly of young children. There are strange anecdotes about a heaven made of water, about frozen rivers of the dead moving across the land. About lights from the beyond tearing up the land. A story of the wooden bridge being destroyed.

The most interesting section of the journal is where the author speaks about the early partnership of the Cabots and the Beuvrys. I didn't realize that in the past our two houses stood together, rather than apart. It's not something taught now—now it's every house standing alone.

The journal has given me terrible dreams: of red lights and fire arching overhead, of Norah's body floating face down on the water. These dreams leave me jerking awake in bed, sweaty hands clutching the sheets, unable to go back to sleep. I finished reading the journal yesterday. The lilting cursive and figurative language of 1876 isn't the easiest to read, and I'm not eager to return to it. I need sleep. And distraction.

After I finish salting in the garden, I head inside, depositing the remainder in our salt barrels. When I come back, I feel Hali staring at me from across the kitchen table. With a smile, I sit down next to her. This table has been in our family for generations. The corners are warped with water; there are places where the wood has swelled and split. It's uneven but strong and has survived many Storms. This table has fed my ancestors and our family three meals a day for hundreds of years, but it might not survive my sister's stony silence.

"Today's going to be *very* lonely if you're not talking to me." I see her resilience deflate. She hates being alone more than she likes being angry.

"I was sitting here wondering, do you ever think this is all for nothing? All the shoring up, all the precautions? I mean, we may die, and you salting those tiny flowers will have amounted to nothing. What's that quote again? 'Sound and fury, signifying nothing'? What's that from?"

I take a drink of milk, probably pulled fresh from our cow out back this morning.

Millie the cow is the love of Jeff's life.

"The quote is from *Macbeth*. You know, it starts with 'Life's but a walking shadow . . .'"

"Ugh, of course you know, you NERD." She pokes her finger under my arm as I swat at her.

"Mr. McLeod would be ashamed of you not knowing."

Hali shrugs. "He was always annoyed with me." She looks away, and I think how truly lovely my sister is, the way the light catches the red in her hair, how the wisps around her forehead look like tiny licks of flame.

"Seriously, though, what if it's all for nothing?"

"Look at it this way. At the very least, we'll make excellent home fortifiers for a zombie apocalypse."

"Literally the best they've ever seen." She pauses. "I'm going to start that new blanket today. Do you want to help me? I think I'm going to do a chunky knit with the white stargazer yarn."

I wrinkle my face; Hali knows how I feel about craft projects, in that I hate them so much. "Sure." I stand to go change out of my salting clothes, when the phone on the wall rings, the shrill sound blasting through our quiet house.

"It's probably Miles again. Give it up, bro." She rolls her eyes. I glance around for Jeff, but he's hiding from this interaction.

After a second, my mother screeches, "Will someone PLEASE answer that, for the love of God?" and I pick up the phone, bracing for his voice as my heart seals shut. I desperately do and do not want it to be him, but it's not.

"Mabel? Oh my God, did you hear already?" It's Norah, and she sounds frantic. My heart speeds up.

"No? Hear what? I have no idea what you're talking about. *Are you okay?*" I hear her take a deep breath on the other line.

"Yeah, I'm fine, and don't freak out. But, Mabel, *they took him.* Miles."

"Who took him? What do you mean?"

Her voice lowers. "Edmund and Eryk and the rest of the boys from school snatched Miles a few minutes ago from the Cabot house. Mabel . . . they're taking him to the Dehset, to dive for his iron whip. *At the Bone Barrier.*"

I suck in so much air that it stings. "Oh God!" I mutter, the phone almost dropping from my hand. Diving for his iron whip is a coming-of-age ritual for the boys on Weymouth Island. Hali, seeing the distress on my face, leaps up.

"What's wrong?" she asks, her face concerned.

"It's Miles; they took him to the Bone Barrier. He's going to dive for his iron whip."

Hali's face drains of color, and she begins voicing all the thoughts running through my head. "What? No. They can't do that. There's no way he's ready! Weymouth boys have had a lifetime to prepare for it. Jesus—Mabel . . . he'll die out there."

The Bone Barrier. . . . "Barrier" means "a marker, a boundary," one that should not be crossed until you are ready, one that holds unspeakable horrors behind it . . . and they're about to throw Miles right into it.

Stop spiraling! Do something!

"Call Edmund on the radio! Tell him to stop it already!" I order.

"He's the one who told me they were going to take him! I begged him not to do it, but he hung up on me. That prat. I think I've had about enough. From what Edmund said, some of the boys heard what the Triumvirate were implying at the meeting— you know, about Miles—and decided to teach him a lesson. It's already happening, Mabel. We're too late."

She's probably right, *but no*—I have to try. Miles might have pissed me off, but he's also made my world light up, and he doesn't deserve what's about to happen to him. He's as lost as I am.

"I'm going down to the dock. Try to meet me there if you can." I hang up the phone without waiting for an answer. *I have no time.* A second later, I'm moving to the front door.

If I stop, I'll be too late. If I overthink, I may not make it.

Hali steps in front of me, blocking the door with her slight body. "Mabel, you can't stop this. You know that. Maybe he'll be fine!"

I yank on my boots. "Yeah and maybe he won't be, and that's on me. I should have warned him about this. I should have remembered this could happen. Argh! How much do you want to bet Eryk Pope is behind this?" For a minute I think she's going to physically try to stop me—*I'd like to see her try*—but instead she hands me Jeff's car keys and curls my fingers around them.

"I know you had that lesson the other night. Try not to wreck it. Otherwise our Guardian will seriously lose his shit." She leans in. "And seriously, be careful. You know how close the dock is to the Bone Barrier. I've never heard of anyone doing this so close to a Storm year. Never."

I pause long enough to let dread wash over me, and then I'm gone, flying toward the garage with the keys in my hand. *I'm coming, Miles.*

Jeff's Subaru is much nicer than Miles's Honda. It's clean inside, with soft gray leather and sleek lines that run across the dashboard. It also hauls. A second later, I'm going at least forty miles per hour down the one-lane road that runs up the middle of the island, not worried who sees me. No doubt when Jeff finds out—and oh, he will—I'll be grounded for life, but will that even matter if Miles is gone?

I clench my teeth as I take a turn too fast. I didn't realize how numb I had become until Miles showed up with his stupid backpack and grieving heart on his sleeve, making me aware of all the things I'd buried away. Damn this kid.

When I pass the road to the Mintus house, I take a small left onto a hidden road and follow a roundabout way toward the Dehset Shore. Up ahead on the cliff, I see the Mintus house, shaded by their famous white pine forest. I'm sure their Guardian, Darcy, will see me flying past their porch and will be on the phone with Jeff, her bestie, in no time. *Great.*

The car hurtles up over the ridge that runs along the northeast end of the island. I slow down finally. The last thing Miles needs is for *me* to be thrown from a car on my way to rescue *him*. The road grows steeper as the tree line disappears, and in front of me I see the stretch of the Soft Shore. Once, when we were hunting for oysters, my father told me that the Soft Shore was a gift to the people of Weymouth to make up for the violence of the Dehset, a gift that provided all we needed, a sea that wasn't wicked. And now I'm headed to the spot where the two shores meet.

Through the windshield, a small wooden fence appears, and I slam the brakes harder than I mean to. My face hits the wheel as the car comes to a shuddering stop. I taste blood on my lip, but I don't have time to worry about it as I fling open the door, leaving the keys in the ignition.

I sprint along the fence line until I find what I'm looking for: a small break that marks the trail down to the Soft Shore. It's a steep series of rocky switchbacks set on a narrow trail, headed down to the shore with no guardrail in sight. My boots skitter on rocks as I make my way down.

The closer I get to the dock, the clearer I can hear the raised voices of teen boys, testosterone punching through the gentle breeze. *Shit, shit, shit.* When I come around the corner, the shore comes into view all at once. I stop at the crest, my breath caught in my throat, taking in what I can see.

My hope was that Norah was wrong and perhaps they were

just passing a skunky beer back and forth on the beach, shyly asking Miles what Seattle girls were like, but no. That's not what's happening.

A group of about twelve boys is clustered on the metal dock that stretches out into the sea, a bold symbol to mark the place where the Soft Sea meets the Dehset. About a quarter mile off the dock, a straight white line bobs in the current, stretching out past where the eye can see, like a divider in a swimming pool.

Only ours is made of the bones of our ancestors.

I see a few heads swivel my way as I loudly make my way down the hill. All the boys I've grown up with are here: Eryk Pope, Edmund and Sloane Nickerson, Ryland McLeod, and Chadwick Mintus. Fallon Bodhmall and Van Grimes have joined the group even though they graduated last year, big hulking followers that they are. They've even brought the youngest ones along: Norah's little brother, James, is here with Hudson Pelletier, both boys standing still as statues and looking terrified. I shove past Ryland McLeod, who stands at the back of the dock, arms folded disapprovingly. I give him a withering look as I pass.

"What the actual HELL are you doing?" I yell as a gust of cold wind almost sends me flying off the edge of the dock. The sky around us is gray, churning the waves into slices that crash against the shore. On my left side is the Soft Shore, lapping peacefully. To my right, the Dehset screams. I push through the pack of hungry boys, sensing their intensity as I go, a storm on the edge of turning violent. When I pass Sloane Nickerson, his hand wraps around my upper arm. He yanks me toward him, not unkindly, and whispers as beads of sweat drip down his brown skin. "You have to stop them. Eryk's gone mad," he hisses.

I look back at him, the disappointment in my eyes clear as day. "*Why didn't you?*" I rip my arm away from him and keep walking, boys parting in front of me like water. I finally see Miles. He's standing tensely in between Eryk Pope, Edmund Nickerson, and Fallon Bodhmall. Eryk's never been my favorite, but my hatred for him flares when I see the grip he has on Miles's shoulder. When Miles sees me, his mouth twists a little, and he looks at me with such longing that it almost makes my legs go weak.

Eryk slowly looks up, a mean glint in his eye, his white-blond hair tousled by the wind. "Why, it's Mabel Beuvry, finally gracing us with her holy presence. What entices you to join us, old friend? That old bedrock of yours finally feeling empty?" He tilts his head toward Miles. "I heard through the grapevine that you prefer the company of this interloper rather than your own Weymouth kin. I didn't think it was true! But judging by the right look on your face, I'd say maybe you have a heart for this Cabot loser." He shoves Miles forward. "Don't be so pissed, Mabel. It's not like we carried him here. He came voluntarily. He wants to be one of us, right, lad?"

Miles growls in Eryk's direction, "When it's nine against one, there's not much choice involved. What brave men you are, jumping a man sleeping in his bed while his uncle and cousins are out!"

"You're not a man yet," Edmund replies. "But after this you will be."

I glare hard at him. Edmund isn't always my favorite person, but he's not who he's acting like right now. "You don't have to help them do this, you know. You're better than this." I turn and address all of them. "Is this going to make you bigger boys?" My eyes fall on James and Hudson, barely twelve years old. "Does exerting power over someone else make you fear the Storm less?"

Fallon Bodhmall takes a menacing step toward me. "You know women aren't allowed here. This is a tradition for the men only. Best get on, before someone calls your Guardian to come and get you." Fallon doesn't scare me.

I whip my head around. "Oh yeah? I'm not the only one breaking tradition here. As far as I know, the Barrier Dive is for boys who *grow up on the island*. Boys who know it's coming and have been seasoned to the Dehset their entire lives. You're messing with the history of this island, and for what? Because you're threatened by some new blood? He's not here to take your shack, Fallon." I see his nostrils flare; the Bodhmalls have the smallest and the lowliest house on the island.

He's pissed as he steps closer to me. "Look, girly, if Miles wants to be considered one of us, he's going to have to earn it." He makes like he's going to shove me backward, but I don't move, even though my legs give a shake, and my eyes remain defiant. Suddenly Miles is there, putting himself between me and Fallon, his narrow figure staring down all of Fallon's hulking six-foot-five mass. Miles's eyes are dark, and I see a whole new side of him.

"Touch her, and I swear to God, I'll put you in the *fucking* ground."

Behind me, I hear Eryk clap with maniacal delight. "Aha! Yes! Yes! THERE'S the city kid I've been waiting for. You've been hiding out on us, Cabot. I knew you were secretly a badass." I notice for the first time how predatory his smile is. "Now, everyone, calm down. Fallon, chill out, for real."

Eryk faces Miles. "Look. I want you to take a second, Cabot, and imagine you're one of us. You've grown up on Weymouth

Island. Born and bred to survive the Storm. You fortify your house day after day, spend your school days learning the stories of your ancestors, speaking words into the stones of your house. Growing up here, you earn the right to defend this island by your sacrifice of a normal life. Maybe you lost a sibling. Maybe you watch your grandfather die in front of you. Or your father." His eyes meet mine. "But by salt and iron and paper, you earn it."

Around Miles and me, a small circle of boys has formed, pressing tighter against us. Miles takes my hand in the crowd, and I lace my fingers around his, squeezing tight. Underneath the dock, waves crash against the pillars.

Eryk circles around Miles and me as he speaks, his voice rumbling beside the waves. "Since you decided to skip all the other steps to becoming a man of Weymouth Island, I figure you can at least do us the courtesy of this one tiny little thing."

Beside me, I can hear Miles's steady breathing; he's trying not to show his fear to the other boys because he knows they'll eat it up, like a bunch of feral dogs.

Edmund points at me. "She's not supposed to be here."

"Neither is he," I snap. "But I guess we're all ignoring rules of conduct today, aren't we?"

Eryk gives me a terrible smile as he faces the rest of the group. "That we are, I guess. You can't cut through all of us, Miles, so what do you say?" There is a low humming that emits from all the boys around us, a steady, low sound that sets my teeth on edge. They press closer to us until there's no escape.

Miles whispers, "Okay," as someone wraps their arms around my waist. I jerk around to find Sloane.

"No!" I whisper, flailing as he yanks me backward, out of the circle. "Stop, Sloane! Let me go." I struggle in his arms, but he's stronger than me.

"Trust me," he whispers into my ear. "You don't want to be in the middle of this right now." I struggle, but it's no use; the boys I used to call friends swarm around Miles, their hums turning into chanted verses I've never heard before.

> 'Tis an island your home; 'tis the sea your breath.
> Retrieve your prize beside the bones.
> Your proud brothers will wait for you
> As you tempt patient death.

CHAPTER TWENTY-ONE

A s their chant ends, the boys watch Miles with eerie still-
ness. Eryk steps up next to him and then signals to Fallon Bodhmall. He carries a small wooden box, warped
by the years and blackened with age.

I know what's inside: a privilege granted only to Weymouth's
glowing boys.

The group goes silent as Eryk holds the chest up above his
head like a sacrifice. If I weren't so scared for Miles, I would laugh
at the seriousness of it all, the intensity of these boys who still kiss
their mums. The chest has three interlocking squares decorating
the top, the symbol of the Triumvirate. Eryk smiles as he lowers
it ceremoniously in front of Miles.

Edmund pushes him forward. "Kneel," he says, his voice
emotionless as Miles stares at him with eyes like lit flint. "You
want to be a part of us, Cabot? Kneel and open the chest."

Miles reluctantly sinks to his knees and flings open the lid of
the chest.

Sloane holds me back. "Calm down, Mabel," he hisses. "It's
not right that he's here, but maybe he'll be fine."

Miles stares down into the chest with a confused face. "What the hell am I looking at?"

"Pick it up and see," Edmund orders, trying to sell his own toughness.

Miles pulls out a small wooden handle no more than two feet long, a small dowel that fits in the palm of your hand. It's nothing special; on the surface, it's completely unremarkable. He turns it over in the gray light. "This?" he says skeptically. "Are you planning on attaching a jumping rope to this?"

"No, idiot." Edmund snatches the wooden handle from Miles. "What you just said shows that you know absolutely nothing about this place. During the first Storm, when almost all our people were drowning in the surge, while men watched their children and their wives perish on the beach, a monk named Gregor Des Roches—" I snort angrily. *Of course, this patriarchal story.*

"Gregor Des Roches found broken pieces of iron. He then wrapped the end around a piece of wood, and suddenly he had a weapon. As the seas raged around him, he defended ten small children with this single piece of iron; it's why we know iron is one of our best defenses against the dead. This weapon changed everything, and you don't even know what it is."

Eryk leans down. "It's a *bloody iron whip, man*—and every boy on this island dives for it." Miles's shoulders are coiled up like he's ready to spring. Edmund keeps chattering on about the Monk Des Roches, but no one is listening.

I've heard this story before, but all the women on this island know a different version. I flash to my mother, pulling a young Hali and me close, huddled in the warm dark in our bedroom. Outside, a snowstorm rages.

"It's time to tell you girls the story of Sister Mary Rose, the bravest of Weymouth women," she whispers, hoping to lull us to sleep. "It was during one of the early 1900s Storms on this island."

"Everyone died," I chirp. "That was the year everyone died."

"Not everyone, Mabel." Hali kicks me under the sheet.

I pull my leg back and then slam it down hard against hers, much harder than she kicked me.

"Stop now, both of you. Sister Mary Rose was one of the original nuns that came over from Our Lady Monastery."

"One of the Triumvirate!" I say proudly.

"On the night of that Storm, several families were forced out of their homes by the dead. Panicking, they ran toward the chapel at the top of the hill, hoping it would protect them. While three cowardly monks hid inside the cellar, Sister Mary Rose waited for the families, helped them inside, and hid the children inside the wooden confessional. She secured the door with a piece of fabric pulled from the altar, where she had been making a flower mosaic with small pieces of iron. When the dead broke through the door, she found herself face-to-face with a man from under the sea with glowing orbs for eyes."

Hali buries herself under the covers with a shriek.

"What happened then?" I ask, breathless.

My mother leans forward, the shadow of snowflakes dancing across her face. "Brave Sister Mary Rose noticed that the dead man avoided touching the iron-covered piece of fabric that she had laced across the door. With a cry, she yanked the fabric from the door and began slashing it back and forth like a whip. She saved the children, and those children would become our ancestors. Afterward, the blacksmith on Weymouth used her design and added a wooden handle, and since then the design has improved every year. And that became the iron whip. The boys dive for it when they're old enough."

I frown. "But . . . why don't we learn about her in school?"

My mother's eyes grow hard. "Because over the years, history becomes twisted. One of the cowardly monks who hid decided to take Sister Mary Rose's story as his own. Who would contradict him? No one listened to women or children in those days. Instead in the chaos, a legend was created of the brave Monk Des Roches, who saved our island with his genius and his glued iron." She tucks the blanket around our chins. "Only the women of Weymouth know the truth of this story. Our sisterhood keeps Sister Mary Rose alive. And while the men have their silly Barrier Dive initiation, we have the truth. The reason that we are all here, on this island, is because of one woman and her little piece of fabric and iron."

"Why did you tell us that story?" I whine. "It's so sad."

"And scary!" chimes in Hali from underneath the quilt.

My mother kisses my forehead; she's so slight, it's like a feather brushing my face. "Because it's important to know that history depends on who is left alive to tell it." The blackness of the hallway dims as my memory fades away.

I'm back on the dock, salty water spraying over my face as Eryk berates Miles.

"It's time." Edmund raises a hand, and all the boys begin pushing Miles toward the edge of the dock. "I'm doing you a favor, mate. We're giving you a chance to earn your iron whip. Every man on this dock, save the little ones, has done it already."

Edmund holds the iron whip over his head, and I think of

Sister Mary Rose swinging it left and right, mauling the dead as she goes.

"All you have to do is retrieve this from the bottom of the ocean. Simple! Get the whip, along with a handful of sand to make it count."

Miles looks relieved. That sounds easy enough. But he doesn't *know*. Edmund walks to the side of the dock, holding the whip casually out over the waves. Relief washes through me; it shouldn't be that hard to retrieve it.

"And whatever you do, don't—"

In a flash, Eryk grabs the iron whip from Edmund's hand and gleefully hurls it far out over the water. It cartwheels through the air and then plunges down into the waves with a splash.

"Oh shit!" gasps Sloane, his grip on me loosening as my mouth drops open. *Shit indeed.* My eyes trace past where the whip landed straight to the floating line of bones only a dozen feet away. Everyone on the dock is frozen in place.

"Idiot!" Edmund snaps, spinning around to face Eryk as the boys explode. "According to the bylaws, it's supposed to be at least thirty feet away from the barrier! That's way too close!"

Everyone is yelling at him, but Eryk only smirks, and I swear I'm going to wipe it off his pretty face. "Who's gonna tell? Seattle can spare a little extra effort for the privilege he didn't earn." He faces Miles out to sea. "Retrieve the whip, and you'll be one of us."

"Or what?" asks Miles. "You're going to drown me?"

I see a slight hint of panic on Edmund's face. "Look, just go get it, man, and everything will be okay."

Miles looks back at me for confirmation.

Can you swim? I mouth, and he kind of shrugs. *Oh God.* I

want to tell him about all the complex dynamics at play here, how this initiation is built on a lie, how Eryk is trying to alpha-male over Edmund because he's jealous of him over Norah, how Miles belongs here and doesn't need to prove it. How he belongs with me, even though I'm furious with him.

The thought stops me in my tracks. *He belongs with me.* It's not some overly romantic statement. It's a hard truth, hard as the rocks that overlook the shore. It's built from the rising waves, the salt on my cheeks, the pine cones in Wasp Wood. We belong together.

The first and the last.

I see the fire in his eyes reflected back at me. He knows it too.

Unspoken words pass between us, and then I struggle to breathe as he leaps into the churning waves.

CHAPTER TWENTY-TWO

Miles is instantly swallowed by the water, and panic rises in me, but then I see his head emerge, black hair slicked back. He begins pulling himself forward, using a lazy forward stroke. My heart sinks in my chest. *Oh no.* I can tell already that Miles isn't . . . a good swimmer. In a pool, he would be absolutely fine, but here, in the ocean, he's barely cutting it—and he's so close to the Dehset border. Weymouth kids know how to swim in the ocean; from the time we can walk, we are trained by our Guardians in waves off the Soft Shore. We know about undercurrents and wave breaks, riptides and tangled seaweed. We're basically our own swim team, because we know that one day the ocean will *come to us.* Weymouth kids are hard. Miles is hard too, but he's the hardness of skyscrapers and neon bodega lights. He's about as useless in the ocean as I would be on a crowded city street.

Now these Weymouth kids are standing on the dock, screaming at Miles to "Go! Go! Go!" I look over at Eryk Pope, who is crouched on the dock, watching Miles struggle with wicked glee.

"Why did you do this?" I snap at him. "Are you so insecure that you need to put someone else's life at risk?"

He gets up in my face, and I see a glint of malice in those glacial Pope eyes. "Because Miles doesn't believe in it, not really. People that come from beyond the bridge don't understand." He looks out to the water, where Miles is about halfway to the barrier. "He will now."

"You're a horrible person when you're sad," I say quietly.

The delight on his face dims. "That means absolutely nothing coming from you."

"Hey!" Norah's little brother pushes forward. "Don't talk to Mabel like that!"

My heart swells. It's charming that scrappy twelve-year-old James is coming to my defense. "It's okay, James. I got this," I reassure him.

"You're too young to be here anyway," sneers Eryk. "Why don't you take your boyfriend and go home?" *Oh no, he did not say that.* Before I was mad, and now . . . now I'm filled with righteous fire as I watch James's eyes fill with tears. I pivot, putting all my weight into a quick, hard thrust with my palm that lands flat against Eryk's chest. He flies off the dock and into the water with a loud *boooosh.* It's the most satisfying sound I've ever heard.

The rest of the group slowly backs away from me as I whirl on Edmund like a madwoman.

"You're better than this," I snap. He puts up his hands in surrender.

I'm interrupted by James, yanking hard on my arm. "Miles!" He points. I run to the edge of the dock. I don't see him, not in the spot where he should be by now; instead there are only choppy waves. Without warning, a horrifying sound rises out from under the water, a mournful moan. Everybody on the dock freezes because we know that sound. The dead know we are here.

No.

I don't wait for permission. I don't wait for anything. I'm vaguely aware of voices rising around me, of Eryk storming out of the water and James trying to stop me, but every other person is inconsequential; they've always been. I fling off my boots, coat, and jeans, stripping down to my tank top and underwear. Then I take a deep breath and move to the edge of the dock. I'm all in; releasing my fear that he'll undo the safe world I've built for myself, shedding the reservation, the burying of my desire, of what I know to be true—we belong. I dive.

The frigid water shocks my body; my limbs freeze as my muscles tense all at once. It hurts like a thousand stinging needles everywhere as I struggle to acclimate as fast as I can. *Move*, I think. Salt water burns my eyes, and I see flashes of black. Immediately the waves are a battering ram that rush over me again and again. After what seems like an eternity, my eyes clear and my lungs take a cold breath. The second my body relaxes, I begin quickly swimming toward where Miles should be, stroke by furious stroke.

The dead are loud and close. A wave crashes over me, and then another, but I don't let them pull at my body; I surge forward, strong arms pulling me deeper into the water, feet thrashing behind me. My father's daughter was a born swimmer.

Another wave crashes into white foam in the distance, and when it dissipates, relief floods through me. Miles is only about ten feet away; I can see his dark hair floating above the water, his lips aimed at the sky as he attempts a pathetic back float.

"Miles!" I scream his name. He looks relieved and mortified all at once. I cover the distance quickly, reach under the water and find his hand; it's freezing, and his lips are an alarming shade of plum. He's not drowning, but he's not exactly swimming, either. He touches my cheek, all inhibitions between us washed away by fear.

"You shouldn't be out here!" he yells, and I shake my head.

"I'm a better swimmer than you are!"

"Yeah, no shit!" His smile fades quickly. "Can you hear them?" I nod. A few feet away from us, the Bone Barrier bobs back and forth on the surface. I glance back to the dock, which seems to get farther away by the second.

"We have to get you back to the dock." I fear he'll pull me under, that I'll have to choose between saving him and myself. Would I choose myself? The thought is alarming. I can feel the Dehset inside me, a blackness taking root in my heart. It's not good to be this close.

"I can't find the whip," Miles sputters. "I tried."

"Leave it, then!" Above my head, the sky churns with gray, and to my horror, I hear words being formed over the surface of the deep.

Come, Mabel. Come see what we know about you.

I jerk back in the water.

"I have to find it," Miles gasps. "They'll never accept me otherwise. I need to do something to prove I belong. I think it landed somewhere over here."

I raise a shaking palm to his face. "It isn't that important! It's not . . . real, that story."

Miles's face is determined. "I can't go back without it, Mabel. I have to stay, because . . ." He laces his fingers around mine. Our eyes lock, and we both understand. He's not doing this for himself. He's doing this for *us*. I want to let the world disappear, sink into him forever. "I have to find it," he whispers. "I have to try. . . ."

I give his hand a squeeze. "We have to be quick." Without words, we let ourselves sink beneath the waves together. Underneath the water, everything is a dark blue. A stretch of obsidian black sand covered with jagged white rocks waits underneath our feet as the shadows of waves dance overhead. After a second, I spot the whip tucked up next to a porous brown rock, blending in—and only a few feet away from the Bone Barrier. I stare at it, unable to believe what I'm seeing, when I feel a hand on my waist, pulling me upward. I surface, gulping at the air.

"Did you see it?" Miles yells, and I nod, salt water streaming into my eyes.

"It's near a rock below us, about ten feet that way," I sputter. The whisper of the dead is growing all around us, sounds bouncing off the waves. I think I hear someone calling my name.

"Don't listen to them," he pleads. "I hear them too, but it's not real." I hear my name again, and my head whips around. *Dad?* Or . . . maybe it's the screams from the dock. It's hard to tell.

Miles touches my face. "Come back to me, Mabel. I'm here. Focus *here*." He is struggling in the water, his body growing tired. If I don't do something soon, we will both drown.

"One dive and we get the hell out," I sputter. "Stay near me, and don't look too long at the barrier." We take our last big breath together and then . . . all is water as a large wave tunnels above us.

We dive down, pushing ourselves toward the ocean floor, the sea pulling our hands apart almost immediately. I kick desperately for the bottom. The whip stares up at me as I grow closer, my fingers reaching out, and then my hand wraps around the rough wooden handle of the whip, a flurry of sand coming up with it. *Yes.* When I grab the whip, otherworldly screams fill the water, and everything goes still . . . *and the dead are waiting for us.*

The Bone Barrier is now only about five feet away from us; the current has pushed us right up against it. It looks like a transparent white curtain—and yet it is made of nothing of this earth. The "fabric" undulates in the currents like linen blown in wind, tethered to the bones that float on the surface. The barrier stretches from the bottom of the sea to the top, a fortress made to hold back our nightmares. It flexes to bind them; it moves with them.

And whatever lies behind it wants to be free.

I hear Miles scream underwater, and then he's gone, tearing upward for air. I understand, and yet I can't look away. In fact, I'm swimming closer to get a better look.

Misshapen skeletal faces ripple beyond the barrier, stretching it farther toward us. Behind it, eyeless holes press against the veil; hands claw at their restraint. The longer I look, the more forms appear; hundreds of deformed faces and broken bodies all writhe together, like a Renaissance painting of hell, where tormented souls entwine together.

The dead of the Dehset are only a few feet away from me.

The shape of a dozen bodies begins pressing its way toward me, out from the writhing crowd. The white mesh of the barrier sinks into a too-wide mouth. White mist rises from the sand around me like an hourglass as the dead call my name.

You know, they hiss. *You know what you have lost.* A hand suddenly pushes through the transparent barrier and reaches for me with unnaturally long fingers. My heart shudders in fear as my grief whispers, *Maybe you should stay.* More long, clawed hands press through the veil, reaching for me, beckoning me closer. It wouldn't hurt to touch them, right? I extend my hand out toward them.

Suddenly two solid human arms tighten around me. Miles is attempting to pull me toward the surface, but together we are sinking . . . down. Beyond the barrier, a hundred delighted nightmares surge forward to receive us as our two souls draw near. The first and the last.

They could take me, I think, *but they cannot have him. I will not let them.*

Adrenaline rushes through me at the thought, and it's just enough to wake me up. I grab Miles's hand, push off the bottom, and kick like a demon for the sky.

We break the surface with a huge inhale as a wave of cheers sounds from the dock. We're alive, but we can't stay above the water for long; Miles is fading. Thankfully, I hear loud splashes right behind us, and when I turn around, I see Sloane and Edmund swimming toward us, a life preserver held between them. With the practiced throw of a lifeguard, Edmund wings it over the water. It splashes down, and Miles and I grab on to it for dear life, resting our arms across each other.

He looks over at me, exhausted. "Do me a favor, Beuvry. Don't join the dead quite yet. We have business with each other."

"Are you guys okay?" Sloane hollers.

"We're fine!" I yell back. No need to linger on how I almost gave myself over to the horrors underneath the Dehset.

"Get back from the barrier!" Edmund yells, as if he's not one of the people who put us here. As my head clears, I remember that I don't belong with the dead; I belong here, between the sky and the waves, beside Miles. Under the water, I pass him the iron whip, pressing the wood and some sand into his palm.

"Take it!" I cough, salt thick in my mouth. "You earned it."

"Not without you," he says. "Let's present it together."

I shake my head. I want no part of this ridiculous ritual. "Nope. You saved my life. Take it." *Sister Mary Rose and I, we know.*

"You saved MY life."

I pause.

He levels me with his intense gaze, water dripping over his forehead. "Why do I feel like we'll save each other's lives again and again?"

I don't have an answer to that.

Minutes later we flop onto the rocky beach, two waterlogged creatures struggling to catch our breath, our minds struggling to process what we saw. Miles is staring at the sky in shock, his chest heaving. He knows. And for the first time, he truly understands. He looks terrified, but then he rolls over onto his side and fixes his eyes on mine. Water drips from his wet hair onto my face, and he cradles my head in his hand, looking down at me as the whole world disappears.

"The first and the last," he whispers. My breathing slows, and just as the world comes back into focus, he leans down over me.

"Mabel . . . *you* are the storm." Then he leans down and passionately kisses me. I taste the salt water on his tongue, the contrast of his warm mouth against his cold skin. His lips press hungrily against mine as waves surround us on the sand. Everyone sees, and not a part of me cares.

As we kiss, I forget the dock, the sea, the dead. His mouth rolls like thunder across mine. His palms are wrapped up in my hair, buried deep in my sopping brown curls. My fingers trace down his wet shirt pressed against his chest. His hands turn my head from side to side as he kisses my face all over; his lips are on my forehead, brushing over my eyebrows, tracing the corners of my mouth, my jawline. It feels so good to be held by him, to have him enfold me like a blossom; I feel his heart beating against mine, two wayward spirits becoming one. He leaves his mark everywhere, and for a golden minute, we are two tiny specks of light against the dark sand. It seems like an eternity passes, when he pulls back, his eyes hungry, his cheeks ruddy with cold. In the meantime, I have forgotten how to breathe.

"You really need swimming lessons, do you know that?" I tease, a smile crossing my face.

Miles smiles. "Only if you're the teacher." He yanks me up, his hand never leaving the place where it has found a bare inch of skin on my hip.

I grin as happiness rushes through every part of me, the bliss of his kiss covering up the horrors we just witnessed together, under the sea. Of the voices that called to us. "Deal."

There is a rush of noise, and suddenly nine loud boys surround us. Miles pauses dramatically before thrusting his iron whip into the air like a champion. The shore explodes with boisterous cheers, and Edmund throws an arm around Miles's shoulders.

"Oi, I thought maybe we killed you. I'm glad we didn't."

"You almost did." Miles stares down Edmund until they both break out in uncomfortable laughter. In that moment, I see that this will be a friendship that grows. Edmund steps aside, and the rest of the boys swarm Miles.

Sloane gives me a hug and whispers into my ear, "I have to say, it's pretty incredible that a boy who can barely swim snatched something from the bottom of the sea *and* made it back to the shore."

"Almost as incredible as someone who saw wrong happening and did nothing to stop it, even though I personally know him to be a stand-up guy." A blush rises up Sloane's cheeks, but I don't have a chance to shame him further because someone is screeching my name.

"MABEL!!" Norah is running down the sand toward me, shoving through the group of boys. "Move, you big jerks!" A second later, she wraps me up in her arms. I exhale, thankful for her pure, feminine energy to counter this madness.

"Hi," I mumble into her shoulder.

"Hi? That's what you say to me? HI? Up at the trailhead, I saw you dive into the water! What were you thinking? You could have died that close to the barrier! Oh my God!" She crushes me against her. "Don't ever do that again, do you hear me? Not even for a cute boy!" I grin as she pulls back to look at my face. "Did you see anything down there?"

"Umm . . ." I have no idea how to explain the dead pushing desperately at the barrier, the shape of their faces under the misty cloth, the mist rising from the bottom of the sea. I shake my head; there's no reason to scare her. "I could barely see with the salt water in my eyes."

"You're lying. But I don't care, because later you are going to tell me all about THAT kiss." The kiss. My heart stops at the thought of it.

Van Grimes throws a heavy woven blanket over my shoulders. "You've got some balls on you, Beuvry! Norah, you going to dive in next?"

She frowns at him. "Didn't you pee yourself when they grabbed you from your bed two years ago?" she asks innocently, and Van Grimes stomps off without a word. My best friend laughs dryly and turns to me. "Let's get you home before you get hypothermia."

I look down; my hands *are* looking somewhat blue, and the tremble in my lips is getting harder to ignore.

Sloane bounces over like a puppy, all his guilt erased, and throws his arms around our shoulders. "Home, nah! These two are coming to the Popes' with us! We've got Des Roches's homemade cider and a bonfire waiting for us. Right, Eryk?"

I get a jolt of pleasure when I see how miserable Eryk Pope looks in his sopping-wet jeans. *I regret nothing.*

He sighs. "I guess you and Norah can join us for the initiation celebration. I'll make an exception this one time."

I bow. "Thank you, Your Majesty." I know he's only inviting us in hopes that he can get some time with Norah.

Norah turns back to me. "Let's go! What else do we have to do today?" *Almost drown by ghosts? Get the best kiss of my life?* "I have some clothes in my bag that you can wear if you want."

There are only two things I want at this moment. One, to kiss Miles again, and two, to go home, change into my pajamas, and crawl under my covers with Hali. I want warmth and comfort; I do not want to hang out with awful Popes or the rest of these boys. But . . . *it's an open invitation into the Popes' house.* Maybe when I'm there I can get some clues about Lynwood's death.

Something that makes the Storm of 1876 journal make sense. *Looks like I'm going to party.*

"Some dry clothing would be nice," I say to my best friend.

With a primal cheer, the boys lift Miles above their shoulders—splayed out like a human sacrifice, his iron whip clutched tight in his hand. I can see he is laughing as they toss him up and down. But beyond that, I see the shock on his face— at the dead he saw under the water, the reality of what we face here. Our island is a strange place, set apart from the whole world, but somewhere in between the sweaty arms of Sloane Nickerson and a wild kiss on a frigid shore, it seems like Miles Cabot has finally found his place in the gate between worlds.

CHAPTER TWENTY-THREE

As I walk up to the front of the house in tight clothes that are not my own, I can't help but stare. It's been ages since I visited the Pope house, but I don't ever remember it looking this . . . severe. This family is marked by their transformative anger, a dark cloud that hovers over their home, one that manifests itself in brilliant and deadly art. With the loss of Lynwood, I'm sure their misery has grown darker. Losing a Guardian means losing the soul of a family.

Norah lets out a long breath. "This is so sad," she mutters before looking over at me. "Did you know?"

I can't tear my eyes away. "No. But I bet Jeff did." The Pope house looks like an honest-to-God citadel. Normally it's an enormous Craftsman made of dark wood, pale blue siding, and a bloodred door—it's quite lovely. But all that beauty has been stripped away by gross fortifications. Where a garden once sat is now a twelve-foot-high fence, topped with coils of iron wire. Parapets jut out from the front of the house, obscuring the lovely rose windows, now covered with heavy metal shutters. Everything is pointy and sharp, barricaded and protected. Steel mesh, generator cages, and iron vines that trail up and over everything beautiful. All the houses on Weymouth are fortresses in their own way, but this is something different.

This house feels paranoid—unhinged.

"Poor Eryk and Cordelia," Norah says softly, but I scoff, not ready to forgive Eryk for putting Miles in harm's way.

"Having a difficult home life doesn't excuse becoming a horrible human being. It just gives context. Either find a way to cope or get help, but don't throw the new kid into the Dehset. There are ways of grieving something that don't hurt anyone, that don't lead to . . . lead to . . ." My teeth start chattering as I stumble over my words, something hard twisting in my chest.

What is happening?

"Whoa, whoa—hey." Norah gives my shoulder a squeeze. "You okay?"

I press my hands over my eyes. I can't shake the sounds of the dead crying out from behind the barrier, the desperate moans accompanied by those clawing hands.

"I'm fine," I finally answer. "It's been a day, you know? When I woke up this morning, I didn't think I would watch the boy I like almost drown in the Dehset."

"So you do like him, huh? I knew it. I mean, I guess it's pretty obvious after that kiss, which looked . . . wet."

I smack her arm. "Oh my God, Norah. Stop."

She pulls me close. "You're so brave, you know. If you can swim near the Dehset, you could do anything that scared you, face anything. You can bear more than you think." She takes my freezing hands in hers, her gaze focusing intensely on mine. "Mabel . . ." She looks like she's about to say something, but we're rudely interrupted by Edmund staring down at us.

"You coming inside, Nors?" My friend withers like a lily under his too-hot gaze, and the moment is lost. Eryk pushes past all of us, unlocking the gates to the house with a silver key looped around his neck. His posture is too proud, acting like this monstrous violation of a home is something to be admired. The gates open, and the boys flood in, except for Miles, who waits beside me on the porch. Edmund sweeps Norah up over his shoulder and heads inside.

"Would you like me to do that?" Miles laughs. "Throw you around? I remember how much you loved it when I carried you up the stairs."

I shake my head. "Last I checked, my legs were working quite well." My tone isn't snarky. Instead it's adoring. Surprising myself, I step forward and push the salty, crusted hair out of his eyes. He shyly touches my lip ever so softly with the tip of his pointer finger. All we want is to be alone, but inside, the boys have begun chanting his name.

"Mi-les! Mi-les! Mi-les!"

He groans in frustration. "Didn't you hear? I'm a man now. Apparently plucking a weapon out of the ocean was the thing to push puberty right on through."

I wrap his hands up in my own. "I did hear that, and I for one am glad. Before an hour ago, you were so . . . boyish. It was almost distracting." I push my lips softly against his palm. This feels so right to me, so why does it feel like I am ripping apart inside?

He tilts my face toward the light. "Hey, I was wondering if we could find some time to talk tomorrow? Maybe take a walk onto the south end of the island or something?"

"You're not missing much. There are some peat bogs, a handful of rocky crags, and a small creek that runs along the length of it. There's a cairn on the very edge, an old child's grave. It's a pretty place to sit."

"A child's grave. Sounds romantic." He leans forward and brushes my cheek with the softest kiss. "Tomorrow, then. It's a date. Then we can kiss all we want." Beneath the fire burning between us, I see a hint of fear. *Why?*

Sloane bursts out to the porch. "Miles, I was looking for you, mate. We're having a toast in your honor. Eryk found his dad's old Scotch in the cabinet." He lowers his voice. "It tastes like expired cleaning solution, but you may have to take a drink for the team, yeah?"

Miles's lip curls. "We're a team, eh? I don't remember that sentiment when you forced me out onto a dock in the middle of the bloody ocean."

Sloane shrugs off Miles's icy tone. "It's not *really* about the iron whip, you know. It was about showing you *who we are*. Whether or not you know it, you looked at us all like we're a bunch of freaks. But this tradition is your olive branch. Be grateful; you now have the same weapon as every other man on this island." He looks over at me with a wink. "And one nun."

I snicker. *Of course Sloane knows.*

Miles shakes his head. "All right, man, I get it. That doesn't mean it didn't suck."

Sloane grins. "Let's go. Are you joining us inside the haunted mansion, Mabel?"

I want to find the dirt on Lynwood, so I shrug like I'm considering it offhand. "I won't be staying long."

"You never do, but we're always glad to have you. Stay away from Eryk, though; he's in a rotten mood." The heavy iron door slams shut behind him.

"Shall we?" Miles reaches for my hand, and even though I know this will set this island aflame with gossip, I let his fingers lace strongly through mine.

Let them all see. It's not like they didn't just see us kissing on the beach.

The second we get inside, Miles is ripped away by the horde, eager to regale him with tales of their own dives. He disappears in a primal wave of male bonding. It's actually the perfect distraction; with all the boys heading into the kitchen, I can look for answers about Lynwood unimpeded. *I need something, anything.* Finding his body unlocked something in me, a shifting of myself. I need answers to make sense of it all. I begin to wander, eventually finding my way down a strange hallway that runs off the kitchen and around the back end of the house.

The walls are lined with mason jars of salt, and the windows are boarded up. A trap stops me before I proceed any farther; straight ahead at the end of the hall sits a metal square mounted on the tracks that run down either side of the hallway. It's essentially an iron maiden: a sheet of flat iron the size of a coffin with iron spikes set inside it. I see how it all works. Someone releases a lock, and the iron maiden slides down the track and splits all the salt jars. The dead would essentially be vaporized with the combination of iron spikes and salt clouds.

It's genius. *It's deadly.* It was in this house that I learned a valuable lesson about traps.

I flash to Hali and me running down the length of this

hallway, hiding from Cordelia because she was being so bossy. Our mothers were in the other room, drinking a mushroom tea and gossiping about the Pelletiers.

"Mabel, hide in here!"

I followed Hali down the creepy hallway and into a room of portraits, where a dumbwaiter sat against a wall.

"This is perfect!" she squealed. Together we pulled the door shut behind us and waited in the dark, giggling into our chubby hands and thinking about how Cordelia would never find us. We had been in there about ten minutes when the dumbwaiter was yanked open, flooding with light. When I looked up, it was not Cordelia looking back at me; instead it was the furious face of her mother. With wide, terrified eyes, she grabbed our arms and roughly yanked us out of the dumbwaiter. Hali let out a cry as Lilou Pope slapped both our faces a single time; we both stepped back in shock.

Our parents had never hit us.

"What are you doing?" Lilou spoke, her French accent sharp and cruel. "You could have died! Why are you in here? Why?"

Cordelia wouldn't look at us as she clutched her mother's leg, her moonish face distorted with fear. "This is a trap for the dead! Don't you see, you stupid girls?" She pushed a small silver latch on the inside of the door, something we hadn't noticed but could have bumped easily. With a loud crash, the floor of the dumb-waiter collapsed, and the whole thing went plummeting down.

"Look down there!" Lilou cried. "Look, both of you!" We bent over the abyss and looked down into the bottom of the shaft, where iron spikes poked upward; we would have, could have died. Messily. Cordelia's mother grabbed both our chins. "You should know better than to play hide-and-seek on Weymouth Island. Foolish girls." She whirled on my mother.

"Isla, you should be teaching these girls how to *survive*."

"And you should be teaching your children how to love," my mother snapped in return, gathering us up in her arms. "Don't ever touch my daughters again."

She never spoke to Lilou Pope after that. I haven't been back in this house since. Yet here I am, creeping down that same hall-way in a house that isn't my own, staring at a contraption that would make a bloody mess of me in seconds. Some things never change.

I take small, careful steps, glancing into the bedrooms. In one, an elaborate gaming chair makes it obviously Eryk's room, and the next one must be Cordelia's, due to the pretty vintage mint color and hand-painted birds dancing across the ceiling.

I should ask her to do my room.

There's only one more room in this hallway, and it's surrounded by a cloud of thin iron rods. *Lynwood's quarters.* I glance down the hallway to make sure no one is following me. From the kitchen, I hear boys chatting, accompanied occasionally by Norah's shriek-ing laughter. I quickly duck inside the room, moving through the narrow passageway of iron spikes, pressing against the antique handle as I shut the door behind me.

When I turn around, my breath catches in my throat as shock sets in. I don't know what I expected, but this definitely isn't it; Jeff's quarters at our house are elegant and refined. They have the weathered look of an old library. I was under the impression that most Guardians lived that way. I try to take it all in, my heart slipping messily inside my chest. A sadness fills me up.

Poor Lynwood. Poor Eryk and Cordelia.

If a bedroom is supposed to be a sanctuary, this place is an asylum. Random clutter towers over every corner; stacks of the *Nova Scotian Register* and the *Glace Bay Weekly* are spread against the hardwood floor. The rug is covered with black paint, spread by a sloppy hand; spiraling lines spread out from the center over what was once a rich tapestry. Random sequences of the same four numbers are scrawled over the walls and the door. A giant wave of white paint covers one entire wall. Inside the wave, pencil sketches of skeletal faces peer out, their mouths distorted. My body gives a shudder. I recognize them from underneath the waves. The smell of something rotten fills my nostrils. I hear the scatter of tiny feet near the back of the room; there are absolutely rodents living in this dank space.

I turn toward the bed, where weapons are stacked—iron maces in a pile, salt wands and guns, axes and swords laid haphazardly across one another like folded laundry. The only thing in the room untouched by the madness is his pillow, and I can still see the outline of where Will Lynwood laid his head every night. Without knowing why, I reach out and fluff the pillow a little, hoping to send love to him wherever he is.

A second later, I jerk my fingers away. *What am I doing in here?* Whatever this is, it's beyond my reach and, more importantly, *not my place.* When I turn to go, however, something catches my eye from the inside of the closet. Just one more thing. My jaw clenches as I push open the door. The closet—unlike the rest of the room—is completely bare. There are only words covering the walls, written hundreds—no, thousands—of times. *It's coming. It's coming,* followed by the numbers I know already: one, eight, six, and seven.

I read the phrase until I'm dizzy and have to look away, but not before I see one last, heartbreaking thing. In the very far corner of the closet, in a very neatly printed square, are two sentences obviously meant for the Pope family.

I love all of you forever. I hope to light the way.

Jesus. My breath catches in my throat. The vulnerability in those sentences is too much for me. These aren't answers. This is just sad. I can tell by this room that Will Lynwood was not in a good place, and maybe this all means nothing, nothing at all. It's just the ravings of someone lost. *I love all of you forever.* God, I'm such a child, looking for a mystery when there isn't one. What am I hoping to distract myself from? I have to leave. I have to go home *right now.* But when I spin around, I bump hard into a body that clutches my arm in the same rough way his mother once did. I look up into Eryk's impossibly pale blue eyes—sharp like a glacier—and they are *furious.*

I'm afraid of him.

"What the hell are you doing in here?" he asks with barely restrained anger. My body tenses as I struggle to pull myself out of his grasp, but his grip is like iron. Everything in me screams, *Get away.*

"I got lost," I sputter. It's the worst possible answer, and I know it immediately.

Eryk's lip curls up in a sneer. "Lost? Somehow you accidentally stumbled down the hallway, through a tangle of iron wire, and through a closed door? I don't think so." He squeezes. "Let's try again, Mabel, this time without the bullshit. What is it that you're looking for?"

I swallow and decide the truth is the best answer. "I wanted to find his journals. I thought . . . maybe they would have some answers about what happened to him." My voice wavers. "I found his body, and it didn't . . . It wasn't right, what happened to him, and I thought if I could just know what he was thinking—"

Eryk stares at me for a long second before he sighs, his arms dropping to his sides. "The Triumvirate was already here this morning. They came while we were down at the docks and took all his journals." He sinks down on the edge of the bed, his hands running up through his messy blond hair as the weapons shift and slide. "They won't find anything; I've read them already. Sorry to disappoint you. He had a lot of theories. His journals were mostly filled with random measurements he took: the weather, the beach, the water, some measurement from a stone in Scotland, who knows."

"How long had he been like that? Maybe you should have told someone."

He snarls at me. "Who, Mabel? Who am I supposed to tell? It's not like we could take him to a doctor on the mainland, not when he was raving about the Storm. It started getting bad this fall. Lynwood was always a bit paranoid, but that comes with the Guardianship. It's their job to be paranoid, to get us ready. But then he started putting more defenses around the house, and when my parents talked to him about it, the fight was so big, they decided it wasn't worth it. And so they let it happen. He had Cordelia and me shoring up *every day* after school until my father finally put a stop to it. After that, Lynwood sort of disappeared into his own world. He stopped sleeping, and I would hear him pacing the house at night, walking in a circle, muttering to himself about the Great Storm and the cornerstones aligning." He looks at the disarray around him.

"But we loved him, you know, and we didn't want the Triumvirate to get involved, 'cause we knew they would send him away. The saddest thing was that he had already left us behind when he died. That wasn't the same man who raised us. Lynwood taught me how to ride a bike, taught my sister how to paint, how to sketch. When I smell the oven, I think he's down there, making us garlic chips, but instead it's just my mum, and she sucks at cooking." His eyes fill with tears. "Lynwood had seen five Storms—and I think that's too much for a person to bear. He said he could smell the Great Storm in the air, that the numbers told him the truth. He tried to latch his contraption to the tallest tree on the island and fell. And I helped him."

The ground drops out from underneath me. Gingerly I sit down, giving Eryk a wide berth. "What do you mean you helped him?"

Eryk shakes his head. "I helped him build his insane wind funnel warning system. I helped him carry it out to the woods, but I didn't know he wanted to climb up so high to mount it. We argued, and I decided that I wouldn't help him do something so foolish and unsafe. It had to be THAT tree. I knew there was no way he could haul his contraption up without me, so I just left . . . but I left the ladder behind. *Stupidly.* And the old man tried to do it himself— stubborn and mad as a mule. I went back a few hours later and found his body on the rocks. But when I heard Norah coming through the woods, I panicked, grabbed the ladder, and hid."

Understanding dawns on me. "*You* moved the ladder. It was you. You watched it all happen." I think back to that day, when I felt like we were being watched.

Eryk fiddles with his hands. "Sorry to disappoint you, but

there is no mystery, so you can stop playing Scooby-Doo in my house." Eryk pushes himself up. "There's only my failure. Maybe if I had helped him, he would still be alive, the fool. I told Alistair everything this morning. I miss him, you know. I was hoping taking Miles to the Dehset would be a distraction." He takes a moment to compose himself, giving his shoulders a shake.

This was absolutely not how I expected my day to go. One minute, I'm shoving Eryk Pope into the ocean, and the next, I'm reaching across the sheets to hold his hand.

"Grief is a clever thing. I hate that you had to see your Guardian that way. I'm so sorry, Eryk. It's not your fault. If it wasn't that day, it would have been the next. It was an accident."

"Yes, well, I can't make it right, now, can I? No, we have to carry on, since that's what we do on Weymouth. Carry on and pretend it never happened. Fares well the house that's ready, and all that crap." He wipes his nose before looking at me. "This is pretty rich, coming from Mabel Beuvry, you know?"

I step back from him, a hint of discomfort running up my spine. "I don't know what you're talking about."

"Oh no? You never think about how we all have to tiptoe around you, pretending that Mabel's fine? You're lucky Norah is always there to protect you." He lowers his face to mine. "News flash: Mabel's not fine." His eyes have a mean glint as I back away. "Just because you're able to lie to yourself doesn't mean we all have to lie for you. And just because you have the best Guardian on the island doesn't mean he can keep you whole forever."

When I turn to go, a headache crackles across my forehead. Panic rises in my chest, and I remember that I *actually hate* Eryk Pope.

"Have you given any thought to what lies in Sentry's Sleep?" he whispers.

I shove him backward, and he gives a sharp laugh. My brain is splintering, like a thread being pulled from top to bottom, starting at the front of my mind, a quilt unraveling. I turn to go, and he blocks my path.

"Get out of my way," I order.

As Eryk starts to protest, Miles walks into the room. "What's going on in here?" he asks, immediately sensing the tension, his eyes combing over the chaos. "Jesus, what happened in here?"

"I was just leaving," I say, before taking Miles's hand and leading him out of the room, happy to leave Eryk's dangerous grief behind.

We're almost down the hallway when I hear his voice call out, "Do yourself a favor, Cabot, and ask Mabel about *her sister*."

CHAPTER TWENTY-FOUR

My cheeks burn as we walk out into the main room. Every single object and person is too close, too oppressive, too noisy. I hear a soft clicking in my ear, like a locust has taken up residence inside my head, and I box my hands over my ears. I'm feeling hot, and I want to rip Norah's tight tank top right off my chest, maybe rip off *everything*. My chest begins to tighten, and my breath comes short and hard.

I'm having a panic attack. Something inside me is unraveling, and I can't have it happen here. I can't. *Ask Mabel about her sister.* Damn Eryk Pope. This is why Hali stays inside, because of people like him. Half of me wants to take him on myself; I imagine the satisfying crunch it will make when my knuckle meets his cheekbone, and the talk that will follow. *Mabel Beuvry* punched him? *Her?* The nonviolent half of me needs to leave immediately. The room is spinning on a slight tilt. I sense the other boys' eyes on me, their instincts picking up on the fact that this girl is not okay.

"Hey, Mabel, what's happening?" I hear Norah's voice in the crowd, see her pushing past Edmund with concern on her face. No . . . not concern. *Pity.* Behind me, Eryk marches out of the hallway, no trace of grief left on his face.

"What did you do?" Norah hisses at him, and I see him deflate.

"Something that *you* should have done a long time ago." His face doesn't look cruel. Instead it's lost. "There's a cost to hiding behind mental illness in our own families. Trust me, I paid it." He looks sadly back at Lynwood's room before slipping past her. Van Grimes hands him a stolen beer. Fallon claps his shoulders. A rush of irrational fear travels through me and settles somewhere underneath my ribs as I bolt for the door, Norah and Miles trailing behind me.

"I've got it," Miles says to Norah, and then his arm is underneath mine, leading me out of the house and out into the humid island air. Above us, the sky is churning with bulbous clouds, heavy as the weight pressing down in my mind. I try to breathe deeply—in four seconds, out eight, like Jeff taught me, trying to keep my eyes on the horizon. Nausea rises in my stomach.

I don't want to lose it in front of him. Not again.

"I need to go home. I can't be here anymore." I try to say it as normally as possible.

"Of course. I'll walk you there," Miles answers, and together we turn toward the road, the silence between us growing heavier with each step. But he doesn't let go of my hand. I'm so embarrassed; I didn't want him to see this side of me, the parts of myself that I can keep contained, never intersecting. Life is safe for me if Hali, Jeff, and Mum are at home, Norah is at school, and the rest of the island is out here. But then Miles came, bearing down on me like a meteor, and every wall I've put up has been blown to bits. All my most vulnerable parts are mixed up, and mixing doesn't work. I can't have him and the rest of it. But I know at this point I can't give him up. Not when he feels like what I've been waiting for. We've just met, but it feels like our spirits aren't strangers. And then there's the way he looks at me.

As the Pope house fades into the distance behind us, the island restores my sanity. My limbs pull back from the coiled position they were in before. *I'm okay.* My inner balance is slowly being restored via the scent of pine needles and Miles's steady presence beside me. There is a pause, and the corners of his mouth turn up when I look over at him. He leans inexplicably close to me. When I return the smile, he looks taken once more, and I'm unable to believe that this boy's want all focuses on me. Do I mention the connection I feel, something otherworldly? Does he feel it too? And does he like me because of it or in spite of it? Does it matter? God, I hope he kisses me again soon. We aren't far from my house when Miles gently breaks the silence.

"So, today's been unexpected," he says with that curved smile of his. "When I woke up this morning, I thought my life couldn't get any stranger, but then a bunch of guys showed up in my bedroom, kidnapped me, and threw me into the ocean. And then, as if that weren't strange enough, the girl that I'm very into shows up on the dock, yelling at everyone like some warrior goddess, and then jumps into the sea to save me."

"You forgot the part where you see the dead underneath the water." A sliver of pure fear runs up my spine at the memory. The faces, the hands pressing against the barrier ...

Miles frowns. "Yes, that was quite awful, and I'm not ready to talk about it yet. I'm sure I'll see it every night in my nightmares, but there was an excellent kiss if you remember. And for some reason, it's all I can focus on at the moment."

I love the boyish blush that rushes up his cheeks. My blood flushes through me at the memory as I relive every second of the kiss.

He looks around at the thick pine trees surrounding us, layers of sharp needles silhouetted by gray light, before clearing his throat. "I do have one question, though." I see a painful hesitation on his face and feel an ache in my heart for him. "Is that what happens to all the people from Weymouth when they die? Do they all join the dead under the water?" Suddenly I know what he's trying to ask. "Like, is my mother under there, since she was from here?"

I stop walking and turn toward him, lacing both of my hands around his closed fist. "No. Listen. My father once told me that the dead that gather under the sea are those that desperately wish their lives had been different. Waiting under the waves in the Dehset Sea is a place for those who *regret* their life. They didn't live the way they wanted; they're rich nobles denied their inheritance, princes who never got to be kings, bitter artists whose work was never seen. Women married to the wrong man while loving another. It takes a lot of regret to regret your entire *life*."

A soft rain begins to patter around us. I pull Miles up beside me. It seems like the place he's always been.

"My dad also told me that those who lived and loved—like us—those who surrendered to the light and the darkness of this world, would never be caught on Weymouth's shores. It's not a place for the world's dead. It's a place for the *waiting dead*, who passed away in the decades between Storms. Somehow, those dead get caught in our gate."

I give his hand a squeeze. "Did your mother regret her life? Or did she have a life full of love that saw loss, like all of us?"

I see tears gathering over his long bottom lashes. "She loved me even as she was losing everything—right up until her very last breath. I know because I was there for it, holding her hand, wishing I was anywhere else in the world, but needing to be there with her." I think about my father's death, surrounded by blood and screams. I would have done anything for him to have a quiet, loving death, for a chance to say goodbye.

"Your mother's not under there, Miles. She's moved on to wherever the rest of the dead go—somewhere good, I imagine."

He nods. "Where autumn never ends and fries are always crisp, and you can swim in public fountains."

"Just like that."

"Okay." He nods again. "Okay."

We resume walking toward the house.

"You know, for a second when we were under the water, I thought I heard her calling me. She wanted me to stay. I thought about it, but only because it would mean that I got to see her again," Miles says.

I don't tell him that I almost *did* stay. What does that say about me?

He pivots. "So, what did Eryk mean back there, when he said to ask you about your sister?"

I bite my lip as my sneakers crunch over the gravel trail. Suddenly there is salty blood on my tongue.

He lowers his voice. "I'm safe to talk to, Mabel. Please." I want to tell him that I know he is, except, how do I begin to explain *Hali*? How can I explain her anger, the way her disappointment hangs around my neck like a chain? Her deep obsession with my time, my whereabouts. The way that she can't walk off the porch without hyperventilating?

"It's called agoraphobia," I say softly. "She can't leave the house or else she feels unsafe, panicky." Sort of how I felt at the Popes'. "It happened after we lost our dad in the Storm. What happened to us that day was too much for her; it broke her mind. Nothing felt safe anymore, so she had to hold on to whatever was left of him—and that was the house, my mom, Jeff, and me. I'm her best friend, her sister . . . her everything." I swallow the lump in my throat. "But it's suffocating to be a person's everything. It's too much."

"And how does she feel about me?"

"Oh, she hates you. *So* much."

He bursts out laughing. "I guess that's fair. Why is that?"

"Because your arrival on Weymouth has shaken up everything. You're a threat to everything she has built up to keep her sanity; she fears you will tear down her forever fortress."

What I'm about to say feels like a betrayal, but Miles feels safe to me. I take a deep breath. "I love my sister, but I want so much from this world, whereas she maybe wasn't meant for this world." *I want you*, I think.

The last house to the sea appears on the hill, the Lethe Bridge rising up behind it like a modern behemoth grown from wildflowers. I see a speck of red hair on the porch, peering out at us from behind the metal shutters.

"She's waiting," I say.

"Let me say hello," he says.

No. *No.* She'll eat him alive. I know it. I can see it now, the cruel smirk of her mouth, the insults, but I think I'm out of options. We walk up the porch, Miles following me as I carefully thread through our traps.

When he approaches, Hali rises from her wicker chair and slinks over to him. "So I guess this is the famous Miles I've heard so much about. Seems our Mabel is smitten by this new boy."

I sigh. "Miles, this is Hali. She's determined to embarrass me in the way only a little sister can."

"Hi." He says it awkwardly, suddenly fascinated by our floor. A blush spreads up his cheeks. He's nervous. It's adorable. He then notices the keyholes under his feet. A second later, he's looking at all the traps around him.

"This is some porch!" he says with awe.

"It should be. We spend every freaking moment out here," Hali snaps, carefully looking over Miles like he's a specimen—taking in his black hair, his handsome face.

"It's like you've never seen a human man before," I snap at her. "Don't be weird!"

Hali looks at me with annoyance but softens when she sees how much is riding on this interaction.

"Nice sneakers," she says finally—forcefully—for my benefit.

"His sneakers?"

Miles turns around, looking amused at our interaction. "Thanks. I got them at Lantern House in the city. Limited edition."

"Yawn. Tell me the real dirt. How was the Pope house?" Hali asks.

"I definitely do not want to talk about the Pope house," I retort.

"And why not?" Miles replies. "It's such a charming place, what with all their barbed wire and weapons just casually stacked by the fire, a gun leaning against the television. A fairy tale, really."

Hali collapses back into the wicker chair. She's bored of Miles already. "I mean, we can't all live at the Gillis house, made of cookies, wishes, and bluebirds. Though, this place has a Gothic charm to it, as you'll soon see. If Mabel lets you inside."

"I'll take him straight to your bedroom," I volunteer.

Miles arches an eyebrow and spins around. "I'm sorry, take who to what bedroom? Your bedroom?" He doesn't even try to hide his delight. "Yes, please."

"Ew, gross." Hali rolls her eyes. "Could you be more obsessed with my sister?"

"No one is obsessed." I'm going to kill her later, for real.

"I would say I'm a *little* obsessed." Miles is fiddling with a latch on the porch.

"Don't touch that!" Hali and I say at the exact same time.

He spins around, his face terrified.

The screen porch door squeaks open. "A good rule of thumb on Weymouth is that if it's attached to a wall, a floor, or the ceiling, walk away. It's probably a trap." Jeff walks out onto the porch with a welcoming smile. *Thank God, someone normal is here.*

"Hey, Miles, I'm the Guardian of House Beuvry. My name is Jeff. We met the other day under the worst circumstances. Hopefully, this time will be a bit better." He reaches out to shake Miles's hand.

Miles gives a strong shake back. "Nice to meet you again. Nice to meet . . . everyone."

Hali sighs loudly; he's not giving her the attention she wants.

She thought she could intimidate him, but that's not happening. She turns to Jeff. "Don't you have anywhere better to be? I was about to interrogate him."

"Do NOT interrogate him," I snap back at her.

"No one is interrogating anyone." Jeff laughs. "So, Miles, two questions: What is your social security number, and what was your most recent romantic relationship like?"

OH. My. God. I throw my hands up in the air. "Are you kidding me?"

Miles just laughs. "The answer is, I don't know and utterly forgettable."

Hali actually laughs. "Okay, maybe I like him a little bit."

"I like him too." I nervously tuck my hair behind my ear as Jeff watches me with a neutral smile. It makes sense—he's never seen me like a boy before, mostly because there were no boys around to like.

"So, Miles, how about you let me pick your brain about Seattle culture for ten minutes and then I will release you, much to Mabel's delight? I made a blackberry-poppy loaf this morning that needs someone to eat it." He gives Hali and me a pointed look.

"I'll definitely eat that!" Miles says, way too excited about a loaf. "Thank you, sir."

"Sir? Please, it's Jeff," my House Guardian responds. "Let me give you a house tour. We'll take our food to go." Hali and I look at each other and suppress a laugh. A house tour from Jeff is going to take *forever*.

As they head inside, I reach out and give Miles's hands a squeeze. "Have fun," I whisper. "See you in about two hours."

"Two hours?" he hisses, but then Jeff is leading him away.

"This foyer was originally built in 1863, but the Storm the following year took out the banister bases here, so we needed to find replacement wood, which meant going onto the mainland. . . ." Then Miles is gone, swallowed inside House Beuvry and its ancient history. I don't feel the need to follow them. Somehow, I know he and Jeff will get along very well.

Instead I'm in my happy place, warmed on the porch and surrounded by all the people I love. The tightness in my chest from earlier dissipates. It's all going to be okay. I can forget Eryk and his words, the anger on his face. He's grieving; I know personally that it can make you do strange things.

I slide up next to Hali and lay my chin on her shoulder. "So . . . ?"

She leans her head against mine. "He's okay. But you—you're the bee's knees."

"I love you." I say it to her plainly.

She stares off into the distance, her mind somewhere else. "I know it."

Thorpe McLeod, December 1926

Dearest Bess,
According to those blasted Grimes weather-
contraptions, indications are strong that the
Storm shall come again in a few days—perhaps
tomorrow—though I fear the wild inventions of
the Grimes family aren't near as accurate as they
hope them to be. If the Storm does arrive on our
shore, I should not be able to pen you again, and
I feel compelled to tell you all the love in my heart,
pushed by the fear that it shall beat no more. I
know that families aren't supposed to aid one
another during the Storm, but I tell you now—I
will die for you, a thousand times over.

Despite all the joys of life and family, I have
known none like the willingness to lie down beside
you and behold the touch of my hand to your
cheek, the breath of your mouth mingled with my
own. You are a triumph of womanhood. Your hair
is the sunlight on the sea, eyes deep like the oak
trees on the ridge, your skin the palest horizon.

Oh, my beloved, if the dead can march from the
sea to the bridge, then I imagine nothing can
separate us. As for me, I will always be near you,
hovering just below your heart, hidden in the
places only we know. I shall be the breeze that
brushes your cheek as the morning mist rushes off
the Soft Sea. The flame your fingers dally over.
The sigh on your lips. Do not mourn me, my lover,
for I shall always be near you.

However, if the Storm arrives and you do see me
later in my skeletal, garish flesh, do not hesitate to
shove an iron rod through my rib cage.

Your beloved for eternity,
Thorpe

Historical note from Reade McLeod: Bess Mintus and Thorpe
McLeod were actually married to other people, thus causing a
large scandal when this was discovered years later. As a result,
the McLeod and the Mintus families have carried a grumbling
animosity between their houses for almost eighty years. Some
houses are meant to be kept at a distance, but some are meant to
be the opposite: existing hand in hand for their time on this island.

CHAPTER TWENTY-FIVE

A few days pass, and just when it seems I'm going to escape the lecture, Ser Jeff tricks me into going out into the garden with him and then proceeds to trap me in between the sea-pea and our overgrown pin-cherry trees. I'm stuck there, a hoe in one hand, garden gloves wrist-deep in dirt, when he pulls off his sun hat and gives me "the look." I know immediately where this is going.

"What?" I ask innocently, trying very hard to focus on pulling tiny, shriveled buds off a curling vine.

"Mabel, don't give me that nonsense. *You know exactly what.* I heard from Katherine about your little stunt at the dock. It's all the island can talk about right now, and the last thing you—we—need is scrutiny. I'm trying to keep our eyes on the horizon, make our house ready—and then I hear my charge has thrown herself into the ocean to rescue the Cabot boy." His voice steadily rises several octaves, and if I don't stop him, he will keep going up and up, so I cut him off with a wave of my hand, standing to face his ambush head-on.

"I know you like Miles, and I like him too. He loved the house tour."

"I'm sure he did. Mabel, you have to be *careful*. You can't attract too much attention."

"Those animals took him from his bed and threw him into the sea. What else was I supposed to do—let him die?"

"Miles can swim on his own, I presume?"

"Not very well! In fact, I'm going to give him lessons."

Jeff throws down his trowel. "Stop trying to change the subject. Katherine told me that Van told her that you both were only feet away from the Bone Barrier. Is that true?"

I shrug, trying to make it seem like it's not a big deal. I only saw thousands of dead bodies twisting under a veil in the ocean. It's fine.

"Mabel . . . is . . . it . . . true?"

I keep my eyes on the pin cherries, their spiny branches almost drooping to the ground. It's odd, them being so low so early in the season. I pick one off the ground, crushing the berry until red juice drips down my fingers. I don't want to answer him, because I don't want to believe it myself. What I saw under the ocean makes the Storm even more terrifying. I always knew they were under there, but I don't think I ever realized just how close they were to our island: a heartbeat, a breath away. How can I explain that seeing them made me understand that our security—our entire lives—is always at risk? We are happily living over a pit of monsters.

"Yes. We were close to the barrier. I saw *them*." I don't share with Jeff that their faces have wormed their way into my dreams. I don't tell him how if I close my eyes, I can still hear their voices begging me to stay. I don't tell him *I almost did*.

"My God, Mabel." He shakes his head angrily. "That ritual

COLLEEN OAKES

has gone too far. Miles could have died—you could have died! Was Eryk Pope the instigator?"

I reach out with my hand and rest it on his freckled forearm. "Yes, but don't do anything to Eryk. He sucks, yes, but the Popes have been through enough. Tattling on them will make Miles's life worse. The boys on this island are *finally* starting to accept him."

Jeff scoffs. "Those boys need better hobbies."

"If it makes it better, I did shove Eryk into the ocean."

A smug grin transforms Jeff's face. "It does, actually. I've wanted to shove Eryk Pope many times." He drives his rake into the ground. "That boy came out angry; I know Will Lynwood loved him but didn't always like him. Not every Guardian has been as lucky as I have."

"Hali and I don't give you too hard a time?" I ask, the sun bright on my face.

"Ask me when I've forgotten the image of you leaping into the Dehset. Mabel, people have *drowned* trying to see the barrier." He sighs. "Is it worth giving you a lecture about this? Are you going to do it again?"

"Not unless someone throws Miles into the ocean again."

"Next time let him drown. Letting another family die is Weymouth tradition."

I inhale sharply at his dark humor. "Jesus, Jeff." This is something whispered about Weymouth, the dark history of the Storms and families. Before the Storm comes, we are a community, always willing to help out. But when the Storm comes? It's every family on their own, probably because we're all up to our necks by that point. I should know, because it happened to us. Jeff leans on the shovel like an American farmer and points to the pin-cherry tree.

262

"That was your and Hali's favorite chore when you were little." His face is shaded by his sun hat, but I see his mouth twist in confusing grief. "You girls loved picking pin cherries for your mother. Your dad loved her jalapeño pin-cherry jam—her mother's recipe. I would always see a jar of it sitting on the counter on my way out the door." I have a quick memory of my father, his strong figure silhouetted in the kitchen windows, a steaming cup of coffee in one hand and a piece of bread in the other, taking in the morning before shoring up the house.

"I remember," I say softly.

"Do you remember that he was slightly allergic to the cherries?"

I look up. "What?"

"Your father had a cherry allergy. Every time he ate the jam, he would get a rash around his mouth—little hives, almost."

I scoff. "Then why did he keep eating it?"

"Because your mother loved making it for him. Because it connected him back to his family on the mainland, the ones he couldn't see anymore. The pin-cherry tree was the one piece of home she could give him here on Weymouth, and so she made it for him, over and over. He loved her greatly, many times to his own detriment."

"Is that why he never said anything about her drinking?" I say softly.

"It wasn't to the point of anything . . . yet," Jeff says. "That came after the Storm. After the deaths." He picks up the shovel again and this time brings the head hard into the earth, uprooting a thistle just minding its own business.

"Have you ever heard of something called the Great Storm?"

263

Jeff pauses. "Why would you ask that?" He's trying to keep his voice light, but I can tell immediately that he's hiding something.

"I'm looking into it. Will Lynwood believed it meant something. Maybe that it was coming?"

Jeff thinks for a long moment. "The Great Storm is a myth, a conspiracy theory held by some of the Guardians. You know how the Storm seems to adapt to our defenses? The theory is that when certain houses are in alignment with each other, the Storm reacts with greater force to help break down the community. It's never actually been proven—mostly because when those Storm years happen, there's not many people left to study it."

I let the shock wash over me. The idea that the interpersonal relationships on the island can affect what happens under the sea is staggering. Then I remember the hands reaching out for Miles and me under the water, the fingers enclosed in white fabric, pushing with all their might. . . . The way my hand in his hand and my lips on his lips feel like it's a passion five hundred years in the making. The undeniable passion I felt for him within minutes of meeting him, like I was always waiting for him. Like we're a Great Storm waiting to happen.

Jeff is still talking, even though I'm a million miles away. "It's just a silly old theory, made up by the McLeod and Mintus families to justify their affair. I don't want you to be afraid of the next Storm. I'm going to get your mother the support she needs so that she can be an asset to us when it comes."

I'm about to ask him what exactly we need help with (though, do I really want to know?) when we hear a yell from the house. We turn to see my mother leaning out the window, waving an actual handkerchief at us.

"Mabel!" she screams. "THERE IS A PHONE CALL FOR YOU! IT'S THE CABOT BOY! HE SAYS HE NEEDS YOUR HELP WITH SOMETHING."

Jeff raises a single eyebrow at me. "At least he's not in the ocean this time."

"Maybe he's lost in his bed and needs help." God, wouldn't that be something?

Jeff's playfulness drops away. "Don't even joke about that, Mabel. Go on, then."

Hali is on the porch when I come in, a knitted cream blanket splayed out over her lap. *The Lion, the Witch and the Wardrobe,* dog-eared to death, is open on her knees.

"Why didn't you help us in the garden?" I ask on my way in, sweat in a neat line across my brow.

"I didn't want to help," she answers, her sharp green eyes meeting mine, her coolness blasting through me as she flips a page. "Besides, it seemed like you and Jeff were having a nice little chat. Someone had to stay with Mother and make sure she didn't fall down the stairs." I crouch down, looking at my sister's face. She's like an abstract painting, all colors but nothing concrete.

"It's not your job to take care of her."

"Then how about you stay and do it." Her voice crumbles a little. "If you would just stay, then everything would all be okay. Why do you *always* have to ruin our perfect thing? You promised you would never leave me, remember?"

I feel a headache beginning. "Don't pull this card," I order.

"What card?" she asks, snappily turning a page in the book.

"The sibling abandonment card. Is taking a phone call really abandonment?" My voice is annoyed as I straighten up. On the illustrated page, Lucy watches as the mice chew the ropes tying Aslan to the stone tablet. "I made that promise to you when we were children, in the middle of a goddammed Storm, so I don't think you can hold me to it every minute of the day."

I try to lighten the mood by swinging her hand back and forth. "Hey, we'll watch a show later or something. Maybe I'll steal you a book from the Cabot house." A new book on the island is like gold, but today, instead of expressing gratitude, my sister grips my hand hard, her nails digging into my palm.

"Can't you feel it coming? Everything's going to change. You shouldn't be with Miles—you know that. You need to be *here*. *With me*."

Her pinkie nail gouges into my skin, causing a flare of anger. "The only thing I feel is you, an anchor around my neck."

She lets my hand fall to the side. I know I've hurt her—but there is no winning here. Then my little sister, who always has something to say, says . . . nothing.

"I'm sorry, Hali. I didn't mean that." My sister won't look at me, so I stomp across the porch. I head into the kitchen, where my mom watches me with concern before handing me the phone.

"For you. He's been waiting awhile," she says loud enough for him to hear. I give her a look.

"Hey," I say, while thinking, *Should I never talk to you again?*

"Hi!" Miles's voice is warm, and I perk up a bit. This is all so silly. "Did this call find you on the mainland? I'm only asking because I've been chatting with your mom for about five minutes. The great news is that we're best friends now and planning a vacation together. Cancun, in the spring. You can come if you can pay your own way."

I laugh. "Sorry, I was outside with Jeff and Hali." I don't tell him about our conversation because the last thing I want is for Miles to walk away from me. "So, what is the illustrious Miles Cabot up to today?" I ask.

"Not to alarm you, but I am bleeding."

My heart seizes. "I'm sorry, WHAT?"

"Well, this morning my cousins decided to teach me how to use my iron whip—you know, the one you pulled off the bottom of the ocean." *Ah.* No wonder he's bleeding.

"Don't listen to those idiots. The iron whip takes years of training with *a Guardian* to master. My father almost sliced his ear off, and he had a gnarly scar on his cheek and shin. You're probably going to lose a fair amount of skin to that weapon." In the background, one of Miles's cousins is yelling at him, Liam probably.

"Yeah, let's just say it was not great. More training may be required."

I pause, hiding the truth under a laugh. "I know a bit, even though girls aren't supposed to touch them, which is so anti- quated and sexist, I can't even begin to understand it." I cradle the phone under my chin and reach for my sneakers underneath the kitchen stools. "Listen to me. Stop what you're doing right now. Put the whip down and walk away until I can get to where you are. Shall I head over to the Cabot house?"

"LIAM, I SAID SHUT UP! Jesus, sorry. No, let's not go there." Suddenly he sounds nervous. "My uncle said there's a beautiful place—the Soft Shore Northern Overlook. How about we make a deal? I'll refrain from using the iron whip until I'm with you, and you agree to ride your bike at a normal speed."

I tilt my head. The Soft Shore Northern Overlook is by the graveyard, an interesting choice, but it's pretty there, a good place to learn about a dangerous weapon. I glance out the front windows; the sky looks fairly clear, though a slight green sheen hangs over the puffy clouds.

"It may rain later, but we can probably squeeze out a few hours," I say, wriggling my toes into the sneakers. "Do you know how to get there?"

"Alistair drew me a map. And, Mabel?"

"Yeah?" I am frantically pulling my fingers through my tangles, half listening as my heart beats faster at the idea of seeing him so soon.

His voice softens. "I love that everything on this island is ten minutes away, but especially you. It feels like I can't go long without you, like you're the only air I want to breathe." And just like that he's gone, upending my day in a second with his words.

My mom peeks her head around the corner of the kitchen cabinets, glassy-eyed and wearing a maroon bathrobe. "You like that Cabot boy." She smiles sadly. "I'm happy for you, Mabel. You deserve something real. It's been a long time since I've seen you so free." She touches my cheek with her paper-thin skin, tracing the planes of my face. "So . . . when do I get to formally meet this Miles? A dinner maybe? With Alistair?" She gives a harsh laugh at the idea. "As if I would let that bastard sit at our table after he left us to die." The warmth between us dissipates.

As I gently take her hand off my face, it gives an involuntary jerk underneath my fingers. I cradle her hand in mine as it gives another twitch.

"Mom." I frown. "Why is your hand shaking?"

She pulls it away from me and clutches it to her chest. "It's nothing, Mabel. It's nothing."

"Isla." Jeff's voice is firm, coming through the doorway, where he stands, knees covered with mud. His tone says, *No more*. They stare at each other for a long moment, and I take a step backward. I can't be here for this—whatever this intense conversation is going to become. I shouldn't have to deal with this, too, not right now. I have enough to think about, like does our attraction put the entire island in danger?

"Mabel, wait!" she calls as I run out the door, but I don't look back.

CHAPTER TWENTY-SIX

Ten minutes later, I aim my mountain bike up the trail toward the Soft Shore Northern Overlook. I press hard on the pedals, plowing my way up the hill to the overlook, my thighs burning with the incline.

Above me, voluminous white clouds circle in the sky as the wind nips at my ankles. I hear the Soft Sea rocking against the sand to my left, and to my right, pine needles and budding oak leaves rustle in the wind. I close my eyes for a minute and breathe in my island, feel its purpose rising through me. I speak to her. *I am here.* I wait for her to answer back and nothing comes, but instead I hear a "Mabel!" on the wind. My pulse speeds up. We're alone, and I feel like it's only a matter of minutes before his mouth is on mine.

Miles is waiting for me where the trail divides, far before the path to the overlook even begins. He grins nervously, and I give him one back as I bring my bike to a skidding stop.

"See. I *do* know how to stop a bike like a normal person. How did you get here so fast?" I should have beaten him by ten minutes.

"Don't judge me. I drove." He gestures with his head to the

road behind the graveyard, and I see Gale, glorious Gale, poking her nose out from behind the trees.

"I judge you," I say, hoping maybe I can drive her again, but when he doesn't return my smile, I immediately get a small twitch of panic; he's being weird. I sense it in the air. I dismount, and when I get to him, he kisses me so softly and carefully that I instinctively know something bad is coming.

"What is it?"

He doesn't answer as I look down at his side. My spine tightens as the hairs on the backs of my arms stand up.

"Where's your iron whip? Miles?" Black pupils like ink stare back at me. "Hey, what's going on?" I nervously step back from him, my heart pounding in my chest. There's no one out here; we're essentially in the middle of nowhere. Around us the pine trees lash and blow; something feels *wrong* in the air. Or maybe it's the way he's staring at me, like he's about to break my heart.

Or kill me.

"I lied to get you here. I'm sorry. But I have to ask—do you trust me?"

"Not right now I don't," I snap back. "Because you're acting different. It's pretty rich to ask if someone trusts you right after lying to them."

He reaches for my hand, and I reluctantly give it to him. He traces his fingers around mine, and a quick relief passes through me. *I know him.* He's acting strange, but I know him. I know he wouldn't hurt me.

No, this . . . is something else.

"Here—take my keys." He pushes cold metal into my hands. "I want you to know that I'm not going to leave you here. Just follow me, Mabel, okay? And hold your questions for a few minutes." My hands tighten around the keys as he begins pulling me toward the tree line, but I have a clear idea where he's going, and I jerk backward.

"*No, thank you,*" I whisper, but Miles continues to pull me through the trees, until a clearing opens up in front of us. I see the starkness of stone through tree branches, see the foliage thinning out. There is the slightest pulse at the top of my head, like a crack beginning to break through stone.

"Miles, no." He keeps pulling me, his touch nothing less than gentle but more abrasive than he could possibly understand. We're almost to Sentry's Sleep now, and the forest floor beneath our feet gives way to a path into the graveyard. Blood pulses in my ears, and everything seems to tilt on its axis. I attempt a pathetic, half-hearted laugh.

"Miles, this isn't the overlook. I've already shown you this, remember? After the party?" I point down the hill, where I can see my house through the trees. "There's a hiking trail that way. We can cut over from here and still get to the overlook if we take the upper road."

"I know why you don't want to be here, Mabel." Miles's voice is emotionless as he gently pulls me through the two single lampposts that mark the boundary of the graveyard. He continues. "I came out here the other night, after our ocean dive. I haven't been sleeping very well, and I was wired beyond belief, so I snuck back out the kitchen window—which really needs to be fortified; I should tell Alistair. Anyway, I ended up back here, thinking about you—and about us." He pauses and quickly closes the distance between us, cradling me in his long arm and tipping my face to his. "That day when I saw what lies under the waves, I was shook. I keep telling myself that Weymouth isn't my fate, that it isn't what my mother would want for me. I was lying so desperately to myself, because if I'm not cool Miles, always trying to escape, then who am I? If I'm not looking for the door, then I may have to face my own grief. And that's fucking rough. I'm sure you know something about that."

Miles reaches out and crawls his hands up my sleeves, his fingers tracing up my elbows. "That night, I saw the light in your bedroom turn on. I knew you were there, in that light, breathing, dreaming, waking. And I realized that even though you are terrifying, I needed to know what Mabel Beuvry dreams about." He pulls me closer to him. "I don't think I have the willpower to be away from you. The next thing I knew, I found myself here." Miles trips toward the marble Cabot mausoleum, feet tangling in the underbrush. I follow him, heart pounding in my ears. He stops when he gets to the veined black-and-white marble wall, where the names of the Cabot dead are carved. "Here I was, having my own existential crisis, but then . . . I saw this."

I look up, and a breath of relief washes through me. *This is what he wants to show me.* Words carved deep into the veined marble:

GRACE CABOT
BELOVED SISTER AND DAUGHTER
TREASURED MOTHER

"Somehow Alistair knew what my mom meant to me. Her body was cremated in Seattle, but he still had this stone placed here. And knowing what I do about Weymouth now and how isolated it is, I know this must have taken a lot of work." His fingers rest lightly on a fresh ring of heather just underneath his mother's name.

"That's when the island spoke to me. I realized why I'm here. This place needs fresh blood to move forward into the future. I can be that. *You* can be that. I have this crazy sense that you and I are fated to change this place for the better, that we're linked. But the strangest thing is that even without whatever island magic is pulling me toward you, you are already everything I could want. Your hair, your lips, even your secrets. I know you feel it too."

He cradles my face in his long hands and kisses the side of my mouth. I should tell him about the Great Storm, about how our aligning might mean bad things for the island, but instead my skin warms at his touch. He's so close, he's what I want, and yet why do I feel like the floor is about to drop out from under me?

"I know you're worried that if you let me in—let us be—that I'll open the doors you've shut and locked inside you. I know that feeling, Mabel. All this time on the island, I thought I was being dragged back to a past that my mother wanted to leave behind; but I was wrong. I'm returning to the place her heart longed for. I'm closing the story." He leans forward like he's bracing himself against the coming wind. "We all have to close our stories, so that we can start a new chapter. You and me, together, the first and last house. We're the beginning and the end." His eyes grow serious. "And we can't do that unless there aren't any more secrets between us."

I begin backing away from the mausoleum as terror ricochets through me. Miles follows me, a slow but purposeful pursuit. *I have to get out of here.*

"Mabel, do you remember the other night, when I dropped you off at your house and was inexcusably rude?"

"Of course. You were kind of an asshole."

"Guilty as charged. But when I drove away from your house, I didn't know what to do. I was falling for someone I knew I shouldn't, someone my uncle had warned me about. I panicked. And after I acted that way, I thought that maybe I had pushed you away." His smile does nothing to quell the panic inside. "That is, until you showed up on the dock with your white cape, screaming at Eryk Pope like there was no tomorrow." He pauses. "I hope eventually you can forgive me for that night."

"I have already, obviously," I reply cautiously.

"I didn't know how to react when you talked about your sister."

Something sharp snaps inside my chest. "She has a mental illness, not a contagious disease. She shouldn't scare you; she's a part of my life. She's a normal girl, Miles."

He takes a deep breath. "Remember when you first took me to Sentry's Sleep, the night of the Nickersons' party?" He chuckles. "That night, I couldn't stop watching as you ghosted around the party, hoping to blend in even though you could *never* blend in, and then you took me here. You told me that the Cabots have their gaudy mausoleums, that the Des Rocheses prefer monoliths, and that the Beuvrys like gently sloped headstones covered with marble thistles."

My headache has grown; it's now cracking down my forehead, tearing at the seams of my temples. The world spins, and the voice in my head starts screaming.

"Mabel . . ." He's trying to be so careful, approaching this with his soft voice and gentle persuasion. It makes me want to hurt him, makes me feral. He continues speaking even though the ground beneath my feet is giving way, and the world bends in the broad, unflattering light of day. "That day, in the car . . . I turned away because I didn't know how to deal with my emotions for someone I couldn't understand. But now I know. . . ." He lays both of his hands against my cheeks, and for a minute, it all stops spinning.

There is only us, right in a way only we understand.

"There is nothing that can keep me from wanting you. Even in your most guarded places, I want you."

What places? His forehead presses against mine, and our lips find each other, and for a moment, in his embrace, I can breathe, and the world rights itself. I'm held and safe—and in return, I hold him too. We anchor each other to the island. There is something about Miles that releases the darkness inside me, the place that keeps secrets. He's a balm, a healer. We're both broken, but when I'm with him, I feel like I can step into the light. I'm not alone.

"But because you mean so much to me, I can't leave you there. It's why I gave you the keys, so you know I'm not leaving." He steps back, giving me space. Nausea rises in my throat. "Look down."

I will my body not to listen to him. I won't. I can't. My stomach churns, and I feel a cold stab of dread moving through my chest, tightening. I turn my head, willing my nausea away, holding on to the thing that's kept me sane all this time. If I look down, I'll be alone once more. The panic rises.

"I'm here. I won't leave you." Moving so gently, Miles takes a nervous breath and tilts my head down. His hands are on my chin as my world comes apart.

We're standing right above the Beuvry family plot. I see my father's grave, and my heart twists painfully, but my eyes keep moving past his grave, until they come to rest on a beautiful white stone, sloped so that it faces outward, away from us. It faces the sea, because she loved it so.

HALIFAX AMELIA BEUVRY
STORM OF OUR YEAR 2012
DAUGHTER, SISTER, FRIEND
LOVED FOREVER AND EVER

Oh, that's right, I think. *Hali's dead.*

CHAPTER TWENTY-SEVEN

I am blown completely apart, like dry leaves spinning in the wind. My head peels open; I can't breathe—my lungs aren't pulling in the air they need. And then I'm yanking away from Miles, legs moving with the only command I can muster: *Go.* I sprint out of the graveyard and tear down the path, branches whipping at my arms as I make my way toward Gale.

"Mabel, WAIT! Shit!" he yells, but he's too late. The car is already unlocked, and I throw it into reverse while the door is still open, taking out several small trees as I go. I spin the wheel, and the car revs around until I'm facing the trail that leads out of the woods. I have to get out of here—not just here, out of Weymouth.

A wailing wind pushes past the open window, deafening until I realize that the wailing is, in fact, me. Miles screams my name from somewhere behind me; I glance at him in the rearview mirror, but a second later I've left him behind. I need to keep moving. I can't *stop* moving, because I know if I do, I'll have to think about the name on the tombstone. *The name on the tombstone.* A new howl erupts from my throat, one primed to tear the world apart as the car bursts out of the trees onto the main road. *I can't, I won't, I refuse.* I leave my body behind.

Weymouth Island flies past me in a gray-green blur as the island narrows. Suddenly the island around me seems so small; I can drive from one side to the other in minutes. I fly past my house on the right, but I don't dare take my eyes off the road. I can't think about where I am going, or why.

Up ahead of me, the Lethe Bridge appears out of the ever-thickening mist. From the outside, the Lethe looks like a normal steel and wire bridge, but that's all part of its deception. Everything—even down to the anchors and the fibers of the deck—is infused with iron, paper, and salt. It holds surprises inside its modern design.

Oh, that's right, Hali's dead. Gale flies over the bridge, water from my tires sluicing down into the river below. Fog surrounds me, the cloaking of our island in full effect as I pass through. It's a lot easier to get out of Weymouth than it is to get in.

Once the car clears the bridge, the fog swirling around it dissipates in a second, and when I look back in the rearview mirror, all I can see is a line of thick trees where the bridge once stood. Weymouth cloaks itself against curious eyes, and I watch as the place that holds all my love, pain, and grief vanishes into thin air.

Now it is just me, left out here in the wild real. Truly alone. And my sister is dead.

Gale hugs the narrow roads as I propel her along the two-lane highway that leads to Glace Bay. My hands clutch the wheel nervously. I see no other cars on the road on my way. We're pretty isolated out here to begin with. It's much chillier here than it is on Weymouth, a sharp reminder that our island is essentially contained in some magic pocket of weather. I fumble through turning up the heat as I think, *Hali is dead Hali is dead Hali is dead.*

"Stop!" I whisper out loud, pushing back the gathering black clouds in my brain. As the car climbs out of the valley, I wonder if my madness and depression have a rock bottom that I can perhaps rest upon? *Where does the trench of my grief end? I will drive forever to avoid it.*

I glance at the rearview mirror as I merge onto Byway 112, and I catch a glimpse of myself. Dear God, I am *harsh* in afternoon light—all freckles against pale skin. My nose and cheeks are blotched from crying, and rings of dark plum circle around my bloodshot eyes. My hair is coiled like a snake on the side of my neck, and my lips are cracked at the corners. I try to wipe underneath my eyes to look less insane, and it's like trying to fix a totaled car with a Band-Aid. When I look back to the road, I scream and slam on the bakes. There is a pale deer standing in the dead center of the road, right in front of Miles's car. Smoke rises from underneath my tires, and the car veers sideways . . . but it stops. In a haze of burning rubber, she stops, and I'm left staring at the deer, now just feet away from the bumper.

The deer blinks its enormous eyelashes twice, staring back at me, before delicately vaulting away from the car and into the woods that lead back to Weymouth. Everything is silent as the smoke from the tires dissipates. There's no one else out here.

It's the quiet that breaks me. A cry escapes my mouth as I lean my head against the steering wheel and sob. She's gone. She's been gone. My Hali. One of the last times I crossed this bridge, she was still alive. There was a carnival in Glace Bay. I remember the lights of a Ferris wheel reflected in my sister's bright green eyes and the smear of nutty sugar on her cheek. Each time we crossed the bridge, it was excoriatingly exciting and predictably disappointing. I turn off Gale, laying my shaking hands against the dashboard. *Hali is dead.* Outside it has started to rain, and the hypnotic sound pulls me back inside myself.

"I can't do this," I say out loud. I mean, what the honest hell am I doing here? *What am I doing here?* I need to go home and straighten things out with Hali. She'll forgive me this little abandonment. It will all be okay. And Miles . . . well, Miles can . . . help.

I've been helped with this before—many times. My memory churns, pulling up the last time that Jeff and my mom tried to show me the truth.

I was talking to Hali on the porch, her long arms curled around her legs, a messy nest of red-gold hair resting against her knees.

"She's not there," Jeff says, carefully stepping out of the house. "Remember what that doctor online said?" I roll my eyes, but he continues. "When you see Hali, when you interact with her, what you are dealing with is a projection of your grief. It's called a bereavement hallucination. They are one of the rare forms of hallucinations that keep the loved one as a source of stability and comfort. It keeps the grief at bay and allows the creator of the hallucination *time* to let that person go. However . . ."

My mom takes my hand, looking over at me. "My love, they can also be a source of considerable distress. Bereavement hallucinations often center on the person's presence—how they *felt*. You loved your sister. You are actively communicating with Hali, which puts this somewhere between a visual hallucination and pathological grief. Mabel, you're not okay."

"Don't listen to these dummies," Hali mutters, and she's right—I don't want to listen. I run to my room. I don't want to know she's gone. Halfway up, I sink to my knees and bury my face in my hands. When I look up, Hali is in front of me once again, sitting on the stairs. "It's all fine. Let's hang out. It's easier this way."

"I should listen to them."

Hali arches her eyebrow. "Why? It's not like they know what we need. There's only us. There is only *this*. *As long as I'm here*, you're not alone." With a sigh of surrender, I lean into her. I know my sister's body like I know my own, the way she always smells a little bit like citrus and sweat. Her feet are rough on her heels, her left incisor is twisted a little—all these details I have promised myself that I will keep safe forever.

I decide to stay. I decide to keep her.

Back in the car, I let out a moan against the steering wheel; it smells like plastic. The rain outside the car window has grown harder, and the shadow of droplets reflects over my skin.

I flash to another time, when Norah tried to tell me while we were sitting in her room. She tells me that my sister is actually dead, and the kids at school are whispering about how I talk to her, how I interact with her. My mind goes to the whispers at school, the way the other kids who aren't Norah and Sloane avoid me. The way Edmund always side-eyes me, how the Popes openly mock me.

I run home, to my mother. I force open her door.

"Mabel? What is it?" I make my way over to her bed, and when she sees my devastated face, her own collapses into a pile of grief. "Oh, my dear. *Oh no*. Someone told you."

"Hali?" It's the only word I can muster. Her hands reach out for me.

"Yes, Hali. Oh love . . . you just needed her so much. It's going to be okay, Mabel, it really is. We're going to get you help. Real help." The comfort of her motherly love evaporates as anger rises within me.

"You'll get me help? You?" My voice is choked with rage. "You can't even get out of bed, Mum! We're here and you're up there, waiting to die—like Dad." She flinches. "Dad would have fought for us, though; he wouldn't have given up! If it wasn't for Jeff, we would be all alone. You left us. Or, just me, I guess. You left *me*. For that!" I gesture to the bottles beside the bed. My mother looks hurt, but she doesn't deny what I'm saying.

I wish for Hali. I don't wish for Hali.

"Listen to me, Mabel. Losing a child, there is no way to explain what that does to a person. It's like your soul being ripped out of your body. I'm not myself anymore. I'm not *whole*. I can still feel her, you know, slipping out of my arms that night. I sense the weight of her body every day, and the only thing that makes it disappear is this."

I don't want to hear any more of this. I slide off her bed, and she desperately trails me to the door.

"I've been saying that we should tell you for months. Jeff and I both agree, but it's never the right time. We've told you before, many times, but you always come back around for her. You've erased the memories of her death because you loved your sister so much and can't bear it!"

When I walk away from her room, down the hallway, Hali is waiting for me at the bottom of the stairs. She reaches for my hand. "Come on. Let's go watch a movie." And then everything is fine once more.

. . .

I slam my hands against the steering wheel, again and again, wanting to hurt Miles, the boy who has brought up all this pain, like dredging the bottom of the sea. Every little, ugly thing I want to stay hidden is floating up to the surface. And here it comes, the memory of the night she died. It's shaded in two colors: a curdling blue-white—the color of terror—or a deep, beating red—the color of blood. First comes the blue-white terror pulsing through my little body as I watch Jeff's father, our Guardian, being dragged down a hallway. My mother carried Hali and me into my father's study, into his closet, struggling under our weight. Ribbons from our nightgowns whirled behind us as I clutched her neck so hard, I drew blood. Everything around us was howling, and it took up every space in the world. That's when *they* came up the stairs. I matched their howls, only mine were the terrified, open-mouthed screams of a little girl. I remember the pungent, metallic scent of fear pouring from my mother's body. I feel her arms protectively wrapped around us both, but we are . . . slowly . . . slipping . . . down into freezing salt water.

My mother clutches us tighter, screaming my father's name as I twist my right hand around her hair like around a rope. Hali never—ever—listens and she pulls away, trying to get to my father. If I close my eyes, I can still feel my mother's hand pressed so hard against me that I can hardly breathe. The other one flails desperately for Hali. The rest of the memories exist in curls of misty white that leap like campfire smoke. I hear my father's thundering voice as he stands like a monolith in front of the open door. I see him try to push Hali back toward us, his eyes wide like a hunted animal's. She won't listen; she stays with him. Seeing my father so afraid blows apart the few last remaining seconds of my childhood. Hali screams. My father rushes forward as the mist takes the shape of bodies. He holds his iron whip out in one hand and an axe in the other. They aren't enough.

The memory slices through me as it turns itself over and over again in my mind, like I'm caught in a tsunami. When I close my eyes, it's there. When I take a jagged breath in, it's there. They say grief is like a wave, and I'm churning in it. This is why I keep Hali in the house. The reality of her agoraphobia is this: I've created a valid medical and psychological excuse for why Hali *only* exists in my world, to protect both other people and myself. I've given her clear boundaries. It's a bit genius, actually. I choke back a soggy laugh. I think of all the times I've begged Hali to come with me, to no effect, how she gets angry. She's been angry a lot lately, because of Miles.

Miles, the biggest threat to Hali. My hands trace the wheel of the car that smells like him. I left him in the graveyard, just like I did before. I can't believe that he still wants to be with me, even though I have an imaginary sister.

The Hali I've constructed to hold back my grief knows that the arrival of Miles will force me to move forward. Miles makes me think about the future, rather than cling to the past, where she still exists. He makes me have to choose.

The car seems to shrink around me as the fortresses I've built for myself crumble and reality comes rushing in. It makes sense that I've kept her around—it's *easy* to see the dead again on Weymouth. I let out a moan when I realize that the very thing that killed my sister is the reason my mind thinks it can keep her *forever*.

The wind pushes the branches up against the car window. My hands are oddly tingly, like shots of electricity are running through the veins down to the tops of my fingers. I wipe away the hot tears streaming down my cheeks. It's getting harder to ignore the crackling of air over my skin and the headache that won't seem to stop. The joints in my knees and ankles ache, and there is a stabbing sensation creeping up my spine and into my jaw. Is this what it feels like, Hali leaving my body, my mind? Because the fact is, if I keep Hali alive in my mind, I will lose everything else.

I curl forward on the seat of the car, wrapping my arms around my chest. I tell myself that her bones are my bones, her ribs are my ribs. She's still here within me. I lean my head into my hands. My body feels like it may implode with all these revelations, but the thought quickly fades into the background as a loud humming sounds from inside my inner ear. The car around me becomes fuzzy and distant, as if I'm floating outside my body. Every hair on my body stands on end, as panic swells in my chest cavity. The rain pounds harder on the window, and suddenly it's all I can pay attention to, the pattern of the drops, one, two, three, like the chiming of a grandfather clock. Eleven drops, and then it starts over again.

Then it's like someone has kicked a chair out from under me and I am falling backward, flailing down through a darkness without end. My heart drops in my chest, my balance thrown off. The rain pounds harder on the window as my heart beats in time with each drop of rain: eleven, eleven, eleven. Oh God, not now. I know what this is now. *The dread.*

Every clock in Weymouth is pointed at eleven right now, regardless of the time, and every fiber of my being is standing alert, attuned to the weather outside. Every cell, muscle, and bone turns toward Weymouth.

The Storm is here.

From the diary of August Grimes,
July 5, 1945

2:45 p.m.
If we lose this war, there will be no hope of
avenging us. Wives, children, and husbands will
be drowned, ripped apart; our every exerted effort
will fall useless against the surge. Panic races up
the main road, a continuous stream of disbelief;
mouths with whispers of the fire to come. A great
storm rising. The rain has already decimated
us. The south end of Weymouth is a soaking
graveyard. I once heard my mother say that to live
on Weymouth is to be sentenced to death. This
island is akin to the mines of Stalingrad across the
sea. This is war.

4:29 p.m.
Our instruments were wrong. The Storm was
supposed to be a week from now. We are not
prepared. Our house is not ready. The Cabot and
Beuvry houses have brought this upon us; may
God have mercy on their souls.

6:22 p.m.

All separate houses have been abandoned to their fate.
No one knows what is happening; the calls on the
radio have gone silent. The siren blares; the sky is red.
Each regiment—I mean, family—is left to their fate.
Elizabeth hides our family in the Keep now, a place
known only to the Grimes family. One can never be
too trusting. Our supplies are strong—our salt barrels
full. The wind has begun to blow. Is it too late to leave
now? Does a strong man leave his family behind?

9:49 p.m.

The water is rising, and I hear a faint scratching
at the windows. My hands tremble as I hold my
iron whip—I have not practiced since I was a boy.
Does it make me less of a man to say I am afraid?

11:58 p.m.

I thank the gods for what they have given me
I thank the gods for what they will take from me

I thank the gods for what they will bring me
I thank the gods for what they will from me

Oh gods have mercy on my—

Historical note from Reade McLeod: August Grimes's body was
never found; he is believed to have been pulled out to sea. His
family survived the Storm in the infamous Grimes Keep, which
seemed impenetrable until the Storm of 1980, when several family
members were trapped inside and drowned.

CHAPTER TWENTY-EIGHT

The Storm. It can't be, and yet I can sense a palpable difference in my body, which is coiled like a trap ready to snap. My previous emotional hurricane has been reduced to a few driving thoughts: *I need to be over the bridge, need to be readying my house.* It's almost painful; every cell knows I'm not where I should be right at this second. The dread deepens as I stare outside; this light rain has a charge to it; the pressure is strong in my ears. With one hand, I roll down the window and reach out, letting the rain fall across my palm; it stings like salt in a wound.

Here I am, in the driver's seat of my crush's car having a nervous breakdown, and here it comes, to destroy everything we love. Hypnotizing sheets of water pour over the windshield as the wipers struggle to keep up. *This is it,* I think. *This is it. God help us.* I turn the key over, and Gale sputters back to life. Every nerve in my body is vibrating like a wire plucked by an invisible finger.

I'm about to turn out onto the two-lane highway that leads back to Weymouth when a car goes flying past me and slams into the side of a pickup truck. The pickup flips around, tires skimming across the water as it spins. Both cars come to a sudden rest in the intersection, horns blaring. *The chaos is starting.* Even normal humans who don't live on Weymouth *feel* the Storm. They can't put their finger on why they feel so strange, but their bodies react with repulsion, anxiety, and fear. Children act out. Dogs go feral. Adults can't sleep the night before. They make up reasons to cover their unease. They'll say Mercury is in retrograde or it's a full moon or the barometer is plummeting.

I glance down the road that would take me away from Weymouth. I imagine a place where not everyone knows my loss, a place where the dead stay dead. The wipers churn back and forth as I stare at the road, temptation twisting in my gut . . . but then I take a breath and hit Gale's right-hand turn signal.

A Beuvry stands against the Storm. My house needs me.

Instead of taking the main highway back, I stick to a smaller side road, pushing Gale as fast as I dare. We whip through the rain, the car clinging to narrow lanes of pine trees. My heart pounds harder as I near Weymouth; my body is trying to climb out of itself.

I'm getting there, I think. *Just hold on.* I flip on the radio. Static fills the air, but I clumsily fumble with the dial, finding my way to 91.12, Weymouth Island's own private station. It's normally white noise, indiscernible from static—so there's no reason for anyone to listen. But today when the dial hits those numbers, an eerie siren fills the car, followed by a chilling monotone voice.

Prepare your houses. Prepare your houses. Prepare your houses.

The voice repeats three times, and then the siren returns, the high-pitched noise building panic inside me. I push down on the accelerator. I wonder what my family is doing right now, and for a brief second I wonder about Hali before catching myself.

Also, oh my God, *I stole Miles's car.*

Up ahead, the road swerves sharply to the left, wrapping around a low foothill with a small river at the bottom, already foaming at its banks. Gale and I fly into the outlying forest and hills that hide our island.

Ten excruciating minutes pass before I spy the two markers for Weymouth appearing between the sweeps of the wipers. The markers are low wooden totems, barely four feet high; they are practically invisible to the naked eye since their wood blends in with the trees around them. They were placed here by the Mi'kmaq people, the original people of this land, long before any of the Triumvirate arrived. They knew that this island was more than just an island and marked it off with the poles to warn their people. They were the first to know it was a gate to something otherworldly—and since they were smarter than us, they left.

Driving *into* Weymouth is much harder than driving *out* of it because it involves driving straight into a line of trees and praying that you're not in the wrong place. I see the passage up ahead, shrouded with mist and looking a bit off-kilter. Something doesn't look quite right about the trees; it's nothing you would notice unless you were looking for it. As I near the trees, I aim the car at the center space between the totems and accelerate straight into a line of white pines. I take a deep breath as trunks rise up in front of me, the seat belt pressing against my chest as I brace for impact. *Sorry, Miles*, I think.

Either I'm right or I'm dead.

They're ten feet away, then five, and then the car is sailing through the tree line; they fall like shadows on either side of my car, a reflection of a forest. A few seconds later I'm driving toward the Lethe Bridge. The river underneath the bridge rages. The fireweed underneath it lashes back and forth in the wind. There is no rain here on Weymouth . . . yet.

I can sense the drop in barometric pressure in my ears. Mr. McLeod once told us that during the Storm it drops more than one millibar per hour. Every vein in my body is pumping blood faster than normal. It's fear and elation. This is what I was born for, made for. My body is pulling toward the island—and toward Miles.

I don't stop at my house as I pass it on the left; I can't stop, not for even a second, not when every minute before the Storm matters—and Miles needs his car. It seems silly, pointless in light of the Storm, but I cannot take his escape from him. If he wants to go before this place falls apart, he has to be able to go. I will not doom him. I cannot carry any more guilt.

I watch as the speedometer climbs to sixty, the car rattling underneath my hands. I pass the other houses and think of the quiet chaos happening inside each one: traps being set, barriers rising, families preparing, all of us burning inside our castles. I think of each family: the Mintus family and their moat, the Nickersons and their boys, the enormous Gillis family.

Please, God, keep them safe. I clutch the front of my shirt in the place where a cross would normally sit. I'm not sure I believe in God, but today seems like a good time to start; if evil exists, then so must the other side, correct? I picked a hell of a time to figure it out.

I spot the Cabot mansion rising up in front of the sea. At the bottom of the gravel hill, Gale hydroplanes across their enormous driveway, her tires spinning as she lurches sideways, water sluicing to either side of the car. I keep control over her—barely—and let out a shriek of terror. Then I'm squealing up the driveway and laying on the horn before yanking out the keys and climbing out of the car. The air is warm and heavy. From the porch I hear yelling, followed by the frantic unbolting of locks and the clicks of machinations, and after about a minute, the front door of the Cabot house swings open, with Miles stepping out, followed by a furious Alistair. *Shit.* For a second, I see myself through his eyes: the wild Beuvry girl with eyes for his nephew.

Miles sprints down the steps, weaving through complex iron barriers, relief stark across his face. My heart pulls away from my chest as, without a second's hesitation, he picks me up, burying his face in my hair. My head swims a little as he pulls back. His face looks terrified.

"God, I'm glad to see you," he says quietly, leaning his forehead against mine.

"Hi," I whisper back, and I suddenly realize we are both bare to each other, scars and all. And even though the Storm is about to consume everything, I still have this moment, this second with him. We don't have time to enjoy it for long because Alistair begins screaming at us from the porch.

"Mabel, what the hell are you doing here? You have to be in *your* home! Go! We have to get inside. If you care about Miles, he has to be inside!" He flicks his hand at me like he's scattering the wind. He's right. I know it. I open my mouth to say goodbye, but then there is a sound like electric fizz, followed by a pure absence of wind. All the hairs on my body stand up. The sound of cannon fire follows soon after, and there is a blur of whiteness, light with blinding coils, the world cracked open. Everything spins in the light, and then there is only blackness.

Breathe.

I am here, though the ringing in both ears makes it hard to steady myself. I roll over, mud gathering at my elbows and slopping against my knees. What just happened? I close my eyes and remember: the light. The sound. *Did I just get hit by lightning?* I painfully sit up, checking my limbs; everything seems in order. I hear a cry.

Beside me, Alistair is leaning over Miles, and for a second everything collapses, but then I hear Miles take a ragged breath in. Alistair chokes in relief, hugging Miles against his chest as he pulls them both up. Not fifteen feet away from us a large maple smokes and billows, a black husk where its trunk used to be.

A loud crack echoes through the air, and I look up in time to see the tree spinning as it collapses. I hear Miles yell my name, but I'm already sprinting away from the trajectory. I smell smoke as it falls behind me, crashing a few feet away. The impact is gigantic, the shock rushing up through my jawbone. I turn back to Miles and Alistair with an astonished look on my face, but my attention shifts quickly from their pale, blood-drained faces to what hovers above them.

The sky.

An unearthly pale green hue stretches out to the horizon, a nauseating shade of warning. Underneath it huge bilious clouds hover over the Dehset Sea, which churns angrily, waves ranging from navy to the palest ice blue, roiling like the inside of a cauldron. Underneath the clouds, bolts of lightning crack down every few seconds, each one accompanied by a vicious clap of thunder. Centuries ago, people believed that hurricanes were manifestations of evil spirits, and that's what this sky looks like: a malevolent spirit.

Alistair steps forward, yelling against the wind. "It's never looked this way before!" he yells. "It's you! Both of you! Goddammit, I think Lynwood was right."

Miles turns to him. "What do you mean both of us?"

Alistair shakes his head. "We don't have time to explain! Get inside!"

Lighting snaps all over the island. I can see strikes hitting everywhere. We all jump as a searing white bolt hits the Cabot weather vane, which diverts the strike down to the ground.

Miles begins pulling me toward the Cabot mansion. "We have to get inside! Come on! We can't stay out here!"

"Miles." I say it softly, but he doesn't stop until Alistair yanks him roughly away from me.

"She can't, Miles. She has to be in her own home!" Alistair's eyes meet mine, and the fear inside them paralyzes me. "No house alone, every house alone, remember? Mabel has to be in the Beuvry Estate; her family is waiting for her." He looks at me sternly. "Mabel, *you need to go.*"

I take Miles's face in my hands. My ears are still ringing slightly, my skin tingling under a phantom sky. It's not unfathomable to think that one of us may not last the night.

"Thank you," I whisper, kissing him one time.

"For what?"

"For waking me up."

Alistair looks as if he's going to have a stroke. I lean forward and press my mouth against Miles's ear. "You can still go. Gale is here." There's nothing I can do to soothe him, no words that can explain what is about to happen. The Cabot house is the first house to the sea; so even though their house is a fortress, they will take the brunt of the impact.

Instead I give him the best advice I can. "If you need to run, run. And don't come for me. Don't." The wind climbs up the cliffside, filling our nostrils with a slightly rotting smell. Above me, lightning crackles across the green sky as the heavy clouds converge to form a strange purple swarm. "This is what you were born for," I say softly.

Alistair drags Miles toward the porch as I toss him the keys. "Come inside," Miles pleads one last time. I shake my head.

They have no time; the Storm is coming for them sooner than it's coming for me.

"Go, Mabel!" Alistair thunders at me as chaos roars toward them.

I meet Miles's deep brown eyes. "I'll see you soon," I whisper. We stare at each other as a series of iron doors begins closing in front of his face. When we see each other again, we will be changed—or dead.

When I turn away from the Cabot mansion, a high, piercing sound fills the air, similar to the siren I heard on the radio. This one, however, is pumped out from speakers fashioned to light posts around the island. The sound of Weymouth's early-warning system stops me cold. One long wail means "prepare your houses." Two short wails back-to-back mean "take shelter." Three means that the dead have come ashore. I pause and listen.

Take shelter.

Over the sea, the monstrous black clouds have sunk so low that they lurk just above the foaming waves. On the shore, the Weymouth lighthouse's usual white light has been replaced by a swirling red that bathes the island in a bloody light. The Storm has begun.

I start running just as the rain begins.

Theo Nickerson, 1963, in a letter to his
brother, Jim

Dear Jim,
Man, I'm so glad that I made it here to
REDACTED *Island. It was a long journey.*
Remember those stories Mom used to tell us about
the dark North? Turns out they're pretty true.

There is so little I can tell you about where I am,
so I'll have to describe it. It would make you
cry to see the way people live here, all campfires
and cold shores. Houses bigger than our old
neighborhoods; the people are white, so white
that they blend with the sand. They'll make
you cry, though, the way they talk about their
families, the people they've come from. We know
a little something about that. I know you and
Mom might not understand why I've left you
for this strange place, **REDACTED**. *I know*
I'll never be able to tell you, but know that I left
for love—love of Adelaide, but also a love of the

whole world. I can't go much deeper than that, but know I would never have left you and Mom for anything less than saving everything.

You can tell these people up here in **REDACTED** *have never been around a Black person. They're either skittish or too nice. You know how it is; meanwhile, I'm freezing myself just trying to fit in with them. We do get the news up here, so I've been following along with the things happening down there, with Rev. King and his people, rising up, saying "No more" to racists. And let me tell you, some of these folks need to hear that.*

I tell myself that if he can do that, then I can be here on **REDACTED***. These old, suspicious families may say I'm a fool for wanting my family to be a part of these* **REDACTED** *houses— things that belong to other people on this island— but I'll tell you something: I'm no fool, and this place needs someone like me. They are living in the past here—and not backward like Jacksonville, backward like it's the 1870s. Even though they're looking at me sideways, and even though some of Adelaide's friends have stopped talking to her because of me, I swear, I will make my mark on this place. I have a feeling that I'm where I'm supposed to be.*

Someday my proud Black sons and daughters will walk these rocky shores and have a house to call their own.

Breathe in that warm Southern air for me, Jimmy; carry me with you, 'cause I'll not be seeing you again. I'll try like hell to protect us all.

—Theo
P.S. Move as far south as you can go.

Historical note from Reade McLeod: Theodore Nickerson was the first African American on the island after he married Adelaide Nickerson. Since then the Nickerson family has become the engineers of the island, updating our defenses while bringing culture and life to Weymouth.

CHAPTER TWENTY-NINE

I've jogged about halfway home up the main road before my path is blocked by an enormous felled oak tree. The hulking giant is lying across the road, its insides still charred and smoking from a lightning strike. A burnt rabbit lies tangled inside in the roots. Nausea rises up inside me as I stare at its dead eyes. *Move, Mabel.* I divert and head north, making my way to one of the many trails that will lead me home. I'm pulling myself up a steep hill covered in wildflowers when I hear the rustling of grass beside me and watch in horror as a stream of black-and-yellow ribbon snakes slides toward me. I try to get out of the way, but it's too late; they slide over my sneakers by the hundreds.

Even monsters fear the Storm.

I'm almost to the edge of the woods, praying the underbrush will swallow up some of the rain. As I get closer, I sense a strange, protective sensation billowing out from the crooked branches and rough trunks. The island is bracing itself for impact, and when I duck underneath its branches, it folds me into a protective barrier of bark and moss. The trail is narrow, shaded over with ferns. The rain increases. I quicken my pace when I think of how panicked Jeff must be; no doubt he and my mother are losing their minds, wondering where I am, while they batten down the hatches.

My lungs begin to burn, and for a brief second I'm thankful for the laps that Mr. McLeod makes us run around the schoolhouse every afternoon. Above me, the sky is holding a biblical amount of water, and when I pause and glance up, it gives way with an audible *whoosh*. Water pours down, only it's not like any rain I've ever seen. Normal rain is lovely, life-giving, tea-drinking comfort. This rain is something different; it's a violent waterfall.

I start to run faster, my mind struggling to find something solid to hold on to as the world seems to submerge around me. *Miles. My mother. Hali. Hali. Hali.* I see her at five, laughing at her pajamas on backward. I see her at twelve, her freckles going from cute to beautiful, her gangly limbs stretching everywhere, teeth too big for her face. I see her at fifteen, reading on the porch, her narrow green eyes full of fire. A breath catches in my throat.

Only one of these memories is real.

I have done something horrible: I *grew* Hali, like a plant on a windowsill. I aged her along with me so that I wouldn't be alone and so I could witness her life. But the truth is that I could never capture Hali in her full, infuriating complexity. My imagination has created just a cheap shadow of who she would have been.

The rain does not care. It pounds down harder, slowing my steps and obscuring my vision. It's getting harder to breathe with the rain pouring down my face, running into my mouth, nose, and eyes. I try to jog forward, putting one hand protectively out in front of me while keeping my other over my eyes in a pathetic attempt to shield them from the rain. The only thing that tells me I'm going the right way is the gravel under my feet and the dim lights of the Gillis house in the distance. I can go there if I *have* to, but I can't stop. If I'm not home soon, I'll never make it there. *I have to be home for the Storm.*

I can still hear the bursts of the siren blasting from the road below; if I wander too far, I'll end up on the cliffs above the Soft Sea—and with the blinding rain, that would be dangerous in a different way. The stink of the other sea is rising in the air, the scent of salt and rot, and underneath that, a sharp, metallic smell—something not of this world.

I run until the rain becomes so heavy that it's physically pushing me down; drops have become a pour, and I lean up against a tree as sheets of rain drape over me like a cloak. My blood begins to cool, and I am sluggish. I close my eyes, fighting the desire to lie down right here. I wonder if I can drown on dry land.

Move. Mabel. Move.

I press my toes into the earth and crawl forward with a growl. I take a deep breath in, arching my back against the deluge, but it's no use. The rain pushes me against the ground, becoming water, becoming mud. A frustrated scream rips through my chest. Just when I feel like I can't continue, a sound rises from the shore, like air rushing through a tunnel. It grows louder and louder until it's an eolian howl that fills the whole world. The hair on my arms stands as I clutch my hands over my ears. The howl peaks and suddenly goes silent, and a second later, the rain stops.

It's as if someone has turned off a faucet. Leaves funnel the remaining water onto the ground, but other than the steady *drip, drip, drip,* the air around me has gone completely still. I stand up nervously, soaked to the core. Not a single breath passes through the forest. When I look up, the sky above me is a churning, malignant dark blue. That's when I realize—this isn't a pause; it's an inhale. *When the wind starts to blow, lock the doors.* I push the soaking hair out of my eyes and start tearing through the forest like a madwoman.

"Go, go, go," I yell to myself, followed by a string of curses. I'm the only person not barricaded in their house right now. Ahead of me, the small field between my house and Norah's opens up. From here, I can see our widow's walk peeking through the trees, and I breathe out in relief; I'm almost there, only maybe a half mile to go. But when I take a step forward, the wind comes for me.

The first gust takes me off my feet. It rips through the forest and throws me forward like I'm a rag doll. My feet and my body fully leave the ground, and I land hard on my wrists in a field full of lamb's-quarters.

I try to push up to my knees, but pain lances up through my wrist and hand. When I look down, I see that a thin branch has pierced through the tender skin between my thumb and pointer finger. Blood is pouring down my hand. I inhale sharply, unable to look away from the horror. I hear the wind gathering itself together again, the inhale before the next exhale, and even though I want to carefully deal with this, that's the one thing I don't have: time. I grit my teeth and pull the branch out, leaving a hole in my hand. Blood splatters onto the ground. The world swirls around me, and I almost black out from the pain. But I hold on, anchored by the sight of blood on my fingertips.

Some consider the first blood from a Storm sacred, our sacrifice for the island. I raise my shaking hands and wipe my blood across the wet soil. I get back to my feet. A second low rumbling pushes out behind me, and another huge gust of air ricochets toward me, carrying every small piece of the forest with it.

In an instant, I am surrounded by swirling coils of wind, hurtling thousands of leaves, branches, and dirt inside them. My feet move forward while I protectively hold my hands over my eyes, trapped in a funnel of underbrush that seems like it could rip my skin off.

Something hard and small bounces off the top of my head. When I peek through my fingers, I see tiny pieces of white beginning to litter the ground like hard, white confetti. They make a clattering sound as they bounce off branches and rocks. I reach down and pick one up; it's wet and cold, straight from the sea.

Oh God. It's bones: small fragments of bone from the Dehset. Bones are falling from the sky. This is normal. I let the piece of bone fall from my hand and into the dark soil.

"Sick."

The moving funnel of wind and bone moves past me into the woods as the wind increases. A small branch whips past my face, leaving a thin slice followed by a warm sensation dripping down my cheek. The woods are still for a second, and then a sound like a train approaching blows through the trees behind me.

I bolt forward, sprinting as fast as I can toward the house. I'm almost there. Using all the sound I can muster, I scream for help, but the wind takes my voice and throws it toward the mainland.

Behind me I hear a horrifying crack as a huge branch hurtles through the trees and crashes into the field, sending a plume of dirt up around it. Another one follows, rolling and crushing as it goes before skidding to a stop. Thin trunks are now being flung, whole trees carried on a bed of leaves, so heavy that the ground reverberates when they land, heavy enough to break a body. I clasp my hands over my ears when one lands beside me, decimating wildflowers in its wake and leaving a sea of crushed purple behind. I can't stay on my feet; if I do, I'll be hurtled forward like these trees, but if I don't move, I'll be pounded into dust by a flying trunk.

I'm trapped. *I'm dead.* This Storm is bigger than anything I could have ever dreamed of, and it hasn't even really started yet. I hear a telltale popping sound from the direction of Norah's house, and I look over in time to see a power line falling near their gardens. It lands in a shower of golden sparks as another tree hurtles overhead, this one an old oak with red-veined leaves. It crashes and rolls away from me. *BOOSH.*

The wind blows me violently sideways as I push against it with all my weight, but it picks me up as if I'm nothing. For a second, my feet leave the ground and my body is thrust forward, but then something grasps tight around my arm, something strong that doesn't let go.

"Hold on!"

Jeff, my Guardian, my savior, is crouching in front of me, his hand wrapped around my arm, the other wrapped around a wooden walking stick, sunk deep into the earth. I clasp on to him, and he anchors me. He curls his body around mine as everything around us lashes, but we stay down, connected to our island as the world rages around us.

"Stay low!" he yells, and I nod, unable to see past the whirl-pool that is my hair. Slowly he begins pulling us forward step by step, fighting against a current stronger than either of us. The bottom of his walking stick, turns out, is lined with a metal spike that drives deep into the ground. We move in the seconds between gusts.

"I'm sorry!" I scream it into the swirling madness, *for this, for everything.*

"You should be!" Jeff screams, all polite decorum gone. "We were never meant to be outside for this part of the Storm! It's a death wish." He drags me forward. "You're grounded forever!"

"I thought I had time!" I yell as tiny pieces of bones fall around us. "I thought it would be fine!"

"So far this Storm has defied previous incarnations!" This is such an obnoxiously Jeff thing to yell in the midst of absolute chaos.

Ahead of us, the Beuvry house rises out of such a thick field of iron and flowers, I barely recognize it. The wind howls in defeat as we drag each other up the porch and make our way carefully through the myriad protections: iron fencing, silver wire coils, shards, spikes, certain death, etc. The ground is covered with salt. My Guardian has been busy.

The wind pulls at us, but it has never met the Guardian of House Beuvry. It will not win. He yanks open the door, takes my elbow, and mutters "Get thee behind me, Satan" with dramatic flair before flinging us both over the precipice. The wind slams the door shut behind us, and everything goes quiet while the Storm rages outside.

CHAPTER THIRTY

It's at least two minutes before we can muster the strength to speak again. My legs shake with exhaustion as the wind continues to batter the house, hurtling all manner of things against our garden and siding. I lay my hand over my chest, trying to slow my thundering heart, worried I may die of a heart attack at seventeen.

"We made it," I gasp, finally able to speak. I lean my head back against the wall, legs spread out before me. I'm alive, and I'm here, in my house. And outside . . . outside is terrifying.

"Mabel, you're bleeding everywhere!" The way Jeff gasps my name hurts my heart; it's quelled panic mixed with anger, anger mixed with fear—the way a father would sound. Jeff turns my face to look at my cut. "Where the hell have you been? As of this morning, all our instruments indicated that the Storm was coming, but the Guardians wanted to wait to make *absolutely sure* before we caused a panic. We wanted to give everyone on this island a few more minutes of normalcy—but that was a mistake. I am deeply furious with you. God, please never scare me like that again."

"I know about Hali," I say. "Miles told me in the graveyard."

He is silent, but after a second he looks up, guilty eyes filling with tears.

"I know you tried to tell me," I say. "Many times."

"When I couldn't find you, my biggest fear was that I would never get to tell you that I'm sorry about everything. All of it. About Hali and your father, about going along with it all because it was easier to not see you in pain." Deep regret crosses his face as I look at him with confusion.

"It's my fault. I kept her," I whisper.

He shakes his head. "No. No! You are the child, and I'm the adult. I should have tried harder to bring you back to reality, and you're right, I did. But you needed Hali so much, and after she died, I was desperate to give you anything to make you better. I would have given my life to give her back to you. It felt like a failure. I couldn't bring her back. My father couldn't save yours, and so I let you *keep* her. It seemed like the least I could do."

I've never seen Jeff like this; he's always a pillar of mystery. He's never admitted to doing anything wrong. How could he? We made him our foundation without giving him room to make mistakes. He glances behind me at the door.

"We have stuff to do. It's fine—" I start to say, but he cuts me off.

"No. It is not fine. This is important, saying these things. We may not have time later." His words are a punch to my chest. "I remember the morning when you came down the stairs, chattering happily for the first time in God knows how long. It had been months since the Storm took your father and Hali, and you hadn't said as much as a word since then. You were laughing, your hand reaching out as if someone invisible was holding it. Grief had turned you hollow, and suddenly there it was, *your light*! You were content, dare I say happy even." He sits back. "It was a couple of hours before I realized who you were talking to and what alternate reality you had slipped into, and by then . . . it was done. You had decided you were going to keep our Hali. And you are a force to be reckoned with, Mabel."

I flash to Miles, his lips on mine, the sea around us. *You are the Storm.*

Jeff continues. "Your mother and I saw how happy you were and so we left you there. We were grieving your father, and at the time it seemed like a small indulgence. We didn't pretend along with you, but we didn't deny it either—until it had gone on for a year. And then two years. And each time we told you, you broke through and then reverted, and we had to start all over. It never took, because each time was like your sister dying for you again and again. There was just so much pain. And so . . . we stopped, because it became easier to avoid what the Storm had cost us if we looked the other way."

His face crumples. "Hali is as much my and your mother's creation as she is yours. By avoiding our pain, we built upon yours, and soon this house became one of secrets." The wind pulls angrily under the door, bucking against its screws. "I should have figured out that you needed someone else to break through the fog, someone outside our family who was brave enough to bear your pain. Not only that, but you needed a reason to move on. You needed Miles."

My composure crumples at his guilt, and I clutch his hands with my bloody ones, wincing at the pain. "I need you too!" I interrupt him rudely. "I'm afraid you'll leave us when it gets too hard! I don't have much family left, and if you leave, this whole house will collapse." *God, it sounds like it's collapsing now.* My eyes search his face. "I don't want you to leave us like Lynwood did. Or because of me."

His eyes soften. "Oh, Mabel. I won't leave this family, *not ever*. The thing that matters most in this world to me is protecting this house and the people in it."

He grimaces as something huge slams against our house and it gives a shudder.

"Here on Weymouth we pride ourselves on our bravery, but we need also to recognize that *true bravery* is asking for help when you need it and humbling ourselves to accept help from others. That's the bravest act there is. And, Mabel, I'm sure going to need your bravery today, because . . . I sent your mother away. Now, let me see that cut."

My mouth falls open as he whips out a first aid kit from his fanny pack and begins treating all the injuries I've acquired between the Cabot mansion and here.

"I'm sorry—what do you mean *you sent her away?*" My voice edges on hysteria as he puts a butterfly bandage on my cheek and smears a numbing cream over the hole in my hand.

His eyes stay steady, but for the first time I see the growing panic behind the calm. "I made a decision for this family. Your mother couldn't be here for another Storm—and, ultimately, she agreed. It's something I've suspected we may have to do for a long time, but I wanted to leave that choice up to her. She's helped us shore up the house plenty, but she wasn't in the right mental place to survive it. The last Storm took her husband and her child. To be frank, she was a liability. I'd rather have her safe on the mainland, and so I sent her there."

God, that's right. All this time, my mom has been mourning her husband and her child, and here I've been satisfied, happily living in my delusions, not even seeing the depth of her grief. Instead I've been angry—at her.

I guess that's the thing about grief—it makes you inexcusably selfish to survive it.

But I won't carry that anger today. She lost a child; I lost a sister, and because of that, I can give her the grace today that she's always deserved from me. I swallow.

"I think you made the right decision," I say finally, surprised by the relief that follows. "And me, with my current mental health—I'm not a risk factor?"

Jeff tips my shins toward him and smears some anti-bac ointment on them. "Nah. I mean, yes, you're definitely mental, but you're smart and fast. You're the only Beuvry I need here today. You and I can defend this house. Your mum will be back, and then we can all start over again—and we can do it much better this time. We'll sit with the pain instead of hiding it. And Miles can help."

"Okay," I whisper, feeling a freedom open in my chest. "But there's something I want to ask you—about Miles and me."

"The surge is coming, and the sun is inching lower every minute." He pauses, listening for the siren; it's still blasting out two wails. "All right. They aren't here *yet*. I'm telling you, Mabel, we will live through this night, and when the sun rises in the morning, we're going to take a vacation somewhere warm and beachy, full of tanned men and drinks with small umbrellas."

I burst out laughing; it's the most real thing he's ever said to me.

"To little umbrellas." We clink invisible glasses. "What do we still need to do?"

Jeff hauls me to my feet. "I've already dropped the hurricane shutters and opened the rain sluice. Water should be moving away from the house as we speak, to clear the way for the surge. We're ready—far more ready than your father was. But we always have more to do." His eyes narrow. "Sometimes it can be hours before the surge; in 1916 it was *almost ten hours* between the end of the wind and the surge. Other years it took only minutes, so we must be ready—and there is something about this Storm I don't like."

I feel it too. Is it because of Miles and me?

"Do you think Lynwood was right?" I ask. "That this is a Great Storm? Is there such a thing?"

"I'm sure we'll find out. You need to go change." Jeff doesn't answer my question, but I see the answer in his eyes. He's afraid. As he begins hammering things shut, I remember what I saw in the Dehset Sea. I see the dead behind the Bone Barrier, clawing their way toward me.

"Afterward, I'll meet you up on Cloudbreak. I'll secure from the top down, and you can do the outside in, once the—" I don't finish my sentence, because all of a sudden the winds that have been battering our house fall silent. We glance at each other, and I nod. Jeff slowly cracks open the front door.

The world outside has been disheveled. Trees have plunged through our iron fencing, which is bent in too many places. There are deep gouges in the earth where the trees rolled, like a giantess has raked her nails through the soil. The oak beside our house stands damaged but proud, but in its branches, a woman's pale blue dress hangs, still as a corpse. There are no birdcalls, no insects buzzing, just things where they shouldn't be, the air so heavy, I could cup it in my hand.

"My God," Jeff breathes. "Go change. Go!" He bolts past me toward the outside perimeter of the house, where I know he will pull out more iron fencing, trigger the many garden traps, and finalize securing the porch—defenses that can't be set until the wind dies down.

I run for the stairs, taking them three at a time up to my bedroom. Adrenaline is punching through my body as I rip off my soaking-wet clothes, flinging them into the corner. I'm utterly disgusting: My nails are black with dirt that spreads up over my knuckles, which are covered with crusted blood. The sharp scent of fear pours off my underarms when I rip my shirt off.

At the top of my closet sits a black duffel bag that serves one purpose: it holds my clothes for the Storm. I zip it open and push back the tissue paper. Underneath sits fancy waterproof gray leggings and a long, tight black water-wicking shirt. I shimmy into them as fast as I can and breathe a sigh of relief when I'm done. It's such a small thing, but not being in wet clothes makes me feel a bit more human. I know it won't last. I yank out my water shoes from their box; fancy, high-tech contraptions that Jeff makes us—*I mean, me*—wear around the house once a week so they are "worked in." I slide my feet in and then pull my seam-sealed, water-repellent jacket out of the bottom of the bag.

After I'm dressed, I pick up my Storm pack from the floor of the closet, a waterproof backpack with all the survival tools to make it through the night: food, water, ropes, weapons, salt, walkie batteries, and even a gas mask sit tucked inside. Last I checked, the dead weren't engaging in chemical warfare, but you never know. I reach inside the pack, double-checking the most important thing that sits tucked up against the side, secured by a single strap of Velcro.

No one knows I have it.

Reaching back, I wring out the remainder of my soaked hair before twisting it into a tight bun and pinning it up against my head; the last thing you want is your hair getting stuck in some trap. *Things Weymouth kids know for five hundred, please.*

I take a few deep breaths, but the sinking feeling I've had since Miles confronted me in the graveyard—which seems a hundred years ago at this point—is still present in my chest. My head is spinning about Hali, something I can't—*no, I won't*—process right now. Like my mother, I'll give myself some grace. I don't have to understand it completely at this second.

It's time to fight.

I dig my fingernails into my palms as I pass my mom's room on the way out. Her door sits slightly open, and so I reach out and close it. Knowing she's safe is a gift. I lean my head against her door, wishing her the peace I know she won't get tonight, when the radio crackles to life next to me.

"This is Alistair Cabot. All houses report."

I listen as others begin reporting in.

"McLeod, Hillary reporting."

"Nickerson, Sloane reporting." *Hey, Sloane,* I think.

"Mintus, Jonathan reporting."

"Grimes, Van reporting." I pause, waiting for the rest. My people. My friends.

"Pope, Eryk reporting."

"Des Roches, Abra reporting in." I hope to hear my friend's voice, and the island grants my request.

"Gillis, Norah reporting." *I love you, Norah*, I think. *Stay safe.*

"Pelletier, Victor reporting."

"This is Fallon, reporting for House Bodhmall." I take a deep breath and click on the radio, making sure my voice is steady. "House Cabot reporting, this is Mabel."

Alistair's voice crackles; he sounds nervous. "It's five twenty-nine p.m., and so far no sign of the surge. Water is rising steadily, wind virtually nonexistent. The Sacred Line stands secure, and House Cabot is ready. Prepare your houses and Godspeed."

The radio in my hands goes silent as I run down past the cellars and into the basement. After I check everything, I lay my hand on the foundation stones, which are vibrating with a strange, low pitch. I reach out, brushing off the dirt to touch words carved in stone, words written by our ancestors. *I am here*, I think. *Be with us.* I check the cellar door (secured) and the fortified walk-out doors (weren't secured but are now). I barricade the entrances in layers, with locks and stones and latches and then finish with bars of iron.

I notice something out of the corner of my eye, and I recoil in horror when thousands of spiders—moving in a large clump— scurry past me, all trying to move upward through the house. The walls are full of scurrying sounds, little paws and clawed feet all looking for escape. My chest clenches ever tighter.

I head upstairs, checking everything on my way, winding out to the porch, trying not to think about how it was Hali's place. With a deep breath, I slip the wooden panel in the floor sideways and find the delicate silver button—*one of the last official steps.*

"Stop." I turn around. Jeff is standing at the door, drenched with sweat. "You have to say the words, Mabel. It's more than a ritual. It's an extra layer of fortification." He doesn't know that I've never done this without Hali, that it feels silly on my own. I take a deep breath as my finger lingers above the button, and I whisper the words.

> *"Iron, paper, salt, silver, and thread;*
> *mind your house; keep thy dead.*
> *Fares well the house that's ready."*

I push the button down into the floor and watch as the porch transforms; metal shutters slam down, and doors swing into place. The iron gears grind below my feet as the entire house closes itself off, curling into its own protection. Our dainty lights go dark, and instead high-powered LEDs click on all over the house. The papers attached to the back of each shutter flutter in the displaced air. I spy a poem from Lady Kasa, one of my mother's favorite poets.

The poem flaps against the wall. *The dead hate paper.*

Iron spikes lower from the ceiling. *The dead hate iron.*

I check the barrels in the salt pantry. *The dead hate salt.*

I grab our salt guns, feeling like a badass as I throw one to Jeff and sling the other one over my shoulder. Trapdoors are opened; secret passageways and clever cabinets are double-checked. I count on my fingers as we go: silver locks, iron frames, iron fencing, metal shutters, iron gates, silver thread, paper nets, iron whip, *check, check, check.* I stand underneath the stained-glass window, the rotating glare of the lighthouse bathing me in its red light. The inside of the house is ready, but a nagging thought repeats itself again and again, like a vinyl turning around and around: *it didn't save them, and it won't save you.* Jeff grabs my shoulder and motions to the stairs.

Without a word, I begin the long climb to Cloudbreak.

Morgan Bodhmall, January 12, 1980

Dear Diary,
What my parents don't know won't kill them, at
least, not in the way the Storm will. That's okay.
I'll break their heart to save my body. My mother's
prayers to the island and my father's daily
scrubbing of the foundation stones—those routines
won't save me. Only I can save myself.

This morning, I packed a bag with enough warm
clothing for a week, my toothpaste, toothbrush, and
the bag of shells I've been collecting with Mother
on the Dehset since I was a child. I love my round
nautilus with shards of sharp bone poking out
and the coiled worm-like gray shells that glisten
with dark plum handprints. And my perfect little
heart of obsidian black. Every day that we collected
these shells together was a good day. They are all
good days here on Weymouth—until they are not.
The Storm is getting bigger every time. No one
wants to say that, but it's true. Everyone knows the
Triumvirate keeps their secrets.

The Storm was yesterday. I can still see it all—the surge, the rush of water, the mist snaking through the forest, ever closer, closer. I can hear the screams of my little brothers in my ears. We came so close to losing it all, even with the defenses. We were not prepared for a winter Storm, for a surge crusting with icicles, razor-sharp and pointed at our homes. Old man Grimes died in the Storm, and his body has already frozen over. My youngest sister has a scar on her face that will never fade. Our island is ice. Our people are lost, houses buried by ice and snow.

I woke up this morning and realized that I cannot stay here on Weymouth. I will not be a living sacrifice for my island. Broderick and Molly live for the fight of it, like the rest of this mad family. But in my heart, I know I was not meant to fight this Storm. I cannot die for this house. When I am gone, my mother will not speak my name. I will not have a grave in Sentry's Sleep. I will not marry a handsome Nickerson boy in a meadow beyond the schoolhouse. But I will live, and that will be enough.

Morgan Bodhmall

Historical note from Reade McLeod: Seventeen-year-old Morgan Bodhmall left Weymouth on Christmas Eve, 1980. While her family does not speak of her, she periodically sends her parents postcards to a PO box in Glace Bay from places like Kauai, Tokyo, and Chile.

CHAPTER THIRTY-ONE

U p on the widow's walk, the changing light catches on the bone shards left behind, like tiny pieces of white confetti. I kick them over the side as I walk. It's a party for the dead, and we're all invited.

Down in the garden, Jeff is shoring up the exterior. I pace back and forth, watching with a careful eye as he raises the iron fencing, layer after layer. Walls, fences, trap, repeat, our house is now a labyrinth.

He looks up to me, and after checking the layout against the schematic that hangs on the widow's walk, I give him a double thumbs-up. He heads inside, and I sag with relief.

We did it. We're ready—well, as ready as we can be.

A second later, Jeff appears beside me.

"How can it still be so beautiful?" I ask, and he simply shakes his head. From here Cloudbreak grants us an incredible view. I can see the entire island laid out before us, where eleven houses hold their breath. My eyes linger on the Cabot mansion, and I wonder about Miles, sitting inside that enormous house waiting for the surge. I feel connected to him even now, like, if I thought his name hard enough, he would hear me. But that's not possible.

Past the Cabot house, the sea fumes—dark, angry, and clear. They'd better be ready. Speaking of ready . . . I hurry over to the walkie. It's not technically allowed, but no one is writing down etiquette infractions right now.

"Mabel to Norah, over." There is a long pause, and I consider that it's possible her parents won't let her talk at all—it's not like we aren't all doing enough. I go to switch it off when it buzzes to life.

"Mabel, switch over to channel 8." I follow her directions, so relieved to hear her voice. "Thank God you made it home!" she explodes. "I saw you struggling against the wind out our bay window, but my mom wouldn't let me leave the house—she said if it got worse, then my dad would go out for you, but then you disappeared into the woods. And at that point . . ." She trickles off.

"It's okay. It was a stupid decision to walk home from the Cabots'; I thought I had more time." I also understand—during the Storm, it's every family for themselves.

"We lost our shed, our power, and our perimeter fencing. My mom and Martha are fixing the breaker now. Was it as bad as it looked?"

"Worse," I say.

"Hey!" I hear James's whine in the background. "Norah gets to make calls on the walkie, and I can't even leave *my station?*" It figures that he's still a huge pain in the ass, even during the Storm. I hear heavy footsteps as her dad clearly approaches.

"Norah, you can't be on the walkie right now—the channels must be kept clear!" I hear movement as they wrestle with it.

"Dad!" I am pierced with the sudden fear that I'll never talk to my friend again.

"Just a second, Mr. Gillis, I promise!" I hear a grumbling reply. "Norah, I want to say thank you." I nervously press my tongue to the roof of my mouth. "Thanks for sticking with me when no one else did. With the Hali stuff. It must have been hard to be friends with someone who wasn't quite there." I hear a sharp intake of breath.

"You . . . know?"

I look up at the churning gray sky. "Yeah. Miles told me. It's been a weird day. I can't wait to tell you all about it."

Norah laughs. "There's something special about the two of you. I can feel it in the air when I'm around you; you vibrate near each other. It's hard to explain, but you both feel like hope. When I first met him in the schoolhouse, I thought, 'This is the one. The one who is going to break Mabel open.' He was the change you needed. How are you doing?"

I close my eyes. "Not great but as well as can be expected, I guess? Learning that my sister is dead and that I'm a bit out of it all in one afternoon would be enough, but then . . . the Storm. I'm afraid, Norah."

"Me too," she says softly.

"Jeff sent my mom to Glace Bay to wait out the Storm."

Her voice is gentle. "That makes sense, but, Mabel, are you guys going to be okay? Just the two of you?"

No, I think, but I lie through my teeth instead. "Jeff and I will get through tonight. Tomorrow I'll worry about what comes next." I sigh. Behind this Storm is another one, a storm made of denial and secrets and grief. I'm not quite ready for that one yet. "At least I can blow off some steam running from the dead."

"Don't joke about that. They probably won't make it to you—

maybe they won't even make it past the Sacred Line. But, if it comes down to it," she whispers cryptically, "just run, okay? Run for the highest ground you can find." Norah's voice is cracking. "I have to go. I love you. Even in the worst of times, you are the best friend I've ever had—"

Her dad's voice interrupts her. "Norah, for God's sake, get off the line."

"Dad, wait—WAIT!" A loud stomping sounds as the walkie switches off. Jeff reaches out for my walkie. In return, he hands me a small bundle.

"EAT," he orders. Inside is a protein bar, a piece of jerky, hard cheese, and an apple.

I tear the bundle open. "Feasting Viking style tonight, I see." We dive into the food with abandon.

Jeff talks through enormous bites. "The Vikings had their own version of the Dehset Sea, you know. Hel—a gray land that rested under the earth. They called it the fog-world. It's where the goddess Hel ruled over the souls." I swallow a big hunk of Irish cheddar. I know a bit about creating a hell to avoid loneliness.

"Is that what Weymouth is? *Hell?*" I ask.

Jeff leans back against the stone wall. "Sometimes I wonder that. I mean, why do we live here? *Why do we stay?* Why not take you and your mother and make it some other people's problem?"

I swallow. I know the answer. This is essentially a test for me. "Because there's not always someone else," I say. "And because this couldn't be fought with governments, with weapons or policy. Because only families are strong enough to weather the dead." I grimace. "Even though there are only two of us here."

"Two is all we need," Jeff says. "No need to overcomplicate

things." The air gives a discernible shift. We match eyes as the pressure around us begins to drop. He reaches up and touches the air with his fingertips. "It's beginning."

We brush the crumbs from our laps and stand to look out over the island. Below us, the tips of the trees sway; blue pines, sharp and fine as needles, move back and forth. Out on the Dehset, the red glow of the lighthouse sweeps over the sea, and we can see black waves rising. The pressure coils around us like a python, hot and heavy.

"The first breath of the dead," remarks Jeff. "Fetor hepaticus."

"Could we *not* with the Latin right now?" I ask, nervously peering over the side. As we watch, the sun sinks lower in the sky, and a thick gray mist begins to roll away from the sea in huge rings.

"You should try to rest," Jeff says. "It'll be a long night."

"What, nap up here? No. That's not happening." I can't imagine sleeping now, not with the adrenaline pumping steadily through my veins. I begin pacing back and forth, counting my steps as I go, repeating rhymes about the Storm under my breath, struggling not to think of Hali.

Suddenly the walkie springs to life, and I hear Alistair's strained voice crackling over the static.

"Weymouth Island, we are called to watch."

Jeff and I freeze. The Storm has officially begun.

Jeff hands me the walkie. "It's your turn."

Something stirs deep within me; my blood awakens. I was born for this.

"May you stand strong on the foundations of your ancestors," Alistair crackles.

I hold the walkie up to my mouth. "Our houses stand so that all may stand."

"Survive the night so that others may live, then turn your face to the sun." The last line we say all together: "Fares well the house that's ready." I think I hear Miles's voice buried in the chorus.

All is silent until a horrifying howl climbs out of the deep as a thousand voices of the dead rise up from below the waves.

"God, that sound could peel the skin from your bones," Jeff utters, his face pale.

The swirling light from the lighthouse turns a deep crimson, and the ocean steadily rises all at once, like a tsunami rising from underneath. There is a muffled cracking sound, like that of a spine breaking, and the metal dock that I dove off to save Miles breaks away from the shore and floats out to sea. Shards of jagged timber are thrust upward in the foaming void before it disappears quickly under the Dehset.

Suddenly the Weymouth siren goes silent. My insides turn to stone as we wait for it to resume, and when it finally does, three long tones sound. Three means the water is coming—and the dead with it.

CHAPTER THIRTY-TWO

S urge," Jeff commands, a single word. I yank open a control panel in the wall beside us. Inside sits a metal lever; I pump it three times and then pull it downward with a hard yank. We watch as the water sluices open in the garden, the driveway, and around the house. Inside the house, I can hear metal gears turning as House Beuvry prepares itself; gutters widen, locks are sealing, and the pipes in our subbasement are opening up.

"Here we go," Jeff breathes as he reaches out for my hand. I tuck mine inside his, and we both look out to the sea. A thick mist roils on the surface of the Dehset as the water churns under the twilight, now an inky black. I lean over the stone barrier, squinting at the sea.

Jeff speaks. "There they are, the bastards." It begins with a pale white glow that flickers up from underneath. Horrifying white tendrils spread over the face of the water until the whole shore is bathed in mist and white. The waves grow higher, climbing up the sides of the cliff walls, not so much a tsunami as a steadily rising wall of water thrust up from below. The glowing wall of water reaches the top of the cliffs, and the spill begins to spread outward from there. The pale water swallows everything as it builds speed, hurtling forward from the shore, the glow of the dead visible beneath foaming white crests. It swallows the shore where I first kissed Miles, swallows the grassy knoll where Hali and I once played pirates.

"Steady now," Jeff says. The deluge of water is plunging toward the Sacred Line. Our holy wall of white stones glitters in the moonlight. Pale smoke curls from the wall's cracks. The glowing waves rush angrily toward it, screaming their way across the east side of the island. I push my fingernails into my palms as I pray: *hold*. It has worked before; there were years when the surge was completely stopped by the Sacred Line, but this wave is bigger than anything I've ever seen. The trees look like miniatures beside it.

"It's not going to stop them, is it?" I whisper.

Jeff grips the wall "No." The stones underneath our feet begin to vibrate as the water funnels toward the Sacred Line.

"Mabel, get down!" Jeff shouts, but it's too late. When the surge meets the Sacred Line, an enormous wave of energy pushes outward at the impact, like a sonic blast. It passes through me, and I'm thrown backward up against the house, Jeff blown over next to me. We brush it off and leap back to our feet, shaken but needing to see. When I reach the wall, every part of me goes still as my eyes and brain struggle to comprehend what I'm seeing.

The water rises up over the Sacred Line as if there's an invisible wall holding it back, like a river stopped by a glass wall. All the way down to the Dehset Shore, water pulsates against the barrier, two forces of nature meeting, neither one able to give. From inside the wall of water, I can make out hundreds—thousands—of pulsating, glowing figures straining against the barrier.

A living wall of nightmares.

"Will it hold?" I whisper. My chest tightens as the pillar of water grows ever higher, as the waves from the incoming sea join the others, the pressure piling the waves ever higher. It climbs upward until it's almost level with the lighthouse. It's *terrifying*. Beside me, I notice Jeff's hands shaking as he grips our stone wall.

"Have you ever felt this island breathe, Mabel?" I can tell he's making conversation to help calm himself down.

"Yes," I answer gracefully, my eyes never leaving the wall of water. "A few times."

"It happened to me . . . twice. Once when I was out fishing with my father in Bridgewater Creek, the water began to vibrate, ever so slightly. Then I felt myself rise upward, and the wind came up to meet my face. I felt the island inhale and exhale beneath my feet. It was extraordinary. The second time was when we lowered your father and Hali into the ground. It was raining that day—"

I close my eyes, remembering the rain pattering on my black dress, the cloying smell of hydrangea hanging in the air. Beside me, Hali was holding my hand.

Only, she wasn't really there.

The Sacred Line gives a shudder, the mist becoming denser as it crowds around the base. The wall of water is beginning to stream down over the sides as Jeff continues his story.

"On the day we buried them, I felt the island breathe once more, only this time it wasn't exhilarating. It was *sad*; its cry moved around me. I'm telling you this because it's important to remember that Weymouth *chose* your family. It chose us. We are its protectors, its guardians, and teachers of its history. Wouldn't you want people like us to hold the world in our hands?" He chuckles.

"I mean, who better than an old gay guy and a mad teenager?"

"You're not *that* old."

He reaches over and adjusts the salt gun on my back. "And you're not that mad."

We smile, trying to quell our nerves, then turn to watch the swell of water, which keeps growing, like soon it will blot out the moon.

"Jesus," Jeff whispers, looking up at it. "Will Lynwood was right. A *Great Storm*." I look over at him in shock. "There's long been a theory floating around that when houses align, the Storm grows stronger. The last Storm was the one that killed your father and Hali. But there was something else happening around that time: Your father and Alistair were very close friends. It triggered a big Storm. We know that the dead adapt to our defenses, but when they sense a strength rising between the houses, they're going to meet it. A friendship made it violent; but think of what a romantic bond, one decades in the making, would do. An alliance between the first and the last houses, tying everything up between them."

"What are you saying?" I whisper, my eyes on the towering wall of water. "That this is my fault?"

"No. That you and Miles are called to change the island— together. Your love and bond are going to become the force they're afraid of. That's what this Great Storm is about—eliminating the threat. I think Lynwood knew that. He knew it was coming when Miles arrived."

I watch with horror as enormous white stones begin being pushed out from the center of the Sacred Line. The ground begins to shake.

329

"Do you remember when we used to play Jenga with Hali?" Jeff asks, and I nod. The edge of the wall begins crumbling as the surge pulses against it; and there, at the foot of this colossal wall of water, sits the Cabot mansion, like a tiny dollhouse . . . waiting.

"Miles," I whisper, my desperation to protect him overriding every other emotion. I hear the first sharp crack; it's like a stick breaking over a knee. Then another and another, until the sound fills the air. The stones begin pulling apart, and Jeff steadies himself.

"Brace!" Liam Cabot's muffled voice screams over the walkie, and before we have a chance to respond, an explosion ricochets throughout the island. The stones from the Sacred Line explode outward, some thrown a full half mile from the pressure, landing with huge thuds. I watch one go wheeling through the Des Roches garden, smashing through its protective fences, while another rolls down the main road, carving destruction as it goes. Our holy rocks fall as the swell of water pours like a shroud dropping through the air. The sea and the dead inside it rush toward the Cabot mansion and crash against the Cabot barricades, swarming up over the sides; the water is at least as high as the third-floor windows. I try to imagine what Miles is going through right now. Is he huddled back with his cousins and Alistair? Is he terrified, the way I was when I was a child, or is excitement potent in his bloodstream? *Keep him safe. Keep him safe.* I'm not sure who I'm pleading with, but I can't stop.

"We should help them," I choke, the agony of watching too much to bear. "How can we just stand here while they could be dying?"

Jeff's face remains unmoved, like a marble sentry. "The

Cabots are a strong people. They'll be okay. Alistair's without a soul already, so the dead might leave him be." He smiles wryly. "Miles will be all right." I know he's lying. "Off this island, in their normal lives, human beings know there is *always* a risk. You could get murdered by a serial killer or die in a car accident or get shot. Here on Weymouth, we're mostly safe. We don't carry as much risk as those who live over the bridge. Our risk comes every ten years or so, and we know what it looks like." His voice is solemn. "And I would rather face death in its true form."

The Cabot mansion sits dark and still as water foams around the outside. The eerie glow of the dead sweeps toward the entrances, looking for places to get inside.

"It's so quiet," I whisper, but that's because the chaos is now inside the house. The horror is coming to them—and it's coming for us.

"All we can do now is wait." Jeff's shoulders slouch. "I know it seems a strange thing to say, but we should try to get some rest."

I almost laugh. "You expect me to rest now? With an army of the dead swarming the house of the boy I kissed today?"

"Sounds like normal life on Weymouth to me," he says with a raised eyebrow and a shrug. "It's your only chance to rest, Mabel. We'll head inside, get ourselves ready. There isn't anything we can do now, and it's going to be a long night." Reluctantly I tear myself away from Cloudbreak and my view of the Cabot house. He's right—there's nothing I can do. I carefully follow Jeff down into the hallway, mindful of all the set traps around us.

We quietly sink down onto couches in the living room. The Beuvry house is as empty as a tomb, and I'm reminded that out of my family of five, only two remain. I cough; there is a dull ache in my lungs that hasn't dissipated since my frantic, freezing run through the woods.

I bite my cheek. "We should check everything again. I can run the checklist backward, start from top to bottom this time."

Jeff leans back on our antique green sofa and puts a pillow behind his head. "There comes a point of diminishing returns. We'll only make things worse the more we tinker. Our house is ready. We're ready." He closes his eyes.

I know there is no way I can sleep, so instead I focus on relaxing my limbs, which feel as though they have been knotted for days. My body slowly begins to uncoil, muscle by muscle, as the Storm rages against our neighbors' houses. The first wave is always the worst; it's what the Cabots are handling now. But then the surge continues, wave by wave. It continues to push the dead inland. We're the last house to the sea—luckiest in some ways but not in others. If the dead get here, they're the strongest of the bunch, and we're the only thing standing between them and the bridge to the mainland. *They're angry when they get here.*

My eyelids begin to droop. The wind, the water, my frantic run across the island, the realization about Hali—it's all too much, and my body begins to take forcefully what my mind does not want to give. And so I fall asleep sitting up on the couch, waiting for the end of the world.

CHAPTER THIRTY-THREE

M abel! Wake up." I'm on my feet before I'm fully awake, which brings a wave of vertigo. It takes a second for it to all rush back to me.

"How long were we out?" I ask.

"We've been sleeping for about two hours. I set a timer." *Of course he did.* Jeff holds up the walkie. There is buzzy static, followed by a prerecorded and looped announcement on our radio system. The rule is, if your house is overrun, you get to the switch, and it sends out the announcement to all the other houses. It's not for aid—no one is coming—but it helps the next house get ready. Right now an eerie female voice plays over and over on a loop. The words fill our quiet living room.

"The Cabot house has fallen. The Des Roches house has fallen. The Pope house has fallen. The Grimes house has fallen. The Bodhmall house has fallen. The Pelletier house has fallen." Jeff looks over at me, his face drawn as he checks his watch.

"What's wrong?" I press.

"Six houses in two hours. Jesus, usually it's two houses in five hours. They've never fallen that fast before." His face is panicked as he flutters through his bag. This scares me: I've never seen my

Guardian undone. "That means we don't have much time. Forget what you're about to see." He reaches into his backpack . . . and pulls out a pack of cigarettes.

"What the hell are you doing?" I ask. "I'm sorry—you smoke? Since when? Who are you?"

Jeff lights up and takes a long inhale. "Since my whole life. I'm always trying to quit, but after Lynwood, I decided to quit trying to quit. For now." He blows out a line of smoke and does it with style. "Don't worry yourself. I'll quit again after the Storm. Something to look forward to." He turns the cigarette over and leans back, his eyes on the windows. "I'm not sure there is a worse feeling than the waiting."

Outside our windows the Storm roars on. The screams coming off the Dehset are horrifying, and I wonder if I listen closely whether I'll hear humans screaming as well. My friends, my people. I run my hands over my face as reality comes rushing back to my sleepy brain. *Are we all going to die tonight?*

I stretch my legs out on the couch; I'm sore all over, which is not a great way to start the night. The smoke from Ser Jeff's cigarette lingers in the air above our heads, lazily circling in the breeze. It's heavy and hazy and smells like the sea: dead, clear, salt. I blink.

That's not smoke.

I realize it the second Jeff does, and we both stand up and stagger backward. It's not smoke. It's *mist*, slowly coiling under the doors like a lazy snake, pouring through rooms and hovering in the air above us. Cautiously I reach out and wriggle my fingers in it; the mist is so thick, I can move it back and forth. *When the mist begins to rise, say a prayer.* I watch it slowly fill up our foyer.

"They're almost here." Jeff hoists his backpack up and over his shoulders. "We should begin. I'll start with the—" Suddenly everything around us begins to shake violently. Pictures rattle off the walls, and furniture crashes face down; our grandfather clock—with hands pointed at midnight—crashes to the floor, glass shattering everywhere. Jeff grabs me and pulls me under the piano, which begins to roll back and forth on its wheels, both of us desperately clutching its legs. Under our knees, the floor rolls; it's as though seismic waves are passing underneath our house. The piano makes a loud cracking sound as one of the legs gives way.

"Move!" Jeff screams, and we both shoot out from the small gap underneath the piano. I lunge for the banister at the bottom of the stairs; Jeff darts underneath the doorframe. Then, like the slowing of a beating heart, the rumbling comes to an abrupt stop. The mist thickens.

"Was that an earthquake?" I yell, trying to keep the panic out of my voice.

"But that's impossible, right? There's never been—" I can see that Jeff is equally shaken as he tries to find an answer. "If the ground beneath us is loosened, there might be more places for the dead to get in, but that doesn't make the most sense, unless it's a—"

I gasp and turn to him, unsure how I know this. "What if it's not them? It's *her*. Weymouth. The island is trying to warn us."

"Warn us about—" But Jeff doesn't get a chance to finish because a wave of seawater smashes through every window on the first floor. I watch him vanish underneath the water, and then suddenly I'm tumbling in a rush of glass and salt water, smashed up against something hard. Everything is water; I have no sense of what is up and what is down; instead there is only chaos. A thousand tiny cuts scratch themselves across my skin as I tumble, a rag doll in a washing machine. Jeff is gone. I am gone. The world is salt water.

I slam up against the foyer wall, water pinning me up against a dresser that once held Hali's trinkets. I gasp a quick breath of air as the fast-rising flood sucks at my legs and chest. Another wave crashes through the broken glass, and it submerges me in brine. As the water swallows me, the screams of the dead under the water become deafening.

Kill them, they scream. I use my feet to push off the dresser and claw upward. When my head finally emerges out of the water, I suck in all the air I can before screaming, "JEFF!"

"Mabel! Over here!" My Guardian is at the end of the hallway, trying to pull himself up on a wall sconce. Our possessions float all around us in a bizarre collision of the human and natural worlds. The water shifts, and I swim as fast as I can through floating picture frames and umbrellas, tree branches, and a broken shutter. Mist is still snaking along the ceiling. I sputter above the foaming waves. "Is this— What—"

"NO!" Jeff yells in reply, his feet slipping. "This isn't normal!"

Chaos bobs all around me as I push my way through the water. I try not to think about what could be underneath.

As I push my way to Jeff, the waves batter the windows around the house and water continues to pour in. We have to move. We have to get *up*. There are traps to reset, processes to keep us safe. My foot catches on one of my mother's antique console tables, and as I pull myself up on top of it, something wet slithers past my ankles. Water foams around me as I crouch on top of the table, my head still spinning from where I smacked it against the wall.

Jeff regains his composure and leaps down into the angry current frothing down our hallway. He almost slips on my mother's lacy doily as he frantically wipes the water off his face.

"This was not how this is supposed to go! We start on the main level with the traps, with the dead coming up from below—"

I cut him off with a yell. "I know. I know! We're supposed to start at the bottom and work our way up, staying above the water as it goes, but that's not what's happening now, so we have to pivot. WE HAVE TO. Right? Forget our plans, Jeff!"

He looks at me with disbelief.

"Yeah, you heard me. I said 'forget our plans'! The next step in the Storm protocol is what? Climb, right? Get to the next floor. That's what we need to do."

"I can't," he says before his face collapses. "We forgot the flue."

My heart sinks. We *have to* open the flue. Otherwise the water will continue to rise, and most importantly, we can't open the lower traps until the water pressure has equalized it from the outside. If the surge had started in the basement, that would have been when we'd have normally pulled it. But now . . . We both glance down the hallway. The flue is set halfway down to the basement cellar in a narrow stone staircase. It's close but currently submerged under about five feet of rolling black water.

The house gives a crumpling, groaning noise, settling under the weight of the water. There is a slight shift of the stone and lumber around us.

"I'll go," I say, and Jeff scoffs.

"Mabel, no."

I'm already taking off my backpack. "I'm the better swimmer of the two of us. Remember when I bested you last year in the Weymouth relay?"

He frowns. "I had a cramp."

"Yeah, well, I have talent. I'm not a kid anymore. You have to let me be your equal today. Otherwise we aren't going to make it."

Jeff grabs my arm; his skin is clammy. "Hurry. It won't be long before this all gets far worse, and we don't want to be separated when *they* come." There's no time to discuss it further. "Remember to pump it up three times." I dive off the console table into the water, which is shockingly cold. I'm *swimming through my living room*. Tiny white pieces of bone bob around me.

I quickly reach the area where the living room spirals down to the basement level. I keep my head above the waves, trying not to think about what lies on the bottom level, what horrors are possibly waiting there.

I take a deep breath and duck under, salt water stinging my eyes as I kick forward, swimming down a staircase. Quickly I reach the landing and find the picture frame that hides the flue, thankfully still in place. I shove it aside, and a portrait of my great-grandmother sinks down into the darkness. Underneath is the pump. I push the handle upward: One, the flue is open. Below me, I hear the rumble of gears as the latching mechanism opens. Two, it signals the pressure change, and three, I throw it upward as my body starts to run out of air. *Done.* From underneath the water, a harsh clanking sound fills the house. My body senses the current change under the water as the flue gate is yanked open. I gulp air as the water begins going down, slowly at first, and then, out of nowhere, rapidly. *Too rapidly.* It's a drain.

My hand shoots out, grabbing on to the flue lever just as my body is sucked downward toward the basement. The water turns white as it becomes a cascade, frothing down the staircase, my body a rock in a raging river. My arms strain as I heave myself back up the staircase, holding on to the railing and fighting the current that threatens to push me downward. Hand over hand until, finally, I'm up and out.

The water continues to lower until it remains at my shins. I splash my way back through the living room, breathing a sigh of relief when I see that Jeff is exactly where I left him. He leaps down with a splash when I appear.

"Head upstairs," he commands. "This level is no longer safe."

Together we shoulder our bags and slosh down the hallway; I look back once at our main level, the place that was supposed to be our base. Our *safe place* is absolutely decimated; the windows are broken, and water is still pouring through. Huge pieces of glass float on black waves.

"Are we screwed?" I whisper as we make our way toward the stairs. All these things meant to trap, to trick, and one huge wave took them all out. We're supposed to be trapping the dead, on the offense. Instead we're just trying to get our bearings.

Jeff checks the staircase. "Don't lose hope yet. Our house is built for this purpose. She won't fail us. Come on." We make our way up to the next level, which thankfully looks relatively normal—and better yet, it's dry. I could almost sag with relief. I stare down the hallway. All the doors are locked from the outside with complex numerical locks; we can get in, but nothing can get out.

Jeff points to the round, reinforced window at the end of the hallway. "We should have a proper look outside." A second later,

I'm stepping on his open hands for an upward boost, reaching for the iron edge of the windowsill. I peek my head over.

"What is it? What do you see?" Jeff asks. What I see chills me to the bone, *because I can't see anything.*

"Nothing," I whisper. "It's like we don't exist. Like we're floating in space."

"What does that even mean?" he asks, and I'm not sure how to answer. The mist around our house is so thick that outside the window is soupy gray, a blustery mini cyclone. As Jeff struggles to hold me up, I find myself drawn into it, pulled toward its hypnotic patterns. Something appears in the window, something long and thin that elegantly parts the mist. I lean forward, but by that time it's too late.

I lurch backward as five long shadows turn into five bony fingers that hurtle straight for my face, exploding through the glass. One of the fingers rips at my ear, and blood flows down my neck. I fall backward, and Jeff catches me as I collapse.

"Got you!" he yells. Fleshless hands shred themselves on the iron windowsill, trying to get at us. Glass falls to the ground as the long fingers try to find a way through the webbing. Every time the strange, misty bones make contact with the iron, a shrill scream fills the air. One skeletal, ephemeral hand is joined by another and another, each one desperately scraping to get inside the house. I watch in horror as finger bones crack off at the joints, leaving the white metacarpal pounding uselessly over the surfaces. Mist conceals the rest of their form, but I glimpse the shadow of an eyeless face.

"But—but we're on the second level," I stutter as blood drips down my chin. I turn back to Jeff, who is watching the window with a petrified expression as the hands proceed to break themselves apart. The sound is horrifying. *Rip, scream. Rip, howl.* There is something about seeing the hands that makes this real in a way it hadn't been before. Very real, too real. I close my eyes for a second, trying to redirect my brain. The pounding stops without warning, and the bone knobs disappear, yanked back into the mist by the monster that wielded them.

Startled, Jeff picks up the walkie-talkie and turns it to channel 6. Buzzing static fills the air, interrupted every now and then by faint screams.

"Turn it off!" I shriek, and he obeys. I clamp my hands over my ears. This isn't how this is supposed to go; we aren't supposed to be taken by surprise.

"Follow me!" Jeff commands, and I nod, thankful *someone* is acting like they are in charge. Every window is now covered with the swirling gray mist, which gives the entire house a strange, silver tint. Mist pours from underneath the doors and through window cracks, from the boards above our heads and through the garden below. It feels like House Beuvry itself is sagging with it.

We cut our way through the hallway as the dead's maw swallows us whole. We make our way toward where the staircase looks down to the lower level, to get a better assessment, but when Jeff turns to point at something, the lights flicker a single time before we are plunged into darkness. The only electricity is the metallic sharpness in the air, one I can taste on my tongue. I reach for him, feeling nothing but the heavy air.

"Where are the generators?" I yell.

Jeff's voice comes out of the darkness. "They should be coming on in three, two, one . . ." His voice tilts upward at the end, splintering as it goes. He is afraid. Nothing happens—only the dark and the mist remain. "Get out your flashlight, now. NOW!"

As I reach into the backpack, the lights flicker and then come back on. A loud hum fills the house.

"Oh, thank God." Jeff sinks against a wall. "At least one thing went right tonight." My heart slows a bit; we wouldn't have made it in the dark. The lights glow and flicker down the hallway, and an enormous crash sounds from outside the house. We freeze as the sound grows louder, like a metal egg cracking open.

"Was that what I think it was?" I ask him, trying not to sound like a scared little girl, but instead sounding like an absolutely terrified adult.

He gulps. "The East Gate."

My mouth falls open. *The East Gate?*

"Do you mean our impregnable wall of iron and silver? The one that is supposed to hold even after the Storm. The thing my father spent his life building?" I see the answer in Jeff's eyes. My knees go weak. *Our barrier*, the thing that keeps the dead at bay, has fallen, and the Storm has barely begun; dawn is still so many hours away.

We're all alone out here.

CHAPTER THIRTY-FOUR

From downstairs comes a loud thudding. Something is battering against the house. I hear the shattering of glass and the frustrated howls as the dead meet our first defenses. It is the sound of trailing fabric, a snake slithering in the walls. Mist curls in slow, uneasy circles up the stairs.

"They're trying to get in through the main level, but they won't. Our defenses are strong there, even if the porch fell in the surge." My Guardian seems confident.

"So they'll circle around the house, to the other side. Or they'll go up. . . ." I think of the hand reaching through the second-story window, cloaked in mist and shadow. My mind is frantically running through all our defenses, but I have a sinking in my chest that says it's not enough. "Are they in already?"

"No, that would be . . . It's impossible. How would they—"

I interrupt him; we don't have time for his long, thoughtful pauses. "Then we should go higher, to Cloudbreak maybe. Up and out."

"No, that's more vulnerable since it's outside the house. You saw what's out there. The safest place should be here, on this level.

If we follow the plan, then we should end up in the study." Our eyes meet in the dim LED lights.

"Then there is no safe place." We both take a second to weigh this hard truth as chaos rages on the bottom levels of the house. The dead are moving through the shingles—I can hear them—as the mist creeps up the stairs. Jeff has gone rigid; I can see in his eyes that his thoughts are far away; his mouth is set hard.

"We need to get to the Keep, then."

"Are you mad?" I sputter. The Keep is essentially a panic room, hidden in the wall between my room and my mom's room, accessible only from the hallway. The dead can't find us there, but also, once we are in, we are shut in for good; the door can't be reopened. It also makes it so that we can't trap them; we aren't helping, and if we aren't helping, then there is a good chance of them making it to the bridge. "If we're in the Keep, the house will fall. We can't do that. You would literally sacrifice the world to keep us safe."

Jeff won't look at me. "To keep YOU safe." Below us I can hear them trying to tear down the porch, unearthly shrieks filling the air when they are burned by the salt, iron, or paper.

"This house won't fall! It can't. I won't let it," I say as an iron resolve crosses his face.

"And I won't let it take your father's last daughter." Without warning, his arm wraps roughly around mine, and my Guardian begins dragging me down the hallway.

"What—what are you doing?" I shriek, trying to get free. God, he's strong.

"I'm sorry, Mabel, but I have no choice." He's dragging me toward the entrance to the Keep. I know exactly what happens next: I'm safe and he's dead. The other huge families of Wey-mouth are fighting together right now; it's him and me trying to hold this house, and soon it will be just him. And he will die.

"NO!" I shriek, fighting back. "Let me help you. We stay together! You promised you wouldn't leave me. We have to defend the house! If they get to the bridge and cross it . . ."

"I'll take care of it," he says through gritted teeth.

"You'll die! Stop, Jeff, STOP! For Pete's sake—" I fight against him, shoving frantically as he tries to gently but forcefully maneuver me down the hallway.

"Mabel, love, you're making this very hard." He grunts as he lifts me off my feet, crossing my arms over my body and picking me up, rushing forward as I kick and twist in his arms, trying to get my feet back on the ground. Above our heads, the sound of the dead intensifies; I can hear their whispers now, pieces of the languages they once spoke, confused and jumbled in their tongue-less mouths. Tears fill my eyes. I cannot lose him. *I cannot.*

"PUT ME DOWN, GODDAMMIT! JEFF!" The Keep approaches on the left. As a last resort, I slam my fist upward against the bottom of his chin, and he drops me suddenly. I scramble away from him. When he looks up, I see blood on his lip.

"Mabel Beuvry, you punched me!"

I spin around to face him. "Damn right I did, you *bloody* idiot! I'll do it again if you try to drag me somewhere for my own safety. You cannot just throw me into the Keep and leave me there. I deserve to be here. This is my destiny too. You can't take it away because you're scared of losing me!" Drips of water are sneaking through the ceiling above our heads, and I try not to think about what this means: the dead are most definitely in the attic.

Jeff's face turns red. "You're the only thing that matters! Don't you understand? Lynwood was right; this is the Great Storm. It's here because of you and Miles! The first and the last house, the strongest houses on the island. You're the only one that matters! You and Miles together are a threat to the dead; something you do in the future will affect this. If I know you're safe, then I can fight. I can keep them at bay. I swear it. We don't have time to argue about it, so just—"

When it happens, we don't see it coming. Jeff keeps shouting, but I don't hear any of his words because a vaguely human shape moves up in the mist behind him. We don't even have time to react before a shrouded, skeletal hand reaches out, curls its bony fingers around his shoulder, and yanks him backward.

My Guardian is torn away from me, his words disappearing as he is flung up and over the banister. A strangled cry comes out of my mouth as his body falls through the air, bounces off the lower banister, and then disappears into the mist below, which swallows him whole. I hear a cry of pain when he splashes into the bottom level. When I look up, a grinning skull-like shape stands unsteadily in the space where my Guardian used to be. Hollowed black eye sockets center on me.

"JEFF!" I scream, totally unhinged. The ghoul moves out of the mist toward me, and without thinking, I pull the salt gun off my shoulder and begin firing it. Salt crystals slice through the mist like tiny blades. They embed in his face, where they grow wider upon impact, dissolving him from the inside out. I fire the gun again and again, until there is nothing left but a swirl of mist.

I sprint down the stairs, screaming Jeff's name. Water sloshes to my shins when I reach the landing. The entire floor is still flooded. I can't see him, can't find him in the tiny waves that fill my house. I plunge my hands into the water up to my wrists in salty cold, but there is no body, no person. My breaths become increasingly short as I slosh around. *Be here, be here, please, God.*

"Where are you?" My scream is pure desperation.

Finally I hear a loud gasp of air to my right. I spin around in time to see a hand push up between the waves, grasping for something, anything. I'm on Jeff in a second, yanking him up, his head emerging from under the water. He coughs up mouthfuls of water as I pull him up to a sitting position, my arms wrapped around his chest. His face is pale and bluish, lips purple, and eyes bloodshot with pain. He unleashes a stream of curses the likes of which this island has never heard.

"My leg, Mabel, oh God!" he yells in agony. "It's broken! I'm so sorry, sorry for everything. I've failed."

"Shhhh . . . Let me look," I order him, gently raising his leg up above the water before my jaw clenches. It's definitely broken. His ankle is twisted the wrong way, and there is a limp lifelessness to everything below the knee. He clutches his side. "I think . . . I think I may have broken a rib as well. I hit the banister on the way down."

"I saw. Nice job."

He doesn't laugh, instead wincing with each breath. He takes my hand, and I know what's coming. The wave of grief that rises through me is unbearable. I cannot lose a second father.

"Mabel, look at me. LOOK AT ME. This is where we say goodbye."

"Oh my God, shut up. Just shut up already."

He tries to make eye contact with me. "You can't get us both upstairs, and there's not enough time. They're here." He grips my arm, his knuckles white. "Leave me here and get into the Keep. Maybe I can play dead. Mabel, I'm ordering you to listen to me." Tears gather in his eyes. "Please."

"Yeah, well, lucky for you, I never listen." I see in his eyes that he understands: I will not let him die here; I will NOT. My mind races as the mist at the end of the hallway swirls into a tall, vaguely human shape. We have to move, but he's right. I can't get him up the stairs by myself. My mind runs frantically through our house, finally landing on a desperate idea.

"Come on, you useless lump," I mutter. With a loud moan, I gather my Guardian underneath his arms and heave the top half of his body up against mine. *God, he's heavy.* Water streams off us as I drag him out of the foyer and away from the stairs. I focus on each step, trying to avoid panicked thoughts invading my mind: *What are we going to do? What is Jeff going to do? The dead are in the house. Has the house fallen already? We aren't ready. We haven't trapped any yet. What happened to Miles? Where is Norah right now? He'd better not die. Shit, shit, shit.*

The water grows shallower near the kitchen, but that makes Jeff heavier, harder to drag. He gives a cry as his broken leg bumps against a wall, but he's also trying to push with the other one to help me along, which is making it harder.

"Stop pushing!" I snap as I grit my teeth, worried I'll crack a tooth. "I need you to be a rag doll." My arms are shaking with exhaustion and my back is screaming, but I can't stop. *He's so heavy. This is impossible.* But also . . . *I have to get him there.* I hear a loud cracking above me, followed by the crushing roar of metal being torn away from the side of the house. Outside, the howls of the dead become a fever pitch, and every hair on my arms stands up.

"They're coming inside." Jeff groans, his eyes rolling, right on the edge of delirium. I let out a primal, female roar as I summon all my strength and drag him down the remainder of the hallway in one long stretch.

Ahead of me on the right is our kitchen; it's raised up from the rest of the hallway by two single stairs, two stairs I never thought about until this second. But now, as I haul a grown man up and over them, they seem like mountains. The doors to the kitchen are locked with a small iron wheel, its code represented by images. Panic rises in me as I struggle to align the symbols. I can't look back.

Star, rain, branch, bird. The lock doesn't open. *Rain, branch, bird, rain.* In my peripheral vision, a misty skeleton in a ratty dress takes form at the end of the hallway. *Jesus.* I try it again, and then I hear Jeff whisper weakly, "Rain, star, branch, bird." I spin the dial, and the lock turns. I kick open the door to the kitchen and drag him through as he yelps out in pain. Once we are through, I slam the door hard behind us, barricading it from the inside.

Our kitchen is untouched. Copper pots hang neatly above the island, reflecting the strange, silver light outside. The counters gleam; all the dishes are put away, and the appliances look extra shiny. A lemon sits on a pile of peaches in a blue-and-white bowl. Outside the door, chaos and death rage.

"Did you clean before the Storm?" I huff, dragging him across the floor.

"Of course." He manages a grim smile, followed by a grimace. "Can't have the dead see our home looking a mess."

At the back of the kitchen, I fling open the door to our salt pantry.

"This is your plan?" Jeff coughs, but he has no energy to fight me. I gently lay him down on the floor and then push into the salt pantry, violently shoving past the barrels. I crumple up a pillow for his head out of empty bags and set his pack down next to it. Then, using every ounce of my remaining strength, I pull his body into the salt pantry.

"What a nice place to rest my head," he says weakly, laying his head against the bags. I rip open his pack and find a bottle of water and the first aid kit.

"Open your mouth," I command, and he listens. I dump four painkillers into his mouth and wash them down with water. "Swallow." He does as I say. "Now close your eyes and mouth."

"Why?"

"DO IT!" I growl in a monstrous voice he's never heard before; even I don't quite recognize it. He follows my directions as I begin dumping salt barrels over his body. Salt pours out, burying Jeff until he is literally a giant mound of salt. The air around me dances and sparkles with tiny salt crystals; they are in my mouth, my hair. Every cut on my body stings. I hastily clear an area around his head and face so that he can breathe and then thickly spread the salt under the pantry door: a warning.

"The dead should know better than to come in here," I say. "I hope." I lean over him and press my hand against his face. "Sleep, and when you wake up, I'll hopefully be taking you to a hospital."

"I told you to go to the Keep." Tears flood his eyes. I've never seen him so vulnerable. "You could stay in here with me. I'll tell you every Guardian secret I know. I can't bear the thought that something might happen to you out there, and I won't be there to help you. Dammit."

I kiss his forehead, tears gathering in my eyes as well. "Jeff. I'm a Beuvry, and I'm almost an adult. This is my house, and you're my family. Let me protect you." I take a jagged sigh. "I can't keep Hali, but I swear I will be keeping you. Also, I'm going to take this." I reach into his pack and pull out a needle. It's a shot of pure adrenaline. We only have one.

He grabs my hand. "Remember the traps. Use your weapons— all of them. Mabel, don't get cornered. Trap as many as you safely can and then get to the Keep, the world be damned. The bridge will have to worry about itself. I would sacrifice cities to watch you grow up."

"*You will*," I say forcefully. "Stay quiet. I'll be back for you." I stand up, acting much stronger than I feel.

He closes his eyes; he's fading. "I love you, Mabel."

Trying not to cry, I shut the door behind me and turn off the light to the pantry. Salt pours out under the bottom of the door; no smart dead would breach it.

I move to the other side of the kitchen, making sure I'm out of Jeff's earshot before I slide down to the floor, pulling myself underneath our marble countertop. The panic I've been holding back rushes forward, rising inside me until a violent sob is yanked out of my chest. I clutch my knees and stuff my shirt into my mouth, silencing the cries so that Jeff won't hear them. So that *they* won't hear. I scream into the wet fabric again and again, my hands shaking and my body following suit. The thought passes through me like a cannonball, blowing apart, leaving nothing behind.

I am the only Beuvry left.

Ser Lynwood of House Pope

I think it's May.
They aren't listening. They can't see THE
TRUTH. For years, I've tried to warn them,
quietly, Alistair and his allies on the Triumvirate;
they see me increasingly as a crazy old man, my
warnings falling on deaf ears as they prattle on
about the politics of the island, or the children,
or other subjects that don't matter. They don't
understand; nothing matters if this family doesn't
survive. I need Crake and Eryk and Cordelia to
live, because it's coming. I hope they will not be
here to see the disaster firsthand. I hope they are
far away. I hope we are all far away. They don't
listen to me; they wave me away like a rambling
man, delusion creeping through my thoughts as
I'm left in my bedroom, painting the truth until
someone finds it.

They don't know that I have read every record
from every Storm. I see the patterns lurking
underneath, mixed throughout the diaries of

housewives and gravediggers, great patriarch manifestoes, and children's rhymes. It's there in the early Mintus letters of the 1920s, there in the Pelletier poems of the 1880s. The island creaks with anticipation of another house alignment, the one that will change everything. I couldn't figure out who it would be all this time—the Gillis girl and the Nickerson boy? But then the arrival of Miles Cabot, and I knew what was bringing the Great Storm, the only thing that can bring it—the alignment of the First and the Last House, an unbreakable one, bonded through love. Because of this, it's likely that one Storm will rise that is unlike the others. I have found these occurrences and have brought them to the proper people, but they don't want to hear it, won't listen to the truth.

The real proof, though, is in the numbers. If you study the numbers of the Storms, the years and the astrological readings, the weather systems, the constellations, and the latitudes of the current of the Dehset, if you study the number of families and the members within them, if you look to historical records of Nova Scotia and the nautical points at which ships turn back from Weymouth, you'll see a pattern, a spiraling, grand pattern indiscernible to all but me. Miles and Mabel will fall in love, and they will have opened the gates of hell—and they will also be the ones to close it.

Especially when they are old enough to change the old ways. I've begun taking notes on this—I have to make my family listen to me. If I cannot keep them safe, what kind of Guardian am I? I have a device that will hopefully help, but it has to be high up so that it can gather the sun before the long night. The numbers are whispering to me; my sleep decreases as my understanding goes with it. I feel the darkness approaching.

CHAPTER THIRTY-FIVE

I let five agonizing minutes pass. Five whole minutes in the dark kitchen, with hell swirling just outside the door. I do my best to ignore the blood pounding in my ears and the way my vision is swirling ever so slightly. There is a tightness in my chest as my thoughts spiral in maddening circles. *This isn't how the Storm was supposed to go.* It was supposed to be an organized thing; Jeff, my mom, and me pulling triggers, setting traps, and making jokes as we move upward through the house in an orderly fashion. We would be ready for them; it would be as we have predicted with all our history, all our information, a lifetime of preparation for this day.

But the joke's on us. We should have known better than to cage a wild thing. The Storm adapts. Lynwood knew it would change once Miles arrived. He tried to warn everyone without putting us in the spotlight. But then he fell.

I hear the dead waiting outside my kitchen door.

"Breathe." I say it to myself over and over again until I finally listen, until I finally force my body to obey. My heart starts to slow, the panic along with it.

"One thing at a time. Just one," I whisper to myself, closing my eyes. "Focus."

COLLEEN OAKES

Okay, what do we need to do next? I hear Jeff's voice in my head, even though my Guardian is feet away, passed out in the salt pantry. It reminds me that the longer I stay here, the higher the risk I am to him. The dead will be looking for us, and when they find me, they will find him.

So that's the first thing I need to do: draw them away from Jeff toward the upper floors. Once they are there, I can trigger the traps. A plan forms, but I'm frozen to the spot, desperate to stay here, safe on these black-and-white kitchen tiles. Ten seconds, that's what I'll give myself, I decide. Ten whole seconds of happy memories before I run.

One, two, three: Miles kissing me beside the ocean, salt on his lips.

Four, five, six: My dad pushing me on the tire swing out back as my mom reads in the shade.

Seven, eight, nine: Hali running around the yard with a stick in her hand, so free.

Ten: What comes next.

I slam the adrenaline needle into my leg and push the release into my body. Liquid lightning floods through my veins as I bolt to my feet and scramble toward the door, then press my ear against it. Jesus. I can hear my heart pounding in my ears as every nerve in my body lights up.

On the other side I hear nothing, but the mist is leaking from underneath it, which could mean everything or nothing. I push open the door as quietly as I can, step out, and then shut it firmly behind me, setting the codes back into place, hoping it will be enough to protect Jeff.

When I turn, there are three dense shapes sailing toward me

with limbs too long, fleshless figures with the shadows of cheek-bones, and cavities where their hearts should be.

Draw them away. "I'm here, ghosts!" I scream ridiculously. I unhitch my salt gun and raise it up as I walk backward, moving away from the kitchen and toward the living room. The dead slowly emerge in the flickering light, and I swallow my horror. A tall figure in a dress made of swirling gray raises an arm in my direction. Fingers of white bone reach out toward me as the air fills with the scent of rot.

I lunge sideways, reaching for a fancy brass candelabra on the wall, sneaking my hand around the center candle. I push back-ward, and a panel on the floor in front of where the dead hover over the water is hauled open with a screech. A second later, nine-foot iron spears jut up straight out of the floor. The dead fall back with a shriek as a few of them evaporate into mist. Most aren't close enough to the spikes to be killed; instead they hiss at me, blocked from continuing down the hallway by an iron fence and a pit filled with shredded paper below it—a combination of a the-saurus, the poetry of Byron, and Dad's old comic books.

It buys me only minutes. I plunge through the house, the dead raging behind me. I hear a hiss in my ear as I pass the library, but I can't stop, not until I make it to the back staircase. I see the entrance ahead of me, tucked secretly behind a bookcase that I have to manually open. I'm almost there when something wet slithers around my ankle, and before I can reach for my salt gun, my feet are jerked out from under me, and I hit the ground hard, elbows cracking against the damp floor.

It's like being plunged into another world. The fog is deep down here, a thick, swampy thing. Pain shoots up through my elbows. I may have chipped a bone. With a groan, I turn over, and when I do, there is a grinning, rotted face right next to mine. A scream rips through me as I push backward, my brain trying to comprehend. She was lying in wait for me, prone on her stomach like a snake. Her smile is hideous, a nightmare of rotted teeth and decaying lips, her face made of mist and bone. As I jerk backward, her body curls like smoke over a fire, but I know if she touches me, I will feel the pain as she rips me apart.

Her loose jawbone clicks like she's trying to talk to me. I can't tell how old she was when she died, since her face isn't quite right; the Dehset Sea has distorted it all into smooth bones and dark holes. Her breath washes over me, reeking of death.

"Get away!" I shriek, kicking back at her. My boot meets her jawbone, and it dissolves into a pile of bone dust and mist. Her head bobs up and down—trying to laugh, I think—as her skeletal fingers reach for me. She slithers upward, reaching for my neck with a howl, and behind her, I can see more of them. Her eyes are two glowing orbs focusing hungrily on me, and for a second, I think, *This is it.*

But I don't freeze; instead I reach down into the front pocket of my backpack and search around for a small cylinder with a plastic trigger on top of it.

A rotted tongue slithers out of the place where her mouth used to be. I suppress a scream as I whip the cylinder out in front of me and press the trigger. A mechanical ticking sounds, followed by a loud pop. I throw the cylinder at the ghost just as it explodes. My world fills with snow; only instead of snow, it's ten thousand tiny pieces of paper floating in the air. The ghost dissolves with a scream as the paper covers her, each part turning into a wisp of smoke.

I scramble to my feet and bolt toward the stairs as shreds of Shakespeare's complete works float down around me. Behind me, the dead scream. It's time to trap these assholes. I reach the bookcase and yank a Shirley Jackson down from the spines; I have one shot at this.

Behind the book sits a metal latch; I turn it to the right and push it back in. The door swings open, and I catch it with one hand as it goes; with the other, I grab one more book—*The Stand* by Stephen King. In one swift movement, I pull the door quickly shut behind me. *Practice makes perfect.*

On the other side of the bookcase, the dead are pushing at the door. I hold it against them, waiting . . . waiting. Then finally I hear it, a metal ping sounding out as *The Stand* slides back into place, now over a notch in the wood. Ten iron rings roll out from in between various books, fall to the ground around the door, form a barrier around the bookcase, and trap any dead that dare to cross them. I hear their moans of frustration as I sprint up the servant stairs in the back.

We almost never use this end of the house. Cautiously I push open the door to our third floor. It's darker than the rest of the house, but it doesn't have the chaos of downstairs. I take a second, leaning over my knees and trying not to think of what I just saw. But the dead don't rest; they don't sleep. I hear a hiss, and they're on me again, flowing up the stairs like smoke.

I slip into the first bedroom on the left, adorned with beautiful black wallpaper and a simple antique bed, a relic that belonged to my grandparents. We only go into this room a few times a year, to shore it up—other than that, it stays barren . . . because it's a trap. The wallpaper is laced with small iron threads, there is salt in the mattress, and the mat under my feet is woven paper. Around me the house creaks and shudders, and then I hear the front door open. Downstairs, a clock chimes. It's midnight. I stand trembling in the room, my salt gun held out in front of me, waiting for the dead. The adrenaline is making me feel alive and a little bit wild. *Come and get me*, I think, but the problem is, they already have. When I look away for a second, something yanks on the bottom of my jacket—the way a little kid would. I glance down and swallow a scream. The *thing* yanking on it is a child. *Was a child*. Rounded bones where cheeks once were catch the light as he looks up at me. His eyes burn with a pale green wickedness, and his hair is made up of curls of mist.

"Mama?" he whispers, so freshly deceased that he can still form words. I wrench away from him, but he ambles toward me with an unbalanced gait. "Mama?"

What the actual hell?

"Mama?" He's almost pitiful until he reaches for my neck. A small hunter-green sack hangs on the back of the antique bed frame, and without tearing my eyes from him, I rip it open. Coiled inside is a paper chain, the kind you make on holidays, only it's covered with words. I hold it out toward the dead child, and he snarls and backs away. Moving quickly, I lay it across the length of the bedroom, creating a barrier between us.

More dead follow into the room behind him, and they begin pushing forward, a dozen glowing orbs all set on me. They shove the dead child forward until he falls directly onto the paper chain. He lets out a wail as his form starts smoking, and I watch in horror as he dissolves.

With a scream, I begin firing shots of salt straight into the mist and don't stop. The dead in front of me dissolve with loud screams, which gives me time to lunge across the room toward the windows. On the wall near the bed sits a little metal bell, the same one my great-grandmother once used to summon her children to her bedside. The bell releases a trigger, which releases a pulley, and a wall of thin iron chains falls from the ceiling behind them. The dead give a wail. They're now trapped between the paper chain and an iron curtain.

"See you later, you prats!" I salute them and roll underneath the bed, where a hole has been cut out of the floor—roughly the size of a grave. I choose not to think about that.

Once inside, I slide a latch above my head and pull myself through the floor to the next bedroom. It's a simple snare trap, executed perfectly; it's maybe the one thing I've done right today. My pride doesn't last long, since when I climb out into the other bedroom—our old nursery, complete with pelican stencils on the wall—I see a horde of the dead waiting for me.

Since I don't have time to execute the traps in that room, I climb out of the floor and sprint past two of them. One tangles her fingers in my hair, but my knife is ready, and a second later some of my curls are left on the floor. Breathing hard, I sprint down the hallway—the mist makes it hard to see, and everything seems like it's spinning out of control. I veer past bedroom after bedroom while, behind me, the dead move slowly *until they don't.*

Up ahead are the two fanciest doors in the Beuvry Estate, and behind them lies a staple of a past age: the Grand Ballroom. I slam hard into the doors, my hands shaking as I try to open them. The words STAY AND DANCE are stenciled over the door, alongside two painted Victorians bowing. Jeff would be so angry if he knew I was heading here. He doesn't like this room, thinks it's dangerous. But my Guardian is passed out cold in the salt pantry, and mist zombies are still coming up the stairs, so yeah, *I'm going into the bloody ballroom.* Finally the door gives, and I step inside.

CHAPTER THIRTY-SIX

I hum as I walk inside the ballroom, my voice shaky as I softly pull old Weymouth hymns from my memory. These winsome melodies I've known since childhood should calm me, but instead they make the atmosphere more haunting. Still, I keep humming, because I need *them* to hear me. I need *them* to stay and dance.

Inside the ballroom, two hanging chandeliers glint in the foggy light. Warm maple molding surrounds a busy geometric wallpaper. It hurts the eye to look at it for too long, but there's a reason for that: the wallpaper hides thin iron bars that run the entire length of the wall. The bars run around the room, from the ground to the ceiling and then across that as well. They run underneath the shiny hardwood floor and across the large windows at the back of the room. The Grand Ballroom is a cage designed to look like old money.

I linger in the dusty silence of the room. I used to come in here to hide when Mom was too drunk and I couldn't face it. There's a single chair in the corner near the window, perfect for curling up with a book. When we were little, Hali and I would roller skate in here to the sounds of American rock bands, Jeff hollering at us to turn it down. I can remember the skates on my feet, hear the Aerosmith lyrics pumping through my body. I continue to hum softly, making sure I'm at the very back of the room—near the windows—when I hear the doorknob rattle once, twice. We want them to think it's a lock, but it's not—it's just a sticky door. Finally I watch as the door slowly swings open, horror rising inside as the dead gleefully follow their prey.

Me. I am the prey.

A tidal wave of mist pours through the door, fanning out through the ballroom like a river, like the adrenaline in my veins. Outside the windows, I can hear the sounds of a war being waged on Weymouth. The dead move around the room in my periphery. I try not to look right at them, but it's difficult, because *they don't move like us*. It's hard to track them. The living move with purpose, but the dead have no sensible flow, no sense to the way they move. They slither, they raise themselves up and crumple back down without reason; there are no bones and muscles to maneuver or to relieve. It messes with my mind, and I can't bring myself to hide the terror on my face.

God, they are *freaking* scary.

"Beuvry . . . ," one of the ghosts hisses through an open, gaping mouth. "House Beuvry. The last house." The dead continue to fill the room; maybe a hundred, maybe two? It's hard to tell as they merge and separate, spirits that aren't tethered to the ground or even to their own being. Two become one; one becomes three. I grit my teeth so hard that a slice of pure pain arrows down my jaw and back up into my forehead. I hate them, I hate them *so* much, and I will trap them here in this ballroom. If I have my way, they will stay here until the sun turns them to dust.

I reach the back of the room, where a silver lever sits in a hollow frame. I wrap my hand around it; the cool heaviness of it makes me calmer. *This will work.* The dead are piling up into one horrifying mass of bodies. I let them come; I let them swarm. I can hear jumbled words being hissed among them.

"Beuvry, House, Island, Girl, Bridge. The First and the Last. Cabot."

God, *bridge*. One swirls out of the pack: a woman on all fours, her head hanging sideways, a peasant's dress swirling around her as if she's still underwater, her hair undulating in invisible currents. She is missing an arm and half a face; and she moves quickly toward me, almost galloping, her mouth open in a terrible roar.

I slam down the latch. The double doors at the front of the room close shut, cutting a few ghosts in half as they go. The iron bars burst out of their wooden stocks with a loud crack, crisscrossing the exit, the walls, and the ceiling. The cage shows itself. A collective cry pushes from the horde when they realize they've been tricked. They can't escape, but I can. I feel a small wave of pride pass through me. I did it. I trapped them. It's surely not all of them, but it's *a lot* of them. *And it's time to go.*

I spin back to the large window behind me. It has an uncomplicated lock at the hinge; it's easy to undo. I've done it a dozen times. Once it's unlocked, the iron bars separate just enough to let a human slide through. All I have to do next is slip through the bars, and then I can lock the window behind me from the outside. *The dead stay locked in, and I am out. Easy as pie.*

I hoist my backpack tight around my shoulders and undo the simple lock. It clicks open, and I move to push the iron bars aside on their metal track. Only . . . the bars aren't sliding, and the window isn't opening. *No. What? No.* My mind won't allow the possibility as I yank desperately on the bars again. They don't budge, and I let out a whimper, my eyes tracing the track above them. This should be simple. It should be set. Everything looks fine on the mechanical side; there is no reason the bars shouldn't move. And yet they don't.

A whimper escapes my lips again as understanding dawns. The lock is open, and the track is set, but there is one other component: a weighted lever on the outside of the room that needs to slide forward. I close my eyes as I frantically, desperately yank at the bars. It could be wedged. It could be broken. It could be . . . OH MY GOD. I let out a strangled cry. *This is my mother, goddamn her.* If she had been here, she would have double-checked this; this was the piece we forgot. Tears flood my eyes as anger surges through me, hot as a nuclear blast and gone as fast. I can't be angry at her when I die. Because I'm going to die in here.

"*Nonononononono.*" I let out a frustrated scream as I fumble desperately with the mechanical track. I pull at the bars so hard, it feels like my arms are separating from my shoulders. Behind me I hear the dead shuffling closer. For a moment, they were confused by my hysterical fear. Life is unfamiliar for them—but not so unfamiliar that they won't kill me.

They surround me from every side until they are ten feet away . . . closer . . . five feet . . . an arm's length. I shove my hand into the front pocket of my backpack, grab a handful of thick salt, and quickly make a half circle around myself and the wall; this will hold them back for only a minute or so. This is the end of the line. There are no more tricks, no traps I can trigger. There is a wall behind me and hundreds of dead stacked ten deep in front of me, and there is nowhere left to go. I think of Jeff saying "Don't get cornered." *I'm so stupid.* I let a terrified, angry cry escape my lips. *It's over.*

I back up against the wall and sink down, burying my head in my hands as the dead press closer; soon I'll be one of them. The thought releases a wave of fear inside me, fear of the pain that is coming. *Will it be quick? Will it hurt?* A desperate wail erupts out of the deepest part of me. *I am alone, and I will die alone.*

I close my eyes and wait for their skeletal fingers to rip me apart. A cool mist curls around my quaking body, and my head begins to pound. Something touches my hand. But instead of the cold, rotted bones I'm expecting, I feel warm skin against my fingers. A hand wraps around my own. It's familiar, every crease and softness known to me.

I open my eyes and see Hali standing in front of me.

CHAPTER THIRTY-SEVEN

H i," she whispers as time stops, as if she never left. I'm trembling, speechless as my eyes well up with tears.

"I missed you so much," I whimper, unable to believe what I'm seeing.

My sister smiles as she kneels beside me and leans her forehead against mine. I can feel the sweat of her brow and the wispiness of her hair. She is so unlike the dead circling around us. They are rot and pain; Hali is flesh and depth and compassion. And yet . . . not.

"You're not real," I whisper. "You're in my head. Just a construction of my grief."

"No," she says, cupping my face gently in her hands. "I'm a construction of your heart. But I'm here, Mabel. I'm here." I lace my fingers through hers, wishing it could be true, knowing I would sacrifice it all for this to be true. Even Miles. Even what remains of my family.

"Are you here so that I'm not alone when I die?" I ask, thinking that it wouldn't be the worst thing. Then I could be with her forever.

Hali's magnificent green eyes spark with life. "No. I've come so that you're not alone when you decide to *live*." She stands up, her hand still holding mine. "So get up. Get UP, Mabel."

All I want is to hold her, to crush her against me, but I do as she says. Around us, the dead uncoil from the mist, their fingers reaching out for me, dissolving over the salt. *Too close.*

My sister smiles gently. "Let's shore up together one last time, yeah?" she asks.

I'm so taken aback by her presence, by what my mind has gifted me in these last moments, that I'm unable to reply. The dread in my chest dissipates, and the world narrows until there is only us. I face my sister, she who is my bones, my breath. Moving in perfect unison, we both cross our fingers over our chests three times before grabbing each other's wrists. We make a gate. Our voices rise through the ballroom as the dead scramble back from our (my) words.

> "*When the sea starts to scream, close the shutters.*
> *When the wind starts to blow, lock the doors.*
> *Keep an eye on the Dehset Shore.*
> *Fares well the house that's ready.*"

Our words spiral up through the ballroom, the cadence of our voices sweeping into every empty crack and rotting stone as we call on the Beuvry ancestors to help us. Hali's hands are wrapped tight around my wrists, my own hidden strength pouring back into me. There has to be something, some exit. Then it hits me: *the fireplace.*

"Yes. Make for the fireplace," Hali says. "And don't forget you have one weapon left."

One weapon left. In my panic, I forgot. Hands trembling, I let go of her to reach inside my bag . . . and pull out my father's iron whip. I let out a long breath as I take the wooden handle in my palm. The wood is soft as butter, worn from practice and the years my father spent oiling it every week. It is the tool that failed to protect us all those years ago. And now it is my only hope.

"Hurry!" Hali urges as the dead slither closer. I slide the release button upward and watch the razor-thin iron whip coil down to the floor. The hundreds of dead are cloistered around me, so close, I can taste the sickly ocean-rot permeating them. I close my eyes and feel my father's weapon in my hands. I have as much a right to it as any boy on this island. And unlike some of them, I'm pretty good.

I take the defensive stance Jeff's father taught us long ago: feet wide, body taut, making myself as small as I can to avoid injuries. *This is going to hurt.*

"Go," she (I) yells, and I begin to move. Hali doesn't step aside and—as if I needed more confirmation that she only exists in my head—the whip passes right through her middle. I turn quickly, but the iron whip catches on my side, ripping away a small patch of skin as it goes. I curse. This is the cost of the iron whip. I let out a cry as I spin again. Hali, my grief, my comfort, moves with me as I make my way toward the fireplace across the ballroom.

The dead dissolve into clouds of mist as the whip passes through them. I move like I'm dancing, swirling in circles that tear holes inside them and through them. They try to escape the whip, gripping at my hair and clothing as I go, but I can't stop moving, not even for a second, not for anything; it's only my momentum keeping me safe. From inside me, I hear Hali's voice cheering me on.

I spin again, and the whip lashes around me, slashing across my head. I'm cutting myself everywhere—a hard strike catches me on the side of my face and hip. My own hot blood begins pouring down my cheek; the whip has ripped through my jacket. The next lash catches me on the side of my shin, and a sharp flash of pain shoots up my leg. I leave my body behind as the adrenaline and muscle memory take over. I'm light on my feet, a ghost. My whip passes through empty eye sockets and rotting torsos. It cuts through the seawater that drips from their mouths. It severs heads from bodies, ribs from waists. It cuts through their outstretched hands, returning them to the mist from which they came.

When I finally look up, I'm almost to the enormous stone fireplace, the mantel held up by two ancient Novantae statues.

Hali is behind me, screaming in my ear. "Climb! Now!" Her hands move me forward as I duck underneath the mantel. I tuck the iron whip back into my backpack. "Mabel, go!" screams Hali.

I begin to climb. The inside of the fireplace is decrepit. Particles of thick dust have been dislodged in the Storm, and they quickly make their way into my lungs. I struggle to breathe, coughing as I climb upward, reaching blindly for outcropped rocks with my hands and feet.

Some eight-legged monster skitters across my hand and up into my hair, but I keep climbing, the rock face cutting into my hands. Thankfully, the chimney narrows as it rises, and quickly I'm to a place where I can brace my legs on either side and move upward. Just when I think I'm getting momentum, one of the stones crumbles in my hand, and I slide down a foot before catching myself, cursing all the way. I pass right through Hali, who is climbing up below me, but I try not to think about it. *Damn, damn, damn.*

I glance over my shoulder. Mist is pluming up from the bottom of the fireplace; the dead know where I have gone—and they are going to try to follow. *Up, up, up.* My feet are slipping, hands slick with blood and dust. My lungs burn, and my legs shake as I push faster. A tunnel of mist surrounds me.

Hali's voice sounds in my ear. "Climb!"

Rain begins pouring down my face, and the higher I go, the wetter and crumblier the stones become.

"If I ever see you again," I say out loud to Jeff, "we're going to have a little chat about the state of this fireplace." Thinking about him gives me an extra boost of energy; I have to make it, because I have to save my Guardian.

"You're almost there!" Hali cheers. I'm not, but it's the kind of hopeful support I need. The voices of the dead are just below me now, and to my horror, a bony finger scrapes my foot.

This time, I practically fly upward, one hand over the other, moving fast and not stopping for anything. I'm almost at the top when I see the thin iron grate that locks the entrance. A few more feet upward and my hands slam up against it, but it doesn't budge.

Behind me, I hear the sound of chattering bones. I push with all my might against the iron grate; it doesn't move, and the sheer panic I've been holding back roars forward.

"PLEASE!" I scream hysterically, yanking on it. "God!" Something small rattles in the corner, and when I take a closer look, I see a lock—a tiny silver lock, the kind you would attach to a diary. I yank desperately on it, raining down curses on Jeff for being so damn efficient. Hali is next to me in the chimney, one hand on my arm, her breaths steady and calm as I pull desperately at the lock.

"Don't look down . . . and don't panic," she whispers.

"I can't . . ." My words are coming up short. Mist circles like a snake around her waist.

"Mabel!" she cries, her fear my own.

"I'm trying! Jesus!" I scream. Something that isn't Hali grips my ankle, and I kick out, my foot passing through glowing orbs, wispy hair, and a rotted skull. I give a last yank at the lock, using every ounce of my remaining strength. It comes apart in my hands, the insides rusted. Thank God for good ol' Nova Scotia rain.

With a scream, I push the grate open and pull myself, hand over bloody hand, out of the chimney and onto the roof of the Beuvry Estate. I have never been so happy to see the sky in all my life, even if it is a horrifying plum-green. I let the humid, salty air fill my lungs, and I feel the drops of rain on my face. For a blissful second, it's just me and the sky—but there's no time to enjoy it.

I roll over and look down the chimney as a horrifying jumble of hollow eyes, teeth, and random body parts surges up toward me. I let the iron grate slam back down upon their faces with barely concealed fury, then stack loose bricks on top of it just in case. There's a bag of salt up here, and I rip it open and dump it over them, screaming "PISS OFF!" at the top of my lungs like a nutter, but also like someone who just survived the impossible. A smile breaks across my face as I watch them dissolve into nothing. Then I slide down against the chimney exterior, all energy quickly draining from my body.

"We made it," I manage, sighing with relief.

Hali looks back at me. "You did it, Mabel. You trapped them!" I know we aren't any safer outside than inside, but I let myself take a few deep breaths as the rain washes layers of ash and dust off my skin. Below me is chaos, everywhere, but for this one moment, I focus on the warmth of Hali's hand in mine, and I let myself keep her.

372

CHAPTER THIRTY-EIGHT

C an we stay here?" I ask softly. "You and me, on this roof?"

"You know I can't stay," she replies, which means I only have a few minutes to say everything I never did.

"I'm sorry I never appreciated you while you were here. I was a terrible older sister."

She laughs. "You *really* were. Remember that time you locked me in the closet, and when I finally got out, you jumped out at me in our dead grandmother's lace veil?"

A laugh mixed with a sob erupts out of me. "Um, that was great, actually! You screamed so loud that Jeff came running, two stairs at a time. He was so young and nimble back then. Now he's passed out in the salt pantry."

Hali gives me a toothy grin. "I had such a crush on him. Even when I learned he was dating Mr. McLeod."

I squeeze her hand. "Me too. I guess the joke was on us." *God,* I think, *what am I doing out here talking to my invisible sister?* I look over at her. "I'm sorry I brought you back again. I wanted to do better. But I've failed . . . again. Turns out I'm pretty broken." A violent cough catches in my lungs, and I bend forward, ash on my tongue. Hali rests a hand on my back, rubbing softly.

"Mabel, kids don't have time to appreciate each other. That's what makes them *kids*. We were too busy living to appreciate it. And that's how it should be."

I touch her face. It's the first time I see the deep cuts on my palms from the iron whip. There's blood all over me.

"We should move," she whispers cryptically. "Look down."

Carefully I make my way across the roof—a slippery maze of pointed eaves and battered tiles—toward the widow's walk. Wincing, I climb up the small ladder that vaults up to Cloudbreak, gripping the freezing rungs. Once I get up, I have no words.

Below me, Weymouth is in utter chaos. Darkness has swallowed the entire island, the only few points of light provided by the houses. The lighthouse is still spinning, its broken crimson light illuminating a new horrifying scene with each turn. The Cabot mansion is almost halfway submerged under seawater, along with the Des Roches house, which looks absolutely decimated. The sirens have gone silent. There are two huge fires burning, one in the trees near the Mintus House and the other at the tail end of the Bodhmall property.

Sentry's Sleep is a tattered remnant of downed statues and foaming water. From here I can see what look like tiny matchbooks floating out on the water. A strangled sound escapes my lips when I realize what I'm looking at: coffins. Coffins bobbing on the low waves, some empty, some still sealed.

Is my dad's body out there? Is Hali's? Nausea rises from my stomach as I force my eyes away from the sight. A thick river of white mist lingers over the entire island, a living thing that snakes a deliberate path up the mainland toward the bridge. The glow of lifeless souls inside it churns back and forth. There are so many of them. They aren't even stopping for the foundation stones. Every-where is overrun. Our home is a sea of glowing souls. I pick up the radio attached to the wall and wearily hold down the button on the side.

"This is Mabel Beuvry. The Beuvry house has fallen. Over. I repeat, there is no one left." Only static answers back. There is no one on the other end. I fling the radio away.

"We've never had control," I whisper to Hali. "We say these words and we learn our history and prepare our houses, but it's all to make *us* feel safe. The eleven houses of Weymouth are a *sacrifice.*"

She watches for a second. "Perhaps. But it doesn't make what we do any less important."

A second later, I hear a scream come from somewhere on the island, the high-pitched scream of a human dying violently. It rips through the air and then suddenly is cut short.

I run my hand over my face. "Do you think Miles is still alive? Is Norah? Is anyone?" Dread fills my chest at the thought. What if I'm all alone? What if I'm literally the last person alive on this island? Despair sweeps through me at the thought, like a spiraling black pit in my chest. Will I be on this island by myself, surrounded by the ghosts of those I love? And if all the houses have fallen, that means there is no resistance left to the sea of the dead that remain; they are clear to move toward the bridge. "No," I utter. *Is it truly just me at the end of the world?*

"Look!" Hali cries, her voice tight and scared, a reflection of what's happening inside me. I crane my neck to look at the front of our house. Black water sucks at the gates and the garden. I glance over it just in time to see long, pale bones lurch up over the widow's walk. A second hand slams down next to it and then a third as mist curls up and over fleshless shoulders. Glowing eye sockets rise up from below.

"Go!" my sister screams. They may have found me, but I have also found them, and there isn't a section of this house that doesn't have something to help. I dash over to the whale-shaped weather vane that sits atop the end of the roof as the dead heave themselves up. I pull the whale downward and duck as thin iron barbs spit out from the wall. They pass through Hali and pepper the dead.

At the same moment, a trapdoor slides open at the end of the walk, triggered by the release of the trap. I slide toward it on soaking-wet tiles as the dead grasp at me from above; there are at least six of them on the roof above us now. *They're everywhere.* I slide into the tunnel feetfirst, and Hali is behind me as we plunge downward, free-falling through the ducts that run the height of our house.

Together we fall through pitch-darkness, the metallic scent of copper in my nose as my body bounces off the narrow sides of ducts. We're going much too fast; I try to slow down using my legs, but it doesn't work very well. Vaguely I'm aware of Hali falling beside me, but then the darkness disappears, and I hit a layer of water that feels like brick. I'm submerged, salt water pouring into my mouth and eyes. Little waves churn around me, pulling me away from the surface. I flail, trying to get my bearings, trying to figure out which way is up. My lungs start to cave in as my hands are reaching for something, anything.

Eventually my fingertips rip across a concrete floor, and I realize where I am: I'm in the cellar. I get my feet underneath me and propel myself up toward the air. My head bursts to the surface. Hali is in the water beside me. I swim over to the cellar stairs, careful to keep my nose in the three feet of air between the cellar ceiling and dark water. Something brushes up against my legs; dead or living, I don't know, but I do know that I have to get out of this room as quickly as possible.

"If I live through this night, I never want to be wet ever again," I mumble through gritted teeth. A second later, the stairs are underneath my feet, and then I'm pushing up against the cellar door, which, thank God, opens easily. I strain to pull the door open against the water pressure before stepping out into the hallway at the south end of the house. Then I let out an absurd, hysterical laugh.

Jesus, I'm practically right back where we started, but when I look around, I barely recognize the house I've lived in all my life. Everything is destroyed, a watery, discombobulated version of itself. My laugh dies on my lips when Hali yanks on my arm—and horror takes its place. Our house is *full* of the dead. They hover at both ends of the hallway, are folded between the railings, and are pressed up against the ceiling. Remnants of our traps float along: folded paper, packets of salt crystals, and iron bars that have sunk onto the carpet.

We have stopped some, but not enough.

They haven't noticed me yet, so I hold my breath as I move silently through the water, hoping to get out of the bottleneck. If I can make it to the porch . . . But as I pass the sitting room, a head whips around from inside it, and when I turn, a very whole Lynwood is staring right at me.

He looks at me through a pale white, partially decomposed

face, and his head hangs from his neck the same way it did on the rocks. He stares at me for a long moment, and for a second I think he remembers me. But then a horrible sound pours out of his open mouth, fingers scratching down a windpipe. He points a bony, skinless finger at me, and with a hollow, inhuman shriek screams, "THE FIRST AND THE LAST!" The dead around me all jerk to attention, as if held by invisible puppet strings. *They see me.*

Hali's fingernails dig into my arm. "Go!" she gasps.

But I can't leave him this way. I won't. Lynwood deserves more than this.

Upon the mantel sit two iron candelabras, heavy and sharp, with elaborately sculpted flowers at the tips. As the ghost of Will Lynwood lunges, I grab the candlestick and plunge it straight into his face. He staggers backward with a howl, suddenly more mist than form. His scream reaches a crescendo, and then he looks up at me with a grateful sigh as his body disappears and the glow in his eyes extinguishes. He's gone. Hali's hand closes around my arm.

I run. Everything is a blur; everywhere I turn, the dead are there. I've never run faster or moved slower all at once, Hali at my back. I pass by the kitchen and see that the lock is soundly secured; there should be no dead inside it, and the water is only inches deep, rather than feet. Jeff should be okay. *Please, God, let him be okay.*

Ahead of me, the entrance to the porch is guarded by two old dead men who seem to be wandering through the hallways without purpose, wailing together as their fingers trail over our things. They want to live again—I get it . . . but I want to live more. I throw two open books from a guest table at them; they scream and dissolve right in front of me, and suddenly the path to the porch is clear. I need to be out of this house.

I dart forward, Hali in tow, and open the porch entrance with a series of locks that slide up to reveal a tiny tunnel at the bottom, big enough for a single person to crawl through. I'm in, Hali behind me, and the panel snaps shut, sealing us inside.

I curl myself into a small ball, burying my face in my knees. I'm struggling to comprehend what I've just seen. What I've just done. I feel my sister's hand on my back, and I know what she's going to say before she says it, because it's me. She is me.

"The bridge, Mabel." Simple words that convey a terrible meaning. "The bridge" means a possible sacrifice. "The bridge" means that I am the last Beuvry standing, and it's my responsibility to protect the entire mainland from the dead. If the dead pass the bridge before daylight comes, they will come across an unsuspecting mainland town with no protections. They will not leave when the sun rises. They will march through Glace Bay and then on to Halifax. The human cost will be enormous, and even worse, *the world will know what we do.* The truth of our island will be out there for corrupt governments to regulate and control, and Weymouth Island will no longer be its own. *The dead cannot pass.* I close my eyes. The name Beuvry means "a person near." Our literal purpose is to be near the river, the bridge.

My last breath for the last house.

I look up at Hali's tear-streaked face, every vulnerability about myself laid bare.

"I can't," I whisper to myself. "I couldn't even save you."

"No one could have. You need to let that go; it's a cancer, and it's eating you from the inside. Your guilt fuels your delusion."

I whimper. "I should have held you tighter."

"You did. But the dead were stronger. You can finish this," she says lovingly. "I know it."

My lip trembles. "None of this is fair. You being gone isn't fair."

"No," she says slowly. "Life rarely is. Grief is fear, but grief is also love." She leans her head against mine, the sister of my heart. "But it's worth it. Always." She touches my cheek. "I think you know this is where we say goodbye, Mabel." She tilts my face toward her. "A thousand of your tears or the most complex denial won't bring me back again. I'm here now, but I can't stay. You have a big, beautiful life waiting for you."

My resolve crumples as I clutch her to me, desperate to keep my sister, even when she is nothing more than a dream. For a second, I close my eyes and see my family as it once was before the Storm: my father, my mother, and my sister, all standing before me. But now it's just me on this porch, holding myself together with too-thin arms, struggling to keep my bitter, all-consuming grief at bay.

"*Look at me, Mabel.*" When I look up this time, Hali is a child once more: a nine-year-old girl with freckles on her face standing in a sopping-wet nightgown. Her hair is soaked with salt water, her green eyes not as vibrant as I remember. This is how she looked the last time I saw her on this side of the world. When she was an actual living thing.

And I know, deep in my heart, that it's the last time I'll see her.

"I love you, Hali," I whisper, hot tears pouring from my eyes. "I *love* you."

She kneels down, cupping her tiny hand over my ear, a little kid telling a delicious secret. "You don't have to keep me to love me." And then, in a breath of wind, my sister is gone.

With a wail, I rock forward to my bleeding knees and begin crawling to the wooden panel on the porch floor. Tears dripping off my nose, I slide it sideways until I see a tiny button appear. *One last time*, I think, before I push the button down into the floor. A familiar, horrendous screeching sound fills the porch. I brace myself against the wall as the porch opens itself up to the outside. Metal shutters peel back, and papers flutter to the ground.

It's like being in a hurricane inside a snow globe. The porch lights flicker, and the light of the moon casts everything before me in horrifying light.

The dead are *everywhere*.

The ones who have made it through our house are slowly moving toward the Lethe Bridge. There must be at least a hundred of them between me and the bridge. Too many. I experience the urge to curl up here on the porch and let them go. But I can't. *I can't.* Instead I climb shakily to my feet and bend down to pick up a broken piece of our gate, blown all the way up onto the porch. It's a thin piece of iron and will make a fine spear. And after that, it may not matter, but I have to get there.

CHAPTER THIRTY-NINE

Clutching my side, I limp off the porch and jog through the yard toward the main road, hoping to head them off any way I can. I'm not enough. I know it. It's over, but at least I'm not being ripped apart inside my house, for one thing. *At least Jeff will make it. And at least I got to say goodbye to Hali this time.*

My footsteps are swallowed by the voices of the dead as I step out onto the road. If the dead see me, they don't slow their pace. They are a slow parade moving toward the bridge, their goal only a half mile away . . . and then they will reach the mainland. The bridge has always been a last resort. With a deep breath, I hold the iron spear out in front of me with a trembling hand. Tears fall down my face. "Come on," I whisper. *This is it. I don't have time to make it to the bridge and hold them back.*

As the mist blossoms in front of my eyes, the shadows within it lengthen. There are more of them than I thought. The dark shadows stretch taller with each step. I square my shoulders as they grow closer, their cries reaching my ears. They are loud, these last strong remnants. I know I won't be enough to stop them.

This is it. I won't get to see my mom's face again. I won't get to help Jeff heal. Miles and I won't get to change this place for the better. We'll never know what the first and last could have been. The island called Miles here, but I won't be here to see it through with him.

I close my eyes and say a prayer. *Let me not feel it. God, let it be over fast.*

The mist parts. I take a breath.

But instead of a nightmare, it's . . . Miles who pushes through the mist, sprinting toward me, screaming my name. It seems like a dream, and I wonder for a second if I'm already dead, but then he's moving past me, wielding his new iron whip like he was born to it. The iron swirls around him like a dancer's ribbon, eviscerating the dead moving toward me in one clean swing. Another comes up behind him, and he whirls around, cutting it at the head. The dead dissipate, and through the mist left behind, Miles looks over at me, standing there with my iron spear.

"You came," I whisper, unable to believe what I'm seeing. "It's supposed to be every house alone!" I move closer to him. A dead man slithers up behind him, and I plunge the iron lance through the man's head, a move I'll maybe tell our children about someday.

Miles grabs my hand and pulls me close to him for a long kiss as mist swirls around us. I lose myself for just a second, allowing myself this tiny, warm pleasure.

When he pulls back, his eyes are hungry. "Yeah, well, I think that rule is stupid, so I came. You and I both know that the rules need to change." I reach out, and he kisses the palm of my hand, covered with blood and salt and dust and who knows what else. "I couldn't bear to know that you were fighting here and I was there.

COLLEEN OAKES

I don't want to be separated from you, Mabel. Certainly not in this lifetime and hopefully not the next."

He gazes down at me. His face is a bloody mess, a depth to his eyes that wasn't there before. Miles is now a kid who has seen some things. The dead keep coming, and Miles is moving around me with a whirling iron whip. He shouts and jumps, and it's obvious he's glowing through and through, alive in a way I haven't seen him before. He's meant to be here. He's meant to be with me.

I don't even have time to comprehend the beauty of this moment before more shadows begin plunging their way through the fog: First it's Alistair and his two grown sons, all sprinting toward the dead as they make their way to the bridge. Liam and Lucas Cabot wield iron weapons I've never seen before, strange mallets and maces strung with iron spikes that release salt with each swing.

I watch as Alistair slides through a set of three dead with ease, but I note that his hair has gone completely gray since the last time I saw him hours ago. Liam and Lucas plunge fully into a horde of the dead, shouting to each other as they go with insane, masculine energy. Are they having . . . *fun?* I blink, still unable to believe what I'm seeing: People are here. They came.

I hear my name being wailed on the wind, and the next thing I see is Norah bursting through the mist with James, her father, and four of her older siblings by her side. They each have their salt guns up and loaded, a deadly combination if there ever was one. There is a lot of blood on their clothes, but they seem fine. However . . . I don't see their mother with them, and my heart drops. *Oh God, no.*

The Nickerson clan follows right behind them: Anjee has a

slim iron lance that she wields like a rapier; Edmund is an absolute brute, his skin drenched with sweat as he moves behind his mother, angrily cleaning up what she leaves behind. Sloane is more graceful. His whip moves around him like they are one, dismembering dead before they ever get close to him.

And suddenly there are so many of us, the island of Weymouth emerging for this last, great push. We always stand together, but tonight, for the first time, we are *fighting* together. This Storm has broken all our rules in an attempt to destroy us, and by this they have brought our power forward. Random members of every family are fighting back the dead as they push toward the bridge. I even see Cordelia Pope speed by on a sweet motorbike, her hair pulled back in a blue bandanna, with lines of blood streaked down her face like war paint, chasing down the dead like the coolest person alive. The whips of the Bodhmalls and the iron chains of the Des Rocheses swirl in the mist.

"Take that back to hell, you ghastly mackerels! Back to the sea with ya!" Jesus, even the reclusive Pelletiers have come to help, and Henry—who is around seventy years old—is flinging salt at the dead with his bare hands, cursing them as he goes. A sob climbs up my throat. They have all come to fight for the last house to the sea.

The weather is going berserk, fighting us every step of the way. Miles screams my name against the wind. I glance back one last time at my empty porch, but Hali is gone for good, as it should be. The sight of my house stops me in my tracks. A glowing infestation of death has taken over the place where I lay my head.

Miles runs up beside me. "What's the plan, Beuvry?"

I look past the dead. "We have to get to the bridge. We can't let them cross it! Come on." I grab his hand and pull him beyond the road. We've almost made it when the lights dotting the island go out and we are all plunged into darkness. The absence of light is staggering; it's as if the moon and the stars have gone out. The darkness has a density. There is no light, no generators; the lighthouse is dark; the only light is from the far flames of the McLeod house. My terror drops to another level; I can sense the dead around us, but I can't see them very well. There is no way we can make it to the bridge—or even ten feet in this darkness.

But I have to try. I close my eyes, feeling Miles next to me, but pushing past that, past the darkness, until I hear it: the river.

"Follow me," I say, and I take his hand. Small, strong random currents of seawater foam around our shins as we quickly make our way down the hill, toward the noise of water rushing across rocks, tripping our way through fields of wildflowers, trying to avoid the scent of the dead, which is overpowering at this point; they are surrounding us, and we can't see them. Miles takes a nervous breath in, and then I see them, the glowing orbs of their eyes, circling us. There are too many, too close, and we don't know where they are.

Miles unravels the iron whip I pulled from the bottom of the sea and pushes me behind him. With his other hand, he squeezes mine, his voice choking with anguish. "It's been a pleasure, Beuvry. And in case I don't get a chance to say it later: I think I'm falling in love with you." I don't get to respond, because then an honest-to-God Weymouth miracle happens. All of a sudden, there is light. A bright, glaring light, coming from the trees and aimed at the bridge. A huge, bright spotlight shines down from Wasp Wood, and we're able to see it all: the throng of the dead around us, our friends and family fighting, struggling to keep the dead back from the bridge. The light is so strong, it cuts through the mist, and the dead seem to wither from it. That's when I realize where it's coming from. The top of a very tall tree, the place where Will Lynwood placed it before falling to his death. Something about the island being plunged into darkness activated it.

His last gift to us. His light. Aimed at the bridge he somehow knew Miles and I would be fighting toward. Tears gather in my eyes.

"Keep going!" I scream to Miles. His arms begin whirling as he uses his iron whip to take out about a dozen dead between us and our path. He lets out a string of American curse words as he goes, making me even more attracted to him. At this point in the evening, I am mad, almost euphoric—and bordering on collapse. The adrenaline is wearing out. We're almost to the bridge. The Lethe appears in front of us, and we fly toward it, Miles clearing the way ahead of me. We reach the road in front of the bridge, and we're too late. They are already crossing over it. There are just too many of them, moving now like a brainless horde over the river. The bright light illuminates the horror of them: their misty bodies, their long fingers, their miserable faces.

I feel a surprising surge of pity for them—but not enough to let them kill us all. We near the end of the bridge. Miles keeps fighting, trying to hold them back. Above me, I hear the sounds of my people fighting, trying in vain to keep them off the bridge. I meet his eyes once, trying to convey everything I feel for him.

"Miles . . ."

"Go!" he yells, and then I break away, leaving him in a pocket of swirling mist and glowing orbs.

The dead don't pay me any notice as I head down from the edge of the bridge, making my way to the small catwalk that runs underneath it. I hear panicked cries from my fellow islanders as the dead reach the midpoint of the bridge; this is our worst-case scenario.

Their panic hits me like a wave.

As I duck underneath the pylons, I catch a glimpse of the world beyond. The line of trees to the west that eventually leads all the way to Glace Bay. Just past that road, people are hunkering in for a rainy night: couples snuggle on their couches; parents are quietly reading to their children. They have no idea that death is marching slowly toward their doors.

They will never thank us, the silent guardians of their world.

I pull myself underneath the bridge, using the metal brackets overhead to steady myself as the wind almost blows me off my feet. Below me, the river laps hungrily at my ankles; it's dangerously close to surging over the banks. Mist pours down through the metal slats overhead, where the dead are passing over. There are no footsteps, only a slithering sound marked with horrifying moans.

Loud footsteps splash through the water behind me. But whoever is coming is too late. I can't wait for them. "Stay back! Please!" I scream. Just ahead, secured above me on the catwalk, I see a small plastic red square mounted underneath the bridge. It bears the sigil of House Beuvry. An exhausted laugh passes through me.

My house. I can only imagine what is left of it.

Breathing heavily, I unlatch the plastic box and open the protective glass beneath. A small piece of paper flutters out, and I barely catch it before it plunges into the river beneath me. It's thick, lovely paper. When I unfold it, I see my dad's handwriting.

Don't be afraid to blow the entire thing up. I love you both.

I choke on unexpected tears. My dad thought I would be standing here with Hali today.

Underneath it, he has drawn four little hearts—one for each member of our family. I press the note against my chest. Somehow my whole family has been with me today, even though each of them is gone. Hali came to me in my greatest moment of need. My mum humbling herself enough to admit she needs help. And my dad, here at the end of all things.

He knew that someday one of us would be here, that we would be the last Weymouth residents standing between life and death. And he trusted us to do it. *Don't be afraid to blow the entire thing up.* Somehow, I know he isn't just talking about the bridge.

I tuck the paper into my pocket. Mist is pouring over both sides of the bridge now; the dead are almost at the end of it. Sitting in the middle of the red square is a small silver wheel. Aided by Will Lynwood's light, I turn it until it gives a loud click, and then I watch as a line of explosives begins to glow a faint purple in the dark night; they're activated. Normally this would be activated remotely, from inside the house, but the trigger is probably floating at the bottom of a staircase at this point. I look at the glowing purple lights. These aren't just any explosives; they're bombs filled with iron, paper, salt, and . . . fire. Our last trap— our last hope. I won't have enough time to make it back to the riverbank, not while I'm exhausted and injured. But somehow I'm okay with it. All this time, all this training, all the gates and the rhymes and the conversations have made me ready for this. This *is* my purpose—and I'll serve it gladly.

I close my eyes and think of my family. I think of Miles. And I turn the wheel once more.

There is a loud, high-pitched whining sound, and just as the first bomb triggers, someone's arms wrap around my waist—Miles?—and then the world *explodes*.

Everything around me lights up: the sky, the ground, the bridge overhead. I'm being yanked backward as the explosives fire, away from the metal that now blazes like molten lava. There is only fire and sound as the world shakes beneath my feet. The river below us is siphoned up into a swirling funnel of heat and water. The screams of a thousand dead fill my ears, the iron bridge above me gives a metallic groan as it sways, and the river rises before our eyes, swallowing all the dead crumpled on the bridge.

I can't do anything but watch as the bridge—the last trap—falls around us with a roar, shaking the ground as it collapses in a smoking heap. Slivers of iron shower around me, cutting into my skin as whoever is helping me lays me on the muddy river-bank. I watch the bridge fall away in a blaze of flame, salt and paper raining down on my face like snow. Something hard and hot explodes against the side of my head, and my vision explodes into stars. The hot liquid pouring down my face is surely blood, and that's when I realize that *it's over*. Even if the bridge is gone, there are still more dead behind the first line. They will not pass onto the mainland, but they can still kill us. Eleven houses were not enough. Our families could not stand. My thoughts swirl, and I'm not sure what's real. Above me, the dead shriek and dissolve, mist pluming outward.

Everything is spinning; my ears ring as the night sky swirls in my vision. The clouds above me are clearing; I spot the constellations my father loved. Andromeda and Pegasus. I think of Miles, of how, like them, we are forever entwined against the black. I turn to tell him, but to my surprise, it isn't Miles cradling me against him. Instead it's his uncle. Alistair Cabot carried me off the bridge, risked his life for mine. *Is this real?* I reach up and touch his face. My hands leave bloody fingerprints on his cheeks.

"I'm sorry I didn't come all those years ago."

I close my eyes. "You came today."

A second later, voices are echoing around me as Alistair lays me on the road. I am losing consciousness; I'm trying to tell them to run, that the dead are still here. The stars in my vision begin to widen exponentially. Miles leans over me, his face almost unrecognizable through the mud.

"Stay with us, Mabel. Please." Suddenly Norah is with him, both of them pleading with me to *wait, to stay*. I smile at them as the howls of the dead are suddenly replaced by a strange, new sound. Weakly, I turn my head, trying to understand what I'm hearing. Are those . . . *cheers?* The sound rises up over the trees. I'm done, I think, but *I'm here*, someone says reassuringly. *I'm here*. But it's too late. I'm already flying away, over the trees and toward the Soft Shore, where no dead wait for me—only the quiet lapping of waves and a well-earned rest.

And Hali. Always Hali.

"Mabel. Look at me." A palm slaps my face. I open my eyes.

The last thing I see before passing out are the first rays of the dawn passing over Jeff's face.

And they are so goddamn beautiful.

Hali Beuvry, May 2012, from her personal diary

Daddy says the Storm is coming soon but that we don't have to be afraid because we're all together and this is our job. I have my doll, and Dad has his iron whip.

Our house is strong, my daddy says.

Mabel doesn't think we will be safe, but what does she know? My sister thinks she knows everything. I know as long as we're all together, we'll be okay. When you have family, you're never alone.

The wind sounds scary outside.

Historical note from Reade McLeod: The Storm of 2012 took the lives of both Hali and Jack Beuvry.

The scented candle in my counselor Harriet's office is almost burned down to the end of the wick; I watch the flame struggle to hang on as it meets the pool of wax. It feels nice being here. There's a comfort I can't quantify in this office, a place where I come to find the most real version of myself. Even if we do have to take a ferry to get here. A boat, an actual freaking boat.

"Mabel." Harriet smiles as I snap back to attention.

"Yeah, sorry."

"We were talking about what tools you can use with your mother to help keep an open, honest conversation going between the two of you. Now that she's back from rehab, it's really important to be transparent with her."

"Right." We talked about this. I wrap my hands around my head, touching the raised scar where a piece of the bridge decided to lodge itself against my skull. "The tools are: Express my wants and needs as the child and encourage her to express her needs as well. Give clear, positive feedback about her progress, and keep my expectations realistic."

"Yes, Mabel, yes, that's exactly right! And I'm sure your mother sees your progress being made as well. You're an inspiration." Harriet grins, the bright summer sun glinting off her glasses. Her lightness is contagious, and I've absolutely caught some of it.

"That's definitely the first time I've been called an inspiration."

Harriet looks at her watch, and I deflate a little—I hate when our time is up. "Well, I have a feeling it won't be the last. I know we've talked a lot about your mother today. Is there anything else you would like to discuss? Hali, for example?"

I shake my head. "She hasn't come back. Not really. There are times when I am stressed or tired that I may see a glimmer of her. But she never fully forms, and goes away as quickly as I notice it."

Harriet thinks my sister drowned in the ocean when she was a child. She knows enough to help me but not enough to jeopardize the island's secrets.

"This might always be true for you," Harriet says softly. "She may always be a shadow lurking at the back of your mind—your trauma manifested—but that doesn't mean she gets to engage with your life. Have you found new ways to healthily grieve her?"

"I've been taking flowers every week to her grave with Miles, and I've started journaling about my memories of her and trying to work them into some poems." I pause. "They're really terrible. Like, incredibly bad."

"Well, they're just for you, unless you wanted to show me?" She looks hopeful.

"Absolutely not." I bite the inside of my cheek. Not only are they very bad, but I could never show Harriet, because in addition to writing about Hali, I'm also writing about the Storm. Sketching the Storm, planning for the next Storm. Notebooks and notebooks of processing. I'm Lynwood without the paranoia.

This time I'm not going to act like nothing happened. This time I want to give the Storm the consideration it needed. Acting like things always have to be the same is a death wish. We can't wait for the next generation to save us.

"No, no . . . I'm good. But I'll keep it in mind."

"That sounds great. Also, your cut looks better this week! What have the doctors said about your healing?"

Harriet believes I was in a pretty bad car wreck the night of the Storm. It's been a solid excuse to cover my litany of injuries: a minor head wound from the bridge that looks pretty major, cuts all over from my time with the iron whip, a hole through my hand, sprained *everything*, and a whole bunch of terrifying memories that I'll never be able to shake. I don't think I'll ever be able to go into the ballroom again, and Jeff is in and out of the salt pantry as fast as he can be. We're all scarred—an entire island with PTSD.

But there's good news. We're rethinking literally everything. Miles and me, helped by Alistair and Jeff, a united front of two houses, Guardian and Triumvirate.

Everything is going to be different from now on. I smile and stand up. "I should head out. Same time next week?" I give Harriet a thumbs-up, but honestly, it depends on the weather. Since we have to take a car ferry from the island to Glace Bay now, a lot depends on the conditions of the water. Hopefully, the bridge will be rebuilt soon—and a new Weymouth will rise from the ashes of the old one. More strategy, less rules.

Outside the door, Miles is waiting in Gale, reading one of Hali's paperbacks. In Seattle, he says, he never got time to read (secretly, I think he thought he was *too cool* to read), but now I rarely see him without a book in his hands. Next up we're starting

The Giver, one of my personal favorites. He hops out of the car when he sees me, his dark brown eyes lighting up with happiness at the sight of my face. The world would be a better place if everyone had someone who looked at them the way Miles looks at me.

"Any crying at therapy today?" he asks, lightly touching my wrist.

"Only at the beginning, but not like last time. Harriet says that crying is healthy, though. Does my face look like I was crying?"

Miles gently turns my face from side to side, kissing my cheeks. "Hmm, I may have to inspect it later. And much closer. Here, and here, oh, and maybe here." He traces his hand down my neck; my blush rises to meet it.

"So . . . lunch?" I say.

He moans and raps the hood of his car as we climb in. "Definitely my second choice of activities right now."

"Yeah, right." Miles loves food deeply. He and Jeff spend way too much time watching the Food Network these days and then attempting the recipes afterward.

"SO! Did you know that Glace Bay has an Asian restaurant? It's called the Blue Bay Café, and it has three five-star reviews, which mostly look like they're posted by the owner, but a man has to know his own food, right?"

"That is a very optimistic outlook." I tuck my newly short hair behind my ear; it's wavy and full, and I love it. For some reason, cutting my hair has helped me process. When I first looked in the mirror, I couldn't believe how much more myself I looked; not only that, but I looked a little bit like the girl I imagined Hali to be. But it's just me.

"I've actually never had Asian food. Not from a restaurant

anyway. I think Jeff once attempted wontons and they didn't take."

"Your white Nova Scotian Guardian couldn't make authentic Chinese? Shocking. Well, you're going to love it." Miles pauses and reaches for my hand. "Hey, I'm proud of you, you know."

"For simply existing?"

He smiles at me. "For allowing yourself to be happy. It's a mountain to climb. It was for me."

"I know." I lean my head against his palm as the car crests the hill that leads onto the main street of Glace Bay. Miles turns the music up, the tattoo on his wrist catching the light. He's introducing me to all his favorite bands, which mostly consist of obscure hip-hop and folk tracks. I look over at him as he bobs his head to the music, taking in that crooked half smile on the side of his mouth that I love.

Below us, small white boats are parked at the marina, where boys chase one another down the dock. Weymouth's dock on the Dehset hasn't been rebuilt, and I'm not sure it ever will be. It's not like people swim in the Dehset, and even though our ancestors built the dock, there's no reason for it to return. Everything is changing, because the Storm changed everything. Beside Miles sits a drawing pad and pencil. We're in the early stages of sketching out a plan. Hopefully, in the future, the dead won't even need to come into the houses. Hopefully, the next time they rise from the sea, they will find themselves drawn into an elaborate labyrinth made out of all our foundation stones *together*. And from the walls of that labyrinth, we'll attack. The entire island. We'll wait out the dawn together.

"Jeff said he wants us to grab some fresh Brie on our way out—"

God, I love this kid. I grab his hand and bring it up to my lips, kissing the small scars he bears from the Storm. He saved me from the dead. I saved him from water. Both of us needed saving. I see so clearly now that we were meant to save each other.

When I touch his cheek, I see the slightest glimmer of red hair in the mirror, a shadow I can't indulge. In the here and now, there is so much to love. I don't need to see Hali, because she's already with me—forever.

We make it into the town of Glace Bay; it's a beautiful September afternoon. Families walk down Main Street; fishermen gather at the pier. Out on the water, waves crash and return to the sea. I watch them play, thinking how eventually these little waves will make their way toward our island, and then into the Dehset. Some of these salt crystals will crust the eyes of the dead; some will sink to the bottom and rest beneath the Bone Barrier. But some of them won't. Some will travel around the entire world.

Miles parks Gale in front of the restaurant and looks over at me. "You want to drive home afterward?"

I smile, the light from the dash reflecting on my face. It's a Thursday, and Weymouth is already bracing for the next Storm. But we have some time, enough for a whole life, I imagine.

I reach for the keys.

ACKNOWLEDGMENTS

Eleven Houses was written during the pandemic. Perhaps you can tell that after reading this story of isolation, paranoia, growing dread, family dynamics, and a heavy sense of impending doom.

All my other books (twelve at this point!) have lengthy acknowledgments of the people who I love and am so thankful for, but after much consideration, I would like to acknowledge and thank *myself*. I wrote this book in the middle of the pandemic, when the world felt like it was ending, and I wasn't able to escape to a coffee shop—or anywhere—to write. The only escape I could find was in the pages of this book, on a lonely, haunted island called Weymouth. I painfully etched this book word by word in moments stolen from the chaos swirling around me. Page by page, I wrote through the sheer horror of it all, through the news that never stopped, through worrying about my elderly parents, through trying to be everything to my only child. I clutched my laptop through anxiety that was like a thundercloud, and over so many sleepless nights and long days, I wrote this book to its unthinkable end point.

While my other books were labors of love, this seemed more like actual labor: a book made of pain and strength in equal measure, one that came roaring into the world like the dead up from the sea. During that time, I lost my father. He would have *loved* this book. He was lighthouses and rocky beaches, Nova Scotian ancestry and dark, salty water. When the world woke back up, I was clutching a hard-fought, tearstained manuscript. I hold it up for you now, thankful to put it into your hands.

This book is a scream. It's therapy, it's beautiful, and it's all mine. It is me.

ABOUT THE AUTHOR

Colleen Oakes is the bestselling author of books for both teens and adults, including the Queen of Hearts series, *The Black Coats*, the Wendy Darling saga, and *Sister of the Chosen One*. She recently moved to New England with her husband and son, and now spends most of her time marveling at trees. Colleen has a master's degree in library science and would love to chat with you about building diverse book collections.